THE LONG CON

Book and cover design by Riki Moss w/Michael Gruber

By Michael Gruber:

The Long Con
An Active Shooter
Amnesia Dreams
The Charles Bridge
Tropic of Night
Valley of Bones
Night of the Jaguar
The Book of Air and Shadows
The Forgery of Venus
The Good Son
The Return

YA   The Witch's Boy

Ghostwritten/published under the name of Robert K. Tanenbaum

No Lesser Plea
Depraved Indifference
Immoral Certainty
Reversible Error
Corruption of Blood
Material Witness
Justice Denied
Falsely Accused
True Justice
Reckless Endangerment
Irresistible Impulse
Act of Revenge
Enemy Within
Absolute Rage
Resolved

THE LONG CON

A Novel

MICHAEL GRUBER

For
Aliceanne

The Long Con

ONE

On a day in June, Bernard Goodrich kissed his wife good-bye, after which she walked out of their West End Avenue apartment to the subway station at 77th Street. Louise Chu Goodrich was a public agency psychotherapist specializing in dual diagnosis—people who were both crazy and addicted— and as a result her client list contained more than the typically tiny proportion of the mentally ill who are dangerous maniacs. One of these, a meth-stoked schizophrenic named Oscar Portillo, happened to be on the station platform that morning, and when the downtown local came shrieking into the station on schedule at 8:27, he picked his therapist off her feet and tossed her into its path.

When the police came to Bernard's door and told him, his first response was a bark of laughter, something he felt awful about afterward, but which the grief counseling literature he later read assured him was quite common. The absurdly impossible makes us laugh. That was what he said to the officers, a large male and a smaller, red-headed woman: "That's impossible. I just saw her a few minutes ago."

"I'm sorry," said the female cop, and he could tell she was, she was youngish and not yet hard-faced, and her eyes were damp, and that look was what made him have to sit down on the couch in the living room, his legs having lost their power to support.

The male cop told him how it had happened, that she didn't suffer, that they had the perpetrator in custody and the female cop said, "You shouldn't be alone. Is there anyone you can call?"

And of course, there was. Bernard pulled out his cell phone, went to Favorites, and called his wife.

After a brief sad period, the cops got that straightened out, and Bernard was able to call his son and daughter. Lawrence screamed and railed; Leslie was largely silent, except for a single gasping wail at the end of their conversation. This sound from his dear girl caused all the energy to drain out of Bernard's body. He curled up on the couch and pulled a shawl up over him, as he was suddenly shaking with cold. Before he closed his eyes, he gave his cell phone to the female cop and told her to push the button for Albert.

Pushing the button for Albert was what one did in the Goodrich family when difficult matters arose. Bernard's elder by five years, CEO of the family business, pillar of Church and community, father of six, Bertie Goodrich was the man you wanted around when disaster struck. Bernard had often expressed this notion to his wife, who agreed, always adding, "but not otherwise."

Bertie arrived forty minutes after the call, with Mary, his wife, and a son in company, dismissed the cops with thanks, and attended to the wreckage of his kid brother's life. Mary made tea and comforting noises. She was wearing black, and Bernard supposed she had changed for the occasion. Mary had always regarded her brother-in-law as something of a challenge, he and his late wife having been the only members of the family she had not sculpted more or less to her satisfaction. The son, Matthew, was assigned the calling of the relatives, who began to arrive at the apartment later that afternoon.

Bernard stayed on the couch, wrapped in Louise's favorite afghan, inhaling her scent, wondering how long it would last. He was thinking about their last moments together, how trivial and quotidian they had been, how unrepresentative of the fullness and glory of their long relationship.

Twenty-nine years. They were planning a trip around the world for their thirtieth anniversary. Bernard had just completed a novel, so there was the book tour to consider, and they thought they could extend that into a pleasure jaunt. He was popular in Germany, and, oddly, Hong Kong and Singapore. He was sure his agent could set up speaking engagements in those places. Louise was longing to visit Vietnam, land of her ancestors, and she had a slew of relatives in Sydney she hadn't seen in years.

What would the last moments have been like, had we known?

This futile thought became obsessive for Bernard in the days and weeks after the event. In fact, they had experienced a minor spat that morning, of the type that any marriage of length has seen and seen off a thousand times. Some stupidity about a piece of plumbing, a special brass handle sold only by a shop on Madison quite near where his publisher had its offices, and so since he had a meeting there, and was going to be in the neighborhood anyway…but he had forgotten.

It was one of the healed scabs of their relationship: her perfectionism about the material surround, his indifference to it, and so they were careful not to peel it up. He apologized, promised to take a cab to the place, leap out, get the brass, and come back with it, and she had said not to bother, she had a lunch meeting in the neighborhood and would do it herself. And he had let her, with some relief mixed with the guilt. She had kissed him goodbye, which is something she did spontaneously when there was any contention in the air, but still it was not what he would have picked from a menu as the ultimate exchange of a long and generally loving marriage.

Of course, the dog helped, Murtagh, his Doberman, the dog helping a cliché he would not have used in a novel, but in the actuality undeniable. The dog missed her too, dumbly; which was how Bernard missed her, so they had a basis. The dog attended the funeral, despite Albert's objections. Albert had taken over the arrangements when it had become obvious that Bernard would not emerge from his virtual catatonia to fully participate, and that the kids were helpless in their grief. He had arranged a Catholic funeral Mass at Notre Dame, the elegant little church near Columbia University that Louise had attended, plus a reception and a burial at Calvary Cemetery. The coffin, of course, was closed.

The family gathered in the apartment after the funeral. Mary had arranged a caterer to provide the canapés and drinks she deemed necessary for any society whatever. Bernard was numbly grateful, and also for the arrangements that sent out the word to Louise's friends and workmates. Louise's mother had collapsed at hearing the news and was in the ICU at Downstate Hospital, so the Chu family did not linger. Bernard had not been particularly close with his in-laws. He suspected they thought that their brilliant girl might have done better than a hack writer, however rich. He wondered vaguely whether he would have much to do with any of them in future, and found he did not much care.

He sat on the sofa with his dog's head never far from his knee and watched his daughter spread the necessary social grease among her mother's family. He couldn't bear to watch her too closely, because in her slim, dark-haired beauty she so resembled Louise at the time he'd first met her. She was even wearing Louise's black Chanel dress. She might die too, he was thinking. People approached him, offering the fruitless, formal condolences usual at such events (If there's anything I can do . . .) He was polite to these nice folks, and only had to leave three times to go into the bedroom, close the door, and weep.

Each time, as he returned to his mourner's throne, he passed his son Lawrence, who sat in his mother's favorite leather sling chair inside an impenetrable bubble of grief. He hadn't moved in hours, it seemed, nor had he partaken of the funeral meats. Bernard patted him on the shoulder as he passed and asked him how he was doing. It was like patting furniture, the response a shrug, a murmur, a small emergence from grief. Bernard knew how he felt, and also that there would be no sharing comfort with this particular kid.

Bernard knew his son was a decent man; he had work he loved and many friends, but his dad was not one of them. Louise and Lawrence had had a thing that Bernard had never been able to penetrate. There was a photograph hanging in the hallway he had just passed, of himself and Lawrence, aged six, sitting on his lap and gazing up at him with adoration. Where did that go? Into the Internet, probably.

Once the kid discovered on-line, that had been it for the relationship. Bernard was an outdoorsy, athletic guy, Louise always described herself as a skilled indoors-woman, and Lawrence was the same. The teen years? Lawrence was neither hostile nor rebellious, merely indifferent, and a natural-born citizen of Bitlandia. Was not a Larry. Would not respond to Larry. Liked that he was named after the Founder, Lorenz Godríc; Bernard had spied the kid signing himself Lorenz. Perhaps that's how he was known to his peers. In the family, he was L.

And as if in response to some strange current of family dynamics, Leslie had become his. She rode horses, she shot, she ran, she tumbled, she swam, she fenced. Bernard came to the meets, he drove for the travel teams, ever faint with admiration. And, almost inevitably, she was also an artist, with vast

5

charming ambitions, to act, direct, write screenplays, make movies. The choice of arty Bennington for college a natural, and after her freshman year she had won a place in a highly selective summer program, with a major Broadway director to show off for. Now here she was in the great crisis, dry-eyed, showing class, the opposite of catatonic, making it all tolerable for the discomforted mourners.

Who departed as the sun faded in the big windows, leaving the diminished family trio alone with enough food-stuffs to feed them for weeks. Lawrence drifted off to his room, now the guest room, and closed the door. From behind it, the inquiring ear heard only the gentle click of the laptop key-board. Father and daughter exchanged a look, the most recent of two million they had exchanged in reference to Lawrence's behavior. The spectrum, they called it, although Louise had disapproved.

"He'll come around," Leslie said to her father as they worked in the kitchen, filling the refrigerator with plastic boxes of food.

"As around as he ever comes," said Bernard.

Leslie said, "Don't be hard on him, Dad. He really got blasted by this. And he's not good at this kind of stuff anyway."

"I know, I know--sorry. My God, I'd give anything to talk to her now. Is that crazy?"

"No. Me too."

"But I mean about L. Did you ever notice that we kind of skirted around that when you were younger? That he was odd? That our relationship was a little off?

"I wouldn't say skirted. We used to joke about it. Mom used to do like a robot when she wanted to get his attention. You know..."

Here a representation of her mother's robot act, the

buzzing voice, the automaton grimace, the jerky slo-mo of the limbs, so accurate that both of them burst into tears.

Bernard awakened the next morning, still exhausted after the usual threesome with Louise's ghost and Ms. Xanax, to the sound of his children bickering in the kitchen. He put on a robe and paused in the hallway to listen; like all fiction writers, he was an inveterate and shameless eavesdropper.

"…that's nuts," Leslie was saying. "What, national security depends on you occupying your cubicle and banging your keyboard? It's your family, for God's sake. You can take more than a couple of days off when your mother dies. You can tell national security it won't ever happen again."

Sound of weeping. "Oh, come on, Leslie. I'm not going to do stuff because you turn on the tears."

"Then fuck you. Go. Get out of here. Scram!"

"Well, *you'll* be here. You're the one he wants around anyway."

"Oh, don't be a jerk, Lawrence!"

Bernard thought this was a good time to make his entrance. They both looked up from where they sat at the counter. Bernard noticed that Lawrence's roll-aboard bag was standing in the corner, with his laptop case propped on top of it.

Bernard said, "Good morning, kids," and to Lawrence, "I see you're going."

"Yeah, Dad, I really have to be in Boston this afternoon, seriously, or I would stay . . . "

"What's going on in Boston?"

Lawrence looked at his sneaker. "Actually, I can't tell you what."

"Secret agent man," said Leslie.

"Be nice, Leslie," said Bernard. "Okay, but here's the thing. L. *should* go and so should you, Leslie. Get back to your lives."

At this Leslie protested that she wanted to stay, that Bernard shouldn't be alone at a time like this, to which Bernard responded that he was not alone, that he had his writing and his friends, and that she had worked so hard for the coveted slot in the Marlboro theater program, and that it would make him more miserable than he already was should she not go back. Her mother would have said the same, he added, had it been Bernard in the closed coffin.

This last worked: tears ensued, Lawrence made his escape, and Leslie packed and caught the 3:15 to Bennington. Bernard spent the rest of that day in the apartment, sleeping a lot, awakening from time to time to take another pill, happy that his kids were not around to see his agony. He didn't work; he did not allow visits from friends.

Some weeks later, Bernard found he had no memory of any of this, or rather he had only bits and fragments, like the traces of a film seen many years ago. He imagined he must have interacted with the other mourners in some way, but he couldn't recall any of it. He did remember the stupid argument with Louise about the brass fixture handles and he remembered Leslie volunteering to drop out of her theater summer and take care of him.

Soon after Leslie had gone back to Bennington, he called his housekeeper into his office and suggested that this would be a good time for her to take a long vacation. He reminded her that she and her husband and kids had long wanted to visit their families in the Philippines. How long, she asked, like two weeks? Take a year, he said, and wrote out a five-figure check. She left the next day, blessing him for a saint. But he

8

was not anything like a saint; he just wanted to be alone, with Murtagh and with his hallucinations.

He heard her voice; he sat in the living room, in his accustomed chair, with a book written (it seemed) in a language he could no longer read, and there would be a sound from the kitchen and the familiar tread and then the uncanny, dreadful sense of her presence in the room. Occasionally, he had night terrors: the bedroom door slowly opening, him paralytic on the bed, her standing in the doorway in her mangled state, smiling. He had never seen her so, of course, but was he not a professional of imagination? He screamed himself awake from these episodes, and swallowed the pink ovals that provided oblivion.

He thought he might be one of those men who wasted away and died when their spouses died, but after some weeks this notion passed. He was drugging himself heavily and not eating, but his vitals were fine. He had a stationary bike that he rarely used, but now he dragged it out and became a fanatic: fifteen, twenty, thirty miles a day at the highest setting, with the headphones on, and every so often a song would come on that had meant something to the marriage and he would break down, sobbing and screaming curses into the empty apartment, and pedal yet faster.

His keyboard gathered dust; his smartphone sat on his dresser top uncharged and silent; he ate takeout, when he remembered to eat. His daughter sent him a weekly postcard, an art print or some ironic cartoon on the front, chat and jokes on the back; his son sent emails, the ding of the incoming message unnaturally loud in the silent apartment.

He answered desultorily: I'm fine, don't worry. Bernard loved his children, but just now the sight of their faces, Louise's eyes in their faces exposing their pain, was more than he could bear. Albert represented the family to the press and to the legal system. The wretch who killed Louise would be tried, and probably be declared not guilty by reason of insanity, but Bernard was uninterested in these proceedings and grateful that he had a brother who relished such things.

So, he lived on. Every morning he was nudged awake by a large damp nose and the rattle of a dragged lead. Then the tormenting moment as he rose out of sleep when he could imagine that the thing had been an actual nightmare and that if he listened, he could hear her light step moving down the hall to the kitchen.

Bernard's apartment was on West End Avenue, four bedrooms, bought years ago when the kids came; God knew what it was worth now. He'd have to rewrite the will; they had both left everything to the other. Pull on the same clothes, jeans, the ancient sneakers, t-shirt, a ball cap and sunglasses, so he would not have to meet an eye, a leather jacket as the year advanced and grew chill. Not literally the same clothes; Bernard may have stopped shaving regularly, but he washed and changed his clothes and ran the washer. Because she would have wanted it; he feared to disgrace her by any extravagance of grief.

During this period, he tried to avoid conversation with anyone but the dog. Murtagh. It was one of Bernard's peculiarities that he talked to his dog. Many dog owners do this, but in his case the dog responded and Bernard could understand what it said. He had been doing this his whole life, as far as he could recall. Children do speak to entities that are not thought to have the power of speech and imagine that these speak back, but this habit typically fades with childhood. It had not, in Bernard's case. He did not actually hear a voice in his head, but words did appear there, along with the feeling that it was not him who produced them. It was akin to what happened when he created dialog in writing fiction, but more intense, for there was the living creature, its brown eyes glowing with sensitive comprehension. Or so it seemed.

"What am I going to do, Murtagh?" he would moan at night.

<Eat. Drink. Piss. Shit. Sleep. Go on walks. Throw the ball.>

"That hardly seems like a sufficient life."

<You could sniff females.>

"Not quite yet," replied Bernard.

But as the weeks passed, it became clear that he was not going to climb into the grave with Louise. As everyone said, life went on, and although this discovery brought no comfort, on it still went. Early in September, the kids came back and selected the things of their mother's that they wanted to keep and they had a dinner in the apartment. Leslie whipped up a stir-fried beef dinner no one really wanted and they all hung around in the kitchen while she wokked, as they had in happier times, and avoided staring at the empty chair.

Bernard watched his kids chatting amiably, L. teasing Leslie about the intellectual deficits of the country club college she attended, comparing it unfavorably to his MIT. She offered a stout defense of the liberal arts, and got the needle in pretty well. He was a mushroom, bleached and desiccated, who spent his whole life staring at a screen, the juice of life was not in him. In fact, Lawrence was a remarkably handsome young man of twenty-two, with his mother's elegant features set atop his father's stocky, dense body, black eyes and hair, inheriting only the prow-like Goodrich nose. Bernard had never been able to get the boy into athletics of any kind, so that the tapping finger comprised his sole muscular effort. As a result, Leslie was right: he was fungus-pale and starting to get plump.

Leslie, in contrast, was a wand like her mom, had that prized Eurasian melding, the almond eyes, the cheekbones, the sculpted mouth, but with solid jaw line and a narrow, high-bridged nose. She moved like Louise, had the same timbre in her voice. On occasion, even now, Bernard had to look away from her, when one of her gestures brought the dead into the room.

Leslie called upon her father to defend literature and the arts from the philistine, and he reluctantly engaged. The son said that technology had changed everything; Bernard maintained that technology had changed nothing. Human experience was mediated by art, and it didn't matter what the medium was. The medium was not the message; the message was still the message. Art was linked indissolubly with nature. No, said his son, nature was beat, was dying, we have God-like powers now, we were going to escape from nature entirely.

The argument grew heated as the spicy dishes cooled, until Leslie said, in just her mother's tone, "Oedipal, shmedi-pal," and they all laughed, after which all three felt that they had passed out of a circle of hell, perhaps even in the right direction. Over the ensuing weeks, Bernard arranged for people to come and take away Louise's books and clothes, while he himself distributed the keepsakes and valuables that appeared in the careful list Louise had appended to her will. Where possible, he used shipping companies. Where not, he doped himself up and made visits, always brief, and heard from many people all about what a wonderful person his late wife had been.

Aside from this, he didn't care to deal with his fellow man. As he had long known, it is quite possible for a professional writer in New York City to exist with minimal human contact. There is no job at the office, no classes to teach, no clients gaping like baby birds for attention. Six weeks after he became a widower, Bernard was back at work on a novel; a little ashamed, true, but grinding out the pages all the same.

Bernard wrote a series of popular thrillers about a young woman named Noreen Blow and her dog, Bingo. The premise of the series was that Noreen was a graduate student in philosophy at a fictitious university in the Philadelphia area, where Bernard had in fact gone to college. She was just doing PI work until she could land her doctorate, and the running gag of the series was that every time she seemed to be about to complete her dissertation or schedule her orals, something violent came up in the locality, which, despite the leafy academic surround, had a murder rate exceeding that of Ciudad Juarez. Noreen's dog Bingo was a huge Dobe just like Murtagh, and the other running gag was that the dog solved all the cases.

Each book was essentially the same: complex preposterous plots, colorful characters, snappy dialog. To save his sanity and his self-respect (for Bernard, whose superior education had taught him that novels were supposed to be subtle, complex, obscure, and full of fine writing, considered genre somewhat shameful) he larded the novels with literary references and, using Noreen and her philosophy department as a foil, inserted the great questions of philosophy into the routine structure of the thriller. *Dog Gone*, his third, dealt with the nature of perception; *Bad Dog*, the next, was all Aristotle and Kant and ethics; *Hell Hound*, covered ontology and the underlying nature of being; *Puppy Love* delved into the Romantic philosophers; and *Dog Is Dead* featured Nietzsche and his atheistic epigones. A minority of Bernard's readers got the joke, and the rest, he imagined, flipped through all that to get to the artfully depicted violence and the dirty parts. He sold hundreds of thousands of copies in paper, each book opening a little higher on the bestseller list of the *Times*.

He had become prosperous from this work, although he hardly needed the money. The family firm, Goodrich & Sons, founded by his great-grandfather, was the second largest veterinary supply company in the nation, and Bernard had a substantial chunk of its stock as an inheritance. "You're such a good writer..." people often began when they encountered him, and he had become skilled at forestalling the obvious follow (so why do you write genre?) with some light remark: it's fun, I enjoy it, it makes people happy, the serious novel is dead, boring, inane, some of the best writing today is found in genre, and similar.

This stance was only true-ish. Like any writer not actually mad, Bernard desired acknowledgement by the current literati. He would have liked to be reviewed by the prominent journals, he would have liked to be invited to speak at literary gatherings, he would have liked to attend festivals and be awarded prizes. These desires were wistful rather than urgent; until his wife was murdered, he had considered himself a fortunate and contented man.

Now his life had a hole in it, and from this pit sprang demons. How remarkable that a small Vietnamese-American woman could have held them at bay for so long, himself all unaware of this service. He thought that the raw grief would fade, felt it was fading already, the familiar face and voice becoming harder each day to bring to mind, this horrible in itself but not nearly as horrible as the nakedness he now felt, the absence of any defense against his own self-contempt, and this, he feared would not fade, might even worsen. He recalled bursts of this sort of despair earlier in his life, but they had ceased with his marriage. Louise could always jolly him out of the hole, and refused to take his megrims seriously. Absent her presence, a sourness prevailed. He was a pathetic hack, unloved, unlovable, virtually friendless, a silly hollow man. He doubted even his dog.

"Do you barely tolerate me, Murtagh?" he asked as he left his building one autumn morning. The dog, heeling precisely by Bernard's right knee, responded to the tone and glanced up with a doggy grin.

<I love you beyond all expression.>

Bernard loved the dog back, but felt it made him even more pathetic: aging phony relies on the cupboard love of an animal. Not to mention his tenuous grip on reality, evidence of which was his belief that he could hear his dog talking to him. A harmless illusion, he had thought, but worrisome now.

They walked west on 77th Street to the park, leaves crunching under foot and paw, Bernard oblivious to the fine blue day, the dog less so. After crossing West End Avenue, Bernard felt Murtagh stiffen and tug against his lead, something he rarely did. Bernard focused, and saw that the rear window of a black Town Car parked just ahead had rolled down and that an arm clad in a shimmery gray silk coat hung from it. Coming closer, he could see that the small hand at its end held a small, stiff brown rectangle: a liver snap.

The dog whined and looked beseechingly at the man, who nodded and slackened the lead, at which the dog darted forward and the hand dropped the treat delicately into its maw. The empty hand now made a beckoning motion.

Bernard approached the black car and said, "Good morning, Elsie."

"Good morning, Bernard," replied the woman in the car, who was E. B. Schriffren, Bernard's literary agent. "Would you like a liver snap too?"

"No, thank you. What are you doing here, Elsie? Am I being stalked?"

"Actually, Bernard, when your agent wishes to communicate with you, the phone or email is the usual route. When authors don't answer email or respond to numberless voicemail messages, for *weeks* upon end, then the agent may resort to ambush, as now. What the fuck, Bernie?"

"The fuck is my wife just got murdered. I'm grieving."

"Just? That was in early June. It's October now. You noticed the leaves falling off the trees? Really, Bernard, I'm sympathetic—you know how much I liked Louise—but life goes on. I have a business to run, of which you are a part. I guess you've forgotten that you have a book out in two weeks. *Mongrel Race*? Ring a bell?"

"That's an unusually dumb title, even for me."

"Your publisher loves it."

"I hate the cover, too. Two mutts running away from a dead body?"

"Your publisher loves that as well. Could you get in the car? I feel like I'm arguing with a squeegee man."

Bernard said, "Murtagh, lie down. Stay!" The dog dropped, panting. Bernard went around the rear of the car and swung into the back seat.

Air kiss, and "You look better than I thought you would. You dropped some weight."

"Thank you. I've started another one."

"A Noreen and Bingo?"

"No, a sensitive evocation of life in a small New England town, involving the death of a child and containing a lot of fine language."

Elsie checked to see if he was kidding. "Well, you know I always say you can write whatever you want and I'll be happy to represent you."

"You do say that, but you lie. You lust after Noreen-and-Bingos. And in reality I *am* writing another. I thought of calling it *Sleeping Dogs Lie*. It's about the morality of lying, and I get into epistemological themes—the Gettler Problem, Nozick's work, and so on. I see a gelid smile. Also, Noreen gets kidnapped and is about to be gang raped when Bingo comes through the skylight. And her face lights up. So—you see I'm alive and working—are we done here?"

"Not so fast, bub. You have a book tour, and I want to make sure you're on it. I sent you the details weeks ago. Check your computer."

"I'm not touring, Elsie. I forgot how to smile inanely. Oh, is that a sigh?"

"We've been over this, Bernard," was the weary reply. "If you don't want to tour, you should not sign contracts obligating you to do so, and I will endeavor to obtain such terms for you in future. But you *did* sign one for this book that *does* so obligate you, and if you want to keep your publisher on board and me as your agent, you will comply. Honestly, Bernard, first class to eight cities, premium hotels . . . what's not to like? Your adoring fans lining up for a few seconds of face time, the bookstore owners caressing you . . . and you're good at touring. I've seen you charm a crowd."

"I'm out of charm just now," said Bernard, working the door handle.

She detained him with a hand on his arm. "Darling, you know I love you, but this is for real. You *have* to tour. Marty is inclined to be understanding about your personal problems, but he's unyielding on this. If you don't go, he says he'll hold us in breach, plus they're talking about pulling all the stops out on this one, full court on marketing, publicity, ads. They want to open at number one for the first time. You could be another Patricia Cornwell or James Patterson."

"Fulfilling my boyhood dream, yes. Why don't we let them breach me and we'll take the book elsewhere. I don't see why all this *unyielding*--everyone knows touring is bullshit."

"But it gets people into bookstores. Maybe they'll buy a latte. Marty has guaranteed that your warm body will appear at the important bookstores, i.e., the ones that contribute to the *Times* bestseller survey that no one is supposed to know which they are, but everyone does. Plus, this is not all about you, Bernard. The marketing and success of a book floats many boats. Lots of people depend on your good behavior. So, play nice. Please, for Elsie?"

Why not? thought Bernard then. He doubted he could feel worse in Chicago or Atlanta. So he said, "Elsie, you're a pain in the ass, but I love you too. I will read the thing on the computer, and I will comply."

"Good. There's a sales meeting tomorrow at Forman's—it's on the schedule I sent you. You have to be there."

"Yes, mom. Can I have my liver snap now?"

There was a muffled burble of music. She pulled a phone from her bag, checked its screen, and said, "That's good, Bernie. Bernie, I have to take this. Kissie, bye!"

"But I'm going to take you," Bernard told his dog as the black car drove off.

<Of course. You would not survive a minute without me.>

The next morning, Bernard shaved, dressed in clean Levis and a black denim shirt, donned a leather coat, topped it with a worn tweed cap and called a car. His clothes hung loose on him, but the persona into which he struggled was tight, sweaty, full of grit. To his surprise, he got through the meeting without snapping. He was made much of, and the dog was spoiled rotten, and called Bingo by everyone they passed in the halls of Forman Bros., Publishers.

Bernard was neutrally cordial to his publisher, Marty Small; he shook the man's hand, arranged for Murtagh to do likewise, was kind and avuncular to the kids on the sales and PR staffs, received praise graciously, uttered no sarcasms, and was out on the street by one-thirty, feeling as if he'd run a cross-country race, a feeling he knew well from the hundreds of such races he had run as a youth.

What knocked him over was the toilet store. Pekko Waterworks was its name, high-end bathroom and kitchen fixtures for the carriage trade, on Madison near 58th. The mermaid taps. That was what he had forgotten to pick up, a pair of elegant brass faucet handles Louise had ordered. She'd had this thing about mermaids, a silly and endearing taste that made it easy for everyone to buy presents for her, and this was an example thereof. She'd seen them in this window, and here they were, lying like jewelry on a plush cushion and it was like he'd been Tasered, tear-gassed, his legs gave way and his eyes spouted water, and he had to sit on a hydrant on the side of the building, his dog whining faintly with concern.

"What's happening to me, Murtagh?" he asked. "Am I actually going mad?"

<I will lick your face. It always helps.>

After a moment, aware that passers-by were staring, he wobbled to his feet and headed west on 58th, then drifted down Fifth Avenue in a daze until he found himself facing the gray massif of St. Patrick's Cathedral. In a daze, he stayed his dog in front of the statue of St. Kateri and entered.

It was full of Asian tourists wearing yellow golf jackets. A handful of elderly people sat in the pews, a few actually kneeling in prayer. Bernard walked down a side aisle and bought a candle at an altar dedicated to Our Lady of

Guadalupe. Bernard had not gone willingly to a Catholic Church--weddings and funerals aside-- since he had come of age, although he had been religious enough as a child, had been an altar server, in fact, and had enjoyed the rituals.

At the age of thirteen, however, while working the ten o'clock Mass at Star of the Sea, he had lost his faith. It remained inexplicable, although he had heard similar stories from other lapsed Catholics he knew. He'd been fine at the Introit, at the Kyrie, at the Gloria, but somewhere between the Sanctus and the Consecration, the whole thing had disappeared. One moment he was inside, and the world made a certain kind of sense, and the difficult or unpleasant aspects of being a Catholic were explained and justified; and in the next, like a kitten dumped from a cushion, he was outside of it all, alone and confused. He told no one of this, not parents, teachers, priest or friends, but continued as he had before, going to church, making the motions, living an accommodating, false life.

He had told Louise, though, she a true believer, a descendent of the old Vietnamese Catholic aristocracy, and she had laughed and told him it was a normal function of puberty, you couldn't handle the old Church's nuttiness about sex, but he knew it wasn't that at all.

Now he sat in a pew and thought about praying, maybe even praying for his wife's soul. That's why they built cathedrals, he thought, to make it difficult to suppose that their immensity and beauty could rest on nothing at all. He didn't quite pray, but nor did he believe that she was absolutely gone. He slipped a dollar into the slot and lit another candle, and as he did he heard a voice behind him say, "It's okay, Bug."

He dropped the taper and whirled around, but no one was there. Of course. Bug, her pet name for him, from Bernard Usher Goodrich, initials seen on a briefcase. Hair standing up on his arms, cold sweat on his face, he left the building, not quite at a run.

Outside, Murtagh sniffed at him peculiarly, as if he had been a stranger. No, that was imagination, like the voice, although so real, so clearly *not* in his head. He snapped on the unnecessary lead and walked rapidly west, wanting to warm up the chill he felt, although he knew it had nothing to do with the weather.

At Fifth Avenue, Bernard saw two mounted policemen and felt an odd pang. It had been a while since he'd been on a horse, but the creatures still lifted his heart. After he lost his faith, he had turned his faculty of worship toward horses. The Goodriches had long owned a place in Locust Valley, its stables stocked with warm-blood saddle horses and jumpers. Both his father, Alfred Goodrich, and his mother, Rose-Marie Usher Goodrich, were competitive riders.

It had been clear to Bernard and his brother from an early age that the horses were rather more important to their parents than the sons were. During the show-jumping season, the couple left their children in the care of servants while they flew around the country and to Europe, their horses following in vans and specially-equipped aircraft.

Bernard had ridden from earliest childhood, and ridden well, but he disliked competition, to the great frustration of his parents. (Albert was the competitor, although, in fact, and to his dismay, a lesser horseman than his brother.) After his loss of faith, however, Bernard changed. He rode thereafter in deadly earnest, and his ribbons and trophies accumulated in the family's long glass cases. At sixteen, driven by some odd romantic quirk, he had decided to take up the Olympic pentathlon.

The family was not entirely pleased by this turn (all that shooting, running, swimming was a little infra dig) but was

21

supportive. Coaches were employed to improve those skills, and Bernard started to rise in the rankings as a pentathlete, first regionally and then nationally. He delayed starting college on the chance that he could make the Olympic team in 1980. And so, he did, last man picked, but on the team and on the way to Moscow.

Except that those Moscow Olympics hadn't happened--the Afghanistan thing--and Bernard had lost his mind entirely, entering a period of his life he had struggled to forget, except for the dogs.

One of the cop horses turned its head and gave him a look and Bernard felt his eyes prickle. How he had loved them.

He turned quickly away, crossed Fifth with the dog, entered the Park and there defied the law against the unleashed. Bernard and the dog played with a ball. The dog ran and leaped, snatching it from the air, dropping it at his master's feet, each time a small thrill of pleasure in the man. The dog could not fill the hole in the man's life, however. That was not what dogs were for. Louise walked by pushing a stroller, but Bernard made himself look away.

They played until a cop showed up and gave Bernard a ticket for being off leash not at the time permitted, after which Bernard and the dog went home. Bernard wrote out a check for the ticket and packed for his book tour. The next morning the dog shipping guy came, Murtagh walked meekly into the crate, and Bernard took a limo to Kennedy. On the LAX end, Sue, the young woman provided by the publisher, was clearly prepped to handle a gigantic, fierce-looking dog as well as her primary charge. She presented Murtagh with a dog treat. He ignored it.

"Doesn't he like Zuke's?" the woman asked. "They're all natural, grain-free."

"He loves them. But he's a Schutzhund. He doesn't take food except from me or when I say he can."

"He's not a Doberman?" she asked.

"He is. Schutzhund is an obedience training method and a ranking system. Murtagh is a level one, the lowest of three. Murtagh, you can have your treat now."

"What can he do?" asked the young woman after the fragment had vanished. "Whadya got?" replied Bernard, and they both laughed.

The hotel was in Century City, and the first bookshop was The Black Dahlia in Brentwood, a low-ceilinged place with skinny aisles so crammed with books as to be claustrophobic. The owner was named Jack Bill Nashe and was a friend of both Bernard and Murtagh.

"Does he still read?" Jack Bill asked, ruffling the dog's ears.

"He does, but he thinks post-modernism is in the toilet."

"He's right there. Could you make him do it when you do the reading?"

"For you, Jack Bill, anything. How's the throng?"

Jack Bill airplaned a hand. "Maybe fifty? I'm tweeting about the reading dog right now. The throng will grow."

It turned out to be closer to seventy, and the back room where the Dahlia held readings was jammed and hot. Bernard brought Murtagh out on the stage, and placed his new book at the sitting animal's feet, at which the dog began to carefully turn pages with its paw, and utter a burbling growl that might have been taken for human speech in an unfamiliar tongue. The effect was delightful: Murtagh looked and sounded wonderfully like a man reading aloud. Bernard enjoyed this aspect of his tours: a bit of the mountebank must attach to any genre author, besides which he was happy to demonstrate the brilliance of his dog.

After the dog read, so did Bernard, the first chapter of *Mongrel Race,* to enthusiastic applause. Bernard smiled back at the crowd and could not help noticing that the woman in the center of the second row was Louise.

He couldn't breathe. His field of vision narrowed to a gray tunnel; with an effort, he wrenched his gaze away and let it settle on a woman in the front row. Jack Bill was taking questions. Where do you get your ideas? Who trained your dog?

He spoke the answers to the woman in the front row. She had a calm face framed by dark brown hair, more pleasant than striking, and her outfit—a light coat in a dead-leaf color over a just darker sweater and skirt—was calm as well, casually expensive in the manner of women who wish to make the impression that they don't care what they throw on. She met his eye so frankly that he had to blink and look elsewhere. After the last question, he was relieved to see that Louise had changed back into an ordinary Asian woman who barely resembled his late wife.

When the questions ended, Bernard sat at a table in the rear of the room with a stack of books beside him, the dog stretched out at his feet, bearing patiently the caresses of his fans, these perhaps even more numerous than his master's. Who poised his Sharpie on the title page and signed books and eventually looked up into the face of the calm woman from the front row. He noticed that she was tall and slender, like a runway model.

"What name shall I put?" he asked.

"Miranda," she said. He wrote, "For Miranda, Best Wishes," and signed it. When he handed the book to her, she said, "Poor Bug. You miss me, But you're not going crazy."

With that, she turned and was gone in the crowd.

Two

Bernard found himself on his feet, staring after the woman, just for a moment until he came back to himself, and felt his face burn. The young couple next in line asked him if anything was wrong. He sat, drank a gulp from his plastic bottle, and brought what he thought must have been a ghastly smile to his face. To Bruce and Shara, Best wishes. Next . . .

Another hallucination, this one more disturbing than the others because it had involved another person, close-up. The fan (Miranda?) could not have said what he thought she had. Had the woman been there at all?

Later, after the crowd had gone, he asked Jack Bill if he recalled her.

"A friend of yours?"

"Never saw her before," said Bernard, "but I'd like to see her again, if I can."

"Not a problem if she bought her book on a card. Name of what did you say?"

"Miranda."

"No last?"

"She didn't give it."

Jack Bill grinned, said, "I love a mystery!" and turned to his computer.

She *had* used a credit card, proving herself one of the blessed few who still paid full retail in a bookstore. "Miranda G. Gardiner, Bank of Hawaii Visa," said Jack Bill. "Want me to do some digging?"

"Could you?"

"What was this, love at first sight?"

"No. I just want to know if I'm crazy or not. No, I *know* I'm crazy. I just want to, you know, check the oil."

Jack Bill said, "Oh, I've been there. Let's go to my office."

Jack Bill had his office above the shop, a triangular room, with a view through narrow windows of the tony shopping street on which the Black Dahlia stood. The office contained a leather couch, a plain wooden desk with a laptop on it and a swivel chair behind, a leather sling chair draped with a serape, a stuffed coyote on a stand, and an old white Frigidaire.

"Want a Grolsch?" asked Jack Bill, crouching in the glow of the open refrigerator.

"Could I have whiskey instead?"

Jack Bill gave Bernard a look. "Well, sure. I got a bottle of Dickel somewhere. Want some weed, too? I also got a tank of nitrous, but I'd have to look for the regulator."

"Just the whiskey, please."

When they had their drinks in hand, and after a splash of beer had been poured into a bowl for the dog, Jack Bill lit up his machine, typed, made a phone call, typed some more, muttered a little, typed, said, "You hungry? I could call out for something."

"No, thank you. Did you find anything yet?"

"Oh, yeah, no mystery there. With a credit card number and you know who to call, it's not too hard to get the dope on someone. Your girl is Miranda G. Gardiner, address in Honolulu, self-employed, excellent credit. She's staying at the Radisson by USC. Want her cell?"

"No. Wait, okay, what is it?"

Bernard keyed the number into his own phone, feeling both silly and excited. "Self-employed as what?" he asked.

"I don't know, but let's ask Mr. Google." More typing. "Here she is . . . uh-oh, you drew a fruitcake."

Bernard came around the desk and looked at the screen. He saw a large portrait of the woman he had seen, clearly Photoshopped to enhance her allure. She was not wearing a turban or peering into a crystal ball, but it was almost that bad: on a violet background cavorted stars, planets, and astrological signs. Small panels set on the page at odd angles showed Stonehenge, Egyptian hieroglyphs, Mayan pyramids, and other mystic crystal revelations. The text announced, in a hard to read script-like typeface, that Miranda was available for psychic consultation via phone and Skype, and in the flesh in Honolulu. There was a schedule of fees, a brief biography, a couple of columns of New Age boilerplate, and a widget where you typed in your date of birth and received astrological advice.

Bernard felt disappointment mixed with contempt, as always when he discovered that a new acquaintance believed in this stuff. Louise had regarded such credulousness as the next thing to pathology, and had been a fan of the various stage magicians and professional rationalists who made it their business to expose claims of psychic powers.

On the other hand, there was what he had just heard the woman say. Practically no one outside the family knew that Louise used to call him Bug. Also, he'd just had a Louise hallucination, and this Miranda seemed to know it. On the other other hand, he could have imagined it. Maybe she'd just said, "Thank you, Mr. Goodrich, I really like your work."

Somewhat to his surprise, he observed his fingers typing a phony date of birth and his email address into the widget.

"Going to give it a shot, I see," said Jack Bill. "She

must've knocked your socks off."

"No, but did you ever do something you knew was crazy, but you just had to see how it played out?"

"Innumerable times. Shit like that usually ends up costing a pile of money and/or occasioning significant wear and tear on the physical frame. Especially with a woman in the picture. I knew a so-called psychic once back when I was with the cops in Oakland. Tiny little redheaded girl, couldn't have weighed more'n a hundred pounds wet, not that great a looker either, but Jesus, when she walked into a room no one could let their eyes set on anything else."

"What could she do?"

"Not that I believe this shit, but she could find stuff. You could say to her, 'Roxanne, where in hell is my sixteen-foot tape measure,' and she'd go, 'Look behind the shed!' And you'd have to figure out what that meant—which particular shed, and so on. But damned if that fucking tape wasn't sitting there behind some god-damn shed, out at a crime scene, for example. She found a missing kid once..."

"Really?"

"Yeah. Why are you interested in this girl?

"I'm not going to hear about the kid?"

"Not just now."

"Interested is the right word, then," Bernard said. "I haven't been *interested* in anything since Louise died. Thanks for the ferreting and the drink."

"De nada, brother," said Jack Bill. "But I'd keep a grasp on your wallet, you hang out with a girl like that."

Bernard shook the man's hand and walked out, with Murtagh at his heels. Behind him Jack Bill sang "Age of Aquarius" in a pleasant tenor.

Out in the street, the waiting black car slid to the curb, they got in, and as they did a chime sounded on Bernard's smartphone. It was a message from Miranda.

> You are emerging from a dark period of loss into a great ex-pansion. Prepare for changes.You need not limit yourself as you have in the past. Look for a guide to appear.

Again the little thrill of revulsion, fascination. Look for a guide, my ass. was his thought, and still there was the memo-ry of her face and voice and what she had said. Or not, if he was nuts.

"Our next stop is downtown," said Sue the Minder as the car pulled into traffic. "You have an interview at NPR."

"Downtown—is that near USC? The Radisson?"

"In the vicinity. Why?"

"You can drop me off thereafter. I'm meeting someone."

He typed a few lines into the phone and by the time they swung onto the freeway the answer appeared. Yes, she would be happy to meet him in the lobby of the Radisson at four-thirty.

"What do you think of this, Murtagh? I seem to be go-ing on a date."

<Have you sniffed her anus?>

"Not yet."

<Sometimes God is a jerk>

Bernard could not disagree.

He entered the lobby with Murtagh on a short lead, and found the space a typical Brown Room, dark wood, maroon carpeting, beige and other unthreatening colors on the uphol-stery. He checked out the seating areas, but no one resembling Miranda was present. He took a chair, downed the dog, and scratched its ears, feeling an unaccustomed sense of anticipa-tion. It was like being in college and waiting in the lobby of the girls' dorm for your date to descend. He passed the time by studying the other people sitting in the lobby--a group of chatting elderly women, a couple with a toddler, a single woman with an ordinary face reading a paper, three guys in expensive casual attire, who could be musicians or software moguls, a bearded man working a laptop. No Miranda.

Then the single woman stood and walked toward him and everyone in the lobby looked up at her. It was impossible not to, she seemed to throw light, or anyway some kind of attractive energy. The three musicians or moguls stopped conversing. The toddler broke briefly from her parents and toddled toward her, the dog pricked up its ears, wagged its tail, panted.

The woman held out her hand and Bernard popped to his feet. He took her hand, cool and dry, with electricity in there somehow, and said, "How did you do that?"

"Do what?"

"I came in, I looked around, I saw you, but . . . it was like you weren't there. I didn't recognize you. And then you just, like, appeared."

"Well, you only saw me for a minute in the bookstore, so...."

"No, I knew what you looked like. I was looking right at you, and you weren't there." She was an inch or so taller than he was, he discovered, which made him want to sit down. He gestured to a chair. She smiled and sat, and Bernard resumed his seat.

"Oh, that," she said. "It's the aura. I can control mine, its size and direction and intensity. When I draw it into my body, I'm essentially invisible. It's handy when I'm writing and don't want to be disturbed."

"And now you've turned it up to high."

She laughed, a bubbling guffaw, like a kid. "Busted. I wanted to impress you."

"And this aura thing is part of your psychic armory?"

She looked bemused. "My psychic . . . ? Oh, no, anyone can do it, but women especially. There's a story about Marilyn Monroe walking down a street in L.A. with Arthur Miller and he says, I can't understand why all these people aren't noticing you, and she goes, oh, you want to see *her*, and she turns it up high and in two minutes she's being mobbed."

"I see. And why would you want to impress me?"

"Because I'm sitting here talking to *Bernard Goodrich*, is why. I'm such a huge fan of your work. I give your books to all my friends. I've read all of them any number of times. I couldn't believe it when I saw you responded to my web page." She smiled, the kind of smile you saw in photographs of political or religious leaders surrounded by their acolytes, that open blazing devotion. Bernard knew he had ardent fans, but had not experienced this smile before. It made him giddy.

"Well, thank you. I should tell you that I'm not really into all this psychic and astrology stuff. I wanted to see you because of something you said at the signing."

A look of puzzlement appeared on her face. "What I said? But I didn't say anything except my name for the dedication and a thank you."

"No, you told me I wasn't going crazy. And you called me Bug."

"But I didn't say anything like . . . Oh, wait. It was probably a visitation. Did you lose someone close to you recently?"

"Yes. My wife died in June."

"And did she call you Bug, like for a pet name?"

"Yes, it's from my initials—Bernard Usher Goodrich."

"Well, that explains it then. I'm not much of a medium, I mean professionally, but a lot of psychics are mediumistic. What did I say again?"

"You said, 'Poor Bug. You miss me so much. But you're not going crazy.'"

"Yes, she wanted to reassure you that it was really her, and she used me. I don't have any memory of when I get used that way, which was why I was puzzled. You thought you were nuts--yeah, we get that all the time. I take it there have been other visitations. "

"I think I see her all the time. I saw her in the crowd at the reading this afternoon."

"Oh, so that was what it was. I got a clear sense that one of the departed was there. Um, Louise, wasn't it? Funny-- that name has been running around in my head for hours, and now I know why."

"Forgive me, Ms. Gardiner . . ."

"Please, it's Miranda."

"Miranda. Forgive me, but, as I said, I don't believe in any of that."

"You'd rather think you're going crazy?"

"No, but . . . I'm sorry, this is all very distressing. And I think I need a drink. Will you join me?"

They shared a booth. She had club soda and bitters; he had a Gibson. On top of Jack Bill's bourbon, it produced something close to a feeling that he knew what was going on. He knew at some level that this was false, but he didn't care.

He studied her face in quick glances as they swerved into small talk: where she was from (Hawaii, rural California before that) what she was doing in L.A. (some kind of New Age conclave called Heart and Spirit, at the convention center). She had spotted the notice about his reading in the paper and, of course, she had to come.

Not a classic beauty, not like Louise, the jaw too long, the brow a little heavy, but her face attracted the eye in the manner of one of the great actresses who parlay an unusual face into a career. Eyes set at an odd angle and very long—wolf eyes—and blue-jeans blue. She wore little makeup--a pale lipstick and some eyeliner; her hair style he thought too severe, and he could not help imagining what it would look like unleashed and flowing around her shoulders. He found himself talking about Louise, something he never did with strangers. He related anecdotes from the marriage, he tried to describe her qualities, what made her lovable.

"She had no bullshit at all in her. Honestly. Purity of heart. She loved her crazies, she gave herself to the lowest of the low. Sometimes I thought she cared more about them than about me and our kids, but it wasn't a problem. Being a writer—well, you tend to live in your own world, and the fictive universe starts interacting with the real one. You play games with words, with the truth. And she wouldn't have it. She grounded me, she put up with none of my crap. Since she died, the world seems unreal, like a dream, someone else's dream I got stranded in. I'm sorry, I don't know why I'm telling you all this."

"People tend to tell me things. What was her month and date of birth?"

Bernard told her, and for a long moment she seemed to go away, her eyes off to the side and her face unnaturally still.

"Yes. Well, she's in a good place. A Pisces. You *would* pick a Pisces. Why did you lie on my site about your date of birth?"

Bernard shrugged and swallowed some of his drink. "I just picked the first date that came to mind. Bastille Day, you know? How did you know I was lying?"

She stared at him, then grinned and let out a sharp bark of a laugh. "Um, because I'm a psychic? What's your actual birthday?"

"If you're a psychic, you should be able to guess."

She stared again, this time with a disturbing intensity. Her eyes seemed to light with tiny sparks.

"You're a Libran. Moon in Sagittarius. Pisces rising. That's what gives you your tenderness of feeling. Your Sagittarian moon combined with your Venus in Leo makes you hide this behind a façade of boisterous masculinity. That's the downside; the upside of the Venus placement, plus your Libran sun, makes you unusually honorable and puts you on the side of fairness and justice. Mercury in Aquarius—that's your intellectual brilliance and your slippery presentation. You're an athlete—that's Sagittarius again, but you're not a superstar. It's because of your moon—your ability fluctuates—sometimes you're perfectly in the groove, sometimes it all goes to hell. It drives you nuts. You have a problem with balance, like all Librans. You have Mars in Virgo--when you feel off-kilter, you tend to oversteer. Louise probably pointed that out to you. You veer between bombastic self-confidence and hypercritical self-judgment. Saturn in Taurus: highly disciplined, maybe even when you don't have to be. It's trine your Jupiter and Mars conjunct in Virgo, which helps you not be a controlling jerk. You're always seeking a guide, but you often don't follow her good advice. What else? Oh, yeah, that Venus: you love extravagantly."

This was so accurate a portrait of Bernard as he knew himself to be that he gaped. She grinned again and bobbed her head, as if embarrassed.

"And if I were a charlatan, I would claim to have intuited that just now. In fact, I ran your chart years ago, when I first started reading your books. Oh, also, because your Jupiter is conjunct Mars, and because Uranus is now transiting Pisces, you're in a period of great emotional upheaval. Your life has been entirely upset, but you are on the verge of a gigantic expansion, professionally and emotionally."

"Don't astrologers always say stuff like that? Great things a-coming?"

"Actually not. And I'm not an astrologer. I'm a psychic. Astrology is descriptive, not deterministic, and I only use the symbolic power of the technique to focus the information I receive."

"Receive from . . .?"

"I have no idea. Some psychics talk about named spirits or beings, but I've never gotten a name. They're just guides. They picked me up when I was seventeen and they've been using me and teaching me ever since. I don't pry into who they are."

She leaned down and scratched Murtagh behind the ears. To Bernard's surprise, the dog lifted his muzzle and rubbed his jowls against her knee, something he'd not done previously to anyone but his master.

"I'm like their dog, I guess," she said. "What's his name?"

"Can't you tell?"

"Now you're making fun of me. It doesn't work that way. It's not mind reading or a trick. Sometimes it's a real burden."

"Sorry. It's Murtagh. He likes you--he doesn't respond that way to many. In fact, he's trained not to. You must have a way with animals."

"Yes, it's my Sagittarius rising. You're good with them too, behind your moon. Also, I grew up on a ranch."

"Really? You're a cowgirl."

"I wouldn't go that far. A hick, for sure. Does it show?"

"Not at all. I would have taken you for a denizen of the toniest salons. Where was this ranch?"

"Near Fresno—a place called Piedras. Horses, burros, and registered Angus. My mom's a high-school principal, which pays the bills, and my dad runs the place-- into the ground, as he would say. That's another reason for the trip to the mainland—they're getting on and I like to check on them a couple of times a year."

"How did you end up in Hawaii? It always seemed like the end of the earth to me—I speak as an East Coast person here."

A small shadow came across her face. "I don't know— it's sort of a long story, involving men. Short version: I was with a guy who moved to Oahu, and I went along. Then he left for Australia and I switched guys rather than countries."

"Still with him?"

"No, not for years."

"You wouldn't move to a place because a man you loved was there?"

"I just said I did. And not just once."

"This relationship survives?"

She gave him one of her sparkly stares. "Are we making small talk or do you have an actual interest in my relationship status?"

"I guess. I was just saying to Jack Bill back at the Dahlia—I haven't experienced interest in a long time, and now it's interesting that you called me by a nickname unknown outside my immediate family, as if you were somehow—what's the word? *Channeling* Louise. So, yeah, I do. Have an interest."

Now she smiled, a look so frank and enthusiastic that it pierced his sad heart. "Since you ask," she said with a laugh, "there *is* someone, but it seems to be winding down. He's in island real estate, a mover and shaker. A Viet-American as it happens, like Louise. He's generous, pleasant, and hot, but he spends a lot of time working and likes me to be available when he has a free moment, never mind *my* plans. Let's say it's become tedious. He's a big fan of your work, by the way, Evan, and he usually reads *nothing* but business stuff. Actually, I've been turning people on to your books for years, my friends, my clients . . ."

She beamed at him. Bernard had thought that *beamed* was a mere figure of speech, but now he observed beams. After a pause, she added, "What surprises me is why you're not, I don't know, bigger."

"Bigger? I do all right. I've hit the list a time or three."

"Four," she said, "out of twelve books. I don't mean that, doing just okay. You should be *huge*, like King or Grisham or Cornwell."

"You should have lunch with my agent. But enough about me. How is your conference going? Anything new in the land of woo-woo?"

"That's amazing," she said. "You don't like to talk about yourself or your status in the literary world. I have to say, I have several successful writers among my clientele and this isn't what usually happens when the subject arises."

"Do they have a Heart and Spirit Festival every year?"

She gave him a conceding grin and said, "Ah, yes, the dear old festival. I come because they pay me and because I like to see my old friends in the biz."

"Why do they pay you?"

"Well, not *pay*--I mean expenses and an honorarium, is all. It's for giving a couple of sessions "

"Psychic sessions, I assume."

"Sort of. I take a bunch of people into next year."

"Do they get to read the *Wall Street Journal* while they're there? If so, I wonder why *you're* not huge."

She didn't return his smile. "Actually, there are psychics who specialize in advising financiers. J. P. Morgan had an astrologer, so yeah, there's that part, but what I mainly do is take them into their own heads, a year hence. They're aware of what concerns their future selves, what they're thinking about, how they are."

"I see. You'll have to forgive my flippancy, Miranda. I'm not used to having this kind of conversation. Does this time travel, so to speak, do them any good?"

"It can. It gives perspective. If something that consumes you isn't on your mind a year from now, maybe it isn't that important today either."

"What if the person has less than a year to live? What would they see?"

"They would see where they were going in their next life, obviously."

"The flames of hell, et cetera?"

"Not exactly. But people have been known to mend their ways after a session."

"Would you recommend that I try it myself?"

"Adding to one's knowledge never hurts, Mr. Goodrich, but unfortunately. . ."

"You have to call me Bernard."

"Unfortunately, Bernard, the last scheduled session was today. Oh, here's the program if you want to splash in the woo-woo while you're here."

She reached into her bag and handed him a well-designed, glossy booklet.

"I'm on page sixteen, in case you want to scope out my public image."

"I saw your website."

She laughed, throwing her face back as she did. "Oh God, that. It's a template from one of those outfits that sell paraphernalia and books for the psychic community. I should fix it, but I never seem to get around to it. I didn't have one until recently anyway, but people kept yelling at me that I had to have a website or I don't exist. I try explaining to people that everyone I'm supposed to help will find me *without* the Internet. But I guess it's a convenience."

"It let *me* find you."

"Yes. But we were fated to meet since forever. Don't you feel that?"

Bernard did, but thought it was crazy. All the grief books said beware of falling into relationships after the death of a spouse. He arranged a pleasant, noncommittal expression on his face, and said, "It would be pretty to think so."

Her face lit. "I love that book. But you're as good as Hemingway."

"Now you're being ridiculous," he said, feeling absurdly pleased that she had picked up the line as the terminal sentence of *The Sun Also Rises*.

"No, but seriously, Bernard, I can't understand why you're not more recognized. None of your books ever got made into a movie—why is that?"

"There've been a few nibbles, but they all fell through. Hollywood is allergic to philosophy, and there's not enough simple sex and violence, although I do try."

"Ivan Kells isn't allergic to philosophy. Did you see *The Void?*"

"I did. It was terrific, but he's an exception. And he hasn't made a film since he won the Oscar for that, what was it, four years ago?"

"Five. Then he went to India to study with Vikananda. But he likes your stuff. A lot."

"And how do you know this?"

"He's a client. I turned him on to your work and he read all twelve in a week."

"Well, I haven't heard from Mr. Kells, so maybe he wasn't impressed enough to bring them to the screen."

"Sometimes Ivan needs a nudge. He almost passed on *The Void,* as a matter of fact. You know . . ." Here she paused and tugged at her lip, a childlike and charming gesture, Bernard thought.

"You know, I should get the two of you together. You need nudging, too. No, don't give me that frown. This is a great idea."

"Okay, I'll play along. Which book would you like to see filmed?"

"Oh, *Dog Gone,* of course. It's my favorite."

Bernard sighed. It was his favorite too. Of course.

Now she began to gush about the book, how you could realize Noreen 's hallucinations on the screen, and contrast those images with the dog's POV, and the incredible scene in the tunnels, where Noreen's being chased by the bad guys, all the while thinking she's somewhere else, locked in an imaginary battle with demons . . .

Bernard listened, mildly amazed—she knew the book better than he did—but increasingly uncomfortable. This was moving too fast, and he was deeply relieved when Sue the Minder appeared because he was scheduled to give a talk at a literary ladies club that evening. They had to leave now if he wanted to return to Century City, change, and get up to Pasadena by seven-thirty.

He stood. Miranda Gardiner slid from the booth, and embraced him in a hug that was not overtly sexual, nothing untoward, but he felt electricity flow, and when she kissed his cheek, the hair stood up on the back of his neck.

"I'm incredibly excited to have met you, Bernard," she said when he pulled away. "Can we email? Can I friend you?"

"Yes, and yes," he said. "This has been a remarkable afternoon for me, too. Thank you. Maybe our paths will cross again."

"Oh, yes," she said. "There's no doubt about that. None at all."

When Bernard returned to his hotel after his performance, he found an email from her on his laptop.

Well, looks like I did it again. The expression on your face when I said we were fated to meet--priceless. So let me offer an apology. I came on strong, because I see things and if I'm not careful I act as though others can see them too. I've got into trouble numerous times because of this and I never learn. But for the record--I'm not a stalker or a wing nut. Obviously, I would love to write to you and Skype too, if you'd like, but the ball's in your court. You can answer this one, and if not, I won't persist. How did your talk go?

Bernard immediately sat down and composed a reply.

Yes, I was a little astounded by you and by your take on things, but not offended or annoyed. As I said, I've never been a believer in all that, and hope you won't be disturbed if I remain so. The talk was the usual--sixty or so women and a dusting of gentlemen, most of whom wanted to know where I got my ideas.They were somewhat more interested in my dog than in my books, I fear. Murtagh had a great time--he loves to have his skills shown off to a crowd. I had him select objects volunteered from the audience and then find the donor, always a hit, and I had him menace, show the teeth and snarl. I am like that too, sometimes; but you knew that already I suppose.Yes, let's keep in touch. Who am I to challenge fate and the stars?

On previous book tours, Bernard had not communicated with home. He called infrequently and did not send email. Nor did Louise reach out to him. They had discussed this and concluded that the tours offered a break from the intensity of their relationship. It was always a big deal when he returned to her-- dinner out, champagne, energetic sex. So, he found it remarkable to be emailing Miranda several times a day, and checking his mail almost compulsively to see if she had responded. She proved to be a witty and amusing correspondent, her emails full of her delight in knowing him, and referring to the film of *Dog Gone* as if it were a done deal.

So, quite beside the Ivan Kells business, which he regarded as mere pleasant fantasy, he was excited about a woman. Ridiculous, really—a *psychic*? But there it was, and with it a soggy guilt. Here was the prospect of a life beyond Louise, presented too soon for comfort. How could he be thinking along such lines, barely six months after the death? But he was.

A line popped into his mind; *I buried my heart in the grave with my darling.* What was that, a song, a poem? He couldn't place it, but he'd felt that, and now here it was back in his chest, warmer and beating with a livelier rhythm.

But what would the kids think? The terror of this thought drove him to the keyboard, where he tapped out a long email to each. The one to Leslie was easier, some funny trip anecdotes, a bit about Murtagh's hilarious performance. He said how glad he was that she was back at her program, mentioned some books on theater he'd picked up for her, described the changes in his feelings, the strange sense of life picking up again, the guilt attached to this, the error of not letting the dead go, how this is not dishonoring the lost loved one, but freeing up the love we felt for her and showering it out upon the living world.

The email to Lawrence was shorter—I'm fine, doing the tour, hope you're well, let me know how work is going, stay in touch, plus several links to YouTubes and articles Bernard thought his strange boy would find amusing or interesting.

Leslie would come back with a complex, heartfelt email, and describe what it was like to play Anya in *The Cherry Orchard.* Lawrence would wait a week and send weird site links, analogous to snapshots of scenery, from the virtual universe in which he spent all his time.

Bernard felt keenly the burden of being the remaining parent, subbing incompetently for the irreplaceable dead. Louise had taken so much of the burden from him, allowing his immersion in the lives of imaginary people, many of whom were in an odd way more satisfactory than real children. Dickens, apparently, had the same problem. Tolstoy, too, and Cheever. He considered the list of authors whose children either despised them or had come to bad ends. It was a long one. Writers should have dogs, not kids, he thought, and then hit the mini-bar and lined up the little empties on the bedside table until he dropped into sleep.

He was in Miami, the last stop before home, when she wrote:

> *Great news. I finally got in touch with Ivan Kells--in fact, he called me for a reading. After, we talked a little about perception and the difference (if any) between what we perceive and the Real, and that got us into how you had dealt with the subject in Dog Gone and I couldn't resist telling him I had met you and how I would love to get you guys together to talk about a movie, and Bernard, he just lit up. By the time we finished, he was talking about Brie Larsen for Noreen and Matt Damon for Wilson, the philosophy professor she has a thing with. I was throwing up I was so excited. Anyway, he'll be in New York next week and we could set up a meeting. Oh, say you'll do it.*

Bernard responded that he would like to meet Mr. Kells anytime and thanked Miranda for her help. He kept his tone cool, even sardonic, but he was conscious of a growing, almost manic enthusiasm. He had always thought his books would make good movies, and he now discovered he was less immune to the allure of Hollywood than he had supposed. Kells.

43

Brie. Matt. And that blizzard of admiration that Miranda was throwing his way. He'd had a rough year, he told himself—why not enjoy this while it lasted?

He spent hours on his computer during the tedious downtime every book tour necessarily included, following up every Google hit on the name "Miranda Gardiner." He discovered she cut a considerable figure in the annals of the New Age —writings on various sites, testimonials to her skill, and besides these, social notes from what passed for society in Honolulu, pictures of her gowned elegantly, laughing at parties in gilt-edged venues.

He began to Skype with her, something he had not done to any great extent before, and was amazed at the sense of intimacy the technology provided. The face was there, and the voice, but not the confusing presence of the flesh. Bernard was happy to be spared that particular vibration, and free of it, he allowed his intimacy with the woman to grow deeper.

He arrived back at the West End Avenue apartment after an evening flight from Miami, during which he had drunk more than was his habit on planes, and upon entering was struck by the most peculiar feeling. He had expected the emptiness, but this was like an amplification of that, as if, instead of standing in a civilized apartment in the middle of a teeming city, he was out on some deserted prairie with the sky domed above and a flat horizon and the keening wind around his ears. He turned on all the lights and moved through the rooms, thinking that perhaps he'd been burgled in his absence, but everything seemed in its proper place. His desktop computer exhibited the page he'd been working on before the tour; the scatter of notebooks and papers on the long table seemed undisturbed.

He made himself a drink he didn't need and sent a Skype message to Miranda. In a few minutes came the Skype burble and her face. After he had described, with no little embarrassment, what he was feeling, she said, "Oh, that's just her absence. It's quite common. It takes a while for some of the departed to understand that they're dead. They linger in the places they knew and around the people they loved. That's why you've been having visitations. Now she's moved on."

"How do you know that?" Bernard demanded, more stridently than he had intended.

"Because I've *been* there, Bernard," she replied calmly. "I've taken people across, dying people. It's something I do. Just try to accept it, all right?"

Bernard took a deep swallow of his Scotch, and coughed, and thought what if the world is different from what I conceived it to be? What if the loonies are not loonies? Echoes of dead beliefs stirred in his mind. He felt a laugh growing in his chest and he let it explode.

"What's funny?" she asked.

"Nothing. Everything." He raised his glass to her image, her open face, her kindly gaze. "I think I just drank your Kool-Aid," he said, and she laughed, too

Three

After the Skype with Miranda concluded (and he felt a strange reluctance to punch the red telephone icon, as if it were another kind of death) Bernard attended to his emails. One from agent Elsie, asking about the new book, reminding him of his deadline; one from daughter Leslie, brief, telegraphic, expressing worry about him, attaching a photo of her theater troupe, all impossibly young and glowing. Clearly, life had resumed for her, and he was glad, but felt distant, and faintly embarrassed about what was happening with Miranda. Another from son Lawrence, which he was happy to see: L. sometimes did not answer for weeks. The text consisted of a Hi Dad and a short stack of YouTube links: stupid guys setting themselves on fire, a goat lip-syncing Leonard Cohen singing "I'm Your Man," a bearded fat guy trying to video a cooking show and making a mess—typical Lawrence, how he expressed love.

After that, Bernard walked around the apartment, examining the paintings and furniture as if he'd never seen them before. It was a peculiarity of his relationship with Louise that she had chosen every object in the house aside from the chair in his office, his desk, and his computer. Now that whatever weirdness in his dwelling had evaporated, he felt a powerful urge to be surrounded by different stuff. In fact, he felt like breaking free of stuff entirely. During this walk-through he felt his nose start to run, and went for some tissues, wondering if he might've picked up a cold on his tour, but then his eyes began dripping as well. He wasn't sobbing or particularly sad, but his body was crying, a steady stream of slow tears. Murtagh came over and put his muzzle on Bernard's lap. A few tears plopped on the dog's head, but he didn't move.

That night he told the pixels representing Miranda about it, and she said, "You need to roll with this stuff and not get hung up on the past. You should be orienting now to the future, which looks really, really bright. Actually I'm glad you called--not that I'm not always glad you call--but the meeting is set up for next week--the tenth. Did Ivan's person call you yet?"

Bernard checked his phone.

"I have a recent call and voicemail from a Monica at Abraxas Productions. Is that her?"

"Yeah. Monica is his scheduler. Don't you answer your phone?"

"I got out of the habit. Where are we meeting?"

"He'll be at the Carlyle--the details are probably in the voice mail. I'm flying out of Honolulu on the eighth, I'll see my folks in California and then take the red eye. The meeting's at one in his suite."

"Not in a restaurant?"

"No. Ivan wants to meet the dog. Your typical New York boîte doesn't take giant Dobermans."

"Can I pick you up at Kennedy?"

"Newark, actually, and no, I'll have transportation."

"But you can stay here, in my apartment. We have plenty of room."

"Well, I had an Air BB reserved. In Jamaica. They said it was fifteen minutes from Manhattan."

"Oh, please. You can't stay in farthest Queens and then have lunch in a suite at the Carlyle. You'd crack wide open from the cultural shock. No, I insist. You can stay in my daughter's room. It has its own bath."

She gave him a considering stare and then grinned. "Sold. I was sort of dreading sharing a bathroom with a strange family. Thank you. There's your Libran generosity again. So, are you writing?"

He admitted he was and told her about the new book. "It's about lying. I'm getting into the philosophy of lying."

"I didn't know lying had a philosophy. It's always seemed pretty straightforward to me. So to speak."

"Demonstrating you're not a philosopher--*nothing* is straightforward. The formal definition is you lie if and only if you assert *p* to X, and you know *p* is false, and you intend to deceive X that *p* is true. This includes the Costanza Doctrine. You remember George Costanza on *Seinfeld*? 'If you believe it, it's not a lie.'"

"Yeah, but there *is* such a thing as the truth."

"True. But lying is strangely independent of what happens to be true. It's a matter of belief. For example, you can tell the truth and still lie. Say you've promised a child a picnic tomorrow and it's pouring rain and the forecast is for rain all week. But you lie and tell the kid it will be fair for the picnic in order to put off her disappointment for a day. Now, suppose tomorrow dawns fair, so you haven't uttered a falsehood at all, but you still lied to the kid. You can also tell the literal truth, but still deceive. Is that lying? When Roman soldiers came to arrest St. Athanasius, they asked him 'Where is Athanasius?' Being a saint, he could not lie, so he said, 'He is not far from here.' The soldiers were deceived, but Athanasius told the literal truth."

"This is all going to be in the new book?"

"As much as I can squeeze in, as usual. The plot so far is that a young woman, one of Noreen's grad students, is the victim of what she says was a gang rape at a fraternity house.

The university investigates and declares she's lying. Noreen decides to find out what really happened, but one of the frat boys is the son of a drug lord, so Noreen gets warned off by thugs. The whole affair is a nest of lies--the boy is a psychopath, so we can deal with how lies appear to someone like that, and there are all the varieties of untruth--deception without actual lying, lies that turn out to be the truth. And maybe the girl is lying too. There's a professor of ethics who's involved, the dean in charge of the investigation is corrupt in the case but basically honest otherwise. . . oh, and I'm going to do a thing about animals lying, so I can get Bingo into the plot."

"Can animals lie?"

"They know what they're not supposed to do, and when they do it, they act like they didn't. I guess that's a lie. I have to do more research though."

"It sounds great," said Miranda. "It's a shame you can't write as fast as people read."

"If only. I have to say it's a little strange talking to you about something I'm writing now."

"Didn't you talk to Louise?"

"Never. I'm afraid Louise didn't take my work very seriously. She didn't read much fiction, and when she did it was usually doorstop sagas by third-world authors and novels recommended by the *New York Review of Books*. Fine writing."

Astonishment appeared on the face on the screen. "But you're a *wonderful* writer. How could she not see that?"

"Because she had a finer sensibility? Because I'm really not that wonderful? She saw my work as sort of a rich man's hobby, faintly silly. It's not surprising, considering what she did for a living, trying to help the most afflicted, really horribly messed-up people. Thrillers about a girl and her dog did not impress her."

"My God. Listen, you can piss on *anyone's* life like

that. I could say that *she* was a rich woman with a hobby, except her hobby was a faintly masochistic immersion in the lower depths, like Marie Antoinette playing shepherdess. Your work gives deep pleasure to hundreds of thousands of people, maybe millions. And who gives a shit what the literati say? I can never get through those high-tone books. I mean, I want to say, just shut the fuck up and tell the damn story!"

He laughed and said, "If only you were writing reviews for the *NYRB*. Really, you're very kind and I don't mind my lowly status in the lit world. I mean, people who devote their entire lives to literature are bound to know a thing or two about it, don't you think?"

"I do not. The problem with those people is that they make their living off of screwing writers and they've forgotten that reading is supposed to be pleasure. You think sexologists have the best sex?"

"They may—how would we know?"

"Sample of one, but I dated a sexologist once. Let's say the earth didn't move. There is such a thing as too much technique."

"That's interesting—where was this?"

A vague look appeared on her face, and she waved a hand dismissively. "In the past. You know, I've been reading *Dog Gone*—for like the sixth time, speaking of excellent writing. It makes me so mad when you diss yourself like that."

"I'm sorry."

"Who are you apologizing to? You should ask forgiveness for what you do to yourself, Bernard. I admit it—you're my favorite writer, and I'm not the only one. I think this thing with Ivan is going to blow all that shit out of your head."

"Unlikely."

"You think?" There was a pause, then, "You know, I have a client in New York who pays serious money for face-to-face readings. She'd probably front the airfare. I could shift around some things and come earlier, maybe day after tomorrow, and stay the week until the tenth. Or would that be too inconvenient?"

"It would be the opposite," he replied, "and I'm picking you up at the airport."

Bernard had his apartment cleaned and filled with flowers. The morning was fair and unseasonably mild, so he decided to walk the dog across Central Park. He had always enjoyed walking an extra-large, glossy, perfectly trained Doberman through Manhattan, the animal not forging ahead on a leash like the goofy retrievers and the terriers in their little tailored coats, but trotting along with its head half a foot from his knee.

There was something almost supernatural about having a shadow with an independent will, a will that was yet subordinate to his own. It was part of Bernard's romantic thing, that went with an antique instinct toward chivalry, with the pentathlon craze, with the desire to not be a mere rich kid but a somewhat dangerous man. What had Miranda said about Jupiter and Mars in conjunction? Bombastic self-confidence, but not a jerk. That felt right, as it felt right to walk a dangerous but perfectly controlled dog through the crowded streets.

Some hours later, having snatched Miranda from the hell of Newark International, having received what felt like a sincere hug and a careful, but warm, kiss on the mouth, Bernard sat with her in the back seat of a black car and asked her if there was any place she wanted to go.

"Is there a saloon? It was a god-awful flight."

"I believe there are several in the city. Any particular one?"

"Is the Algonquin still around? When I was a kid in the sticks I read all those stories about witty sophisticates hanging

51

out there. And now that I'm a witty sophisticate myself, it'd only be natural to haunt it. Besides, I need to pee."

They sat in the comfortable dim of the Algonquin's Blue Bar with the rest of the tourists. Bernard was doing nervous drinking, now on his second Gibson; she was drinking a concoction of beer and tomato juice on ice, sipped through a straw.

Bernard asked her if she was disappointed with the apparent lack of scintillation.

"Not really," she said. "It's a shrine. No one expects the Virgin Mary to appear at Lourdes any more, but they go anyway."

"Speaking of which, did you ever do anything miraculous yourself, like predict a disaster and save thousands?"

"Not really—it's not my department, it seems, although I guess the thing with Ivan sort of counts."

"What thing?"

"He was going to take a helicopter to scout some locations and I called him and told him not to. He didn't, and then the helicopter exploded right after takeoff. That's how we met, actually."

"And ever since, he's been the slave of your mystic powers? Is that why he agreed to meet me?"

"Not my slave. He often doesn't follow my advice."

"And what happens then?"

She shrugged. "It's not always like the helicopter thing —a clear vision. Usually it's cryptic and subject to interpretation. For example, something very big *is* going to happen to you, and I think it's this thing with Ivan. But it might not be. You gamble, right?"

"Actually, that was Louise. Her China vice, as she used to say. She got me into it. We used to fly to the islands and play; and Foxwood a couple of times. I got to like the James Bond aspects. Baccarat and so forth. Why do you ask?"

"Because this deal could crash, but a week from now you could casually buy a lottery ticket and win a hundred million dollars and then we'd look back and go, oh, *that* was what it was, the good fortune, not Ivan Kells and *Dog Gone*."

"That seems less than useful."

"True, but on the other hand, I've been doing this for eighteen years, and I've developed a feel for what's right for a client. This is right for Ivan and it's right for you, even though you're not exactly my client."

"So you're telling me full-speed ahead, don't listen to the naysayers, if any."

"I am. Quite aside from my relation to Ivan, and my relation to you, it's just a fact that the sense I get on the negative side is always a lot more defined than on the positive. Like, my sense that something good is about to happen may be subject to interpretation—there really *is* good coming, but we may not know exactly what it is, like I just said. But when there's a malign force in the field, if someone means the client evil, then it's clear as a bell. It's hard to explain."

"I guess," said Bernard. He munched an onion from the drink he'd just finished. It had been quite a long time since Bernard had drunk two Gibsons at a sitting, and he found himself thinking that Louise would be miffed if he came home smelling of gin. The thought must have done something to his face, or maybe Miranda really was psychic, because she said, "What's wrong?"

"Nothing. A little drunk, I guess. Have you anything in mind for the rest of the afternoon?"

"The Statue of Liberty?"

He laughed, rather more heartily than the remark deserved. You'll have to go without me, I'm afraid. I never drink like this in the afternoon, and I am going to have to go lie down for a while. You can have the car to take you around and then we can meet back at my place and have dinner."

"Actually, a nap sounds good," she said, and so he called the car and they got in, and as soon as they were rolling Bernard leaned over and planted a rich, tongue-filled kiss on her mouth. Miranda responded in a pleasant enough fashion but without real ardor. He pulled away and fell back on the seat, his forehead asweat.

"Wow. Sorry, I don't know where that came from."

"I do. You and I are entwined in a psychic field. The only entwining psychic field most people are familiar with is sexual love, so you naturally wanted to express it like that. And you're loaded, as you say, so there go the inhibitions. It happens all the time with clients."

"Did Ivan?"

A grin, and, "Would that violate client confidentiality? Maybe not. So, yeah, big time, but we got past it and now we're pals."

"Pals, eh?" said Bernard. "You and the dog." It sounded bitter and he immediately regretted the comment.

She shifted her body and met his eye. "Look, *pal*: this is a complex situation, and one you haven't been in before. Let's just hang loose and see what develops."

"I'm fine with that," said Bernard woozily. "I just want you to know that I'm not going to, you know, *leap* on you when we get to my place. If that's a concern."

"I know that."

"How do you know that? I just *did* leap on you."

"I'm a psychic, Bernard," she said, and patted his thigh. "Relax."

Four

He had the dream again, and awakened in a sweat, surprised for a moment to find himself fully clothed and lying on the bedspread, with his shoes on. The dream was that the whole past year had been a nightmare from which he was now awake, and he wanted to tell Louise about it, and in the dream he wandered through the apartment calling her name, thinking about how they would laugh. Seven-ten on the bedside clock. He had slept for four hours. Those Gibsons. That kiss. A shudder of embarrassment as he slipped from bed. He washed his face, brushed the foulness from his mouth, and went down the hallway to his daughter's old room.

He scraped a knock on the door. Nothing. He pushed it open and peeked in. The throw pillows that usually occupied the head of Leslie's bed had been neatly stacked on a chair, on the back of which hung a pair of jeans and a red sweater. She was lying face-down, deeply asleep, it seemed, with Leslie's appliqué quilt (pandas) thrown over her. One long, tanned, naked leg could be seen where the covering had slipped away.

Bernard stood there, breathless, watching her sleep, trying to deal with his feelings—an erotic throb such as he'd seldom known, tenderness, peculiarly mixed with fear. Minutes passed. He heard the dog moving in the living room and soon it appeared at his leg, pressing its warm strength against his thigh, like a guardian of virtue.

He patted its head and sighed. "You want your walk," he whispered.

The day had darkened and turned distinctly colder. As he left his building with Murtagh, Bernard noticed a black SUV with tinted windows double-parked on the avenue. Its engine idled, throwing puffs of vapor. Ordinarily he would have hardly given it a glance, but as he moved past there was a motion behind the glass on the driver's side, a glint of reflection. He slowed and took in the driver—a middle-aged black man in a hound's-tooth driving cap and a leather coat with a fur collar. The man had a brush mustache and was looking straight ahead, but Bernard was sure that the glint he had seen had been a camera and that the man had taken his photograph.

Or not. Perhaps another of the odd semi-hallucinations he'd been having. Paranoia? A fan? He dismissed the thought and moved on west down 79th Street to Riverside Park. Under the parkway, past the sunken stone circle where they had the café, out onto the path. No cops in sight, so he gave the dog a run; squirrels were pursued. On the way back, they passed a man on a bench, sitting behind a newspaper. The weather was not the sort that tempts New Yorkers to linger on park benches, which earned an extra look from Bernard. Leather car coat, and there was that hound's-tooth cap.

I'm hallucinating again, thought Bernard, as he quickened his step, but why a nondescript black guy with a hound's-tooth hat and not Louise? He stopped and pretended to adjust the dog's collar so that he could look down the path. The bench was empty.

I am not going to go batshit over this, he said to himself, more than once, as he walked homeward; the intensity of missing Louise and her counsel like a toothache. But at least he had Miranda.

"Describe this guy," she said when he returned and found her up, working on her laptop in the dining room, and told her about what he'd seen (or not).

He did, in as much detail as he could recall.

"Okay, so what's going on with you now?" she asked.

"What do you mean?"

"You're nervous, right? You're about to plunge into a deal unlike any you've ever done before. You're freaking out and this is a result. You're not being followed or photographed. But you do project your fears outward, just like you projected your grief. My advice is: stop being scared."

"I'm not scared when you're around," he said, thinking that it sounded like a line from a dumb movie, but true nonetheless.

"I know. That's why I'm here."

"You think you were sent by cosmic forces to cause a movie to be made out of one of my books?"

"For starters. What would you do if you were world-famous and so rich that money was like nothing to you?"

Bernard shrugged. "I don't know. Probably buy an island or a big ranch and get sexually weird. That seems to be the default, although I don't like the part about germaphobia and letting my fingernails get real long. I wouldn't go that route, probably."

"You joke, but who knows? Maybe you're going to go through these huge changes so you'll be at a certain place at a certain time and meet a certain person and that will change the world for the better. The main thing is, go with it. Don't fight greatness, Bernard. Seriously, it's not good for you and it's not good for the world."

"Okay. But maybe *you're* the person I'm supposed to meet, and maybe *we're* supposed to change the world with all this money and fame I'll be getting."

She laughed at that, closed her laptop, and said, "Yes, well, the connection is there for sure. I've felt it since we met in that book store."

"Be still my heart."

"You think in terms of romance, because your wife is dead and you're alive and so am I. It's a cliché: wife dies, man jumps into bed with the first available. But I'm not available, or not just yet, and fate has other things on the menu besides sex."

Bernard was about to ask to see the menu when his phone rang. It was Kells's office, calling to set up the meeting.

He put the phone away and said, "We're on for the tenth. They're couriering over draft contracts right away. That seems strangely fast for Hollywood. In my limited contact with movie people, I've noticed that everything takes forever. They always have to go to another level to get the green light. Films are in production limbo for decades. Your guy really knows how to get things moving."

"That's because Ivan has his own green light. He funds his films with his own money and contributions from a select group of people."

"What people?"

"Big shots. Silicon Valley moguls," she said, waving her hands to indicate largeness. "A *very* select group. My sense from talking to Ivan is that he's interested in letting you in on the financing. That would be unprecedented. You could get seriously rich."

"Really? I thought I was already."

"Oh, Bernard. What's your net worth now? Twenty million? Thirty?"

"Around there. Why?"

"Because Ivan is not just talking about a movie. You'll see when you get the full presentation. He thinks the Noreen-

Bingo thing could have real legs—that it could be a franchise, like James Bond. Multiple films, cartoons, musicals, product tie-ins, the works. You could have ten, fifty, a hundred times what you have now. If you became a partner."

"Yes, but I'm not all that interested in that end of things. I'm a little uncomfortable being as rich as I am. What I'm looking forward to is actually making the film, working with Ivan and the movie people. As far as the money stuff goes, that's my agent's call."

Bernard was looking at Miranda as he said this, and was disturbed to see an odd look appear on her face, as if she had become suddenly drunk. Her mouth slackened, her eyes lost focus, and the bright something of her aura, which had comfortably enclosed him, seemed to vanish.

"Miranda? Is something wrong?"

She returned to herself, but still seemed off-balance. "What? Oh, no, I just had a thought . . . about my dad. I shouldn't worry, but I do—you know how it is."

"Yeah, I do. With me, it's my kids. Meanwhile, on this deal, I guess I am worried. All these pretty toys I never expected, and I'm afraid they're going to be snatched away at the last minute."

She patted his hand, yawned, and replied in a curiously off-handed way, "Everything will be fine, Bernard. Try to stop fretting."

But he did fret, and later he excused himself, and retreated to his office to do some research on Ivan Kells and his films. To his relief, a note under the news section of Kells's bio stated that he was entering negotiations to make a major motion picture based on a popular book by the thriller writer Bernard Goodrich. Brie Larsen was being talked about for the star.

59

When the contracts came, Bernard called a cab and went to visit Elsie Schriffren. He told her about the remarkable events of recent days, omitting the Miranda thing, and handed over the contracts package.

"There's a meeting at ten on the tenth at their lawyer's office. Can you be there?"

"Try and keep me away," Elsie said. "But Bernard, this deal will not go down until I have personally reviewed every line of every contract. I hope that's clear going in."

"Could you do me a solid and read over them now? Just to see if I'm crazy. I'll go wait in your outer office and improve my mind by reading from one of your big-time literary clients."

She cracked the fat package and waved him out. He sat on a comfortable couch and perused Elsie's latest prize winner, a thin novel called *The Lingering Rain*. It was full of fine writing, and had not a single murder in it.

Bernard asked, "So, what do you think?"

"I think you lucked out, pal," she said. "They're offering gross points. That's unheard of for a writer in Hollywood. Mr. Kells must be blinded by love. If this takes off like they're saying, you're going to be a very rich man."

"I'm already a very rich man. Though apparently I'm now going to be worth more dead than alive. That life insurance policy is a little strange, don't you think?"

"Not at all," she said. "It's standard practice. They can't get funding without insurance on the principals, and you're a principal. When they start casting, the stars will be insured, too. A whole shit-load of money is going to be floating around this thing. And none of it is going to be yours, bub."

"I figured you'd catch the part where they want me to invest. Why can't I? I've got the money. . ."

"Because the first principle of my business model is

that money only flows one way—from someone else to my clients. It's like the Mississippi. You want to invest, buy mutual funds."

"Right, and anyway, this isn't really about money. It's about doing something really terrific and fun." Again, he did not mention Miranda.

"Yeah, well, excuse me but it's always about money. Even my little fifteen percent is making my head swim."

"Time to start looking for a place in the Hamptons?"

"At least Quoge," she said, and they both laughed.

He cabbed back to his building. A chilly rain had started, and the wind had a nasty edge, so that pedestrians suckered by the fine morning were buying cheap umbrellas from immigrant vendors on the street. Maybe he would get a place in L.A., since he was probably going to spend time there. Venice or Santa Monica, jetting back and forth; private jetting, of course.

He was grinning like a monkey as he opened his door. As he entered his foyer, he heard a series of guitar chords, a tune he didn't recognize, folksy but somehow not American folksy, that tinklingly repeated twice and on the third time was cut off, to be replaced by Miranda's voice, speaking low.

Bernard walked through the apartment and stood outside the door of his daughter's room, feeling foolish and sneaky, listening to the murmur of her voice, until she said, "Goodbye, Mom. I'll see you on the way back."

He pushed open the door and found her sitting on his daughter's bed.

"You're here," he said. "What was that music, your ring tone?"

"It's a slack key riff, from Gabby Pahinui playing *Hi'ilawe*. It's sort of famous in Hawaii."

"Your mom called?"

"Yes, change of plans. I thought I had a week free but I have to get out to California."

"Now? I thought you were going to hold my hand when I met Kells."

"Sorry, no. I can stay tomorrow and the next day, and then I'm flying to SFO and driving a rental to my folks in Piedras. What, were you lurking outside the door eavesdropping on me?"

"Yes. I'm cringing with shame. Also cringing because I'm terrified that you're going to vanish."

She seemed to come back into focus and stared at him. "Vanish? Why would I vanish?"

"You know, like the Lone Ranger. Come on, Tonto, our work here is done."

"You think that? Good God, Bernard. Making this happen, Bernard Goodrich and Ivan Kells, it's just like the most important thing I ever did in my life. Do you think I'm not dying to be part of this? I expect to have a little folding chair with my name on the backrest."

"Really? I guess I'll have one too. We can watch the stars cavort together. God, I have such butterflies, though, like this is all going to be snatched away. And what if I can't do it? Can you fix my abject cowardice with your mystic rays?"

She grasped his hand. "Oh, will you stop. All Libras fear big changes. But it's going to work out. It really is."

"Yes," said Bernard, delighting in the presence of her small warm hand in his. "I can feel it too."

This was a fib. He was terrified still. What he actually felt, to his immense surprise, was the dawning of love.

He took her to dinner at a big noisy bright-lit joint on Broadway, burgers and fries, washed down with egg creams, which she hadn't had before, and they talked, throwing chunks of their lives at each other, stories from childhood, beloved movies, the eccentricities of their families--the conversation of people becoming fast friends. Bernard hadn't talked so much in years, or found so avid a listener. Walking home, they held hands.

Back in the apartment, he put her on the sofa in the living room and poured them both some wine. He sat next to her, took off his shoes and addressed the dog.

"Murtagh, go fetch my slippers. I think they're under the bed in my room." The dog trotted off and returned right away with the slippers in his jaws.

"That's incredible!" she said. "How does he do that? I mean understand speech."

"Dogs understand lots of words, but Murtagh's been trained more thoroughly than most dogs. I guess he has a vocabulary of sixty or seventy words by now, don't you, boy?" The dog wagged his stump and pressed his muzzle against the side of Bernard's knee.

"Was it hard to train him?"

"Not really. It just takes patience and consistency. It's his nature to want to please, and to have useful work to do. Training channels that. All dogs are trained. Some of them are inadvertently trained by assholes to be nuisances, but they're trained nonetheless."

She patted the dog's head. The dog uncharacteristically endured it. "It's amazing anyway. He looks so fierce, but he's just a lamb."

"No, he really is fierce. But his fierceness is channeled into service to me, to protect me if necessary."

"Good thing I'm not dangerous then."

"Yes, a good thing," said Bernard, thinking: my girl, you are the most dangerous thing that's ever been in this room.

They drank the wine, and their conversation turned more intimate. Bernard talked about his marriage and his parents, and Miranda told him what it was like growing up with aging hippies on a ramshackle farm in California's Central Valley. As she talked, he studied her face until she stopped and said, "The way you stare at my face--it's a little weird, if you don't mind me saying."

"Why weird? Don't you look at people when you talk to them?"

"Yeah, but not like that. Why do you?"

"It's part of what I do--close observation. Did anyone ever tell you that you resemble the actress Sean Young?"

"I do not!"

"Yeah, except she's what we call a conventional beauty. It's why they picked her for the android girl in *Blade Runner*--that unearthly, almost inhuman perfection. But your face isn't symmetrical, hence not as conventionally beautiful, but also more interesting. For example, you have a widow's peak, but it's off-center. Your left eye is slightly higher than the right and tilts upward slightly more. On the right side of your mouth, the lips are a little fuller than they are on the left. Your left ear is set at a different angle than the right and is a tiny bit higher."

As he mentioned each feature, he gently touched the relevant flesh.

"So--not quite as attractive as the young Sean Young. Is that a compliment?"

"*More* attractive for the imperfections, I'd say."

She sighed and leaned back on the sofa. "Bernard, I adore you, but I'm not going to go to bed with you just now."

"Yeah, I sort of picked that up. There's a sexual energy going on though."

"Uh huh. Big time. I think I mentioned already about

psychic entanglement and sex, and that's one reason. I need to be clear in that department until this whole Bingo thing is resolved; and also, I can't like *start* anything until I decide what to do about Evan back home. But I like the way you kiss."

He kissed her then and she kissed back. His joints turned to jelly. He said, "I'd love to spend tomorrow with you. How about if I give you the nickel tour of the city? We'll rise early."

"Don't you have to write?"

"I *will* be writing. Writing is five percent tapping on keys and ninety-five percent thinking about which keys to tap. You'll inspire me."

Now came the genuine smile.

Bernard spent a relaxed and delightful day with Miranda. Like most native New Yorkers, he had always taken the City's infinite marvels for granted: the native thinks, they're always gonna be there, so why ever go? Now he experienced the joy of showing the great Babylon to someone who'd never seen it before, not only the big attractions, but the kind of things that they print in the front of the *New Yorker* that one always pages through without reading: obscure art galleries, tiny museums, new restaurants, cabaret acts featuring people one had believed long dead.

At night, they returned to his apartment and drank some more, smoked her excellent Hawaiian weed and got giggly, and there was some discrete necking, of the type that conveys the message: we can't do it now for various reasons, but we *will* sometime later and it'll be cosmically great. Perhaps he was not quite in love with her yet, but he'd bought his ticket to Loveland, and he was sure she had, too.

Ridiculous, really, the bereaved falling for the younger woman, a stranger; the banality of it oppressed him, but not enough to stifle his enjoyment (and what a terrific word that was-- the process of injecting some situation with joy, enjoyment, so different from entombment, his prior state.) Often, he was brought up short by a kind of déjà vu, the same sense of being extra alive he had enjoyed (!) when he was competing: dense physical pleasure mixed with pain, an almost out-of-body experience, a God-like view of flesh in action.

He insisted on driving Miranda to JFK for her flight to San Francisco. She said she'd take a cab, that it was too much trouble, but he pointed out that he owned a car, and thus it was no trouble at all. Really, it was that he wanted every minute with her he could get.

"Why don't I turn off at the next exit?" he said as they rolled toward the airport in heavy traffic on the Van Wyck.

"Would it be faster?"

"No, I mean let's not go to the airport at all. We could go north. Tour New England, see the foliage. Or we could we could visit Glen Cove, where I grew up. You could meet my brother, although I'll admit that's not much of an attraction. But we could ride horses. You could show me your cowgirl chops."

She laughed and said, "No, I'd love to, but I promised my Mom I'd be there tomorrow. My Dad isn't all that well."

"Oh? Nothing serious, I hope."

"Just old age. He's a lot older than her, and he's never been too tightly wrapped, and he's not nearly rich enough to pass off the crazy shit he pulls as eccentricity. She wants me to talk to him, especially about his driving."

"I could get on the flight with you. We could talk to him together. It would be more convincing, no? And you could give me the tour of Piedras."

"It wouldn't be as interesting as the last few days, I'm afraid. Not much of a museum and gallery scene in Piedras, and fewer piano bars."

"I wouldn't mind. Or I have this phone app that you can use to order a seat on a private jet. We could fly directly to Piedras. And then to Hawaii..."

She gave him a look. "Can I take a rain check on all that? You know I'll see you again."

"But I *don't* know that. You'll get on a plane and you'll be gone. I find that an unsatisfactory situation. How do you know I'll see you again?"

"Because I'm a psychic? Really, you'll be out in L.A. a lot working with Ivan, and I'm like *always* in California. Speaking of that, it's occurred to me that my life in Hawaii may be winding down. Lots of expansions and transitions in my chart, just like in yours. Who knows, a year from now we could be hanging out together."

"In my Malibu place."

"Right, you'll be in Malibu. I'll be in Echo Park or Encino. Seriously, Bernard, could you please not worry? Everything will be fine. You're taking the plunge and I'm proud of you for that, and from now on it's all going to be fantastic."

"I'll call you."

"I doubt you'll get through. The cell service is barely a rumor."

"But your parents have a landline."

"Why don't I call you?" she said firmly, and he had to be content with that.

He wanted to park and come into the terminal with her, but she refused to let him. It was stupid, she said, and besides she hated long dreary good-byes. So they got out and he embraced her and inhaled the fragrance of her hair until he felt her making withdrawal movements, and then she gave him a long serious kiss and was off, trailing her little rolling suitcase behind her.

Bernard drove back to the city, trying to keep the glow alive while turning it, as he did with all strong feelings, into fiction. He had decided that Noreen was going to meet a guy in this one, an important character, and they would enter into a passionate, committed relationship. The dog would not approve, and there would be some amusing jealous encounters.

Bernard's car was an elderly Mercedes he'd inherited from his father, the last of a long lineage of Mercedes the old man had owned, which he'd replaced every three years with a new version of the same model. Yes, owning a car in New York was silly, but Bernard felt oddly naked without private wheels. Maybe he'd drive it across the country. Maybe he'd drive it across the country with Miranda!

"How would you like that, Murtagh?" he asked the dog, who sprawled on a blanket across the back seat. "New smells. Many new poodles to terrify. We could get a place with a big yard, how would that be?"

<I could tear a squirrel to pieces.>

"If you could ever catch one," said Bernard, and turned his wheels toward home.

68

Five

She wore a blond wig, long and curly, and a little red leather jacket over a pink t-shirt flecked with sequins. Tight white jeans and cork-soled sandals completed the outfit. Her makeup was heavier than her face required; she carried a big white leather Fendi knockoff bag and towed a cherry-red roll-on behind her as she hurried to the gate. The impression was showgirl or something less respectable.

She drew glances, as her outfit was meant to do. Her identification and boarding pass named her as Lucinda Truman, and she was about six hours old. Her birthplace was a stall in a woman's bathroom in JFK. Before that, the body she inhabited had been known as Miranda Gardiner, but that person was no more, her ID cut into small pieces and trashed, her clothing separated, stuffed into plastic bags, and distributed among a number of refuse cans along the route to her gate.

Now she entered another bathroom, this one at Sea-Tac airport, and did it again. Lucinda's outfit and wig vanished into the trash. From the Fendi knockoff came a faded blue t-shirt printed with *Autodidact from Dogpatch* in cracked white letters, an aloha shirt (red oleander blossoms and parrots on a yellow ground), baggy knee-length shorts, and yellow flip-flops, what the Hawaiians call rubber slippers. She combed out her hair, pulled it into a ponytail, pinned it up and stuffed it under a slightly dingy Day-Glo pink ball cap, embroidered with a leaping marlin and "Maui." She stuck a small round mirror with a magnetic back to the door of the stall, used it and a wad of wet-wipes to clear Lucinda from her face, and finished by inserting dark contact lenses. The transformation took just over ten min-utes. She was good at it; she'd done it before, a lot.

Now she was what she sort of *was*, a Hawaiian return-ing home to the islands, and the identification she carried said she was Marvel Gafney, which was as close to a real name as she cared to come, although it was not exactly the name on her birth certificate. She went into the first-class lounge and or-dered a vodka tonic, drank it quickly and ordered another. She hadn't had a serious drink during the operation, not that she drank much as a rule, but it was nice to be released from the restriction. Not drinking hard stuff during an operation was part of the protocol. Following the protocol to the letter had been drilled into her by Overby, why they could do what they did and never get caught, why a high-school drop-out from the sticks of Oregon now had four point seven million dollars stashed in various off-shore bank accounts.

She had spent the previous three days doing business in connection with those accounts, and those of her associates, having flown from JFK not to fictitious parents in California but to Tortola in the British Virgins, a pretty island dense with shady bankers. In Road Town on Tortola she strolled the pleas-ant Swiss-clean, palm-lined streets, and visited smallish offices behind shined brass plates, wherein dwelt financial institutions handling tens of billions in tax sheltered or ill-gotten dollars. There she passed envelopes, and often received envelopes in return. This was how Overby liked to do business. He distrust-ed moving money via computer.

Nor did Marvel much care for it, having just used a computer to steal several million dollars from Bernard Goodrich. It occurred to her, therefore, while seated in the comfortable offices of Mr. Poggett, her own banker, to inquire about the security of her personal millions.

Mr. Poggett, who looked remarkably like the little rich guy depicted in the game of Monopoly, assured Marvel that the bank would never make a transfer via computer unless it originated with the computer registered to the client, and even then the bank would send a text message to the client's cellphone that contained a code number. The client would have to enter that before the transfer went through.

"Yes, but if an intruder had both that computer and that cell phone in hand," Marvel responded, "the transfer would still work."

"If the intruder had the password and account number, yes," Mr. Poggett admitted. "But I cannot recall such an intrusion. You'll agree," he added with an avuncular smile, "that such an event is extremely unlikely."

"Perhaps," said Marvel, whose life had been dominated by extremely unlikely events, "but is there a safer alternative?"

"Oh, yes, madam. We can prohibit any transfers out of your account except via registered letter, to be confirmed by a telephone call from the bank to a number included in the letter?"

"Fine," said Marvel. "You'll see to it?"

The banker nodded. "Of course. Very prudent indeed, Ms. Gaffney. Will that be all?"

"No, I'd like fifty thousand in cash. Dollars, please."

Marvel had spent more time on Tortola than her business strictly required because she felt uneasy about what had happened in New York and rather dreaded returning to base with her perfect record marred. How had it happened? She'd been over the moment many times in her mind, that first day with him in his apartment, after their naps. Everything was going as planned. She had the sexual net out, and she felt him enclosed in it. She'd proposed the investment, with the subliminal message that if he went along, he'd have her as part of the deal. Then he'd said that stupid thing about not being interested in money, and about letting his agent handle it, and in the next breath the whole thing had collapsed. She'd completely lost focus, and by the time she came back and reestablished contact, she knew the thing was doomed, in the way that a basketball player knows the instant the ball leaves the fingertips that it will be a mere brick.

She should have thrown a tantrum and made him ditch his agent, but for some reason she hadn't, and so they only got the identity theft loot, which paid for the cost of the operation plus a very modest profit. She did not look forward to explaining the debacle to Overby. It would be the first grift she'd run that had not stripped the mark to the bone.

Besides that, she felt extremely odd. She was on a beautiful tropical island, and its beauty oppressed her, although she lived on a beautiful tropical island. Something was going on in her head that was not entirely her. Why had she made that arrangement with the bank? Yes, she'd been concerned about computer security—who wasn't? But never enough to make such a change, and why had she asked for cash? The five tight bricks of hundreds in her bag seemed far heavier than their actual weight, like lumps of glowing plutonium, a crazy thing to do, but the words had just appeared in her mouth. Then there was the dread: she had forgotten something in the protocol, something in the long list she'd memorized years ago, and she couldn't bring to mind what it was. It griped at her, and brought her close to panic at intervals.

Like now. She sat in a bar and ordered a shot of tequila. She drank it down and ordered another. When the barman set it down, however, she leaped up, threw some bills on the bar, called a cab, picked up her things at her hotel, and went directly to the airport, where she took the first flight to San Juan,

Puerto Rico. From there she returned to JFK and bought a first-class ticket to Seattle, connecting with the flight she was now aboard, headed for Honolulu.

Taking her seat, the flight attendant greeted her by name, which was fine, relaxing even, like slipping out of tight heels into fuzzy slippers, the resumption of her base identity after being someone else for so long. Marvel, not Marvelle. She had a story to explain the odd name, if anyone asked. It was, like the eyes, a convenient lie.

An uneventful flight, during which she tried and failed, as always, to sleep, and failing, and not wanting any of the films available, opened her laptop and its book reader and selected from a list of classics Overby had provided: *The End of the Affair,* by Graham Greene. She fell into it, as often happened, read continuously, rapidly, and was nearly done when the plane began its descent into Honolulu International. As she shelved the book in the electronic library, she noticed that she still had the mark's books stored there. She'd read them all, of course, highlighting certain passages for memorization, and reading all the reviews she could find, so that she could pose as a serious fan. A few keystrokes and the books joined Miranda Gardiner in oblivion. She stopped in the ladies' on the way out to remove the contact lenses.

From the chilled terminal, she strode out from under the shadows of the arrivals ramp until she stood in full sunlight, delighting in the heat on her skin. She wore large round dark sunglasses all the time in Hawaii, sometimes even indoors and at night; she didn't care for people noticing her peculiar eyes. She shut them and turned her face to the sky, enjoying the red light-show the tropical sun made on her retinas.

A honk. It came from a candy-red 1957 Cadillac El Dorado Biarritz waiting in the roadway. She walked to it, flung her bags in the back seat, and got in. The driver was a big elderly haole with a leathery pockmarked face capped by a tan bullet dome. His name was Freeman Overby, called Win by everyone, and he was the guiding spirit of the criminal enterprise for which Marvel Gafney worked. Throwing his arm around her, he pulled her close and mashed a kiss against her cheek. She returned the kiss and said, "Thanks for the lift. I was expecting Jumbo or one of the Cars. To what do I owe?"

"They're otherwise engaged and I sprang at the opportunity. This vehicle yearns for a pretty girl in the front seat, plus I get a little thigh contact. Makes me wish I was seventy again."

"It's pathetic when you pretend to be pathetic. What about the squadrons of teenage hookers you're supposed to run?"

"A myth, which I decline to suppress. I even spread it."

"Why?"

"Because I'm a criminal, and criminal opinion is stupid as concerns sexual potency. To the limp dick is attributed limpness of resolve. When people do make that misjudgment, I am quick to correct them, but it's a pain in the ass, and in my old age I prefer to minimize such pains."

"You do too have girls. Amy Ting? She was at the gym in Kailua on the next treadmill, and she told me."

"Told you what?"

"That you were hot--for an old guy."

Overby laughed. He had a loud, jolly laugh; infectious, so she laughed too.

"That shows that, contrary to the saying, you can indeed con a conman. Perhaps young Amy was being paid to lay that trail. And young Marvel bought the con."

"Well, anyway, *I* think you're hot. You'd be a total stud if you lost, like a hundred pounds."

Another booming laugh. "Bring out the carrot sticks.

Tell me, why do you think I'm hot? Is it my unearthly physical beauty?"

"No, I don't care about that, I mean short of positively hideous, like the Elephant Man. Your mind is hot. You know stuff and you tell me about it without making me feel like a stupid hick, like I thought of it myself. And you pay attention; like when we're together, you're totally focused on me, and not because you want to get in my pants."

They were driving along the Pali as she said this, and the words had no sooner left her mouth than she was struck with a powerful recollection of Bernard Goodrich looking at her and describing her face. An intense, undesired heat flowed in a wave through her vitals. The shock of it made her gasp.

"Something wrong?" Overby asked.

"No," she replied quickly, "I'm just, like, a little nervous. The op didn't really go."

And why was she thinking of Bernard Goodrich? She had never thought of a mark after the con played out. Never.

"So I understand. What happened?"

A mild tone. Overby was always so when something went wrong; he hardly ever raised his voice. But she had seen hard men quake in fear before that schoolteacher's calm delivery.

"I don't know," she said. "I *had* the guy. He was eating out of my hand and I still couldn't close it. He just wouldn't invest any of his money in the film."

"I understand he had his agent with him."

"Yeah, the bitch. It would've been good if she'd stepped in front of a bus. Maybe a gentle shove."

"Yes, but we don't do violence in our racket, as you know. I assume you followed the protocol and all the scripting?"

"Absolutely. The mark took me to JFK for bye-byes; I

waited and doubled back and went to Rudy's hotel room, the guy who played Ivan Kells? I monitored the breakdown from there. All I can say is everything sounded perfect, but the mark wouldn't budge. I guess some people don't want to be fabulously rich. I'd already stripped his accounts when I was alone with his home computer. He had no security at all. But of course I could have done that without the movie scam – without bringing everyone else in. I'm sorry as hell, Overby. Maybe I'm losing my edge."

"Don't obsess, dear. We'll make it back on the next one. You're still the best little put-up girl in the business."

"She breathes a sigh of relief. I was scared you'd go ballistic."

He laughed. "I think my ballistic days are over, dear heart. I cultivate calm in adversity. As should you. But back to what you were saying about attraction. I tend to agree with you, although virtually all people male and female are boring as pigshit, and it takes a great effort to maintain even cursory interest. I think it was Casanova who remarked that getting a woman into bed was easy--all you had to do was listen to her with genuine interest. As I do to you. In the present case, I believe we turned up a great rarity—a mark without greed. Such people are impossible to con with a put-up based on money. For those, you base the put-up on love, but we don't run that sort of con. The main thing was you followed the protocol, plus we got over two million off him. Hardly chump change. How did it go in Shore Town?"

"Fine, no problems," Marvel said. A thrill of panic, quickly suppressed; the wrapped hundreds seemed to send out rays. Was he suspicious? Was nice Mr. Poggett Overby's guy? She told herself to cut it out. She was home, Overby liked her; everything was just fine. Except for the forgotten thing.

They were silent for a while after that, and Marvel relaxed into the dense calm that comes after escape from danger. She studied Overby's face with a sideways glance from behind her shielding sunglasses. Massive jaw, scarred by a thin white line that curved from his ear to his left cheek, bulbous nose, thin lips. A piratical face. He wore mirrored sunglasses, too. Like her, Overby didn't care to show his eyes, although his were ordinary matching blue ones, hard and brilliant. Overby was an excellent detector of bullshit, but she believed herself to be a somewhat better purveyor of the same.

Then it struck her. *She had not disposed of Miranda's cell phone.* It still lay in a pocket of her suitcase. Incredible stupidity and an awful violation of the protocol.

She thought the stupidity would be emblazoned on her face, but Overby glanced over at her with a smile and said, "So, Marvel, what're you reading lately?"

"I read *End of the Affair* on the plane."

"Yes, and what did you make of it?"

"Good writing, I guess, but I didn't get it, the ending, I mean. Okay, she dies, but then she comes back, or what? I didn't like it all of a sudden turning into a ghost story."

"Not a ghost story, precisely. Greene was a Catholic. He was saying that Sarah had achieved a kind of sainthood through her sacrifice, through love. She gave up her affair with Maurice when his flat was bombed out. She promised God she would give up her lover if God spared his life. After she died, miracles occurred. So, a religious story, not a ghost story."

"I don't see the difference."

"That's because you're a little heathen, dear," said Overby, with a kindly smile.

"And you're not?"

"No, I'm an apostate."

"What's that?"

"Someone who's been exposed to the true religion but

denies it. I was once an altar boy, did you know that? A dignity I share with Adolf Hitler and many others of the same ilk. I believe we occupy a lower circle of Hell than such as you, who don't know enough about religion to even be decent atheists."

They had just entered the tunnel. Overby gestured broadly to its roof.

"Just now, I suppose I am a devotee of Pele of the volcanoes. Megatons of rock above us, below us a sea of boiling lava. One little twitch of Pele's divine ass and we would be no more, a thin stratum of red jam in the matrix. The old Hawaiians were extremely religious people, for good reason. And look. There's the fabled light at the end of the tunnel, just another minute and we're safe again. You know, I've spent an unfortunately large portion of my life in dangerous circumstances, and I never fail to pray at those moments, to a God I believe is perfectly indifferent to my fate. It's a human reflex, like a swallow or an orgasm. We can hardly help it. Greene certainly couldn't, which is why he converted. And why I like his books."

The big car shot from the mouth of the tunnel and there for a moment was the Pacific: pacific, vastly glittering, stretching blue and infinite before them. Marvel's heart always lifted at this view, not solely because of its conventional beauty, but because it represented, even more than the air voyage, the end of the operation, and her return home.

They began the long winding descent to Kailua. Marvel had forgotten, as she always did when away, the preposterous beauty of the island, and thought that maybe it was impossible to hold such gorgeousness in memory. If it was, she imagined, no one would ever leave, and if they did, they would weep without cease.

Now something occurred to her and she asked, "What's Sami up to that he needs Jumbo and the Cars?"

"He's buying a hotel in Hong Kong. Apparently, besides the lawyers and accountants, one needs an entourage to buy a Chinese hotel, don't ask me why."

"An entourage of muscle?"

"The gentlemen he's dealing with are connoisseurs of muscle, it seems. I advised against it, but you know Sami. He grows tired of having his money exist only as digits. He wants show, he wants to cut a figure."

"Yeah, well, it's a little weird to have all this cash and not be spending any of it."

"I believe we spend quite a bit of it, as a matter of fact. Is there anything you, personally, lack that money can buy?"

Marvel ran the question around in her mind, and concluded that there wasn't, just then. She lived in a splendid house, splendidly furnished. She could hire a private jet. She could walk into one of those clothing shops in Ala Moana that catered to Japanese tourists and clear the shelves. But she was not a collector. She had no urge to compete with other rich people for rare items. She rightly feared the attention that living large brought, and thought also that even had her money come from a trust fund and not crime, she would feel the same. Her upbringing had encouraged lying low, besides which she now had more than she had ever imagined, and while she knew how the nouveaux riches went buy-crazy, she herself was not that type. And wasn't there something a little creepy about, say, wanting your own Van Gogh?

"My *precious*," she said mimicking the hiss of Gollum in the movie.

Overby laughed, the great booming noise drawing attention from passersby. They had stopped for a traffic signal on Kawailoa, in the center of elegant Kailua town.

"You have it right, my dear. Now that we're taking in serious kale, I'm afraid our Sami is starting to find our operating plan a little pinching. Not good, but he doesn't listen to me. Do you think you...?"

"Oh, God, no. Sami doesn't listen to a word I say," Marvel replied. For her own part, the plan (the Plan, as she thought of it) made perfect sense, and she found it a thing of genius. Overby had devised it when he and Sami Choi had arrived from the Philippines ten years ago, and its principles were stupidly simple. Draw no attention. Live clean. Do one crime at a time. Don't spend a dime that hasn't a plausible legitimate source. Pay your taxes as if all your income came from such sources.

Overby had spent almost twenty years as a Central Intelligence Agency operative in east Asia. He spoke the languages, knew the customs, understood how to clean up after an operation. No one was entirely sure what Overby had done for the Agency, but Marvel had gathered that it involved setting up fake businesses to funnel money in directions useful to national security. He'd had to leave government employ shortly after Vietnam wound down, under circumstances he did not discuss, but the experience had rendered him almost insanely careful in pursuing his new profession.

Avoid any suspicion, that was one of his sayings; and also, no evidence, no suspicion. There were checklists that every member of what he liked to call the *apparat* had to memorize, and then burn the paper it had been written on. These made up what he called the Protocol, and Overby was its enforcer. Although he found it difficult to enforce on Sami Choi, for obvious reasons.

"That's the rub, isn't it," said Overby. "Your crime lord sometimes finds it hard to follow the rules. Also, it's hard for someone who can, in theory, whack anyone who annoys him, to listen to good advice. That's why crooks get caught. Oh, well, I expect we can concoct a legend to account for all Sami's money. I suppose a hotel can be an efficient money laundry."

He was silent for a moment, chewing his lip in thought. "And now that I think about it, cutting a figure in Asian real estate might come in handy someday. I could worry about being more visible, but I'm too old to worry. Don't you worry either, my love. You've done very well. You're a careful girl with a good head on your shoulders. Read *The Power and the Glory* next. It's not so ghostly. And here we are."

The Cadillac had stopped at a driveway on Makumanu Drive in Lanikai, a development just down the coast from Kailua. Only the peaked roof of the main house could be seen from the street, beyond a high brown-painted lava rock wall and hedges of oleander and hibiscus. The driveway itself was blocked by a wide steel gate faced with bamboo slats.

"You'll come in for a drink?" Marvel asked.

"Not now," said Overby, "I have some things to do back at my place."

Overby had a house somewhere behind Diamond Head. Marvel had never been there, nor had she heard of any of their associates ever doing so. Nor had Overby ever picked her up at the airport. A long drive there and back, when they could have sent some kid.

"Then, tanks, eh," she said, "be seen you." Overby laughed. Marvel spoke terrible pidgen and Overby refused to speak it at all, thinking it patronizing in a haole. She hauled her bags out of the back seat.

"See you at the party, dear," said Overby. "Give my best to Sami. I hope his deal was concluded satisfactorily."

The Cadillac reversed and drove off. Marvel swung the gate open, latched it behind her, and walked up a path lined with ti plants to her front door. Inside, she called out, "Hello? Anyone home? Sabine? Dado?" But neither the housekeeper nor the yard man answered.

Actually, that was good. She needed a little time alone. She started to make herself a drink, she had the tequila bottle out and open, but then she remembered the cell phone. She put the bottle away and went out into the garden to think.

The garden lay at the center of a compound comprising the main house; a second, smaller house in the same island style, somewhat Japanese, dark timber topped by brown tiles; a low ranch-style cottage directly overlooking the beach; and a four-car garage with apartments above it. The buildings were arranged to enclose a substantial garden centered around a huge mango tree, in the shade of which lay a terrace paved with smooth black stones. The second house was divided into apartments for the staff. Sabine and Dado lived there with the two Cars. Jumbo Wedge, Sami's main muscle guy, lived above the garage.

The cottage was an original Lanikai beach house, miraculously preserved when the developers bought the parcel and built the other two houses. Here dwelt Esmeralda Abizu with her computer systems, because of which everyone called it The Data. Marvel walked through the garden, past citrus trees and palms of various kinds, bougainvillea and hibiscus in pink flower, breadfruit and custard-apple, cacao and mango, and paused at the cottage. Esme was probably there, headphones plugged in, staring at her screens.

Such compounds were not uncommon in Hawaii. Extended families, known locally as 'ohana, lived together in several buildings on the same property. 'Ohana was what Jumbo and the Cars called what Overby and Sami had brought into being, and it *was* sort of like a family, in Marvel's view, although how would she know? Family had not been a big thing in her life until she got together with Sami, years ago in Macau.

Marvel considered going in and telling Esme she was

back, but rejected the notion--she was not really *back* until she'd cleared the protocol and trashed that damned iPhone. She went back to the main house instead. In the bedroom she sat on the edge of the huge teak bed and opened her suitcase. It was, of course, nearly empty, containing only a plastic bag full of her personal gear, makeup and so on. Why hadn't she dumped the phone along with Miranda's dull, elegant equipage? An uncomfortable mystery, like that strange shivery thought about Goodrich. She retrieved the thin white slab and stuck it in the front pocket of her shorts. Now, instead of relaxing in the garden with a drink, and maybe a joint, she had to go back into Kailua, find a trash barrel and get rid of it.

She left the house by the back door, entered the garage, and got into her car, a Porsche 911 convertible, in primrose yellow. This had been a gift from Sami on her last birthday, presented with a wide red ribbon around it. She had bawled unashamedly, as she often did when he gave her something. Until she'd hooked up with Sami Choi, no one had ever given her a thing that did not come with nasty strings attached.

Jumbo's Lexus was missing, which meant that Sami and them had gone off in two cars, Sami's Bentley SUV as well as the Lexus, which meant they had brought an extra crew along, which meant they had used cash and needed two vehicles worth of muscle. Odd, maybe, but not her concern. She drove off, the wonderful little car calming her as she drove, thinking of how really terrific her life had turned out after such a miserable start, living in paradise with a Porsche, you couldn't beat it with a stick. She turned on the stereo and it picked up her iPhone playlist. Nirvana surrounded her. She sang along, feeling teen spirit.

Marvel entered Kailua town in perfect obedience to the traffic regulations and speed limits, which was one bad thing about the protocol, a car like this and you couldn't open it up because the 'ohana had to be invisible to the law, avoiding even petty violations. She parked at the Starbucks, ordered a venti latte, sat at one of the outdoor tables and drank from the cup. When the coffee was half gone, she popped the plastic lid, slipped a miniature of Southern Comfort from her bag and poured it in. She sipped, leaning back in her chair, enjoying the day and the typical Hawaiian scene, more like a foreign country than the America she came from. She waited for the liquor to relax her, to help the switch from her speedy operational rhythm to Hawaii-time. It failed to come. She remained oddly jumpy, as if she were still on the grift, working the mark, her senses tuned high.

She'd be fine when that phone was gone, she knew that, and, draining her drink, she dropped the cup below the table top, slipped the smartphone into it, and snapped the lid back on. But it seemed curiously difficult to stir from her chair, yes, it took a real effort to move, almost as if she'd been bound by duct tape, and ... there, she was on her feet, up and staggering like a toddler over to the trash can.

Walking back to her car, she thought she'd start to feel better, but no. In fact, she felt worse; she hadn't felt this bad since she'd worked the tables at the casino in Macau, when she realized that the pit boss was on to her skimming.

The skin on her face felt tight and her stomach was full of ball bearings. She put the cup on the passenger seat and started the engine. She was on Kawailoa Road before she noticed it sitting there, and almost caused an accident by jamming on the brakes. The cup flew into the foot well. She swerved to the side of the road and sat, trembling, as the truck that had been behind her honked and passed.

She wished she still smoked, as this would have been the moment to light up and consider things in a calm and rational manner. The cup and the cell phone had been dropped into the trashcan at Starbucks; she had a clear sense memory of doing that. Then it had appeared on the car seat. It was not there now. Carefully, like a kid looking under the bed, expecting monsters, she snaked her foot into the passenger foot well.

Nothing. Okay, some kind of illusion. Jet lag? She had never suffered from jet lag before. Probably just a brain tumor, nothing to go nuts about. She laughed to herself, thinking about how she'd tell this amusing story to Esme, then started the car, pulled out into traffic. The first time she tapped the brakes, however, the cup rolled out from under the seat where it had been hiding and sat on the rubber mat, rocking slightly, *real fo' true,* as the Hawaiian locals say.

So that was weird, a little glitch in consciousness, could happen to anyone, easily corrected. She pulled into the next driveway, a convenience store, took the cup, walked to the outside trash barrel and was just about to drop it in when a *Something* appeared in her head and told her to keep the cell phone. It was not exactly a voice, but it was definite, like the assurance that came with figuring out a puzzle or a math problem. The sense of rightness was familiar enough, but it did not come from her.

Nothing like this had happened to her in a very long time, not since she had seen her Aunt Ethel's ghost winging away from the deathbed, (to Hell presumably, if there were any justice, Marvel had thought at the time) so this came as a surprise and concentrated her faculties. An undoubted excursion from normal reality and a quite specific order had been given. Stress, she thought, I'm stressed from the operation and from not junking the iPhone, and these hallucinations are the result.

Her hands trembled and sweat dripped on her face and under her arms, even though she never sweated, not even on the hottest days. That tremble. Parkinson's? She controlled her breathing, suppressed the fear. She was good at that, had practiced long at the art. When she felt under control again, she started the car and drove back to Makumanu Drive.

In the garage, she found all the cars were back. She stuck the Miranda cell phone in her pocket, a lump of fuming lava. Somehow, she doubted she could get rid of the thing until this strange mental defect had been diagnosed and cured. Or maybe it would resolve by itself; weird mental glitches sometimes did, she knew, so there was that hope. The notion that she had actually been spoken to by a being not of this plane never entered her mind. She knew there was no other plane and no beings resident there, for Marvel was perfect in her suppression of belief in non-material phenomena. She thought all of that was irremediably low-class, a reminder of what she had escaped, crappy little shacks in Dogpatch with stupid signs announcing Psychic Readings, patronized by the most pathetic suckers.

Now Marvel used her remarkable powers of amnesia to recreate the persona she inhabited between jobs while resident in Lanikai, different both from the one she presented to Overby while discussing great literature and the one she had used to seduce Bernard Goodrich. She did this easily and unconsciously, like an octopus or chameleon changing color when moving from a light to a dark surround. Her face changed, becoming coarser; an antic light shone in her peculiar eyes; her walk developed a slutty strut; her voice became more raucous; her vocabulary diminished to the level appropriate to the tenth-grade drop-out she really was.

This performance always amused Overby, although he never let on he was hip to the con. It was a thing between them, a kind of edge each had over the other. She walked down the breezeway toward the front door of the main house, under a long trellis heavy with bougainvillea, the light around her eerily purple.

The core of the 'ohana, except for Overby, had gathered in the living room. Marvel made her entrance with a loud, shrill scream, ran across the room, and jumped into Sami Choi's arms, planting a thick kiss on his mouth while the others cheered and chanted "MAR-vell. MAR-vell"

This was her great moment. A long con is always the work of many hands. The people who had actually run the con against Bernard Goodrich were hirelings—the false Ivan Kells, the imagined Hollywood producers and staff of the phony law firm, the Asian women who provided the hallucinatory presence of the dead wife, and the minor supporting cast had all been paid in advance for their services and then vanished into whatever identities they chose to occupy.

But of the working con artists, only Marvel was a member of the inner circle, the only one of the 'ohana who had been out in the cold, bearing the risk. She was the astronaut, and the other people in the room were like the white-shirt-and-tie guys in Houston, vital, of course, but an entirely different order of hero. The indispensable girl, Overby called her, and since she had spent almost all of her life being as dispensable as chewing gum, she reveled in this glory.

Each of the gangsters now came close for a congratulatory embrace. First, as always, came Esmeralda Abizu, the BFF, a mighty hug and many kisses. Abizu was their computer and electronics guy. Recruited by Overby out of a hacker collective in Philippine Olangapo, she had a story even sadder than Marvel's.

That was one bond, and another, the wonder Marvel felt at her pal's spectacular accomplishments. Orphaned at ten, living on the streets, she had somehow begged enough to fund her education in computer science in the Internet cafés of that low-rent Manila suburb. By age fourteen she was running a variety of Internet scams, specializing in identity theft. Overby had trolled for just such a genius and nailed her when she'd attempted to steal *his* identity. Then, instead of punishment, he'd drawn her into a larger and vastly more profitable trade, yet another life experience she shared with Marvel.

Next came Yoshi Tanaka, who lightly squeezed her shoulders and avoided the kiss, for which Marvel was grateful. Tanaka's story was obscure. Marvel had gathered that he was a former salary man, fairly high up in some *zaibatsu,* who had fallen into the kind of utter disgrace still possible in Japan. Apparently, embezzlement and peculiar sexual tastes might be forgiven individually, but not in combination, especially when the former paid for the latter.

He had fled to Macau, where he worked as a bookkeeper for a casino, which was where Choi had found him. He was perfectly honest as long as he could pay for his vice, and was besides a genius at organization. He was in charge of operations: he hired the subsidiary grifters, supplied fake paper, constructed identities, moved the necessary funds. He was perfect in an insectile way, like a wasp is when it constructs the nest for its paralyzed prey.

Now Marvel felt herself lifted from the ground and flung into the air. She shrieked, as was expected. Two immense men were tossing her back and forth between them like a beach ball, accumulating any number of friendly cheap feels as they did. They were both "locals," in the usage of Hawaii, which meant in this case that they were Hawaiians plus bits of other gene pools, all obviously contributing to largeness. Haulani Ford and Ray Honda were called the Cars, both because of the happenstance of their surnames and because both of them were approximately the size of compact sedans stood on end.

"That's enough, you buggahs!" ordered the remaining person in the room. He was not quite as large as the Cars, but big enough, and thick with sculpted muscle where the Cars were blubbered like orcas. Clarence Wedge, known as Jumbo, scooped Marvel from his subordinates and pulled her into a warm hug, held perhaps a moment too long.

Marvel didn't mind. Jumbo was smart and funny and paid her attentions, even more than Sami did, some weeks. He'd been a Marine, done two tours in Helmand province, won a bronze star, earned a bad conduct discharge for striking an officer. A *hapa* from Waianae, he'd come home from the Corps and into bouncing at low-end night spots in Waikiki, had bounced a guy too hard and done three in Halawa. When Sami Choi required a bodyguard on arriving in Hawaii, he'd asked around in the likely places and Jumbo's name had come up. The Cars came with him, both of them Waianae boys some years behind Jumbo in the high school where they'd all played football.

Marvel was not sure why Sami needed a bodyguard, since they were posing as squares in Lanikai, and having three obvious thugs in the 'ohana tended to smear that image, but her boyfriend had explained that they dealt with some bad actors over in China, where the con money got laundered, and these actors might let on to some other bad actors that there was a *hapa* black-Vietnamese-Chinese guy in Hawaii who had a very large chunk of liquidity, some of which he might part with under the proper circumstances, such as being kidnapped or having his girlfriend kidnapped. There had been a certain snappish tone to this explanation, as there often was when Marvel made inquiries about the inner workings of the biz. She kept doing it, though; it was a never fail for getting his close attention.

Although Marvel regarded the recent operation as a failure, no one else seemed to--apparently two million was still serious money on Oahu. The Champagne popped, Dom of course, and they went through a couple of bottles, the Cars also drinking Courvoisier mixed with ginger ale, and listened as Marvel related the story of the operation with gusto, although she left out the part about Goodrich analyzing her face and comparing her to Sean Young. Why? She had no idea.

As usual, Sami hung back, after that solid kiss and a proprietary ass squeeze. He felt that his dignity as a crime lord would suffer if he indulged in hijinks, so he sat in a lounger, smoking and sipping Champagne. Occasionally, Marvel sat on his lap and wriggled, to exhibit her status as the girlfriend. Whether Sami had any real feelings for her was a subject that never arose at the Lanikai house. She knew he liked to fuck her, among others, which seemed sufficient, especially after a few drinks. But he had never looked at her the way the mark had, and this memory was, she now noticed, immune to the forgetfulness of intoxication.

Overby showed up around eleven with a fat bag of *pakololo* he had grown himself. His old man's hobby he called it, a careful program of breeding and horticulture, that delighted him because he had a medical ticket from the state of Hawaii that allowed him to cultivate the marijuana.

It was a merry sativa hybrid and after much of it had gone up in smoke, Jumbo and the Cars left for Chinatown in Jumbo's Lexus for some gambling and sexual exploration. By this time, Esmeralda had passed out as she usually did on these occasions. Though a genius, she failed to understand that she could not absorb as much booze and dope as people with ten times her mass. Marvel got her into bed, and when she returned to the main house, she heard Overby and Choi arguing. She hung back, feeling the nice party vibe blow away like fog before a sea breeze. She hated any contention in the 'ohana. Childhood memories clawed at her spirit; but she stayed to listen.

Overby was complaining about Sami being too obvious,

throwing his money around town. Then there was some lower conversation. The subject seemed to have changed. Sami was saying something about an operation, about "closing it out like usual, with the insurance," and mentioning Esme being "on the job, a couple days, tops." Overby's response was muffled, but Marvel was able to extract the phrase, "the mark's out of town. That's something. We need to get Jumbo on it."

Overby's voice had become louder during this last sentence, which meant he was approaching the shoji screen beyond which Marvel lurked. She took off, running hunched over to the garden and then down to the beach. She stripped to her underwear and plunged into the warm waves.

Marvel, daughter of Oregon, had not been much of a swimmer before arriving in the islands. Jumbo had taught her how to swim, and to surf and kite board too, and she had become strong in the water. She swam out through the black waves, crossed the small surf and bobbed on her back under the starry dome until her limbs ached.

What had they been talking about? She wondered about this as she floated under the stars, and about why she felt it necessary to sneak and eavesdrop? She understood, without knowing how, that she had heard something she was not supposed to hear. And why was that, why these secret conversations? Was she somehow being screwed over? While it was possible that Overby and Sami had other stuff going on, as far as she knew there was no operation that needed "closing out as usual." That there might be an entire universe of grift in which she was not involved stung her, but she retained her loyalty to the 'ohana, the strange home she had made for herself here. Stoned as she was and bobbing on the gentle waves, her irritation soon passed. Let them have their little secrets, she thought; I've got a secret too.

When she returned to the house, she dumped bra and

panties on the floor of a bathroom and came naked into the living room, where she found Choi alone on the big leather sofa drinking cognac from a bottle, with Metallica's *Sandman* roaring at maximum volume on the stereo. She flopped on top of him like a tuna on the deck of a charter boat and they had their traditional welcome-home coital extravaganza. They did it on the sofa, on the rug, atop a table, and at last he carried her, still impaled, to their bedroom, where they fucked one another into oblivion.

She awakened at three-thirty, heart pounding. Cell phone!

After checking that Sami was in deep sleep, she threw on a kimono, grabbed up the peccant device and went over to Esmeralda's Data. Marvel had a small, neat room there, where she could get away to do the considerable research necessary for any long con and compose the scripts the subordinate grifters would use. It had a day-bed, a desk, a chair, floor-to-ceiling bookshelves, a sink, a mini-refrigerator and a microwave oven. The wall facing the sea was almost all glass, which was the main reason she had claimed it as her own.

The cell phone was of course quite dead. She plugged it into a charger, thinking that if, for reasons she did not care to consider she could not simply trash it, she could at least do a full reset and destroy any resident data relating to the scam.

Goodrich's novels were still there on her shelves, which was odd because after an operation closed, housekeeping ordinarily swept the property for evidences of past association with the mark. And indeed, there was an empty space on the bookcase where she had stored the folders and notebooks with information about all the things Miranda needed to know and all the information Esme had gathered about the mark. But they'd left the novels. Was that Overby? She'd confessed to him that she found the novels charming, and had expressed her wonder at that. She never read such light stuff, for Overby had made her into something of a literary snob, a very rapid transit in her case, from semi-literacy.

Because you're becoming Miranda, dear, he'd said. Miranda *loves* that trash. And they'd laughed.

She took one down. It was by chance *Dog Gone,* the subject of the phony movie in the con. She opened it at random, read a few pages, then paged backwards to read the whole scene, then back to the start of the chapter. She was starting to read from the first page when she came out of the fictive trance, cursed, and threw the book across the room.

At that moment she heard the little chime from the revived cell phone, the sound that meant Miranda was getting a message. She snatched it up, stared, and felt the hairs stand up on the back of her neck. It was from Bernard Goodrich:

I don't care about the money. Tell me your story.

Six

The day after Miranda left, Bernard and Elsie had met with Ivan Kells and his associates in the offices of a Midtown law firm.   Kells proved to be intelligent and witty, with a knowledge of the Goodrich oeuvre that rivaled Bernard's own. His plan for the movie might have been lifted from Bernard's own brain, so closely did it track the images that had crossed his mind when first he'd tapped the book out.

After this bravura turn, Kells had to leave for a meeting at CBS, and the rest of the meeting was given over to legal and financial matters, a sausage that Bernard had no interest in seeing made. Fortunately, with Elsie there, little was required of him. He daydreamed, therefore, about Miranda and about how much fun he was going to have in L.A., working with Ivan, having Miranda full-time at his side. The talk concluded, Bernard was asked to sign sheaves of documents, which he did like an autopen. When they were out in the elevator lobby, Elsie danced a happy little jig, and sang the first verse of *We're In the Money*.

"Quogue is in the bag, eh?" said Bernard.

"Oh, Quogue!" said Elsie. "Southampton, with a helicopter pad. My boy, this is going to be *huge!*"

Business thence concluded, Bernard tried to slip into his usual routine—preparing meals, walking the dog, writing the new book—but found said routine unsatisfying, even irritating. He snapped at Murtagh, who retreated sulkily to his bed and refused to converse. His old life seemed impossibly small —how could it ever have satisfied him? He paced, he ate take-out Chinese (something never allowed in the home under Louise) standing over the sink and waited for his new and larger life to begin. He longed for Miranda.

Who did not call, although she had promised to, and neither did his new partners. What about that vaunted velocity? Don't fret, Miranda had said, yet he fretted. In the park he spotted the black man in the leather coat twice, or maybe it was a different man, or maybe there was no following man at all. He read some books on the grieving process, but these failed to mention hallucinations.

When the silence from the authors of his larger life stretched too long, he called the number Ivan Kells had given him and got a recorded message saying the number was not in service. He looked at the number on the tiny screen, dialed it again and got the same result. Then he Googled Ivan Kells, found a number for Abraxas Films in Los Angeles, dialed that, and connected with a secretary. He told her who he was and asked to speak with Mr. Kells or Mr. Trotter.

"May I say what this is in reference to, sir?"

"I'm Bernard Goodrich. This is in reference to the Bingo Pictures project."

A pause. She said, "I'll connect you with his personal assistant."

"Hello, Mandy Forbes," said a pleasant voice.

"Hello, I seem to be having trouble reaching Ivan. I'm Bernard Goodrich."

"The mystery writer?"

"Him. Can you put me in touch? This is about Bingo."

"Bingo?"

"Uh huh. Ivan and I are partners in a production company called Bingo Pictures that's going to make films out of my books. I'm surprised you don't know about it."

"Yes, so am I. You've discussed this project with Ivan?"

"Of course I've discussed it with Ivan. I had a meeting with him in New York a few days ago. We signed an agreement. Ivan and I were supposed to get together in L.A. next week to begin work on the script."

"I'm sorry, Mr. Goodrich, but that's impossible. Ivan's been in Costa Rica for the last three weeks on a shoot. And, sir, I have to say that if Ivan was planning a project with you, I *would* know about it, and I don't. I'm sorry."

Bernard was sorry too. He broke the connection and called Miranda in Hawaii; the recorded voice told him to leave a message at the tone. He did so, asking her to call him immediately, aware of the strained note in his voice. He searched for Gardiners in Piedras, California, and drew a blank. He went to the law offices where he and Elsie had signed the contracts. At first, he thought he had exited the elevator at the wrong floor. There was the wooden door, but the silvery letters were gone and the office seemed deserted. He used his cell to call the lawyer's number, and, pressing his ear to the glass panel at the side of the naked door, he heard, just, the faint sound of a ringing phone.

At his side the dog picked up his mood and became nervous. He growled at a couple in the elevator going down; Bernard apologized, but felt like growling himself.

Out on the street, he spotted a Chase branch and tried to withdraw two hundred dollars. The machine told him he had insufficient funds. Starting to sweat now, he entered the bank and sat down with an officer, a Ms. Tan, who brought up his account records and told him that his two accounts had been emptied via transfers originating from his home computer.

"You say I requested it?"

"Yes, sir. A transfer that large requires safeguards, of course: address, date of birth, social security number, and your mother's maiden name. And your PIN."

"And that transfer went through to what account?"

"Let me see. A corporate account at . . . that would be the Harbor Trust Bank, in the British Virgin Islands. Is anything wrong, sir?"

"No, no," said Bernard, "just checking. You wouldn't have the number of that bank, by any chance?"

She did, and he called it, and for a wonder it existed, but the woman on the line wouldn't give him any information about the balance in the numbered account because he was not an authorized person on that account. And, no, she could not tell him who *was* authorized. He would have to be an authorized person before she could release that information.

Bernard paused in the bank lobby to call his brokerage, and was not entirely surprised to find that his IRA had been looted too. In all he had lost a little over two million dollars.

Out in the street, Bernard punched up Miranda's number again and listened to the recorded voice for a while. He recalled the one time he had dropped acid in college, and thought this feeling was like that, familiar objects had lost their meaning; simple tasks had become impossible. He remembered very well wanting a drink of juice from the little refrigerator in his dorm room and not being able to figure out how to open its door, and thinking that was quite amusing.

This whole thing would be amusing too, when the explanation emerged. Firms did move and there was no reason he should be informed about the leasing plans, and clearly something had gone wrong with the communications at Kells's firm. A secretive genius? He thought about Orson Wells, Howard Hughes. Mainly, he thought about Miranda, about how she looked on that Hawaiian terrace, what had she called it? A lanai, with palms in the background and a white orchid in a clay pot.

By the time he had settled into his car, these alternate realities had started to fade. He recalled signing various papers and sharing banking information with the movie people, and of course Miranda had been alone in his apartment with his computer. His desktop was not password protected—why should it be? And the passwords for his banking and brokerage were stored in it as well.

Still, he could not quite accept that Miranda was part of a . . . what should he call it, a confidence game? They had wanted him to actually invest in the movie deal, and if Elsie had not been there he might have liquidated assets to do so. He might have lost everything.

His knees were shaky when he arrived at his building and took the elevator to his apartment, talking to the dog, who had picked up on what he was feeling and become uncharacteristically nervous and whiney. The door opened, the dog stiffened and growled, and there was the black guy with the hats, standing right in front of his door.

"Murtagh. Get 'em!" said Bernard.

The target's mouth gaped as he saw what was coming toward him. He reached into his jacket pocket an instant before the dog sprang high, knocked him down, and clamped teeth around his neck.

Bernard was happy to see that the man did not struggle. Murtagh had done this for real only once before, against a knife-wielding mugger in Riverside Park, and in that case there had been considerable blood. The fellow had sued Bernard (unsuccessfully) but it had been a bother, for a guard-trained Doberman is considered a deadly weapon by the state of New York, and the burden of proof in such cases is always on the dog and master.

The man still had his hand in his coat.

"I certainly hope that's not a weapon you're reaching for," said Bernard.

"No, it's my ID. I'm a private investigator."

"Then let's see it. Please move slowly."

Bernard took the laminated card from the man's outstretched hand and learned that he had captured Levon G. Ewell, indeed a P.I. He handed the card back, feeling that he had crossed some strange threshold, from normal life into noir. Like most people, Bernard had experienced myriads of fictional P.I.s. In real life? Only L. G. Ewell.

"Can I get up now?" Ewell asked.

"After you tell me why you've been following me."

"I haven't been following you, or not just you. I've been following *them*. Could you please call off your dog? I'm harmless."

Bernard told Murtagh to let the man up, and the dog instantly obeyed, taking up an alert position a few feet away. Ewell climbed shakily to his feet.

"That's some dog you got there, Mr. Goodrich."

"Yes. What do you mean, *them*?"

"I believe you've been associating with a gang of con artists. I hope you haven't given them any money."

Bernard let out a low groan and said, "You better come into my apartment."

When they were inside, Bernard said, "I'm going to drink some whiskey now, Mr. Ewell. Would you care to join me?"

He did care to. Bernard poured generously of Famous Grouse, and they sat on stools at the kitchen counter and drank.

"I would've given them *all* my money," said Bernard, "if my agent hadn't stopped me. As it was, they stole everything they could get by using my home computer. As I say the words I still can't believe it. I was talking to Ivan Kells, a famous man . . . it was as real as talking to you now. Realer. *You* might not be what you seem either."

Ewell ignored this last, and said, "Yeah, they're smooth. Don't blame yourself too much—they're done this at least once before and gotten away with it."

"I can understand that. The embarrassment is too much to bear, and exposing that to the authorities, your family and friends finding out . . . oh God. I guess con men depend on that."

Ewell said, "You bet, Mr. Goodrich. May I ask how much you lost?"

"Around two million. And may I ask what your interest is?"

"I have a client with a story a lot like yours."

"Who?"

Ewell shook his head and said, "That would be confidential, sir. I can tell you that this gentleman was somewhat older than you, lost his wife of forty-two years, a very close relationship, and then some four months after she died, this young woman meets him cute at a hockey game, and she says she's a psychic, has messages from the great beyond—from the man's late wife, you understand. She has a lot of details about him, her, their kids, their marriage, et cetera.

"Okay, this guy is a retired real estate developer, had an estate a little shy of thirty mil. Based in Short Hills, in Jersey. So, the woman says the late wife feels guilty, she was too hard on the hubbie, she should've let him pursue his dream, and now he should go for it. And the girl, the young woman, this psychic, she goes, yeah, and I know just what your dream is. Ready for this? His dream is he wants to own a professional hockey team.

"That's the convincer for the guy, because he never talked about it. He's a hockey fanatic, has season tickets for the Jersey Devils, and so forth, and it turns out this woman knows the owner of the Devils. He's a client of hers, doesn't move money around unless he talks to her, she happens to know he's interested in selling a piece of the team, he needs cash to cover some positions, but it has to be on the hush, because the market can't know that he's liquidating. She arranges a meeting between the bereaved guy and this billionaire and . . ."

"Don't tell me—not the real owner."

"Of course not. The real one is on his ranch in Montana. They produce a look-alike, apparently, and a bunch of legal and financial types, all supposedly associated with reputable firms--they have offices, they have web sites—a complete world, and totally fake. And of course the woman is there, encouraging, smoothing things over, giving him the old pursue-your-dream business."

"This girl, this woman, the psychic—did they get involved, have an affair?"

"No information on that, so far. You . . . ?"

"No. What did they take him for?"

"The whole thing? Neighborhood of twenty-five million. And this guy had lawyers and accountants up the ying-yang, and never once consulted them. Because of the secrecy. . . the guy must've been blown away. He's a regional mover and shaker but now he's meeting with one of the biggest guys on Wall Street, he's gonna sit in the owner's box. Well, I don't have to tell you."

"No. And now he's hired you to get his money back?"

"Oh, no, sir. The victim is deceased. I'm working for the daughter."

"I see. How did he die?"

"He was a diabetic. After the scam went down, he drove

to his country place in the Poconos, alone, drank a lot of scotch, and apparently succumbed to a diabetic coma. The county coroner found no evidence of foul play, I should mention. It's common for surviving spouses to pass away within a year of the spouse's death. The scam probably hurried him along, if you ask me."

"Yes, probably. Tell me, Mr. Ewell, how did you find me?"

"You're listed?"

"No, I mean how did you know a scam was being run on me?"

"Oh, that was Jack Bill. We were with the LAPD together, back in the day. I was fraud, mainly, but I served on some anti-gang task forces with him. We've kept in touch. I happened to be talking about this case, and he goes, uh-oh, a pal of mine, got some money, just lost his wife, and a girl claiming to be a psychic comes out of nowhere and he goes after her. Too much of a coincidence, right? So, I started staking out your place, seeing if I could get some snaps of the players."

"Did you?"

"A few. I'll show them around, see if I can come up with ID. I assume you'll be going to the police here in New York."

"I don't believe I will," said Bernard after a moment's consideration.

"Why the hell not?"

"Because I think it unlikely that the local police will do anything significant to catch these people. I was a fool, I got taken, and I'm disinclined to endure shame and opprobrium on top of the financial loss. It was an expensive lesson and I just want to move on."

Ewell finished his drink and gave Bernard a sad and

disappointed look. "It's the girl, isn't it? You think she really loves you."

Bernard finished his drink too and said, "I believe I'm going to ask you to leave now, Mr. Ewell. I'm grateful for the heads-up, but I think our interests diverge at this point. And I really must get some writing in today."

Ewell took a business card and left it on the table. "Suit yourself. Give me a call if it turns out you can't handle things. I expect I'll be around."

When Ewell was gone, Bernard sat down in front of his laptop, shut off the Internet, brought up the file for *Sleeping Dogs Lie*, and, suppressing recent events, forced himself into the refuge of the fictive universe. It was in fact something of a family legend, that Bernard could write through anything-- sickness, family crises, disasters both natural and man-made-- and while his family might joke about it, Bernard was conscious of a vague resentment from his loved ones, and thought Graham Greene had been right about every serious writer requiring a sliver of ice in his heart. Yes, sometimes the imaginary people were more interesting than the real ones. And almost always more controllable.

He wrote steadily until three, when he took a break to walk the dog. Leaving, he noted that Ewell was still in his car, down the street. Returning, Bernard had a brief conversation with Tony the doorman, Tony being that doorman (there is one in every building) who can be tipped into providing special favors.

Back at his desk he completed his usual bag of a thousand words. He had described the maybe villainess-maybe victim at the novel's center and illuminated her character through dialog. He would not venture into her head, because the reader was not to know what she was thinking. Nor did Bernard at this point.

Yes, much like Miranda here. Ewell had been right. It *was* all about the girl. Or woman; but he couldn't help thinking of Miranda as a girl, there was something so light and fresh about her. Could that be entirely a construct, an element of the con, could they have analyzed him so completely as to understand that, having lived for decades with a woman of utmost seriousness, a heroine battling the worst of human degradation, he would necessarily be game for a creature of air? He had to doubt that. No one was that good an actor.

But he *had* been suckered by the flattery, and by the villains' exhaustive understanding of his work, not only the surface elegance of the thriller's plot but also the deeper layers, stuff he had hardly been aware of himself. Again, there had to be something real there. And there was, for Miranda (and he knew it had to be her, personally) had divined his thirst for a different life.

Now, in his shame, the idea of continuing to live in his apartment, with the books, appliances, bibelots, and pictures from his years with Louise, seemed a positive horror. A break of some sort was necessary for his emotional survival, and if it could not be the lie served up by the confidence gang, it would be something else, someplace different and distant and empty of the reminders of loss. He began to think about where that might be.

The dog rose from his bed, stretched, yawned extremely, walked over to where Bernard sat and rested his muzzle on the man's knee. Bernard looked into the dark and sympathetic eyes and said, "You know, that's a good idea, Murtagh. We should leave."

He wrote an email to his brother, explaining what had happened, saying he was leaving on an extended trip with no clear final destination and asking him to extend hospitality to his daughter for an indefinite period. He did not describe these doleful events in the emails to the kids, but said he was too depressed to live in the family home and that he wanted to get out of town for a while.

Twenty minutes after he sent these, his cell phone rang, and it was his daughter, Leslie.

No "Hi, Dad, how are you?" but a cry: "What happened?"

"Nothing happened. I just have to get out of here. I'm going nuts."

"Is this connected with the movie thing? The scam?"

"You know about that?'

"Of course, I know. It's burning up the cousins network."

"Shit. Bertie wasn't supposed to tell anyone."

"Well, he told Mary, and that's like posting on Instagram. You got your identity stolen?"

"I did. Unfortunately they didn't go far enough. I wish they had stolen it all, so I could be someone else."

"Oh, stop. How much did you lose?"

"A lot, but not as much as I might have. I would have given them the whole farm, if Elsie hadn't stopped me."

"They said you're going away now. Where are you going?"

"I don't know. Away."

"That's infantile, Dad. You have to let us know where you are."

"I will. But don't nag me, dear. I'm a little fragile now."

"Sorry. But are you okay? No bad thoughts or anything?"

"Nope. I'm good," he lied, and after signing off with the usual declarations of love, he felt extra shitty for not having the courage to spill the truth. A *psychic*? Yes, there was a level of stupid you couldn't reveal to your kids, lest they start thinking poor Dad can't handle his affairs anymore. As if to ward against this and to show he was still a citizen, he sent a brief email to Elsie, explaining what had happened and begging her not to tell anyone.

He shut down the laptop and stowed it at the bottom of a leather Gladstone bag he'd inherited from his father. He added warm clothing, all light and washable, and other gear suitable for a substantial stay away from home. In fact, he *was* leaving home; the thought struck him now, the reality of it, hard enough so he had to stop packing and sit on the bed for a moment. He would not return here. He would call a realtor and have the place listed. He would do it all at long distance. There were firms that cleaned out the apartments of the dead, and he would hire one. He'd get a good price for the apartment and the contents, not a small consideration now that the con gang had stripped him of ready cash. He would have them extract Leslie's gear and send it out to the House, as the Goodrich family's stately home in Locust Valley was known, then pack the physical corpse of his former life into crates and take it away, and someone else would have a life in this space.

He wandered through that space now, lingering in Leslie's room, studying the memorabilia of what appeared to be a perfect life. He'd helped make that happen and then screwed it up in the final innings. She would never come back here, and it was his fault. Photographs, awards, souvenirs, toys that would never be played with but were too significant to junk: the ballerina on the mirrored box, the grinning horse puppet, the blue dinosaur. He took this last down from the shelf. Its name was Otto, he recalled, once a transitional object, always within reach between ages two and four, now displayed ironically. Bernard carried it into his bedroom.

One more thing. From a high shelf in his closet he brought down a plastic box. Setting it on the bed, he opened it with a key. Lying on gray finger-foam was a High Standard Trophy .22 caliber semi-automatic pistol. Accompanying it in the case were four magazines loaded with .22 long rifle rounds and an extra 7.3 inch barrel with an integrated AWC Mark II suppressor.

It usually lived out at the House, where Bernard was in the habit of walking out to a bit of wasteland on the property and plinking away at paper targets. He used the suppressor to avoid a racket that might annoy the neighbors, not to mention his sister-in-law. Bernard had received the pistol as a birthday gift from his father, back when he had started training for pentathlon. It was significant that the elder Goodrich had not known that pentathlon competitors shot specialized air pistols, nor did Bernard so inform him, but accepted the gift with gratitude. Mr. Goodrich so rarely took any notice of what his son was doing that receiving something not absurdly wrong made for a red-letter day.

Bernard took the pistol off the foam, worked the slide, aimed at nothing and squeezed off a phantom shot. The Trophy was wonderfully accurate, and Bernard had kept, as he said, *his eye in* during all the years since. He had no problem putting ten shots into a circle the size of a quarter at fifteen meters. He reflected that, of all he owned, he was taking only a computer and a gun. Some significance there, but at the moment he could not quite articulate what it was.

He finished packing, ate a bowl of canned soup, had a glass of wine and waited. The phone rang: Elsie. He declined the call; there was a level of shame he was not prepared to endure just then. Immediately the phone rang again. This time it was Tony, telling him that the guy had left his car for a meal or a pee break. While the car was unattended, Tony had called the towing company, and at this minute, the car was being pulled away.

Bernard took a look around. The place seemed strange now, like a house in a dream, or that of an acquaintance, rarely visited. He thought, I have become not the person who lived here, more or less happily, for over twenty years with a woman I loved. She was the anchor, the cement, the root, and yes, also the governor of the marriage, the one with the more serious work. They used to joke that he was like a fifties wife with a hobby that surprisingly made money, like writing commercial jingles. Or *he* joked. Louise had not liked to examine the marriage—I do psych all day, she always said. I need a break.

Odd how these thoughts accumulated, as if exuded from the walls. The grief counselors said it: the spouse being gone, all the negatives from the marriage, no longer suppressed by daily affection, boil up distressingly. This thought: that an anchor is also a drag, that cement is entombing . . . and this is why he had fallen for Miranda's con so easily: the dream of a new life, rootless for once, like a soaring bird. To the apartment he said, "Goodbye, darling;" to the dog, "Murtagh, get your ball. We're leaving."

Driving in the Mercedes on 72nd Street, heading for the northbound West Side Highway he passed a wrecker pulling poor Ewell's car. He thought it would be impossible to explain to the man what he was doing or why.

"Where to, dog?" asked Bernard.

<I only follow,> replied the dog. <But fields would be nice. Or a beach.>

"How about just disappearing into the blue?"

<I am your guard dog, Beloved. >

"Blue it is," said Bernard, and at that moment the destination flashed into his mind, so that he laughed aloud. The light changed and he accelerated onto the highway, a truly marvelous feeling of release flowing into his bones.

Seven

Bernard drove north out of the city, through cold rain, the big cream Mercedes eating up the Taconic, then the New York Thruway. The short day ended in shiny blackness, but still he kept going over the slick roads, stopping only for fuel, and to tend the dog, and to consume coffee and the semi-disgusting soggy pastries available at the service plazas.

At Newburgh he left the highway, found a shopping mall. There he bought a box of .22 long-rifle hollow-points, and two Alcatel pre-paid cell phones. Back in the car, with the engine running against the chill, he enabled one of the phones, then transferred a select set of contact numbers from his iPhone. He included his children, his brother, his agent and, after a brief hesitation, Miranda Gardiner.

A strange thing to do, he thought: he wasn't exactly on the lam—why shut down a smartphone and use a burner? He concluded that it was part of shedding his old life. People say of their smartphones, "My whole life is on that." Precisely; and he wanted another life now. He used the burner to send Miranda a text message and, nearly hopeless, stared at the tiny screen for some minutes before driving off.

The heater fan was on high, as was the fanny-warmer switch, but Bernard was still cold. "It's the pathetic fallacy," he remarked to the dog. "I'm cold inside, so nature reflects this by sending dark clouds and freezing rain. It might even turn to snow."

<I like the snow. You could throw snowballs and I could catch them.>

"Yes, but they might close the highway. Or there could

be an ice storm and we could skid off the road or into an on-coming truck. That would perfect my disaster, and place me in my proper demographic, bereaved spouse succumbing to accident, just like Mr. Ewell's late client."

The dog had no comment. It was settling down after a disturbing couple of hours listening to Bernard scream curses and slam his hands against the steering wheel. The dog had contributed to the noise as best it could, barking and howling, and it considered the exercise a success. The man had begun to laugh then, although the smell he gave off when he did was not the usual laughing smell.

Now he was quiet, but putting out an unfamiliar scent, one that set the dog's senses on edge. It had scented it just recently, when the man had commanded it to strike the other man down and hold him, a war scent, but somehow colder, somehow combined with the base scent that identified the master. The dog circled carefully on the quilt that covered the rear seat, dropped down and went to sleep, but growled and thrashed in spasms.

At every stop thereafter, Bernard sent the same text to Miranda's cell phone. No response.

Something about his current mental state was oddly familiar, Bernard thought, and it came to him around Kingston that it was very much like what happened when you fell off a horse. One moment you were in perfect control, the horse attentive to your aids, nicely collected for the jump, and then in the next second, chaos--you were in the air with your heart up in your throat and then the violent shock that blotted out the world for an instant that seemed to go on a long time. Afterward came the pain and the awareness of the body, the terror and the gingerly exploration of movement and feeling that provided relief: no paralysis, no broken bones. You were hurting, but intact; you got up and remounted the goddamn horse.

Bernard wondered where the horse was now.

He left the Thruway at Plattsburg and took Route 22 north into the sparsely peopled, heavily forested forehead of New York, where the mapped Empire State seems to butt against Lake Champlain. He was nearly at the Canadian border, now driving through bursts of wet snow, when he made what the denizens of his destination called the last left turn in the United States of America and drove for eight miles over a crunching, pitted gravel road that the Monarch of the Autobahns did not like one bit.

The dog was up and alert. Bernard could feel the panted breath near his right ear. He said, "Do you remember this place, Murtagh? We are traveling to your natal spot. You were born here six years ago this August. Dougal, Fosbergh, Clancy, and Girarde were born here, too. They were all my dogs before you."

<There were no dogs before me. I would have chased them away. But there is a familiar smell. It is from the past; yesterday or even before that.>

"They don't know I'm coming," said the man. "I thought it best just to show up. Absolutely no one knows I'm here."

<I know you're here.>

"Well, yeah," said Bernard. "But I trust *you*."

Bernard's memory of the road was unimpaired, although it had been many years since he'd driven it for the first time. Or had been driven, in a black car that had picked him up at the Plattsburgh airport. He was accompanied by Carnaby, who had served under his father in the Navy and worked for him still around the House, and had been given the responsibility of delivering the errant son to the Monastery of St. Roch for a period of rehab and recuperation.

He admitted that he had become a little unpinned after the Moscow Olympics were cancelled: all that work, and making the team by a hair, and he knew that was his chance, that he was not quite good enough to be an Olympic pentathlete in any case, and by the time Los Angeles rolled around he'd be four years older and not any faster at cross-country.

People felt sorry for him. He was bought drinks and he drank them. There was about six months in there that he didn't quite recall, only that there was a good deal of clubbing in Manhattan, late nights fueled by booze and coke, driving fast under the influence, often in his Mercedes 450 SL convertible, then the rich kid's car du jour, colored the lustrous brown of a mink.

Then the inevitable—a bad wreck on the Long Island Expressway, up a down ramp, swerving to avoid an oncoming bus, crashing into barriers. He'd walked away from it more or less intact, but the girl in the passenger seat had been thrown out and emerged from the event a paraplegic. So he had to live with that, and the legal business, the DUI, the lawsuits from the girl's family. Though not quite Chappaquiddick, it was still a disgrace, and he had not handled it well, nor dealt well with the guilt. He couldn't drive, but he could take cabs to his dealer. He mainly snorted heroin and took Oxy. Again, the inevitable.

After a period of amnesiac blackness lasting a week or two, he had awakened strapped to a bed in a private clinic. Opening his eyes, he saw a fleshy woman in her fifties with an I-can-help-you face. He didn't want help; he wanted death, but what he got was a succession of nurses, doctors, tests, and lawyers. And his parents and family, which was the worst of all, and then the kindly face returned.

Her name was Carol Braun and she was a psychiatric social worker. He told her he wasn't interested in what she had to sell and she said fine, but we have to spend three hours a week together. We could spend them in companionable silence. The rules were he couldn't read or doze off or watch TV. All he could do for an hour was talk to her--or not talk to her and instead think about his sad life and be miserable in the prison of his skull.

After seventeen minutes of watching the wall clock jerk its long hand forward, he told her his tale of shame and regret, hoping for sympathy, like you read about convicts in prison cozening volunteers into helping them bust out, but while she listened with a kind look, she refused to encourage the hard luck story. She thought he'd been stupid and said so, but he'd been saved for something and now had a second chance. There were plenty of people who didn't even get one chance, and who was he to whine? *That* was what was shameful. He was better than the story suggested, she said, and what he had to do now was turn the determination that had made him a star athlete towards something else.

What?

What didn't matter, but it had to be hard physical work and it had to help others.

Bernard hadn't realized that psychiatric social workers talked like this. In fact, as he would learn, she was very nearly unique in her profession. He took it all in, both the shame and the passionate desire to do better, to do something that would impress this woman who seemed to *get* him in a way that his mother did not.

His physical wounds at least were quick to heal. Despite his recent efforts at debauchery, he was shockingly healthy, Olympic fit, and they wanted to move him out of there. The parents had arranged for a bed at the kind of place where rich, naughty kids got stashed while the disappointed parents (we gave him *everything*!) got on with their busy lives; but he had a violent antipathy for such places, which typically held the sort of people who had been his companions in vice. He never wanted anything to do with those idiots again.

In fact, he was not a black sheep at all. He'd had a bad few months, was not addicted, was not anti-social, wanted to get back to real life. He was motivated, had learned his lesson, and so on, and he poured all this out to Ms. Braun during their last session.

She listened, and when he'd run down, she said, "Even if all this is true, you still have a problem with the courts. You're under adjudication. Reckless driving, DUI, reckless endangerment. And that Frances Goring, the girl in the car. That counts against you, what happened to her. So, you're ordered into a program, unless you'd like a year in Rikers. Which I would not recommend."

"Is there any other choice besides jail or the funny farm?"

Her answer, after a near minute of tense silence, was completely unexpected.

"I might have a third choice for you, but I have to ask you two questions."

"Ask."

"The first is, are you religious? It says on your forms you're Catholic. Are you devout?"

"Of course not devout. I stopped going to . . ."

"I don't want to hear that. Say yes. Mass every Sunday, Lenten fasts, the whole deal."

"Actually, I have stigmata, but I never talk about it because I want to remain humble. What's the second question?"

"Do you love dogs? But the answer to this one has to be the truth."

It was a funny story when told later, how she'd pushed the system to the limit, got his parents and the court officials and even the Cardinal Archbishop into the act, with the story of a good Catholic boy, an Olympian no less, who'd suffered a crushing blow and had gone astray, and now wished to spend his time in religious contemplation and prayerful repentance. A generous contribution from the family to the Archdiocese, and the thing was done. Instead of Shady Acres, drugs, and group therapy, he was off to St. Roch for an indefinite period in the hands of the giant Carnaby. He never saw Carla Braun again. By the time he returned to the city, she'd moved on, had been a temporary hire, no one was quite sure where she'd gone or if she was still in New York. Unlisted number, of course.

When the Internet arrived, she was one of the first people he'd Googled, but no luck. When he'd told Louise the story, she'd said, "Angel. Sometimes in my line of work, angelic forces take over, exactly the right person with the right client and the right solution." Louise had searched the social worker registries too, and found nothing, and they had both laughingly agreed that Ms. Braun was an actual angel, and they would call upon her from time to time during the inevitable hairy patches that occur in any long marriage.

He thought about this as he drove, how that little joke was gone, how he would never have that bit of schtick with anyone else. He felt a taste of the original sadness.

"I'm blue, Murtagh. Help me out here."

<Seek food. It's warm enough.>

"That won't cut it, dog. I lost my wife."

<I can easily find her. I know the scent.>

"Do you still remember her?"

<Smell. Voice.>

"Me too."

Then they turned a final curve of the wavy road, and a small stone cottage came into view, and a peeling sign:

St. Roch Abbey
Cistercians of the Common Observance

Registered Dobermans

This last was written on a small white plank suspended under the sign proper.

"You're home, Murtagh," Bernard said.

<I am not home. I am the dog at home, but there are many dogs here.>

"You'll have to get used to that, I'm afraid. But you're still the dog at home."

Bernard stopped the car and looked through the window of the cottage. He could see a figure sitting in a ladder-back rocker, indistinct through the blur of the window screening, but clear enough to show he wore a white monk's habit. It was the doorkeeper's cottage, and that must be the new doorkeeper sitting there. During Bernard's first stay with the monks, the doorkeeper had been a wizened little fellow, somewhat dim, whom everyone had called St. Dom, although not to his face.

It had struck Bernard then as a little unseemly, a simple man so mocked by his brother monks, but it turned out they were entirely serious. "Brother Dominic has more holiness in his little finger than there is in the rest of us put together," one monk had told him when he'd questioned the usage. It seemed that the local people were in the habit of dropping by for a chat with Brother D when they were troubled or in despair, not an uncommon condition in that bleak country, and he would listen and tell them not to worry, that everything would come right. Or not, in which case he would just tell them not to worry. A sort of holy fool, Bernard had assumed; but at the time, he was not interested in holy fools. He was interested in staying at St. Roch just long enough to convince the court that he was a reformed and chastened man, and thus remove the legal hook.

Bernard got out of the car and let the dog out of the back seat. The screen door opened with a springy croak and the monk stepped out into the chill air.

"Welcome back, Bernard," said the monk. "I'm glad to see you again."

"Brother Dominic?" said Bernard, amazed. The monk had seemed an old man to the Bernard of thirty years ago, but here he still was, looking remarkably the same, somewhat north of the sixties, although he had seemed that old when Bernard first laid eyes on him.

He hadn't thought about that day in decades, but now it all came back to him. Brother Dominic had looked with his mild blue gaze and said, "You will find a new life here." That was it, no further counsel necessary, and of course, he *had* found a new life. He'd spent the better part of his twentieth year at St. Roch, autumn winter and spring, while the toxins leached out of his body and his spirit renewed.

The monks prayed at the canonical hours, matins, prime, lauds, and the rest, and Bernard prayed with them, rising in the small hours, chanting the psalms in the freezing chapel, continuing the endless cycle of prayer that was the core purpose of the monastic life. Prayer and work, *ora et labora*, St. Benedict's rule, which the original twenty monks led by Robert of Molesme in 1098 were following when they fled the luxuries of Cluny and founded the first reformed monastery at Citeaux, the town whose Latin name the Cistercians took as their own. Bernard had not known a Cistercian from a chimpanzee on arrival, and no one had sat him down for a lecture. The knowledge of the ancient tradition of which he had become a tiny, temporary part had seeped in over the months.

117

He learned that all monks living by the Benedictine rule must earn their way in the world through the sweat of their brows. Some make fruit cake, others sell honey or fine soap, others run retreats. St. Roch sold dogs, registered Doberman Pinschers, and not puppies, not even pets, for the most part. The work of St. Roch was training dogs to Schutzhund standards; that is, perfectly obedient tracking and protection dogs, capable of demonstrating their skills in Schutzhund competitions throughout the world. As such, they were prized by security services and private clients as bomb-sniffers, trackers, and personal protection dogs. St. Roch dogs were discipline jocks, the Olympians of the pooch world, and Bernard, recognizing kindred spirits, fell in love.

He worked like a dog. A monastery is as rich in menial tasks as it is in spiritual gifts, the former being one route to the latter according to the Rule, and Bernard was generously endowed with all the scut work on offer: peeling vegetables, chopping and hauling wood and ashes, cleaning leaves from gutters, scrubbing floors, and similar work that heretofore he had seen only servants do.

The reward for ten or so hours of this was an hour with Brother Andrew and the dogs. The Cistercians of the Common Observance did not practice perpetual silence like their brethren of the Trappists, but they were not a talkative bunch, except to the dogs. Brother A was a dry stick of a man, red-tanned of face in all seasons, hands scarred like a chew-toy, around fifty, but seeming ancient as the stones of the priory to young Bernard. His training philosophy, presented over the weeks via short gnomic bursts, was that we men were obliged to do God's will and the dogs were obliged to do ours. This was the main requirement for a happy life, in both man and dog, and training was largely a matter of teaching dogs how to be happy.

The first time Bernard heard this remark, he didn't understand it, or understood it as a rationalization: it was convenient, he supposed, for a trainer to believe that making a dog do what the trainer wanted might be pleasant for the dog. It reduced guilt, perhaps, the sense that it was a little harsh to break the will of an animal; in blunt terms, to enslave it. Bernard was then still of the opinion that doing as you pleased was the basis of happiness.

Once, when feeling frustrated that the dog he was training was not doing what he wanted it to do, he'd expressed this notion to Brother Andrew. To Bernard's surprise, the monk seemed as shocked as if Bernard had suggested opening a brothel in the south cloister.

"Is that what you think?" he'd exclaimed, and when Bernard had offered a mumbled confirmation, said, "Why, you have the whole thing on its head. The dogs aren't our slaves. They're our *masters*. Look, what do you suppose we're doing here—I mean all us monks?"

Bernard gave the book answer: "Working and praying?"

"Yes, but why dogs? Why not fruitcakes? Not that there's anything wrong with fruitcakes."

Bernard had wondered about this himself, and had no answer.

Andrew did. "We're here to see if a small community isolated from the world can actually do God's will, can actually love God and our neighbor as ourself, can stop thinking of ourselves for five minutes out of all the time God gives us as a gift. The dogs are a kind of sacramental, like rosaries or statues; training them gives us a heightened insight into pure obedience. We're not nearly as good at it as they are, but I live in hope that I can learn to heel, sit and stay when God commands at least as well as our worst dog."

"I understand," said Bernard.

"Understanding is not the point," said Brother Andrew. "It has to be in the bones, as it is with young Canopus here." He patted Bernard's trainee. "Speaking of the worst dog."

"You know, it's strange," said Bernard, as he continued up the gravel drive from the gatehouse to the main priory building, "I haven't really thought about this place in years. Even when I come up for a new dog, my memory is pretty vague. But now I have all these vivid recollections of the first time I was here. You know how they house a dog to be trained with each brother? Of course you do. Well, they gave me a dog named Canopus . . ."

Murtagh had no opinion on dogs named Canopus nor was he inclined to sympathize with a dog that could not hold an out-stay until death intervened. Father Ambrose, when Bernard related this experience to him in his study sometime later, laughed as he recalled the animal.

"Yes, the wretch flunked the out-stay. I suppose Brother Andrew assured you it wasn't your fault."

"Yes," said Bernard, smiling too. "He said some dogs just couldn't run off to a distant point and stay there if someone wasn't watching them. There was nothing to be done. A pet."

"Pet" was not a compliment at St. Roch.

"Yes, it's sort of the doggie *pons asinorum*. You know the term?"

"I do. In medieval schools, if you couldn't master the proof that the base angles of an isosceles triangle are equal, they figured you couldn't benefit from any more formal schooling."

"Yes, off to the bake house, with you, the wine press, God wants you as a hauler of heavy objects. A dog that won't work out of the sight of man is like a Sunday Catholic, someone who acts the scoundrel six days a week and then gets all pious for an hour in the pew." The abbot paused, signaling the end of small talk, and then added, "So, Bernard, it's wonderful to see you, but also unexpected. Unless you're looking for another dog."

Bernard told the abbot what had befallen him.

"How dreadful. My very sincere condolences on your loss. I suppose it's a convention to say, is there anything I can do, when of course, there isn't."

"Actually, there is."

"Oh?"

"Yes. I can't bear to be in the apartment we shared, and I'm not up to starting a new establishment. I was wondering if I could stay here for a while. I'd work and be part of the community, obviously."

"Well, well. I would have to take it up in chapter, of course, but I see no real objection. It's a surprise, though."

"Thank you, Father. Why a surprise?"

"You seemed a particularly . . . secular figure. I read over Father Adrian's notes on you. That was his opinion."

Bernard looked at the man across the big, plain table. Fr. Ambrose was of the breed of fleshy monks, a large man with a strong-jaw and a wide forehead beneath his silver tonsure. Fr. Adrian, abbot during Bernard's earlier court-mandated stay, had been a man of the scrawny ascetic breed.

"I didn't know you made notes."

"Well, yes. We're always on the lookout for vocations, and young men in diversion from prosecution are a good source. Your bad boy often makes a good monk."

"But not me. Like Canopus, I turned out to be just a pet."

"Yes. And now here you are again. As I say, we will have to have a formal vote, but you've been a patron of this place for almost thirty years. The roof that keeps off the snow I see is starting to fall is your gift. We owe everyone hospitality, of course, but you have a special claim. I believe the chapter will see it that way, too. Meanwhile, I can certainly offer you a bed for the night. Will you be joining us for vespers?"

Bernard was exhausted from the drive and all he wanted was a bowl of soup, food for his dog, and that bed; but he said he would.

After vespers, Bernard joined the monks in the refectory. Before sitting to their meal, each monk fed and watered his dog. The dogs were at different levels of training, but all had enough manners to eat in the presence of other dogs without snarling or theft, and to sit quietly at foot while their monks ate and listened to the lector read a passage from Scripture. Most of the monks were older than Bernard, men in their sixties and seventies, but there was a solid minority of younger men, which he understood was unusual these days. He thought it must be the dogs.

He attended compline, too, the second evening prayer, at nine p.m., and then retired to his cell, an eight-by-ten foot volume with cheap industrial carpeting on the floor and white plaster walls. A small double-glazed window looked out on blackness and showed him, in reflection, someone he hardly recognized. The bed was neither hard nor soft; the sheets were rough and washed thin. At the foot of the bed, a dog's pallet. Wall pegs did instead of a closet (a white novice habit hung from one) and a desk, a lamp, a chair, and a small pine dresser completed the secular furnishings. A prie-dieu occupied a corner, under a large, vivid, polychrome crucifix.

The idea that people require eight hours or so of uninterrupted sleep is modern, and untrue. For over fifteen hundred years, monks living under the Benedictine rules have risen every three hours to give voice to prayer. Within a few days, Bernard had slipped back into the ancient rhythm: vespers at six, compline at nine, matins at midnight, lauds at three in the morning, followed in three-hour intervals by prime, tierce, sext, nones and vespers again. Bernard knew he had little religious sense. As a youth he had read Merton's story of conversion and entry into the monastic life with admiration, but no sympathy for the choice, or for the mental or emotional state that could prefer it to success and sex.

Now, however, he got it, why people throughout the world and throughout history turned to God when fate stripped them of worldly pleasure, and why many people who have access to worldly pleasure decline it in favor of an ascetic life. If you allow people to remove from the world, arrange their lives in patterns of constant repetition within the larger pattern of the liturgical year, give them hard work to do, and oblige them to set aside big chunks of time for speaking to God, those people are going to change. St. Benedict was no dummy.

Bernard had done this all before, but as a man condemned to it. Now he was here of his own volition and what it reminded him of was not that first visit, but his training for the Olympics. The changes in the body and the spirit were just as radical, and they came surprisingly fast. For the first time since Louise's death, he got to sleep without Valium. He worked at the tasks served up by the rota, he sang the canonical hours; time began to flow for him in different, smoother channels. No decisions, no emotional tangles: peace.

In his limited free time he tapped away at his new novel. He didn't know if it was any good, nor did he much care. It was just something he did in the way that the dogs followed a scent trail.

As for the life of the place: he didn't have anything as fancy as a religious experience, but he increasingly felt the presence of Something Else in the spaces of the monastery, like the pressure of a breeze or the feeling of cloth on his back.

Sometimes, reflecting on this, an absurd smile broke out on his face, and he observed similar zany expressions on the faces of some of the other monks. It was like nothing so much as the tongue-lolling smile on the face of a happy dog. Had he a tail, it would be wagging enthusiastically.

"Now I'm just like you, Murtagh," he remarked to his dog.

<Not quite.>

No, not quite. Bernard had modified the canonical routine. After each session of prayer, he sat on his cot and used his burner phone to send a text to the false Miranda.

I don't care about the money. Tell me your story.

No answer, of course. Bernard considered it part of his religious practice. The abbot had not asked him the obvious question. Given his situation, why had he not gone to the police? A good question—Bernard had asked it of himself, and had no real answer, except that he wanted to know if what he had felt in the presence of the girl, what he had felt *coming* from her, was a mere artifact of the con, or something he had cooked up himself out of loneliness, or real. And he couldn't do that unless he could be alone with her again, with the law not involved. Until he had determined that, he felt he could not go on with the rest of his life.

Eight times a day he sent out this secular prayer, and eight times a day the cell phone indicated that the message had not gone through. There was never an answer, which suggested that the thing was shut down, sitting in a drawer somewhere, unused. She wouldn't maintain the account and so eventually the carrier would cancel it and revive the number and a stranger would receive it and ignore it and that would be the end of that practice.

He tapped out the message anew each time, although he could have easily copied it. It was part of the ritual. He hardly needed to look at the keyboard anymore. One day, after prime, with weak winter dawn-light filling his cell, he typed and sent his message, then put the phone away in the drawer of his desk. He went to work, which this week was acting as an agitator, the trainer in the padded suit who incites a dog being trained to attack. It was vigorous work requiring great concentration, for the agitator has to slowly build a dog's confidence, doling out victory in small increments to build a dog who will attack anything on command and not otherwise.

As he did this, he found to his surprise that a Buddhist legend he'd heard once was rattling around in his mind. A sage tells a seeker that there is a certain stone on the road that is the essence of the Buddha and gives him a carved stick of ancient provenance. When touched on the Buddha stone the stick will turn to gold. So the man travels the roads of India, stooping and touching every stone, until he is an old man, bent double from this effort. One day he notices that his stick has turned to gold. He has no idea how long it has been that way or what stone did it.

At nones, after chapel, he went back to his cell and drew out the cell phone. He typed out his message and was about to press the Send button when he happened to notice that under his last message appeared the tiny letters "Delivered." He had no idea whether this was the first one so marked or the twentieth, and this made him laugh out loud and remember the man with the Buddha stick. Then he typed a different message.

Eight

I haven't contacted the police. I don't intend to. I just want to know who you are.

Marvel stared at the message in its cartoonish bubble, still legible despite the violent shaking of the hand that held the smartphone. After a minute she switched the phone off, gripping the thing so tightly her knuckles went white. Why couldn't she make it disappear through a mere act of will? She was looking at death in the black glass. Not only was its existence the gravest violation of Overby's protocol, but even in a less disciplined gang, the possession of a second cell phone was prima facie evidence of duplicity, of betrayal.

She knew this, she agreed with this, she knew she should have destroyed the phone, and the fact that she'd been unable to do it filled her with a kind of terror she had not experienced before. She had been in plenty of danger, from the law, from brutal and desperate men, but she had always felt competent within herself, had always believed she could sneak or talk her way out of any peril whatever.

So her inability to perform a simple and necessary act was like waking up paralyzed or blind for no discernible reason; no, *worse*, because if those things had happened there would be people around to help, they would nurse her and take her to doctors, well, not Sami, probably, but Esme would, as she herself would have for Esme, and Overby would figure out who the best doctor was for unexplained blindness or whatever and get her to his office. This case was different, however, as there was no one on earth she could talk to about it. Esme would be horrified, Overby wouldn't trust her anymore, Sami . . .well, she didn't want to think about what Sami would do.

Right, don't think about that, think about what *you're* going to do, breathe, suppress the panic, focus. She was good at this; Overby had spent hours with her, training her in poise, in self-control--when everything is batshit, you can always control your breath, that was one of his sayings, and it was true: after a few minutes, the devils were gone from her belly and she could think clearly again.

Turn on the phone. When the home screen appeared, she pressed the buttons that brought up the reset dialog, and sweaty-handed, pressed the one that reset the phone, returning it to factory specs, and . . . Oh, good, it worked. Whatever had prevented her from ditching the phone in the dumpster was apparently not against a mere reset. Crazy thoughts, there was no "whatever," and now she was safer, Miranda had been fully erased. All that was required now was to pull the SIM card.

She looked for a paper clip, but someone had taken all the paper clips from her desk, which was crazy, there were always paperclips around, and so then she looked for a safety pin, a straight pin, anything--okay, here was a push-pin from her cork board, that should work.

But somehow it did not, the pin was slightly wrong for the little hole, it wouldn't engage, or maybe she was doing it wrong. She wasn't a tech person, Esme was the tech person, maybe she should go across and ask Esme to do it, ha ha. The chime sounded again--an incoming message. *Ignore it*, she told herself; but she pushed the icon.

> You should have ditched this phone, or trashed the SIM card, but you didn't, or my messages wouldn't have gone through. We can both feel that slight silvery connection, completely inexplicable. I should hate you, right? And you should by no means answer this. But you will. Tell me your story.

She read this several times and her thought was, he's running a con. Marvel knew that some of the things that squares thought were true about her profession were very often not. For example, you would think that someone who'd been burnt in a con would be extra careful, once bitten and so on, but the fact was that people who'd been conned were even better marks than they'd been before. And you *could* con a con man.

How to play it was the question, and from this point Marvel abandoned any thought of following the protocol. This terrified her, but also provided a strange elation. Because why? Because her work with Overby and company represented the longest time that Marvel had existed under a discipline not of her own devising since she'd run away from Springfield, Oregon and Aunt Ethel, nearly twenty years ago, and it had begun to gripe. The violation of protocol was therefore a refreshing naughtiness, essentially harmless: it wasn't like she was going undercover for the cops.

The thought of cops. That last message. What was his game? Was he being straight about no cops involved? Of course he was. Marvel could not have explained how she knew this, but she knew it beyond doubt, like she knew she was breathing and sitting in a room in a house in Lanikai. She also knew, also no idea how, that she couldn't get rid of this cell phone. She thought of the scene earlier at the dumpster, how the phone had appeared on the car seat even though she had a clear memory . . . No, she didn't want to think about that now, it made her face and hands clammy and sent a little bubble of foul nausea into her mouth.

Back to this damned persistent mark. Here another character strayed onto Marvel's internal stage, and this was the crazy girl. Maybe she should tell him about Contrary Annie, that was what Aunt Ethel had called her, and it was so, from the first glimmerings of consciousness, Marvel responded to nearly any directive with objection, and when compliance was compelled, as it often was in Aunt Ethel's house, immediately there began the hatch of some subverting scheme.

Overby had, of course, seen this when he'd first recruited her, he'd said it was a virtue in a grifter, but only when bound tight to a higher discipline. You're always going to shoot yourself in the foot if you don't learn to control it. He gave her a lot of stuff about Coyote the trickster spirit, the god of the grifters, who makes sure that in the end the grifter outsmarts himself. Hence the protocol, ever the protocol, the steel discipline that separated their 'ohana from the ranks of the small time, the jailbirds and fools.

Marvel was grateful for this lesson, she liked being in a family of sorts, she very much liked being rich; but she had certain resentments. Overby always said that the put-up, the first grab at the attention of the mark, was the key to any long con. Marvel was the put-up girl, and Overby often expressed the opinion that he had never seen or heard of a put-up girl to equal Marvel Gafney. Despite this, she always had the feeling that she was not exactly in the innermost circle of the 'ohana, the conversation she had recently overheard being a good example. They were treating her like a kid or a dummy, and she didn't like it.

Wouldn't it be interesting to have a little play of her own, kept secret from Overby and especially from Sami, who was starting to treat her like one of his guys--do this, do that--like she didn't have a brain, only an ass, and she wished he could be a little more discrete. Every time she came back from one of these operations, she would stumble across foreign female paraphernalia in their bedroom and it pissed her off. She got back a little by flirting with Jumbo Wedge, letting him feel her up when they were out together, surfing or kiteboarding or hanging out with the Cars.

Not that Jumbo would actually hit on her, or not that she would actually get dirty with him, because that would be an honor thing with Sami. Overby, who missed nothing, had explained this in some detail, how if she let that happen Jumbo would have to take out Sami, or the opposite, and that would be the end of this, she had to admit, quite lush life.

At any rate, this thing had occurred, never mind the weirdness angle, and she very much wanted to screw with the protocol in a way that was dangerous but not *too* dangerous, and also--here was the truly strange part--there was something about Bernard Goodrich, that pulled at her in a way that no other mark ever had. To assure herself this was true, she considered the other six operations she'd done, and how the men had been.

The first was an oil-shale guy with a ranch in Montana. She couldn't recall his name (Tom something?), but she remembered he had always called his ranch a "spread," like in the movies. Helen was the dead wife. He was a country and western fan and he'd always dreamed of hosting a C&W festival on his property.

It turned out that the pretty stranded motorist he'd rescued knew all about music festivals, she'd been a publicist for George Strait, she'd worked at the Grand Old Opry, knew 16th Avenue in Nashville like the back of her hand. She was sure George would love to headline his festival. She'd call Rich Font, his agent, right away.

And although Ol' Tom Something had a rep as a hard-bargainer, a tough guy in a rough business, she'd had no trouble at all with him, the scripts worked great, the grifter who'd played George Strait's agent was perfect. She'd had to listen to endless hours of fucking country music, but they got $8.4 million off the sucker; almost worth it, was the joke around the 'ohana.

The second was Kyle or Lyle, he'd been a senior airline executive, vice-president for operations—Delta or United--retired, moved to a bloated house in Rancho Mirage just in time for the wife to get cancer. Alice May. (Why did the dead wife's name stick when the guy's, the mark's, faded? She didn't know.) Marvel showed up a decent four months after the funeral, posing as a widow whose late husband had run a small inter-island air service out of Kingston, Jamaica. She'd inherited the concern and didn't have a clue what to do with it. Oh, Kyle or Lyle had been in the airline business? Oh, he'd always wanted to run his own airline? What a fortunate coincidence then, that they should have met at this elegant charity reception.

The mark had a set of hands on him, though; she thought rape was a real possibility, although the protocol said she had to go with it, pretend it was the hottest thing ever. Overby said actually having to fuck the marks was unlikely, the scam typically drove thoughts of sex out of their brains; they assumed sex with Marvel would be a part of the triumphant conclusion of the dream. That one netted $6.4 million.

The next was a real estate guy, Davidoff, from New Jersey. A hockey fanatic, always wanted to buy an NHL team, but couldn't quite afford it. Sally was the dead wife. Then he met a young woman at a Bruins game who'd worked for a billionaire hedge fund guy, a guy who had organized a syndicate to buy the New Jersey Devils. Would Davidoff want to get in on the deal? Why even ask? That had been their biggest score so far, $25 million. She recalled the mark had a particularly rank smell.

The fourth was a dentist in Brookline, Massachusetts. The dead wife was Ellen. It'd been her money, and she'd kept it tightly in hand, which meant George couldn't fulfill his dream of opening an art gallery in Chelsea until breast cancer removed her from the picture.

This had been an unusually complex one, because going in they didn't have a clue what the guy's dream was, so they had to get Marvel to meet him cute, and do the dating business for a while and after she'd found it out, they had to set up a fake gallery in New York, which she could then find for her new boyfriend, and which was coincidentally for sale. $4.4 million. Marvel had acquired a broad if shallow knowledge of contemporary American art to carry this one off, based on a deck of index cards she'd had from Overby, which also included a bouquet of jargon phrases about art that could be applied to any work. As a grifter, she'd felt right at home in the contemporary art scene.

The next two she recalled rather more vividly because it was their first, so-to-speak, walk-in. The original mark was Ted Haley—the guy had owned the largest GM-Chevy dealership in greater Atlanta, and had a passion for NASCAR racing. Dead wife was Kate, a car crash, ha ha.

Big beef of a guy, Marvel recalled, always had a drink in hand, stank of cigar smoke. His best bud was Ryell Abbot, also a NASCAR fan, also a recent widower. Judy. In real estate, Marvel remembered, built huge numbers of tacky houses in Fulton County, and did half her work for her on Ted, he thought her deal was the greatest thing ever and how terrific that her brother was a young driver currently burning up the circuit, and dissatisfied with his sponsorship.

Would Ted like to meet him? Why even ask? Unfortunately, Ted died happy of a heart attack just after he'd transferred $16 million to set up a racing team built around the speedy brother, and Ryell had asked Marvel if the deal was still open. Of course it was and they'd been happy to take $10.7 off him.

Marvel felt no guilt at what she had done to these men. Overby had explained his attitude toward confidence larceny: they were providing an expensive service, the answer to the question, what do you give the man who has everything? Their gift was a dream. These men lived more intensely during the con than ever before; their eyes were brighter, their juices flowed, they were engaged with life again.

Also, did you really think that the money a man earned during years of hard work ought to go to some spoiled brat of an heir who'd never labored a day? Far better to redistribute those dollars to hard-working grifters. Marvel was not entirely sure she bought the economic argument, but she was convinced that she had brought something positive into the lives of the men she'd swindled. It was like a very expensive ticket to a private performance, where for a time your fantasy becomes real.

She now discovered that ruminating on marks past gave her a peculiar feeling of sickly tension, to alleviate which she pulled her stash box out of the lower desk drawer and filled a glass water-pipe with a fat lump of bud.

After a couple of major hits and the usual coughing, her thoughts turned back to her grifting adventures, which seemed a lot funnier than they had a few minutes ago. Sex, for example. A sexual charge was a necessary distraction. When a attractive younger woman professes interest in an elderly man, his mind may not stay as sharp concerning business as it had been. The trick here was to deliver that interest provisionally, to get him thinking about the delights of the future, but without making him actually frustrated.

Thus she always feigned a current boyfriend or husband, unsatisfactory in many ways, eminently dumpable in favor of the mark, as long as the mark behaved himself, did not act at all like the brutal, insensitive boyfriend/hubbie, whose derelictions could be related in detail so as to arouse the paternal sympathies and prevent excessive grab-ass. Marvel had discovered the fictitious boyfriend shortly after she grew breasts--it was very nearly her first con, for she had the ability to extract sympathy and the desire to protect from even quite brutal men. I'd really prefer you, was the seed she planted in their animal brains, but I would never, like, *betray* anyone.

What she'd told Bernard about her aura was perfectly true, perhaps the only true thing she'd told him. She could fill a room with it, draw every male eye to her; and she could pull it tight about her and become dim, a barely perceptible shadow. She had learned to do this last while being raised by a woman who hated and feared her and hurt her whenever possible. A man had taught her the sex scam, for his own reasons.

She was out on Lanikai beach, the sand strip narrowed by a high tide, ebbing now she reckoned, her experienced eye unaffected by the dope. The buzz of which allowed her to think more deeply about Bernard, he of the messages, who was not going to call the police, and of the feelings he engendered. In fact, as she knew very well, she actually *had* the fictive feelings she shared with the marks, she *was* delighted with them, she *did* imagine a future with them, she *did* share their dreams. Or at least the persona did, the artificial being she created for the con; like any great actor, she was able to put *herself* into the character so that it had genuine life.

But Bernard had somehow been able to see the intelligence behind the mask, to touch the person she knew herself to be. *And no one did that.* She hadn't been *seen* that way since the age of ten, when her grandmother died. Overby thought he knew her, thought nearly that he had invented her, but he was seeing merely the next layer down, the steely surface—cynical, ironic—of a stone grifter. She recalled that thing Bernard did when he described her face, and it clearly wasn't entirely about her face, she felt herself *seen*, and she felt that even if she'd drawn in her aura to zero, he would still be seeing her in that way. Plus that whole Sean Young thing, what was he saying with *that*?

Just thinking about it made her feel strange, as if something vital to her survival were slipping out of control. She hated it. On the other hand, she had to credit an intense curiosity about Bernard Goodrich and what he was up to. Those other marks were merely working their futile dreams, and Marvel had been a dream-element. But it had seemed as if Bernard had been more interested in her than in making the movies. She recalled the way he looked at her when he should have been looking at the other members of the crew, making their various pitches.

A storm was passing to the north of the Islands, kicking the surf up and making a palm-rattling wind. Marvel left the beach and went back to her room. She picked up the Miranda cell phone and tapped

What do you want from me?

No, this is nuts, she thought, I'm going to find a paper-clip, pull the SIM card, zap it in the microwave and forget about this . . . but here was the answer.

Not really sure. It's a compulsion, and you must have it too, or you wouldn't be in contact. Where do compulsions come from? The same place as attractions and inspirations? Would that be outer space? The gods? Do you really think you're psychic or was that part of the scam? So many questions. Let me back off here—I am writhing with curiosity—and just waiting for whatever you want to say. As long as it's the truth. You and I both live by making up lies, but let's not let that leak into this exceedingly narrow band of connection. Let's have one thin line of honesty now, hmm? I think it might be good for us both. What do you say, Miranda?

What *did* she say to that? Overby always said that in the espionage game, when you target someone as an asset, encouraging the first betrayal is the hardest part. You had to find the right combination of resentment and reward, the resentment typically establishing a conscience-salving rationale for accepting the reward. (The cipher clerk's superiors didn't recognize his talents--he'd show them. They wouldn't give him that promotion? He'd promote himself!) In her case, the device in her hands was evidence of that primal treason, and what reward was this man offering her?

It hardly mattered. She felt something move in her, some barely perceived dam crumbling and her thumbs worked.

> How's your dog?
> The dog is fine. He sends regards. How're you, Miranda?

> It's not Miranda it's Marvel.
> That's an unusual spelling. Do you say it Mar-VEL?

> No. It's MAR-vel, like Captain Marvel.
> Your parents must have been very impressed or very hopeful to hang that one on you.

> My parents had nothing to do with it. My Gran started to call me that when I was a baby. Because of what happened when my folks died.

???

> They drove off a bridge into the McKenzie River in Oregon. It was January. I was strapped into a car seat in the back of the car when it went into the water. They both died on impact and I was under water for a long time.The cops thought it must have been close to half an hour, but the water was so cold that I wasn't damaged. It happens, especially with small kids. I was just a baby, ten months old. It's a known fact, nothing miraculous about it. But I was the miracle baby on the news for a week and after that Gran

started calling me Marvel. That and the psychic stuff.

?? I thought it was part of your scam.

It is. But I have a history with it too. When I was a little kid I could find lost things. I saw stuff. Dead people, a little clairvoyance. I thought everyone could until Gran set me straight. It's like luck. Some people are just lucky and when they come to casinos, believe me, the pit bosses can spot them and they get barred. But psychic readings and 'you will meet a dark stranger'? That's bullshit, neon signs on storefronts in crappy little strip malls. But I use it in my grift because it works.

What's your real name?

What's "real" in this context?

Point taken. So your parents died in an accident—then what happened?

Not exactly an accident. They were running from the cops because they'd just robbed a bank in Eugene. They were bank robbers when they weren't running a gas station in Springfield. That's where I grew up, just outside Springfield, Oregon. Dogpatch.

Dogpatch?

What the nice people in Eugene called where we lived. Mobile homes in the woods, busted cars in the yards, broken appliances out front, nowhere to go but Eugene, if that's a place to go at all. We had a double-wide on a half-acre, which is like aristocracy in Dogpatch. Gran worked at the post office and we had some money from the publicity about the miracle baby. People who'd pass right by a starving kid on the street pour money on the same kid when something weird happens to her. A lot of stuffed animals too. A sad story, but not as sad as some.

Your grandmother was a taxpayer? I mean not a criminal.

Right. She was . . . I don't know, simple? Not smart, anyway, but honest. A decent woman. An actual Christian, only she didn't go to any church. Her sister was the big church lady.

That must be a story.

Yeah, I guess. Aunt Ethel took me in when Gran died. I lived with her and her son, my Uncle Claude, for five years until I went to the juvie.

What did you do?

I thought this was about my grandmother.

Come on, Marvel. Keep the flow going.

Fine. Like I said, she was an actual gospel Christian. Feed the hungry, clothe the naked and so on. She was a soft touch, always had a dollar for any bum who wandered by. When I got a little older, it made me nuts, because we didn't have all that much and I wanted stuff, all the shit the other kids in school had and I didn't, and she was giving money away to bums. She was nice to me, I give her that, but she was nice to everyone. No, that doesn't sound right--I mean she treated me like I was a miracle every day. I think she felt bad about the way her daughter--I mean my mother--had turned out, and she blamed herself. I was a second chance, you know?

Did they know about your story in Dogpatch? I mean at school and so on.

Oh, yeah, everyone knew. But most kids had a story like that. I mean since the sawmills closed and they stopped most of the logging, the major business in that part of the world is cooking Keith and growing pot.

I mean cooking meth. :)

I figured. So, you were raised by a loving, decent woman. And yet...

My life of crime? Look this suck, tapping into a little phone screen. If you want more of this shit, get yourself a new email account—actually, get a bunch of anonymous accounts, and send email to kite-girl121 at gmail.com. It'll be easier.

But the real reason is? Remember, we agreed to play it straight.

Ok really, I'm just not ready to go into all that, plus

I'm in an insecure location right now.

Damn, I didn't think of that. Look--If you're in danger from
this, let's forget it.
No that's part of the fun. Talk to you later sucker.

As she shut down the phone, Marvel felt her body suf-
fused with a feeling both familiar and strange---strange, because she wasn't on the water. Throb of heart, jump of belly,
that heightened reality that came from risk, from doing something hard and physical and dangerous just right. She'd had it
on kiteboards, on surfboards, she'd felt it diving in caves, on
wrecks, that feeling you had at the edge of danger, living at the
thinnest margin of control. Overby would shoot her himself if
he knew what she was doing.

Plus, she *hadn't* told a lie. She'd just had an interaction
with a man, a conversation in texts, in which she was not manipulating for some advantage. Marvel's case was very like that
of a householder who steps out of his front door one morning
and finds a dead stegosaur on his front lawn. The event is so
clearly impossible that the mind skitters away from what the
senses are telling it and tries for a period to hallucinate the
former reality.

Thus it was in-fucking-possible that a man she'd just
taken for two million dollars would be about anything other
than getting his money back, and yet Bernard seemed uninterested. She wanted to think that this was the put-up to a subtle
long con he had started to run on her, but her highly sensitive
radar for perfidy was not beeping. She hadn't been this curious
since the dawn of sex.

And that must've been why she'd made that sponta-
neous move to switch to email—she wanted a wider bandwidth, she wanted more space to tell things and be told things,
and—it now dawned on her—if they were connected via computer, they would eventually be able to Skype. As she consid-

ered this, she had another, happier revelation: she no longer needed Miranda's phone—and there was a trash barrel near the public beach access not fifty yards from her door.

She found a paper clip in a drawer in which she had vainly searched twice for paper clips, pulled the SIM, and placed it in the microwave oven. Crackle pop. She put it and the phone in a plastic grocery bag, stepped into slippers, and walked via the beach to the trash barrel. She tossed the phone in and walked away, as the sweat that had popped on her skin went cool in the sea breeze. She was actually a little surprised when she returned home and found that the phone was no longer in her possession.

Hilarious with relief, she ran back into the bedroom, where she stripped off her clothes, slid into bed and used her mouth and hands to attract Sami Choi's interest. He responded sleepily and mechanically, which was all she required to achieve an oblivion strong enough to wash all her recent tension away.

Sami, however, was not entirely pleased. Raised in the environs of a Manila brothel, he had learned early that girls really didn't like sex and that if one pretended to it was for money or some advantage she wanted to extract from a man. After this bout, therefore, he turned suspicious.

"So, where did you go just now?" he asked her.

"Out. I was restless, so I went to the beach."

"The beach. What, you want to get a moon tan?"

"Yeah, it's supposed to be good for the complexion. The moon beams."

"Uh huh. You meet anyone?"

"Meet who? It's the fuckin' middle of the night, man."

"So that'd be a good time to meet someone, if you didn't want nobody to find out about it."

"Who would I meet? My secret boyfriend? The FBI?"

"You tell me."

The problem was she couldn't see his face, just the shadowed oval of not-dark, so she couldn't read his mood, nor was she able to judge how serious he was. Sami was prone to interrogations at any odd moment. Usually she didn't mind--it was part of who he was, and one reason he had survived so long in the underworld. Now, of course, she was indeed hiding something, but here the darkness worked in her favor, and she was excellent at controlling her voice.

She let out a sigh. "It was just a walk on the beach, Sami. I do it all the time. I drink, I wake up in the middle of the night, I walk for a while, and then I come back. Baby, believe it, it's not *me* you have to worry about."

She felt him stir, stiffen. "What the fuck's that supposed to mean?"

"Only Overby was filling my ear with shit about how you're throwing money around, attracting attention from parties we don't want to notice us. He's not happy."

"Fuck Overby!"

"Was that a figure of speech or an order?"

A pause; and then he laughed, and the tension drained from them and he threw an arm around her and asked her what she wanted, and she invented something, a diving trip to the Big Island, charter a boat, take some time off together, and he agreed, satisfied (as she knew he would be) that the recent ardor was not about avoiding suspicion but only a manipulation on her part, easily satisfied by an empty promise. They might charter a dive boat, but he'd back out at the last minute, and Jumbo or Overby would go with her. Really, he was easy to control, all of them were easy.

As she dropped toward sleep, the notion occurred to her that maybe Bernard wasn't so easy, or even that she didn't want to control him, nor he her, that this connection might be unlike any other in her long experience with men. But, no, that was stupid, she was having illusions. Soon she'd be thinking like a mark, about *romance*. But what would *that* be like, this her last thought before sleep took her.

The next morning Marvel sat at a table on the sun-dappled terrace eating a papaya with yogurt and reading a news feed on her laptop. As usual, she was the first one up, except for Sabine and Dado who, as far as she could see, barely slept at all.

Reading the news was a practice to which Overby had introduced her, and it was still a little weird, as if she were a citizen and not a grifter, but Overby had said that all knowledge added to power, and so she plowed through the feeds that Esme had set up for her on politics, the markets, entertainment, and crime.

She finished her first cup of the house's excellent coffee and was about to go to the kitchen for another when Sabine came out with a pot and a tray, poured her a cup and served a plate of croissants with butter and marmalade. Marvel was enough of a low-end American to be embarrassed by servants, but she took comfort in the fact that Sabine and Dado were not just servants but Overby's spies in the compound, and also responsible for cleaning and destroying any physical evidence connected with the family's illicit dealings.

She aspired to an easy camaraderie with Sabine, based on her own former status as a cocktail waitress and casino dealer, but while Sabine was friendly enough and informal in the Island fashion, she maintained her distance. Overby had found her in the P.I.; she was from a southern island of that nation, a small, strong woman of indeterminate age, with frizzy black hair pulled back in a rubber band and smooth, dun skin.

They had a brief conversation about the weather, and the surf. Lanikai was not a surfer beach, but the wind would be strong enough today to launch kiteboards and Marvel mentioned that she might be going out later. Sabine said that Overby had called and said he would be here for lunch. Marvel knew this already because Overby had sent everyone an email calling an all-hands meeting for after they ate. It would be about the next operation, probably, which was a little too soon after the last one, in Marvel's opinion. She could typically count on at least two months break, but maybe Overby had found an unusually sleek mark in a situation where time pressed.

Meanwhile, as always, there was the beach, the sea, the sun. And the wind--from the way the tallest plants in the garden were flapping, Marvel figured it might be gusting twenty-five knots out in the bay. She went back to the bedroom, donned a pair of board shorts and a t-shirt from Japan that read "Lizard Bitches Fly Auntie." Sami lay like the dead, head swathed in bedclothes against the windows' light, snoring. Not a morning person, nor a beach person: a denizen of the darker regions, was Sami, a sitter on bar stools, a cruiser among night-spots.

Jumbo Wedge, however, had risen with the cockerels and was doing sit-ups when Marvel knocked on his door and let herself into the apartment above the garage. Two rooms, plenty of light, containing little. Jumbo had decided early that the quarter of him that was Japanese would rule the other three quarters to the extent possible. His dwelling therefore resembled a set from a samurai movie--tatami floors, white walls hung with framed Hiroshige prints, and fabric banners printed with the *mon* of samurai families, whose blood Jumbo believed flowed in his veins. The furniture consisted of a futon, a couple of low cabinets, some wicker baskets, and a lacquered Sendai

chest on which was set a *katana* and a *wakizashi* in a teak
stand. For reasons she could not explain, Marvel did not care to
look at these swords.

As there were no chairs, she sat on the tatami with her
back against the wall in a corner where the sword stand was out
of sight, and leafed through a kiteboarding magazine. Marvel
loved the kiteboard, but not the sport, the constant competition
for the most dangerous, outrageous trick, the endless elabora-
tion of gear, the whole masculine thing. She was not a natural
athlete like Jumbo, and felt uneasy when getting air. What she
liked was the speed, and the control of speed. She had clocked
thirty-five knots and had ambitions to join the fifty-knot club.

Jumbo finished his exercise and they went out to the
beach with their gear bags. It was still early, and Lanikai had
not yet filled with Japanese tourists, the result of this rather
mediocre, narrow beach having unaccountably been mentioned
in a Japanese travel guide as the best beach on Oahu. The wind
was indeed doing a steady twenty-five from the northeast, ideal
conditions. Half a dozen kites were already up, darting colored
patches against the clear blue, back and forth, their riders jumping the small waves, and more could be seen beyond Flat Island toward Kailua. Marvel rigged her ten-meter kite, probably
a little large for the conditions, launched it into the sky, waded
into the shallows, stepped onto her board, and powered up the
kite.

She loved this more than practically anything, holding
the might of the wind in her hands, dashing across the surface
of the ocean nearly as fast as a car on a freeway. Really, she
thought, kiteboarding was the perfect sport for bad girls.

Nine

Bernard stared at the screen until it went dark. Should he have asked her for a photo? Bernard was something of an internet virgin, a relic of the telephone and handwriting era, and was conscious that he was feeling his way. What was correct in this kind of . . . he supposed he had to call it courtship, but it was clearly something more baroque than that. He was corresponding with a woman who had stolen his money and was actually endangering herself by this communication. Or so she said. It was entirely possible that she was sharing his texts with her gang, laughing heartily at the poor fool Goodrich, and perhaps even plotting to strip him further. Marvel, as he now must learn to call her, was way beyond his experience, but he had made a deal with himself that, if she asked for money, he would shed a tear and cut her off. He didn't think she would, though, for reasons he couldn't explain, except to the dog.

The two of them were in the monastery office, Murtagh on the floor working on a piece of rawhide, Bernard in a un-monastically comfortable chair with his laptop on a borrowed desk in front of him. The monastery, somewhat to Bernard's surprise, had a satellite uplink to the internet and an office suite containing every modern device. Brother Anselm, or Brother IT, as he was known, had explained that St. Roch had an international clientele for its dogs, and was plugged into the Schutzhund competition circuit worldwide. Being connected was essential to the high-end dog business, besides which, the Benedictines had invented the whole *idea* of being connected more than a thousand years ago, and had been doing communications technology since goose quills and parchment. St. Roch also boasted its own cell tower, and reception was excellent.

As she'd requested, he now set up half a dozen email accounts and sent the first one through to the mailbox Marvel had given him with "test" on the subject line and a blank body below. He thought it was a good sign that she had asked for an email correspondence, but just now he was at a loss for words to send her.

Oh, that loss for words. On the few occasions when he had taught a writing class, Bernard always made a lameish joke that was nonetheless packed with bitter truth. Writing was easy, he said, what was hard was thinking up what to put. And then he would go off on why this was so: most people had no problem talking—why should writing be different? Because in talking, we accepted a world that existed already, and texting was similar. But writing—especially writing fiction--was making up a new world, even if you thought you were describing a world that you could see and feel.

And he would talk about the peculiar phenomenon of some fictional reality replacing experienced reality in memory and influencing behavior thereafter: it was just like the movies, we say, when some disaster occurs, and we remember the movie version, not the actuality. Few students got this, he found, which was why teaching usually depressed him, and why he hardly ever did it.

Now he could not think of what to put because he could not yet construct a representation of the recipient. Beyond that, he barely understood why he had reached out to her, or why she had responded to him. Correspondence created a world, too, the world of the relationship, and here, of course, there was no relationship. Their contact had been fraudulent, a nullity; but now there was a thin basis of truth—maybe. He studied their recent texts. At least he knew her real name, or a nickname she used, plus the sketch of an origin story. But was it real?

Bernard's thriller required a certain amount of research and so he was reasonably familiar with searching the internet, at least at the Google/Wikipedia level. He tried *Marvel bank robbery Oregon* in the search box and got a miscellany of useless hits. The same with *Miranda Gardiner confidence racket* and a few other likely combinations before he gave up. He brought out his cell phone and read Marvel's texts again, waiting for an idea, but nothing arrived.

After a few minutes, the screensaver on his computer cycled on, a family slide show: Louise in an apron, grinning and holding up a chocolatey spoon, not expecting death; Leslie, aged twelve, making a silly face; Lawrence as a teen, head poking around an old CRT monitor, showing the usual suspicious, slightly confused look he wore when not relating to a computer . . .

Yes, that would be a way to check. He wondered why he hadn't thought of it before, except that connecting with his son was always a little fraught. Bernard punched the Lawrence line on the cell phone's contact list. True, it was two hours past compline, eleven at night, but time flowed differently in a monastery where sleep came in brief intervals between the canonical prayers. High-tech companies, perhaps the modern equivalent, kept similar hours.

"You're only as happy as your unhappiest child" was one of Louise's sayings, and when she said it, she meant this one. Lawrence was not exactly an unhappy child, but he was definitely on the spectrum. Louise had decided to join in the unhappiness, and her attitude had cast a pall over Bernard's relationship with his son. Bernard himself was somewhat obsessive and socially withdrawn (and let's forget for a moment the whole dog-talking thing) and thought the kid would have a reasonable life if left alone and protected from the ministrations of the docs. Despite docs galore, the kid had nonetheless flourished sufficiently to get through college and grad school (MIT, computer engineering) and land a job with a Boston firm doing classified work for the National Security Agency.

"Goodrich." His quiet, neutral voice.

"Goodrich too," said Bernard. "How are you, Lawrence?"

A pause before the answer. "Okay. I heard you went crazy."

"Where did you hear that?"

"Uncle Bertie. He said you blew all your money on some movie deal. True?"

"It's complicated."

"Where are you?"

"In a secure, undisclosed location. Actually, I'm in something of a jam and I was hoping you could help me out."

"A jam . . . like with the law?"

"No, I . . . I fell into bad company; a gang of con artists took me for a ride. A long con, if you know what that is."

"Yeah, I do. What did you lose?"

"A lot. But I have a line on one of them, a woman. She says her name is Marvel."

"As in the Captain?"

"So she says. It might even be true. One thing you could do for me is find out whatever there is on the net that connects to her."

"Last name? Anything else but Marvel?"

"Gafney. And there's another thing. Apparently, her parents were bank robbers in eastern Oregon. They drove off a bridge and died. She was in the car and survived. It must have made the local papers. This'd be maybe twenty-five, thirty years ago."

"Okay, shouldn't be a problem. Is that it?"

"No, something else, and it could be more important. You know, there's a trope in thrillers where the detective looks over a mutilated corpse, and something clicks in her head, and she goes, 'These marks look too definite, too practiced. He's done this before.' She knows she's got a serial killer on her hands and off we go. This thing that happened to me is like that, practiced. Plus, I had a conversation with a private detective who's looking for a gang that did somebody else exactly like they did me. They're terrifically slick, which means they've done it before, which means there should be a pattern you could find."

"Search terms?"

"You tell me. Based on the PI's story, I'm thinking they must target people like me. Older guys, recently bereaved, long-term marriage, they go a little nuts behind it and the gang takes advantage, shows them they could have a new life . . ."

"That's what they pulled on you? A new life?"

"Guilty. So, can you help?"

"Maybe. Tell me a little more about how they operate. This was more than one person, yes?"

"Many more," said Bernard. "It started with the woman, Marvel, only she called herself Miranda Gardiner," and then, somewhat to his own surprise, he found himself relating the whole story, sweating up the phone from the shame of it. Lawrence listened without comment, except for a few requests for clarification. After that, the empty sound of the air waves. Bernard thought he heard the tapping of a keyboard.

"Well?" he said at last, into the hissing silence.

"Sorry, I'm a little stunned. They took you for two million dollars?"

149

"Around there. But I was thinking, with all that arranging, dozens of operatives, all those fake companies . . . they must have left traces."

"I'm sure. I'm thinking they probably used the dark web to organize it."

"I don't understand."

"The dark web. You have your TOR servers. What? No, not Thor. TOR stands for The Onion Router, like the skin of an onion? They allow users to preserve their anonymity online by relaying traffic through a series of routers so you can't tell where a message originated. Then you have your encrypted sites, encrypted email and so on. Obviously, it's ideal for any criminal enterprise. Is there a class of confidence operators hirable in major cities? Do they travel for jobs? How does someone organizing a long con contact these people and pay them? And so on. It has to be done the way every other kind of commerce is done nowadays, but it also has to be secret; so, the dark web. You've probably heard about the Silk Road—that was a dark web operation, commerce in dope and kiddie porn."

"Vaguely. Can you penetrate it?"

"An Oedipal question."

"Excuse me?"

"If I told you, I'd have to kill you. Let's just say the government has a continuing interest. Let me poke around for a while and I'll get back to you."

"Thanks, Lawrence, I appreciate it. How are you doing, by the way? Are you still with that girl, Mariah?"

"Marina. Not so much. I work all the time and can't talk about what I'm doing. It makes relationships hard. Harder, I should say, given my personality."

"Maybe you should try something else."

"Yeah, maybe. Look, I was in the middle of something when you called, so . . ."

"Okay—thanks in advance for the help."

"No problem," said Lawrence, and broke the connection.

Bernard had by now learned to sleep when he had the chance and so went immediately to bed, and awoke for prayers at matins, which, belying its name, was midnight, and then again at lauds, or three in the morning. After prime, he went to join Brother Gabriel, the Dog Master, again dressing in a canvas suit and agitating a series of trainees. It was rough work, springing out from cover and pretending to attack Brother Gabriel and being sincere about it, too, so that the dog would grab him and knock him down and hold on until the release. This activity reminded him dolefully of his relationship with his son.

He always felt a little blue after speaking with Lawrence, but of course the subject matter of their most recent conversation deepened this almost to black. *I'd have to kill you?* Was that even funny anymore? He thought of calling his daughter, a perpetually sunny person, but no—rejected by the son, laying that weight on the girl: pathetic.

After the training session, he returned to the data center and opened his laptop to his novel in hopes that work would distract him, but he couldn't get the motor started. The dialog clanged; the whole thing was tedious beyond bearing. Even the dog character was wrong. Well, it happened—*I'll never write again!* —the first time terrifying, the ten thousand five hundred and fifty-second time, not so much. But neither did it improve his mood.

The actual dog picked it up. It had been snoozing on a mat that, like all the dog beds at St. Roch, had been stitched from the forty-pound burlap bags that the kibble came in. Now it rose, stretched, yawned and walked over to Bernard, where it rested its muzzle on his knee and rubbed.

"Yes, I know," said Bernard, "snap out of it. I will, eventually. I didn't realize that when you're a victim of a scam like I was, the pain comes in waves. You think, you're past it, you're intact, you still have more resources than ninety-nine percent of humanity, you have your health, you can work, you . . ."

<You have me.>

". . . I have you, yes. And I thought I was basically okay, and then it hits like a blow, heavy and smothering, like a pillow the size of Montana, the shame, what you did, what *I* did, that crass, teeth-hurting stupidity, the death of self-respect, everything turning foul and stale, because they didn't just take your money, they took your sense of yourself as a competent man. And I just got a wave of it telling the whole **shitty thing to Lawrence. God.** It'd be like if I did something to you and, I don't know, made it so you couldn't smell anymore."

<That's just stupid. The first thing you said, about being intact, wasn't. There's someone here.>

The dog's ears pricked and it turned to face what proved to be Brother IT emerging from behind the fabric wall of the cubical. As he did, the tower bell rang for sext.

"I thought we'd walk over together," said the monk.

"Yes, let me just save this." Tap-a-tap. Bernard said to the dog, "I have to go to choir. You can go back to sleep."

<I'll come with you. Although this is the greatest bed I ever slept on.>

So, to sext, by tradition the sixth hour since dawn, or noon. The middle of November now, getting frosty, the leaves crunching on the path as the two men walked to the chapel with their dogs. The tolling bell had a curiously hollow sound in the still, damp air. For a monk, Brother Ambrose was reasonably voluble. He had two dogs boarding with him, Terra and Neutron, both yearlings in the final phase of their Schutzhund course. Since dogs at St. Roch lived with the monks, most doubled up like those with Brother Ambrose, for in these fallen times there were more dogs than monks.

"Go play," Br. Ambrose told his dogs and off they went, racing along the road in into the broad stubbled field beyond.

"They've been training all morning, you'd think they'd be tired, but no," observed the monk.

Murtagh looked up from his usual position at Bernard's knee.

"You haven't been doing anything but sleeping on kibble bags, you slug. Go get some exercise!" Murtagh dashed away after the other dogs.

The two men walked silently, content with observing the beauty of running Dobermans.

"Well, let them have their fun," said Brother Ambrose after some minutes of this. "It's an afternoon off—we have a feast day, you know."

"So I gathered," said Bernard. "What saint is it?"

"Not a saint at all—today is the Feast of the Dedication of St. John Lateran. We will do psalms that mention buildings, of course. Twenty-four: open wide the doors and gates, lift high the ancient portals. And eighty-four: how lovely is your dwelling-place, Lord God of Hosts. Charming. The liturgists never miss a trick, as always. Have you ever been there? I mean the Lateran."

"Actually, I have. I even attended Mass there once. Good choir, I recall, and a somewhat gloomy building."

"Yes, you get the sense that being the cathedral of Rome is something of a disappointment to it, since the Bishop of Rome now presides elsewhere. I believe it was used as a brothel to raise money for the church, back in the day. Tenth

153

century or thereabouts—one of the many bad Pope Johns, perhaps the one who was strangled by his fourteen-year-old mistress because he refused to make her newborn bastard an archbishop. Oh, it's a wicked old church, all right. The current wickedness can't hold a candle."

The monk was grinning as he said this, and added, "I love feast days, don't you? There'll be meat at lunch, perhaps sausages, eh? We make a good sausage here, from our own pigs." He patted his belly, which was that of a man who liked his sausages. Bernard cast a sideways glance to see if he were being put on, but no, Brother Ambrose seemed to be a man who had slipped into an antique persona, in a peculiar balance against his obvious skill with the latest technology.

"Where are those dogs?" said Brother Ambrose. He pulled a shiny whistle from his cassock and blew silently. There was barking, and shortly all three animals came dashing across the field and gamboled like puppies around the legs of their humans.

Bernard asked his dog, "Did you enjoy yourself, Murtagh?"

<I did. We found a dead thing, but I didn't roll in it.>

"That's exemplary self-restraint," said Bernard, giving him a pat. "You're achieving monastic discipline already." He had forgotten he was in company and felt a flush of embarrassment.

Brother Ambrose seemed to catch this, and the reason for it, and remarked, "That's interesting, Bernard. Many people talk to dogs, but only a few hear them respond. Brother Gabriel was telling me the other day you're a born dog handler. Have you considered, ah, staying on?"

"If you went co-ed, maybe."

The monk laughed with enthusiasm. "The old Adam still untamed, eh? Well, it's not for everybody. I was married too, for nearly thirty years. No kids, unfortunately. After Marjorie died, I worked myself into a nervous breakdown and then wound up here. It's not an uncommon story at St. R."

"How do you stand it? I'm sorry, is that an awkward question?"

"You mean no sex? Everyone's first question, voiced or not. I suppose it's grace, in the end. Some of us suffer more than others, depending on how we deal with the animal spirits. But even in a good marriage sex declines in importance. The world deplores that, of course—the secular ideal seems to be a randy teenager—but here we practice love of everything, all creatures great and small. Our brothers, of course, and the dogs, as a way of loving God as He loves us. I mean, that's Christianity, isn't it? And our, you might say, dirty secret is that if we prepare ourselves by living the Rule sincerely, God will give us a kind of physical pleasure that exceeds sex, as His love exceeds human love. You occasionally run into monks and nuns with that blissful smile on their faces. That's why."

"Like Bernini's St. Teresa, you mean?"

"Just like."

"A spiritualized version of sex."

"No, I mean physical. Of course, God supplies us with physical pleasure—He made our bodies to feel it. Why would He ignore it when we direct our love to Him instead of to another person?"

"This has happened to you?"

Brother Ambrose laughed again. "Now I've got you interested, haven't I? But let me draw a modest veil over my own experience. To share it, you would probably have to stay, and it's not like it's guaranteed."

The following day, prime having been read and chanted at six in the morning, the monks and Bernard filed from the

155

chapel into the freezing dark, shuffling carefully past patches of ice, back to their cells, all but Bernard, who walked instead to the data center, where after rubbing his hands to relieve his stiff fingers, he switched on his computer. On his usual account were many emails: from his agent (three), from his brother, from his sister-in-law, from thieves and beggars, from merchants and fans, but he ignored these in favor of the one on his new anonymous account, from *kitegurl21*.

> This is crazy I don't know why I'm doing this--
> say if you're there

Bernard, near dizzy with elation, attacked his keyboard.

> I'm here. I'm of your mind as to crazy. But as La Rochefoucauld says, sometimes in life situations develop that only the half-crazy can get out of. Maybe we're both in that kind of fix. Too bad you're not a real psychic or you could figure it out.

He sent it forth. There was a frustrating delay while he waited for an answer. He imagined her typing and the complex virtual dance of the mail packets, and then his machine chimed for incoming.

> Maybe I should consult one. Do you believe in that stuff?

> Not really. Although I'm hanging out with people just now who believe all sorts of weird. Also, I talk to my dog and he answers back. So if you're looking for rational materialism, you came to the wrong store. Also, we have a connection, you and I, that's inexplicable on a purely rational basis. I should hate you and want you to be punished, but I don't. You shouldn't want to have anything to do with me—in fact, you're probably violating all kinds of criminal rules and maybe risking your life, just to keep in touch with me. So we're in a strange region. Mean-

while, tell me about your grandmother. What was it like growing up in Dogpatch?

Why do you want to know all that shit?
    I'm doing research. When I know everything about you, I'll be able to con you better. Turn about is fair play.

But really.
    It's an uncontrollable urge. It's part of the writing jones, I think, besides which I feel lopsided. I'm supposed to be the concealed observer, examining everyone, and now the situation's reversed. And I have a taste for the exotic. My late wife was a Chinese-American woman whose parents were boat people from Vietnam and in the first weeks I knew her all we did was tell stories about our lives and our parents' lives. It was fascinating, and of course, we found we agreed on just about everything important. Most people just love to talk about themselves I find. Don't you?

No. I told everything to the man who recruited me, but that was operational, what he called vetting. But I have no one to talk to about my sad life. Grifters tend to live around what's happening this minute, plus they lie about everything, so why bother?

    The boyfriend's not interested?
The boyfriend prefers me to keep my mouth shut, except when sucking his dick. He's from Vietnamese boat people too like your late wife, small world.

He didn't immediately reply to this message, which was an obvious challenge. She's testing, he thought, see if a little grossness will turn me off. No such luck, dear. He waited. It was a little clumsy using email to have a conversation, but on the other hand the necessary delay was a little delicious, like passing notes to a girl in school. The wait was rewarded with:

The Long Con

You still there?

Of course. About Grandma . . . ?

Oh God. Okay, you asked for it. Her name was Lucille. Small woman, smaller than me when I was grown, but that could've been her age. I mean I always thought of her as real old, but she was probably in her fifties when she got me. Just had the one daughter. There was a son too, my uncle, Ralph. I had to figure all of this out from pictures in albums she had, and questions, although Gran was pretty tight with information. Ralph didn't come back from Vietnam, there was a colored picture of him on the wall, in uniform with the flag behind him. I guess that was one of her heartbreaks and the other was my grandfather dying on her. He was a timber beast and when the jobs dried up he took to drinking and died in his truck out on 128, a head-on with a log truck. Timbering killed him twice, that was one of Gran's sayings.

The other heartbreak besides those was my Mom. Carol Mae. Carol Mae wouldn't listen from an early age, according to Gran, no matter how hard she was switched. As soon as she grew her tits she was off with the boys, and not just boys either. Seventeen, she ran off with my father, whose name was That Stinker, he must've been nearly thirty at the time, still living in a double-wide on the other side of Springfield, with his mother, That Whore. Pregnant with me the next year. That Stinker worked in a gas station in Waterville, shit job, never enough money, plus that was when crystal started to come into the great northwest and he smoked up most of what he made. Carol Mae was always coming around Gran's asking for a handout and after a while Gran told her that unless she left That Stinker she wouldn't give her any more, she said he'd have to find another job, because she wasn't supporting any jailbird. That Stinker had done a jolt in Salem for armed robbery and when Gran cut them off, he went back to it. He had a fast car and a gun and my mom went with him, driving, with me in a car seat in the back. You heard that Joni Mitchell song, I was raised on robbery? That was me.

They did mostly convenience stores, liquor stores, like that, and then my dad figured he'd expand the business into banks, so one day they knocked over the Oregon Pacific Bank in Eugene and took off east with the cops after them. It was January, like I said, and raining and the roads were slick with the bridges icy and she turned too sharp to get onto the Armitage Bridge east of Blue River, busted through the guard rail and into the McKenzie. I told you what happened after that already.

So there was Gran with the Miracle Baby to take care of, and I guess she did the best she could. She kept me away from That Whore anyway, who showed up when the fame money started coming in. God, I haven't thought about this shit since forever. Are you bored yet? I am.

Not bored at all. But I have a call I have to take. Don't go away.

The call was from his daughter.

"God, you must be crazy," she cried.

"It's nice to hear from you, dear. How's the play going?"

"I just got off the phone with Lawrence. What's going on with this woman?"

"I don't want to talk about it. As you can imagine, the whole thing is intensely painful."

"Where are you? I want to see you."

"I'm fine, baby. Don't worry about me."

"Don't tell me not to worry. You're clearly incapable of looking after yourself."

"I said I'm doing fine. Look, I got scammed. I was vulnerable and I got fed a fantasy. You remember your old boyfriend Rufus? He was going to mount a play and you gave him money and it all went up his nose and there were other girls . . ."

"Dad, I was sixteen. You're a hundred and five."

"Not quite," said Bernard, "but point taken. I was old enough to know better." He heard the warble of another call and said, "Darling, this is Lawrence calling and I have to take it. It'll be all right."

159

He broke the connection and let Lawrence's call come through.

"Did you find anything?" Bernard asked.

"Actually, I did. Your girl is Marion Bliss Gafney, born Springfield Oregon, 28 August 1987. Parents were Carol Mae Gafney and Stanley Forrest Riddell. As we knew already, both parents died while escaping the police—this was on 10 November 1987. The kid was in the water over twenty minutes before the cops could get a drag on the car. There was a good deal of local press at the time, the Miracle Baby, et cetera. Little Marion, or Marvel as she was known later, was raised by her maternal grandmother, Lucille Dwight Gafney, 1936-1994. Beyond that, there's nearly zip. No credit, no bank accounts I could find for either Marion or Marvel. She's a high school drop-out, went to Thurston High for two years. Then nothing; she's a ghost."

"That's good, Lawrence, thanks. What about the other thing?"

"The other thing is on a whole different scale. It looks like you were right about the victimology. Did you ever hear of a woman named Kim Haley White?"

"No, who is she?"

"She's from Atlanta, well-off, well-connected, fiftyish. You should check out her web site. I'm sending you the link now."

"What's the connection?"

"Her father. Ted Haley of Ted Haley Chevrolet, big time auto dealership in Atlanta, got ripped off by a gang headed by a woman who called herself Marcia Gilbert. Those familiar initials again? They took him for around sixteen mill. He was going to sponsor a

NASCAR racing team, apparently his lifelong ambition. Then he died. Shortly after that, his best friend, Ryell Abbot, also a rich widower, got taken for something over ten million. Then he died too, heart attack. Both men died alone in motels in rural counties. The county medical examiners found no evidence of foul play.

"But Kim was suspicious. She says—this is on the web site—that her dad had high blood pressure but was otherwise healthy. He died of a massive stroke. The family doctor didn't see it coming. He was on blood thinners and statins and his issues were well-controlled. Same with Abbot. He had heart problems, but had recently had stents put in and was doing fine. Well, two men die, just after losing their wives, from previously reported conditions, just after losing a pile of money to the same con artists. We start to see a pattern, or Kim does."

"Wait a second—she thinks these men were killed? Murdered?"

"She does. And there's the guy your P.I. told you about. I found him, too. Douglas Davidoff of Short Hills, New Jersey. Real estate developer, gave up thirty-five million to a syndicate headed by a Wall Street guy to buy the New Jersey Devils hockey team. Melissa Garrett, ha ha, was the girl who made the introduction to the fraudulent financier. Mr. Davidoff died, too, also in a rural county, also alone. He was diabetic. Went into coma, although he was carrying plenty of insulin at the time.

Also, at least three other cases fit the pattern: an oil shale guy from Montana, a dentist in Brookline, Mass., and a retired airline executive. All of them had

161

contact with an attractive woman who set up the scam and all of them ended dead within a week or so of the final rip-off. Also, each one of these victims was heavily insured, with the payout going to shell corporations. Apparently, the insurance investigators have been active in all the cases, but the medical examiner reports ruled the deaths natural and they had to pay out. It gives one pause, no?"

"That's impossible," said Bernard.

"What do you mean?"

"Well, the implication is that this gang ripped off older widowed men and then had them killed, collecting insurance in the bargain."

"Yes, but what makes you say it's impossible?"

Bernard was about to say that it was Marvel, that Marvel could not have been party to such an atrocity, but instead replied weakly, "It just does. It's preposterous, like a plot in a bad thriller."

"But it would be even more preposterous to believe that the clear pattern we're talking about—scam on rich widowers, girl with the same initials involved, insurance collected by shell corporation after a lone death in a rural area—that this pattern is due to chance alone. I'd say your original instinct was right—they did it before, many times, and . . . look, Dad, you wouldn't be in a rural area right now, would you?"

"Don't worry about me, Lawrence. I'm fine. I have Murtagh with me, and nothing's going to happen. Look, thanks for all your help on this. Have you got anything off the dark web yet?"

"Not yet—that's going to take some time. Look, really Dad, where are you? I'm getting worried."

"Don't, please," said Bernard. "I'm in a safe place."

"Fine. Look, I'm also concerned about your computer."

"I'm using my laptop."

"I mean it could be compromised. When they were scamming you, did you go online and check out these people? I mean the law firm and all that."

"Of course. It all checked out perfectly."

"That's what I thought. Okay, I'm going to send you Team Viewer right now. Install it. It'll let me take control of your machine. Do you know how to ..."

"Install a program. Yes, I'm not a complete idiot."

"Not complete, no. Okay, sending."

Bernard did the necessary operations and experienced the mild dismay of seeing his cursor move to a remote command. He felt sympathy with his dog, who also lived in a world in which he was required to perform sans comprehension of the larger picture.

Forty minutes passed. The line stayed open, but all that came through was the click of a keyboard and faint mumbling. Lawrence had always talked to himself while online. Bernard, who had spent the time in an unpleasant reverie concerning his recent disasters, jumped a little when Lawrence's voice came back. The dog growled.

"Yeah, you had a kernel-based Trojan in there. Basically, they could read every keystroke you made, and when you accessed a website they could feed you any phony information they wanted. I scrubbed it, and unless they're a lot better than I am, which I doubt, you have a clean machine. Try not to click on any unknown links."

"Thank you, Lawrence."

"Not a problem. Your government is watching over you."

After Bernard got off the phone with his son, he sent:

I'm back. I'm dying to hear the rest of your story.

He waited fifteen minutes, but no new message came through. He closed his machine.

"I refuse to believe she's a party to murder," Bernard said to the dog. "I mean, if she was that kind of person, I would know, wouldn't I?"

<You have to rely on your nose. Don't just sniff the air—you have to get down in the footprints.>

Ten

The big whiteboard had been hung on the wall of the living room. When Marvel walked in at ten the next morning, she saw that it was covered with Asian faces, the names neatly printed under the various photographs. The mark was someone named Zhou Feng-yi, and the others were the people close to him—wife, children, political and business associates, children and mistresses. Marvel took a cup of coffee and a sweet roll from the credenza and sat in one of the sling chairs next to Esme. Sami, Jumbo and Tanaka sat on the long leather sofa, Jumbo relaxed in aloha shirt and board shorts, Tanaka sitting stiff in shining loafers and tan slacks, with his bland aloha shirt tucked into his waistband, the infallible sign in Hawaii of terminal tight-assedness. Overby was leaning over Sami, trading whispers with him; Sami looked at Marvel as he listened, not a friendly look. Marvel smiled at him and got a curt nod in return.

"What's happening, Esme?" Marvel asked. "A little soon to start another op. We're going after a Chinese guy?"

"No, this is a big one, fucking huge, maybe nine figures. Overby wants to start on it right now, something to do with the Chinese government cracking down on crooked officials."

"That's a lot of figures," said Marvel and studied the face of the mark. Arrogance and fear shone from it, good soil on which to build a con..

Overby's conversation with Sami ended and Overby took up his stance at the whiteboard. "All right, people. I introduce our new mark, Mr. Feng, the Deputy Governor of Jiangxi Province. This has the potential to be by far the largest operation that we've ever done and . . . oh, Marvel--we won't be needing you on this one."

Marvel started and sloshed her coffee on her thigh, barely feeling the burn.

"What?"

"Yes, you won't be needed. You can go."

Marvel looked around. The others averted their eyes. She rose, her face hot, and stomped out through the kitchen. She look a long walk on the beach, cursing to the gulls and the foreign tourists, angry and a little frightened. What was Overby doing? Was she actually being *fired* from the gang? She went back to the house, got into her car and drove to Kailua.

Fifteen minutes later, she was in Starbucks with the laptop out looking at

Are you still there? I'm dying to hear the rest of the story.

which somehow did a good deal to salve her rage. Marvel had never had anyone dying to hear her story before, especially not a guy, and it thrilled her more than she had imagined. She knew Goodrich had to be working some kind of con on her, but she didn't care.

This is what the marks felt like, she concluded, and it was no wonder that they kept getting knocked over. Could you have that feeling, of a man being interested in *you*, the actual human being you knew yourself to be, rather than an invention, an imposture, and not set yourself up for a rip-off? *You go to my head.* Wasn't that an old song.? *Like a something something Burgundy brew.* It was—her grandmother had played it, she still had vinyl records that Marvel was not allowed to touch when she was a little kid. By the time she got interested in music, Gran was dead and she was living at Aunt Ethel's, and music was not in the air much there. Yeah, it went to her head, and she had to tell him about all of that, too, and she both feared this and felt full of an unaccustomed desire to unburden. She thought this as she pecked away, and also about how different this was from how Overby had extracted the same information, it wasn't anything like an interrogation. It would be a gift. Thoughts of Overby (that bastard!) continued, until (shockingly!) the man himself walked through the door of the Starbucks and, unsmiling, approached her table. She barely had time to bring up her book reader.

"Good morning, Marvel. I'm surprised to see you here. Sabine makes very good coffee."

"I'm more surprised to see *you* here. Aren't you the one who's always saying I'll be goddamned if I'll pay three bucks for a cup of coffee?"

"I'm not here for coffee. I was passing on the street just now and who should I see in Starbucks but our Marvel, looking like she's writing her memoirs. By the way, what were you working on just now?"

"I wasn't working. I was reading that book you recommended, *The Power and the Glory*?"

"You were typing, in fact." He fixed her with his famous stare.

Marvel dropped her eyes, as if embarrassed, and sighed. "For God's sake, Overby, I was making *notes*. On the fucking book. So that when I finish it I will be able to read them and hold up my end of a high-tone literary conversation at the next meeting of the Criminal Compound Book Club, with a paranoid old guy who may be losing it right about now."

Overby lowered his bulk into a straight chair. It creaked. "God, I hate these places; and don't you bite my head off, please. When I saw you in here, I wondered why you, having access to excellent coffee on demand, comfortable loungers, and a wifi that is far superior to the one here, and *secure*, should have chosen to sit and type using a public wifi at a sticky table surrounded by noisy strangers."

"I'm sulking," said Marvel, in a sulky voice.

"Are you? May I ask why?"

"You may. I'm sulking because I'm pissed off. I guess you can figure out why, Overby. What were the words? We won't be needing you on this one, dear. You can go. *You can go?* The fuck, Overby. I'm the put-up girl, or as you have often said . . ."

"Marvel, stop talking, we . . ."

". . . *often* said, the best goddamn put-up girl you ever saw. And now, when there's a really . . . "

"I said *stop talking!*" said Overby in a hiss, with a look that she had not seen directed at her before; she recalled how many people Overby had killed, and shut her mouth.

He stood, gestured toward the door; Marvel closed her laptop, put it in her bag, and followed him out.

When they were on the street, Overby draped his arm around her in a way that was both fatherly and menacing, depending on how she wanted to take it. Marvel decided to go with the former.

"Now you're pissed at *me*. I'm sorry, Overby, that was dumb."

"And uncharacteristic. You must be angry indeed. For my part, I regret having irked you. I should have given you the courtesy of an explanation beforehand, but old habits, and all that . . . at the Company, we never briefed except on a need-to-know basis, and since we all had more than enough to do, well, being left out of a show was often a relief."

As they walked slowly down Kailua Road, Overby pointed and asked, "Is that your car there?"

It was. Overby said, "Let's go walk on the beach."

They got into the Porsche, and she drove the short hop to Kailua Beach.

"I thought you had skin cancer," she said as they left the car.

"My dear, the likelihood that I will escape my enemies long enough to die of skin cancer is extremely small. But it's nice of you to care."

"You don't even like the beach. You never go in the water."

"I love the beach," said Overby. "It's nearly impossible to set up a listening device to pick up conversation over the sound of surf and wind. Walk on, please."

They walked along the dry sand, past tourists and locals, under the swaying casuarinas. Overby said, "I never quite got the craze for sitting on sand and staring at the water. As for swimming, there are pools."

"Not for kiteboarding."

"No, but when I risk my life or I'm required to travel uncomfortably while wet, which I have done more times than I can count, I like to get paid for it. Look, I'll forget your deplorable breach of security and you'll forget my boorish dismissal of you and we'll return to our usual close working relationship, agreed?"

"Whatever," said Marvel.

"Yes. Do you understand what I'm trying to do with this Chinese?"

"I don't."

"Then I should fill you in. First, there's the matter of one Levon Ewell. Ever heard the name?"

"No. Who is he?"

"He's a private detective hired by the daughter of one of our clients, now deceased. Davidoff?"

"The hockey guy. He's dead?"

"Sadly, yes. His daughter thinks there was something fishy about his death and of course, as the heiress, she would like to get her hands on the money. So she hired this Ewell."

"*Was* there something fishy?"

Overby looked startled at the question. "No, of course not. The man was old, he'd just lost his wife—such people often die in the same year as their late spouses. My point is that Ewell is asking questions, questions that we can't afford to have asked. And others are asking questions too. Ted Haley's daughter, for one. You recall Ted Haley? NASCAR man? In any case, there is inevitably a certain pattern to our operations, and our security depends on no one looking for such patterns. Now that people *are* looking, I have decided that we can no longer do as we have done, no matter how profitable."

"Meaning?"

"Meaning we're closing down this particular style of long con. It's been very good for us, you admit—we've netted just under eighty million over eight years. Now I think we should move on to bigger game."

"Bigger than eighty mill?"

"Far bigger, and more satisfying. Because it's China, the biggest country in the world and the second largest economy, and all of it mired in absolute corruption. The amount of cash floating around China looking for a safe haven is . . . I don't know, an astronomical number—a *trillion* dollars left China this year alone. And now we're in the midst of one of the regime's routine crackdowns on this, which is of course not about corruption at all, but a form of political jockeying. Those who lose political battles are the ones targeted, which means that hundreds of corrupt officials who are politically vulnerable will be running around like headless chickens trying to find a place to stash the loot.

"And these are stupid people, Marvel. Morons. Compared to them the old men we've ripped off are models of acumen. They're mainly jumped-up peasants, and what do peasants want? Well, gold, of course, but that's impossible to hide, and after that, they want property in hard currency nations. The small fry go for condos in Vancouver and New York, but the major players need bigger acquisitions. They want to buy resorts, hotels, solid investments they can actually see with their greedy little eyes. That's where we come in."

"Brooklyn Bridge?"

"Smart girl. Only in this case it's the Cascadia Paradise Golf and Tennis resort. It's outside Vancouver, four hundred ten rooms, two eighteen-hole courses, very de lux. Zhou Feng-yi, is the mark, as you heard. He is, or was, the Deputy Governor of Jiangxi Province. He expected to be promoted to the Central Committee this year, and the fact that he wasn't bodes ill for his chances if there's an investigation of provincial finances. Which there will be. Mr. Zhou has somewhere north of one hundred and twenty-five million in a Panamanian bank account that he'd like to buy a Canadian hotel with. I intend to oblige him."

"Who owns this hotel?"

"A shell corporation called Coastal Resorts LLC, registered in Panama. Also gangsters, but from Russia. It's for sale at an asking price of a hundred forty million. We intend to offer Zhang a bargain at one-twenty."

"Fine, but how come I don't get a taste of that?"

"Because it's not your kind of grift, dear. It's in Chinese, for one thing, which you don't speak, and Sami and I do. For another, it's China. You were in Macau, you saw how they do business. Women are decoration and presents, not players—I mean in most cases."

"Yeah, but what do I do? I mean if you don't need me on this job."

He grinned at her, shading his eyes with a hand. "You don't have to do anything, kid. You're rich. You've been working hard for nearly ten years, right? Take some time off, rent a villa in Tuscany, tour the world. You look doubtful."

"Wait, you're shining me on?" Marvel cried. "I thought we were a team."

"Let's not yield to sentimentality, Marvel. We're a criminal enterprise that has to make some changes. We made a really major change when we moved here from Macau and Manila, and this is another. It's a requirement of the business. We can't continue as we have for reasons I've just explained, and I've responded by seeking new and larger opportunities. It's an opportunity for you as well. You have money and leisure ..."

"Oh, fuck leisure. What about the 'ohana? You think you can just mess up all our lives without any discussion? I mean, come on, Overby--I'm a grifter. It's what I do. And what about Jumbo and the Cars, and Esme? They get a pink slip too?"

"Not at all. Muscle is always in demand, as is digital intel. As are your skills, if you'd only give me a chance to explain. I must say you've become spiky recently, and I'm not sure I like it. What's wrong with you? Some little feud with one of the group? Sami not treating you well?"

Overby gave her a searching look, and she felt a recurrence of the fear bubble that had struck her in Starbucks. "No, everything's fine. Go ahead, I'm sorry--what did you want to explain?"

"Thank you. As I said, I'm moving our operation into the far more profitable international areas I've described. The Zhou op is just the first of many I have in mind. As I've said, you're the best put-up artist I've ever come across, but for you to function in this new arena, you'll need languages. Mandarin for starters, and then Russian, maybe Vietnamese, too. Surely you can grasp that the intimate manipulation that lies at the heart of your achievement requires that you communicate with your mark in his own tongue."

"You want me to learn *Chinese*?"

"I want you to take a break, and figure out what you want to do with the rest of your life. If that includes working this new racket with me, then I'd be delighted. But the languages are part of the deal."

"Overby, how the fuck am I going to learn Chinese? I'm a high school dropout."

"As are many fluent Chinese-speakers. Don't be dim, Marvel. When I met you ten years ago, you were a bar girl who'd never read a serious book. I saw the mind under the makeup and I lit it up and now you're better read than ninety-nine per cent of the people in our moronic nation. If you're game, I will place you in a total-immersion program with a native-speaking personal tutor, and in six months' time you'll be able to do again what you do so well, but in Chinese."

"I thought you said that the Chinese don't like doing business with women."

"Perhaps I exaggerated. A beautiful woman who speaks the language well enough to flirt, who, let's say, promises greater intimacy, is a special case."

"You're planning on pimping me out, in other words."

"Oh, for Christ's sake, Marvel. What the hell is wrong with you? Have we not run seven highly successful operations together? Did I ever ask you to actually drop your pants? It'll be the same kind of deal, but in Chinese. Really, kid, do as I say, take a break, and decide if you want to be a player on a much bigger stage or not. Let me know when you make up your mind!"

With that, Overby turned abruptly and walked off back the way they'd come, and Marvel turned and followed him, like a whiny girl who'd driven Daddy furious with her unreasonable demands. Of course, Overby was right, and right to get angry, and she was just being a bitch with that remark about pimping. It had been an instinctive nastiness, a response to the scales falling from her eyes.

Marvel had not much experience with daddy, but the feeling was familiar from her efforts to fill the dad-shaped hole with a number of men whose main interest in her was, can I use you, or not? That was always the question, and the answer, of course, was yes; this is how Marvel becomes known, how Marvel knows she exists. This was love, or so she had always called it. So, she would submit, but, as always, with a sneak on the side.

So she trudged along and plotted, reflecting that she had not run anything serious on the side since she'd joined Choi and Overby's crew, because until now she had been the star of the show, and had imagined that her life had become different. Now she knew that this was no longer true, had never been true, there had never been an 'ohana, she had always been a mere tool, although kept polished in a velvet box.

She watched Overby's bolohead bobbing before her and considered how much the man had done for her. She was not a bar girl anymore, nor a casino dealer, nor would she sink again to that level. Her life had been unusually full of surprises, reverses, opportunities. She was accustomed to these, and was not by nature someone who harbored resentments. Her instinct was loyalty. It was like surfing or kiteboarding, she thought, observing the kites blossomed out on the bay: you subjected your body to the perils of wave and wind and learned to control those mighty forces to get a ride. There would be thrills.

So she would meet his expectations, she would learn fucking Chinese or Russian or any other damn thing he cared to teach her. But she would also keep up this uncanny liaison with Bernard Goodrich.

She passed a haole tourist couple with their blanket and folding chairs, a pair of blondies with two small children and the bags of impedimenta that seems required when taking kids to the beach. The woman was rubbing sunscreen on her pale little girl; the man was looking out to sea, and as Marvel passed him, he gave her a look. She turned his head, as the saying goes, although the beach was full of younger women wearing butt-crack bikinis, and that made her feel good, and she gave him a smile and a fetching glance and put a little extra thing into her walk as she passed. Overby had said there were some women who drew the male gaze, a power independent of any particular excellence of feature, and that she was one of them.

The man was staring now—she felt his interest washing at her back. On impulse, she pulled out her iPhone, turned, gave him a grin, and snapped a picture of his staring face.

At the moment the shutter clicked, she felt odd, as if her head had grown two sizes and was full of helium, floating without weight on her neck. Instead of the woman with the child, she saw *herself* sitting on the beach. There was a man with her, with his back turned away, and she knew that he was *her* man, and he was not Choi. He was a haole man, some inches under six feet tall with an athlete's body, deeply tanned. He turned to speak to the other her but before Marvel could catch a glimpse of his face he turned back into the tourist, who had now focused his attention on his other child, who had started to whimper.

Marvel shuddered and stuffed this memory back in the drawer where she kept all the uncanny events that had speckled her life from earliest childhood. That stuff couldn't happen, everyone had told her again and again that it couldn't, she had been punished for seeing things invisible to others. So it hadn't happened. She paid no more attention to it than most people pay to the occasional déjà vu; less, because people will talk about those and Marvel had never mentioned the contents of that drawer to anyone.

"Wait up, Overby!" she yelled, and dashed forward to link her arm with his.

She said, "How do you say, 'I'm in,' in Chinese?"

"You might say, "*Xie, xie, fei chang rong xing.* It means 'Thank you, it's an honor,'" Overby replied, and squeezed her hand. "I'm really pleased, my dear. Talk to Tanaka—he'll find you a tutor. So—what did you make of *The Power and the Glory?*"

They walked back to the car discussing that book. Marvel had not quite finished it, but she was more expert at fakery than any sophomore English major and as a rule in these discussions, Overby did most of the talking. She listened enough to catch his drift, but her mind was off on an idea she'd just had about how to stay in touch with Bernard from the comfort of home.

Marvel went back to the Data and found Esmeralda in her dark, windowless office, sitting in her Aeron chair before an arc of four large flat-screen monitors. She was working, fingers tapping, ear buds in, the whole of her consciousness focused on the dozen or so windows she had running on her screens. Esme had clearly been at it for some time, as evidenced by the abundance of dirty coffee cups and food-clotted plate-lunch Styrofoam clamshells on her desk. She wore a yellow aloha shirt that was wrinkled and none too clean. The room smelled of fast foods and dirty girl. Marvel watched for a while, not wanting to break her friend's concentration, but after a few minutes Esme stopped tapping and spun her chair around with a scowl on her face. This turned to a gold-punctuated smile when she saw who it was, and she popped out her ear buds.

"Don't tell me," she said, "I look like shit."

"You look like someone who just broke the internet. How long have you ...?"

"I don't know—what day is this? Wednesday?"

"Thursday. What in hell are you doing?"

"Hacking for Win. It's this new thing. Wait, are you supposed to know this?"   Then, realizing what she'd said, she drew in a breath and brought her hands to her face in embarrassment. "Oh, God, I'm sorry, but Overby said . . ."

"Not a problem—the man filled me in on Mr. Zhou. What's your end?"

"Oh, you know—right now I'm doing phony web sites, for the lawyers, the shell companies, the title insurance, and connecting with Overby's people in China. We're going to run intercepts on Zhou's cellphones and computers."

"Can you do that in China?"

"Enough money passed around and you can do anything you want, as long as you don't mess with any the big cheeses. Which our guy is not. His data security is a joke too."

"What's the joke? I mean how do we penetrate? I know you can do it, but I never knew how. Are there lots of white numbers moving down the screen, and then the password is his dog's name?"

Esme snorted. "Right, like in the movies. In real life, we crack the systems one of two ways—salvaging paper or social engineering. On this one, paper worked."

"What paper?"

"People write down their passwords. They shouldn't, but everyone does, usually on a Post-it stuck on their monitor, or if they're real security freaks, inside the desk drawer. We bribe the office cleaners to give our people the passwords and whatever's in the wastebaskets."

"And if there's no paper?"

"Then we call the mark's IT guy and pretend to be from the host system and make up a story, like we had a crash and need to reset all the passwords. Could you give us your password and we'll send you a new one? Or, please reset to this temporary password for half an hour. Social engineering."

"This actually works?"

"All the time. People are stupid, brah. I get into their machine using the password and put a virus in the system. Then I own it—I can track every keystroke, so even if they make up a new password, it doesn't help."

"But *you* write down your passwords in your red notebook."

"True, but I have a lot of passwords that I need to have on hand, plus, nobody is going to wander onto the property and look through it. That's one reason why we have Jumbo and the Cars. Anyway, about this guy Zhou—I got everything he owns. I know where he keeps his money, his off-shore accounts, pictures of his wife and kids, dirty pictures of his girlfriend, all his emails . . ."

"They're in Chinese, though."

"Yeah, Chinese, but Tanaka's got a translator team working."

"If you have his off-shore accounts, why are we going through the scam? Why don't we just transfer all his money over to us?"

"Good question, but as a matter of fact, I don't have his account password. I mean he's stupid, but not stupid enough to keep his account password on his computer. Plus that kind of transaction can only come from a computer registered with the bank. Otherwise, people would be hacking off-shore bank accounts all the time, and they don't."

"Oh, God," said Marvel, "I think I have my password for my BVI account on my laptop."

"Oh, Marvel. After all my lectures. Tell me it's encrypted."

"Um . . ."

"I can't believe you, girl. What the fuck is wrong with you? I'm sending you an encryption program right now."

"Will I understand how to use it?"

Esme rolled her eyes, as she always did when people confessed to having no clue about computers. "It's nothing. There's a tutorial in the program. It's basically a text editor and whatever you type into it gets encrypted, and you need a password to get it out. I'd change your account passwords too. Use three English words separated by punctuation marks or digits. It doesn't have to be fancy. Nobody hacks by guessing passwords, unless the password is 'password,' or the first six digits. The important thing is never write it down. Make up something you can memorize, okay?"

"Can I use it to encrypt email?"

"Yeah, if your recipient has the public key. Who are you writing encrypted emails to?"

"I was going to tell you . . ." Here Marvel lowered her voice and glanced around conspiratorially. "I met this guy . . ."

Este's eyes goggled. "No. From here?"

"God, no. I'm not that crazy. No, I met him in a chat room, about kiteboarding and stuff, and I thought he was, you know, cool . . . and funny. So we took it to email."

"Steamy?"

"Getting there. Want to see a picture?"

Did she!

Marvel showed her the iPhone portrait she'd taken of the haole tourist on Kailua Beach.

"Cute!" said Esme. "Is he from the Islands?"

"No, he's mainland. But . . . it's hard to explain. He actually *likes* me, you know? I can talk about life with him, and feelings. I don't get much of that around here."

"You can talk to *me*."

"Of course I can talk to you, Esme, you're my best friend, but I've never had a *guy* like that. I like the separation, you know? Like it's not just, oh, talk, talk, and when are we getting into the sack."

"Do they know about this?"

"God, *no*. And really, you can't tell anyone, not Overby or the Cars or Jumbo and especially not Sami. They wouldn't get it, and the other reason I'm telling you, besides I tell you everything, is I was emailing him in the Starbucks today and Overby walks in and wants to know what I'm doing typing into a computer away from the house."

"Oh, shit, Marvel. What did you do?"

"I made up some story. But the main thing is, I can't risk going off site for this. I'm going to keep in contact, but I'm going to do it right here. I mean, if it's cool with you."

Say yes, Marvel thought, and made her face vulnerable, and, not surprisingly, Esme smiled and rose from her big chair and gave Marvel a hug.

"Hey, sister, you know me—keeper of the secrets. Shit, Sami found out about this he'd throw a fit. So, are you going to meet up with him? What's his name, by the way?"

"Jake Barnes," said Marvel, secure in the understanding that Esme had never read, nor ever would read, *The Sun Also Rises*. She felt bad about conning her friend, as she often did in such situations, but not bad enough to refrain from so doing.

They chatted pleasantly after that for a while, Esme taking advantage of the new and dangerous confidence to fill Marvel's ear with her own sexual and romantic exploits. This girl talk was something Marvel normally enjoyed, She hadn't had much of it in her life, trivialities about clothes, exercise, body image, where to shop for this and that, and men.

Esme had a long-standing thing with Ray Honda, although Ray had a wife and family in Waimanolo with whom he spent a good deal of time. She also had a new boyfriend, a haole she'd met in a Waikiki bar, and she'd been driving him around in her shiny red Audi convertible, but had not yet stayed the night with him in his condo. She wanted advice on this point, whether revealing the haole would make Ray jealous enough to finally leave his wife, or whether she should forget Ray entirely and cultivate this guy, who unfortunately was a resident of the mainland.

Marvel spun something out, using the language of the advice columns in magazines, as always amazed than anyone would ask her for dating advice considering how low she had scored in that game. But Esme regarded Marvel's relationship with Sami Choi as some kind of romantic ideal, largely because of Marvel having fibbed about it for years, conning both Esme and herself, a little.

Esme was far more of a romantic than Marvel. Absent any encouragement from Ray, she still awaited Mr. Right, an expectation fed by television rather than her lived experience. Marvel had given up explaining that romance was not to be found by getting loaded in rough Waimanolo saloons every weekend and waking up, marked with bruises, next to some strange dude. Esme caused fights when she had her high on-- Marvel had seen her provoke into battle a trio of Samoans whose combined weight was well above half a ton. She had been barred from a number of dives for this reason.

On the other hand, given what she did, it was difficult to hang out with men who were not on the grift or part of the shadow-world of Oahu, because all of it was secret. Marvel knew that on the few occasions that Esme had dated a taxpayer, Jumbo and the Cars had gone to have a word with the sap and the guy mysteriously stopped calling. Did Esme know this too? Probably--she was a genius, after all. Marvel thought the knowledge that she was caught in a net like any mark might have been behind her crazies on Saturday night.

As Esme chattered on about her guy stuff, Marvel had the peculiar feeling that something was draining out of her life, this being sense that she was part of a family, that Esme was an actual, rather than a counterfeit, friend. She felt thin sweat break on her face, and the room grew misty. Esme rambled on and then stopped—she'd asked a question.

"I'm sorry," Marvel said, "Pinkie?"

"Yeah, Pinkie, Ray's brother. Do you think he's okay? I mean he's kind of a square, has a straight job with the Hawaii Power, but maybe I would do better with somebody like him." She laughed. "I mean, Ray would probably be relieved, and least the boys wouldn't scare him off. Or worse, you know, like they do . . ."

Something came over Esme's face, a darkening of the brown skin, and her black eyes went opaque and dropped.

"What does that mean, 'worse, like they do?'"

"Nothing. I just meant, maybe they wouldn't, um, discourage, if it was kind of in the family."

Marvel had met Pinkie a couple of times, a very large local person, who seemed impressed by his brother's prosperity and the freedom with which booze and weed were dispensed at his house. Marvel cleared her throat, forced a smile and said, "Sure, he's a nice guy."

"You think he's cute?"

"Totally," said Marvel, and Esme hugged her again and said she had to get back to work on the Chinese thing but not to worry about using the computer to email Jake Barnes.

Marvel walked out of the house to the shed where all the sporting equipment was stored, racked surfboards and kiteboards and the colorful bags that held the kiteboarding bridles and lines. She stripped off her clothes, moving automatically, her brain on hold, and put on her worn flowered bikini. She went out to the beach and sniffed at the wind. It was a good day for riding, and half a dozen kites were flying, bright lozenges of color against the blue. The trade wind was blowing fifteen knots, she judged, nicely cross-shore, and she went with her ten-meter Cabrinha Switchblade and her usual Airush Vox twintip.

She positioned the kite on the beach, facing the ocean, folded the lower wing tip, and dumped sand on the leading edge. She used her electric pump to stiffen the struts, hooked on the lines, untangled them and laid them out upwind, put on her harness, and hooked the control bar and safety line to it. She placed her board in the wet sand near the gently rippling edge of the sea.

A pull at the control bar--the kite shook the sand off and rose into the air. Stepping into the stirrup of her board, she powered up the kite and was off, flying over the sparkling surface.

Marvel did her best thinking on her board. Her body knew how to fly the kite, leaving the higher centers of her brain free to range wherever.

Like they do.

The phrase gnawed at her mind. It was a slip, some information she was not meant to know. It was not "nothing." Unlike Marvel, Esme was a terrible liar: a lie showed clear on her face, like acne. Not a grifter, Esme.

183

What was it that Jumbo and the Cars did that was "worse" than scaring off an unsuitable guy? And, again, what was a confidence gang doing with serious muscle? Overby had just said there was always a need for muscle, but why? The story that it was to protect the 'ohana from local gangsters was obvious bullshit. The petty crooks that made up Oahu's underworld could not possibly be a danger to a group so cleverly hidden in plain sight. Besides, the whole point of a con was that you didn't *need* muscle, the marks *gave* you the money.

Then there was that conversation she'd overheard on the night of the welcome home bash. "Closing it out like usual." "The insurance." "Esme's on the job." The mark's being out of town as a good thing. What mark? What insurance?

Like they do.

It had to be something they did to the marks after the breakdown, this "close out" thing. That Jumbo did. She thought of how Jumbo had taught her to kiteboard, the hours he'd spent, his patience and good humor. Yeah, he'd killed a man, but that had been an accident and he'd hinted about what he'd done out in Helmand Province, awful stuff, yes, but he was basically a good guy.

She had to know, and thinking this, she turned the kite to shore. He'd taught her how to do this as well, to steer back to the stop she'd started from, not easy, but she'd mastered the technique and now she did and landed close to the house. She depowered her kite, feeling slack and weakly flapping herself.

Back in her room, at her laptop, it did not take her long to go through the names of the marks. Dead, all of them, of natural causes, the web articles said, but that was beyond belief. All of them? The mask of cold sweat fell again upon her brow as she thought, no, one still survived. She brought up her email and wrote him a letter.

Eleven

As the days passed at the monastery, moving deeper into dark autumn, Bernard found it increasingly difficult to spend a lot of time tapping at keys and thinking of what to put. He wanted physical activity, hard work, and so he began to train. He ran along the roads, with the dog loping alongside, until he was exhausted and disappointed at how he had let the once Olympian body decline. He volunteered for the wall repair crew, and spent hours lifting the dense gray slabs. He shot at paper targets with his silenced pistol, and got his eye back in. After every liturgical hour, he did push-ups and crunches in his cell. Since the one thing Bernard really knew how to do besides writing genre fiction was physical training, his body responded. The city suet melted off his gut, he grew more flexible, muscles appeared again. The dog thought it was amusing. One day on the road, it happened to remark,

<I don't see why you bother. You'll never run as fast as me.>

"You're quite mistaken there, pal," said Bernard between pants, "Over a sufficient distance a human being can outrun any land animal on the planet."

<Ha ha.>

"Just for that, I think I'll get you into training, you slob. How would you like to go for second-degree Schutzhund?"

<If you desire it, my Man.>

So, Bernard asked for and received permission to train Murtagh for the second degree of Schutzhund. The tracking phase of this trial required following a scent along three sides of a square, each 150 paces long. The dog had to follow a scent trail, find an object dropped by the judge about midway on the path, then continue along the track and locate a second object at its end. This track was about a fifth longer than the analogous course run for Schutzhund I, which proved to be a problem.

They had been at it for hours now, in the chill damp, and Murtagh would not run the longer distance. He locked on the scent going out, as always, but only for the 125-pace length of the shorter run. At that point, he would leave the scent and jog right, as if following the path he'd already mastered, and then, sensing he'd lost the scent, would start casting, which was a grave and disqualifying sin in Schutzhund competition.

The bells tolled Sext.

The dog got up and headed for the chapel, near which was the heated shed where the dogs waited out choir. Murtagh liked the shed, a fiesta of sniffing anuses and play battles. But never a bark, of course.

"Hold on there, bub!" said Bernard, at which the dog looked inquiringly over its shoulder.

<What now?>

"I know it's sext, but I am not a monk, and not under monastic discipline, nor are you. We're not leaving until you get this right. What can I do to make you understand that you have to follow the scent for a longer run and not make that turn?"

<I don't understand.>

"Yes, yes that's the fucking *problem*!," replied Bernard, forgetting himself so far as to express his annoyance and frustration, which one did not do in dog training at this level.

<I don't see it that way. I am a willing dog. If you say what to do, and if I don't do it, it means you haven't said it right. You're the Man. >

"You have a point. Well, let's try it again, okay?"

<You're the Man. >

"Okay, let me make another pass with the scent and we'll see if you can run the longer distance this time. Stay."

Bernard took the scent bag and began to pace off the 150 steps of the first leg. This time, however, as he passed the zone of error at 125 paces, the light bulb lit.

He spread a heavy smear of scent at this point, wielding the scent bag with abandon and marking a path past the false turn heavy enough to serve as the olfactory equivalent of a strobe light. Murtagh picked up the proper line easily and didn't miss a turn on the rest of the course.

"Good dog," said Bernard.

<Thank you. It certainly took you long enough to figure it out.>

"I've become slow. But I thought it was particularly brilliant of you to finally learn that you were on a differently shaped course."

<I always knew that.>

"Yes, that's what you always say when you learn something new. It's a mark of stupidity in humans, but not in dogs. Let's move along the field and try it on a fresh course."

They did and Murtagh ran it without trouble, even without the heavier scent application at the wrong turning. With this victory, Bernard decided to call it a day and the two walked back toward the refectory for lunch. He wondered why he had not figured out how to cure the error, a solution so obvious in retrospect, when the dog had first made it. He concluded that he was distracted by the woman, Marvel.

"How crazy am I, Murtagh?" he asked as they trod the crisp, dead leaves. "Has my reason been unseated? I lost my wife, a woman who was blazingly honest, who could barely tell a convenient fib, and this was one of the main things I doted on, you could always tell exactly where Louise was coming from. It was enormously relaxing for a professional liar like me to be with a woman like that. So that alone should have shaken my sense of reality, and then I lost nearly all my ready money, and that should have undermined me even further. But I don't *feel* undermined. I feel okay, great even."

<Because you have a good dog.>

"No, really. You remember what I was like after Louise was killed, and I thought that was it, I had my life, and everything else will be a footnote. But it hasn't been like that. I saw her in that bookstore, and bang. That was it, she was what I wanted. How nuts is that? It was just like that with Louise. Passionate, God, yes, but *sane* passionate.

"Neither set of our parents would have picked either of us off a menu for their kid, but that was all the transgressiveness there was, because who really gives a shit about that racial stuff nowadays, and it was a great marriage. It wasn't like falling in love with the child of bank robbers and a master criminal in her own right. Yeah, *falling* is the appropriate verb here, tumbling, helpless, the whole bit. Something cosmic just clicked in and my goose was cooked.

"And she knows it too, I can feel it. She's fighting it, she's scared, but she'll come through. Unless, as I say, I am seriously deranged. Erotomania as a result of loss. I haven't heard from her in over twenty-four hours, and I'm starting to get worried. I have no idea where she even is. I wouldn't mind that if . . . well, the fact remains that I'm *not* sure of her at long distance, I want to see her and touch her, I need more bandwidth. I don't know what to do, Murtagh."

<You *would* be sure if you could sniff her vagina. Get your nose right up in there. That never fails.>

"Thanks for the tip, Murtagh," said Bernard. "You *are* a good dog."

He was an exceedingly good dog after lunch when Bernard worked him into the protection training Brother Gabriel was doing in the yard set aside for that purpose. The yard contained six blinds; small canvas teepees capable of concealing a man. The first task in a Schutzhund II trial was for the handler and dog to walk among these and for the handler to send the dog to investigate each in turn, using only voice commands and hand signals. Murtagh caught on to the searching after only a few tries, and when he found the agitator (Brother Gerard in a heavy leather and canvas bite-proof suit) he set up the required racket, but refrained from biting the sleeve after only one correction.

In the next phase of the training, Bernard acted the part of an officer taking a suspect into custody. He shouted for the agitator to come out of the hide, patted him down and inspected the inside of the blind, after ordering the dog to guard. Murtagh did not wander off or follow his master into the blind, which was good. Then, at Brother Gabriel's signal, Brother Gerard broke and ran.

"Get him!" ordered Bernard, and the dog took off in pursuit. He grabbed the sleeve, whereupon Brother Gerard roared and struck Murtagh across the back with a "stick" made of bound reeds. Then he froze and Bernard shouted, "Out, Murtagh!" but Murtagh did not release, but instead wrestled the monk to the ground, snarling and testing whether his outfit was really bite-proof or not.

They worked on this problem for a good half hour, at which point Brother Gabriel told Bernard that the dog needed more work on the release. Not dropping an attack on command was the worst infamy in Schutzhund, and a total disqualification.

"I'm sorry, Gabriel. I don't know what got into him. He's never refused an out before."

"That's all right," replied Brother Gabriel, "he'll be fine. Just work on releases for a whole day. He's feisty, and I'd rather have a feisty dog than a wuss."

Bernard and Murtagh walked back to the data center and when they were out of earshot, Bernard said, "That was disgraceful, and after you did so well on the search, hold, and bark. What in hell got into you?"

<He hit me.>

"He's *supposed* to hit you. It's part of the trial. Did it hurt?"

<That's not the point. It's the principle of the thing.>

"What principle? That you can't be hit? Maybe I'll start hitting you myself. Would you bite me and not let go?"

<That's different. I love *you*.>

"I know Murtagh, but if you don't knock it off, you're not going to make Schutzhund II."

<I will obey. But it's against my nature. I am a feisty dog.>

Bernard said, "Oh, shut up!" and strode on. He was truly angry, and annoyed at himself for being so, because he knew he was taking out on the animal his frustration with another creature who was not behaving as she ought. Thus, he felt a near-orgasmic rush of relief when, upon opening his email, he found kitegurl21 had made contact again.

We need to talk, now. Are you on Skype?"

"Well, well," said Bernard, staring at the screen and the few words. "What now, Murtagh? What do we need to talk about, I wonder? Is this an extension of the con? Maybe she just wants to find out where I am, so she can send the killers here. Murtagh, you're a guard dog, and I have to say you missed this whole deal. Why couldn't your mighty nose sniff it out, huh? What's your advice now?"

<She smelled right.>

"She smelled right? What does that even mean?"

<No fear. She wouldn't hit me with a stick.>

"Yeah, you're probably right about that," said Bernard, and sent his Skype address. The program warbled soon after, and in the next moment he was looking at her face, and the audio was carrying the sound of wind and surf. Her hair was roughly tied back and a different color, and her face wore a different expression from any he had seen on it before, but it was the same woman. He grinned at her like an ape.

"There you are," he said. "So that's the real Marvel? My God, your eyes are two different colors!"

"Yeah, yeah, look we haven't got any time for small talk. We have a serious problem."

"Besides the fact that you're far away? Where are you, by the way? Near a warm sea, I gather."

"Never mind that. I've found something out, or I think I have. Oh, God!"

She ran her palm over her head, as if to massage her brain.

Bernard said, "You've discovered that you can't stop thinking about me. I have the same problem, but with you."

"No, be serious. Look, I've found something, like, really bad, about our, you know, our racket . . . I mean, I could be wrong, but . . . "

She bit her lip in a manner he found charming. She couldn't quite bring herself to say it, he concluded, and his heart lifted. He'd been right. She didn't know. On the other hand, she was a superb actress. If this was another con, she was carrying it off brilliantly.

He said, "You've discovered that your gang has been murdering the suckers," and was rewarded with what he thought was his first look inside the onion that was Marvel Gafney. Her eyes widened, her jaw dropped, her heterochromic eyes popped. She looked fourteen.

"You knew this? How the fuck could you . . .?"

"I had help," he answered, and told her the story of meeting the private eye, the suspicions this had engendered, and their confirmation via Lawrence and the wonders of the Internet.

"I assumed you were not aware of that aspect," he added.

"Aware? That they were *murdering* people? Fuck no, I wasn't *aware*. I'm a grifter. Grifters don't do fucking *violence*. That's why they're grifters. Oh, God, what am I going to do? They'll think I'm an accomplice."

Her voice had risen to an unpleasant screech.

"You should get out of there," said Bernard calmly. "Where is it you are, exactly?"

"In Hawaii. Where are you?"

This is it, thought Bernard, the breakdown, as they call it in the con game, where the burnt fool's bandaged finger goes wobbling back to the fire, as Kipling has it. He stared into her digitized peculiar eyes, seeking duplicity, but all he saw was panic and confusion. He thought, oh, let the killers come. If she's false again, if these feelings I have are delusion, then why live?

"I'm in St. Roch Abbey, in northern New York state," he said, and managed to keep his voice from wavering. "You ought to come here."

"What? Are you crazy? Why would I come there?"

"Not crazy at all," said Bernard. "We know they're after me. If you take off, they'll for sure be after you. You know the whole story, you're incredibly dangerous to them."

"But I didn't *know* about the murders!"

"That would be hard to prove, assuming you ever had to, but in any case, you know it now, and they can't let you go."

"What do you mean they can't let me go? I'm not under suspicion, I could get on a plane tomorrow and no one would say a thing. In fact, I was just encouraged to travel by Over ... a guy in the crew. He said I could rent a villa in Tuscany."

"An excellent idea. We could meet there."

"Oh, don't be stupid. Look, I don't know what weird shit is going on in your mind, but we don't have, like, a relationship. I mean, I don't want you to die, but that's the extent."

"Oh, don't be stupid *yourself.* You know very well there's a connection between us. I feel it, you feel it. I didn't ask for it, and I don't know what it is, but it's real. Meanwhile, if you're not under suspicion now, how long do you think that will last? You're sneaking off to email and Skype me. Maybe someone is watching you right now--why is Marvel out on the beach with her laptop? It's inevitable they'll find out and kill you, but probably not before forcing you to lure me into a trap, and then we'll both be dead. You have to break away now, today, just leave everything and get on a plane."

"You don't understand. They can find you without me. We have an expert hacker working for ....Oh, God. Are you still using the same computer?"

"My laptop. Why, what's wrong?"

"Asshole. I'm an asshole too. Christ, what was I thinking? Don't you understand? We own your computer."

"Owned, I believe. My son found a kernel-based Trojan in there and excised it."

"Really? Okay, that's good. So they didn't get anything, the email or . . ."

"Not that good. I think the emails may be compromised. He did it after we started emailing, so if they can get hold of your computer . . ."

"Shit. But Esme couldn't have known about it yet, or I would have seen it on her face. She's a hacker, not a grifter. Besides, why would anyone check my computer? And the emails are encrypted. No, I think I'm okay for the time being. But, oh, God. This Skype isn't encrypted. I'll wash the session, take off the whole program."

"Leave now. Fly to New York. Come here!"

"You're being stupid again. What possible reason would I have for making it easier for them? If they know I'm connected to you, it gives them one place to look instead of two."

"No, if you're here we can watch each other's backs. Besides, this is a particularly good place to hide."

"Really? A what-do-you call-it, an abbey?"

"It's a monastery that trains guard dogs," said Bernard. "Believe me, no one's going to sneak up on us here."

"Did your dog tell you that?"

"He would, if I asked him. Come on, Marvel, you know that's the smart thing to do."

"It's the dumb thing, Goodrich. Look, I'm sure you mean well, but these guys I'm with are good. A few dogs won't keep them out. My suggestion is move, and keep moving. That's what I intend to do. Now I have to get out of here. I have to show up at the party tonight with my game face on, and hope they haven't found those emails."

"You're going to a party?"

"Yeah, some of the crew are going off to set up a major score. Usually, it's me they're sending off, but not now."

"Another grieving widower?"

"No, something else, a much bigger deal, as a matter of fact."

She looked away from him, and took a deep breath. Her eyes met his and she said, "So long, Goodrich—you're probably a nice guy and it's too bad you got involved in all of this, but that's life. I suggest you try to have a nice one while you can. Keep moving!"

With that, she signed off. Bernard was left with a blank Skype screen and a wail stuck in his throat. He immediately tried to resume the connection, but the software only warbled futilely. He banged his fist on the desk, knocking over a jar full of pencils. The dog alerted at the sound and growled inquiringly.

<What?>

"Relax, Murtagh. I'm just being stupid again. I seem to be pursuing a woman who thinks she wants nothing to do with me."

<That's not stupid. If she wants you to mount her, she'll wait and put out scent.>

"Thank you. You know what's also stupid? Getting dating advice from a dog. Come on, it'll be vespers in ten minutes, and after that, I have to talk to the prior. We may have to leave this place."

Bernard intercepted Father Ambrose as they both arrived at the refectory before the evening meal and told him a modified version of his strange story. He asked if the prior thought he should leave, as representing a possible danger to the inhabitants.

The prior slipped the question, but asked, "So you believe that, hm, actual *assassins* will be coming here after you?"

"Not as such. I don't think they'll try to actually kill me on the grounds. I think they'll try to lure me away and then arrange a plausible accident or apparently natural death."

"How would they lure you?"

"Well, the woman I told you about. She may be in their power. And of course they could threaten harm to another person I cared about. Or they could just slip in at night and carry me off, I suppose."

"Well, not that, at any rate. A ninja couldn't slip into St. Roch undetected. As for chasing you out, that is not the Benedictine way. We've protected a lot of people this past millennium, and we can still do it, although I admit it's been some time since we had to. Stay as long as you like. In fact, we can use the occasion to practice patrolling the property at night. Our night program has been disgracefully slack, and this is a means of repairing it. So, we are in your debt. Besides that, Mrs. Lincoln, how are you getting on?"

"Great. I feel twenty again, but better, having solved a number of life problems and with a terrific dog of my own. We're working him up to second level."

"Yes, so I hear. It's not unusual for them to balk when you change dimensions on them. Here, as you know, we can course in any of a dozen ways, and so our trainees get used to following their noses and not the geography. There's a homily there about trusting faith and not pining for some imagined future. I should make a note. Ah, I smell bean soup. We make wonderful bean soup, but it has its usual effect and one is glad one sleeps alone in a cell. Choir is another matter, ha ha!"

Laughing, the prior departed to his chair, surrounded instantly by those monks and staff who wanted a word. Bernard looked at the rota by the door to see if he had drawn any tasks, and found he was assigned to bring supper to Brother Dominic. The ancient monk's knees were shot, and he had received permission to live out his days as a sort of anchorite in the gate house, and have all his meals delivered.

Brother George, the cook, gave Bernard two insulated bags, one large enough to hold a container of soup and a chunk of the abbey's excellent bread, and the other half that size.

"What's in the little one?" Bernard asked.

"Ice cream bar. Brother D. likes his ice cream bar. Maybe he'll do another miracle with it."

"What do you mean?"

"Brother Dominic's miracle? This was years ago—Brother D. was just about to eat his ice cream when a woman comes rushing up to the gatehouse. One of his regulars it seems, and she had to talk to him. So, he puts his ice cream bar in his desk drawer—this is in July, by the way, hot as the devil. Well, the woman stays a good long time, and after she leaves, Brother D. recalls his ice cream. What does he find? A couple of hours at least in a hot drawer and it's still cold as a miser's heart, not a trace of melting. It's a famous story around here."

Bernard took the bags without any comment but a smile and walked out of the kitchen, then up the steep path that led to the gatehouse. He thought that while he didn't believe in miracles, he could certainly use one about now.

Twelve

What am I doing? What the *hell* am I doing? This like a drumbeat, boring, insistent, the hideous, inescapable elevator music of her life. Once again, *again*, she was diving into something that would screw up her life, and she couldn't help herself, demons drove her over the edge. Again.

Why couldn't she help herself? Her thoughts as she punched keys on the lap top, annihilating every trace of Bernard Goodrich's presence, although she knew at some level that Esme could penetrate into the guts of the machine where only the computer kahunas could go and find traces Marvel hadn't the skills to excise. Even *that* was a stupid thought, because if they were suspicious enough to vet her computer, she was doomed anyway--there was no way she could stand up to an interrogation by Overby.

But in order for it not to come to that, she had to make plans. Always have at least two ways of escape, she'd learned that from Overby himself, although he was talking about ditching an operation, not leaving home. Was it even home? That was the killer—she'd been conned. They'd played her, they'd understood that she wouldn't have been able to con the marks if she'd known that Overby was going to have them killed, and so they hadn't told her.

Marvel looked around her little room, at the bookshelves, the desk, the day-bed, the wide window giving on the bright beach and sea. She loved this room, which now had become a jail cell. How had she been so stupid? Yes, that's what the marks all must have said, when the breakdown arrived and they saw that all they had believed had been a lie. What hadn't been a lie? Well, a lot of it, of course, because you can't bring off a big lie unless it's surrounded by a padding of truth.

Truth. Overby and Sami had truly saved her life back in Macau. Overby had truly educated her and trained her for the work, taken a Oregon hick and turned her into a woman who could go anywhere, converse with anyone. That he had done it to make her an instrument did not detract from the reality of that accomplishment.

She made herself stop these thoughts by sitting at her desk and making a list (yet another Overby contribution—when crazy happens, sit down and make a list!) So she wrote and crossed out and rewrote, and while she did this she became aware of the sound of a bass voice from Esme's room, and heavy steps, and the complaint of a burdened bed.

That was Ray Honda--apparently he had made it up with Esme, or she had decided to forget for the moment about his wife and kids in Waimanolo. More truth and lies there, because it was certain sure that Esme was her friend, that Jumbo and the Cars liked her—the deception or secret didn't change that, and anyway, what friends didn't have some hidden place where the friendship didn't care to go?

And all that fun. Marvel hadn't had much fun in her life, not after her grandmother died and she'd moved in with her Aunt Ethel and Uncle Claude, not much fun at all in that house, and not much fun with the various men, and not in the bars and casinos she'd worked. But these last years in Lanikai had been a post-graduate education in delight. In the pauses between operations the 'ohana had run a perpetual beach party.

She stopped scribbling and succumbed to an unexpected pang of sorrow. They'd given her the sea, the warm ocean of the Islands, for free, as a love offering, and it was so strange at first, guys who just wanted to be with her, to teach her stuff, without necessarily wanting sex in return, although, of course, Jumbo wanted to, but not that seriously, not so it became annoying. She remembered being with the Cars in the water, at a swimming beach, Lanikai or Kailua or Laie, no surf, deep pools. Esme and Jumbo were there too, with some of his old football buddies, and they had got up a game of water polo, with Marvel as the ball. They handled her as they did their own children; it was common to see a refrigerator-sized man wade out with a toddler and fling the child like a beach ball into the sea, while the haole tourists gaped in horror. Playing with those immense brown men was like being translated into a childhood she had never had, feeling tiny and secure and hilarious. One of the golden days of her life, that one.

And the food—who could have conceived of such food in the land of her birth, where a burger and fries were the summit of culinary imagination? She had learned to eat poke and poi and weird seafood, sea urchin roe and octopus, and eating fish she'd seen actually swimming a few minutes before, then wriggling on Jumbo's spear and then roasting over coals.

And laughing, it seemed they were always laughing, cracking up in pidgen, obscure, ancient local jokes she could barely understand but laughed at anyway, helped along by the cubic yards of top-end pakalolo they all smoked all day.

There was Sami, too, although Sami had issues with the water, and the sunlight. He didn't have much to say, outside of business and making arrangements for his personal comfort, but that was okay because of the sex. Until she ran into Sami in Macau, Marvel had not thought to connect sex with serious pleasure. She had started messing around with boys like the other Dog patch tramps when the time came; it was just part of the scene, it arrived with the weed and the music, Nirvana Wilco Pearl Jam Sleater-Kinney gushing from the car speakers in the butt-strewn parking lots of burger joints, at best a way to get a guy with good dope and a car to pay attention, at worst a way to get out of a situation, something to distract a cop or a boss, no biggie except when the dude was one of the ones who liked hurting. Like Duane. She'd been in love with Duane, and then he'd gotten himself stupidly killed and she hadn't thought about him for a while.

But now she did. At the time she'd thought that putting up with Duane's little ways was a fair enough exchange at the time for escaping from Dogpatch. He'd inadvertently schooled her in faking both pleasure and pain, and also the trick of leaving her body while it was being used, to float off into a calm, dim space, and think song lyrics, a form of the magic circle Gran had described. Duane had brought her to Macao and got her into big trouble and Sami had stepped in and saved her ass and . . .

Why was she thinking of all this old shit now? Because it was over for her, the whole 'ohana thing, and that would include sex with Sami. In bed, he was like Haulani Ford or Ray Honda on a surfboard, or Jumbo with a kite, perfectly focused, balanced, attuned to the various forces, which in his case meant generating the last increment of pleasure in her body. An artist in that way, Sami, though largely an asshole in the other zones of life.

She rose now, gave a little shake to cast off unpleasant feelings, blessed Mr. Poggett of the Shore Town, BVI for securing her money from any manipulations that Esme was likely to try after learning that Marvel had defected, placed her list and her laptop into her capacious Prada bag, slid into rubber slippers, and departed the house in her yellow car. Driving swiftly, but accurately, she made it to the Bank of Hawaii branch in Chinatown in under thirty minutes.

A Hawaii driver's license in the name of Amanda Davis shown to a Chinese-American gentleman in a blue blazer (name tag: A. D. Fong) gave her entry to the vault, where Mr. Fong removed a safety deposit box from its rack. He left her alone at the table provided for such customers, of which there were remarkably many at this particular branch. The true Ms. Davis had lost her wallet to a pickpocket in a Waikiki club, whence it had entered the substantial local market for such items. Marvel had purchased it for two hundred dollars.

Marvel opened the flat box with her key, an item kept secreted behind a wad of tissue paper in the toe of a cowboy boot in her closet. She was pretty sure no one in the 'ohana knew about the key or the safety deposit box or what was in it. Overby could probably surmise the existence of the contents, since it was part of the operating procedure he had so carefully taught his pupil. She recalled that conversation, for he'd stressed the importance of keeping her getaway arrangements secret from everyone. "Even you?" she'd asked at the time.

"Even me," he'd answered. "I might be grabbed and have to sell you out."

"Then how do you know I won't sell *you* out and split?"

He'd smiled then, at his protégée's response, and answered, "Well, you can never be sure what I know about, can you?" And they'd laughed.

The box contained the fifty grand she had picked up in Tortola. (How had she known she would need cash? She refused to think about that now.) It also held a complete set of identification papers—birth certificate, passport, California driver's license, work ID tag (with photo), and two credit cards—in the name of Alison Hill, of Los Angeles.

It is more difficult than it once was to adopt the identity of a dead infant, but clerks in public records offices sometimes need a little extra at the holidays and it can still be done. The real Alison had died in a house fire, aged two, along with her parents, but the concocted Alison had done well for herself. She worked as a producer for Sony in L.A., had Facebook, Linked-In and Instagram pages with many contacts, owned a nice condo in West Hollywood, and had excellent credit. She had substantial balances at several local banks.

Lighting up her laptop, Marvel used her Marvel Gafney Visa to buy a round-trip first-class ticket to Rome from Honolulu via Seattle, made a reservation at the Hassler for two weeks, and similar hotel reservations in Florence, Venice and Amalfi. Then she drove to Ala Moana Mall.

First to the post office, where she shipped the laptop to a P.O. box in Miami and sent the bank form by registered overnight mail to her Virgin Islands bank. After that, she visited the Apple store, where, using the Alison Hill Amex card, she bought an iPhone, a MacBook Air, and a carrier bag. The t-shirt guy helpfully arranged an iPhone Sprite account for Ms. Hill, and she walked out, another satisfied Apple customer. At a coffee shop, she disposed of the intricate packaging and placed the Mac in its carrier and the iPhone in her bag.

Then to Neiman Marcus, for a party outfit. She chose a Paco Rabanne dress of gold mesh, and a pair of Giambattista Valli sandals, stiletto heeled, with nine straps enclosing the arch and the lower calf. She stared at herself in the store mirror and felt herself occupy the outfit, becoming the kind of woman who would wear such clothes. Marvel was natively a board shorts and t-shirt person and regarded high-end dressing as part of the job. There wasn't a dress code for parties at the Lanikai house, but Marvel thought it would be cool to bail out of there looking fabulous, and also thought it might distract Overby. Overby had, in fact, taught her how to dress.

She recalled the long sessions with him in this store, and others in the mall, popping in and out of dressing rooms with a fortune on her back, twirling for his inspection, and then again and again to the point of exhaustion. When she was younger, she had dressed herself through theft, and it still felt a little off to actually pay hundreds of dollars for a garment and walk out of a store without that particular form of tension gripping her vitals. Since Overby had entered her life, clothes had become either costume or distraction, concealment rather than adornment. But passing the elegant women in the dressing rooms, she felt, besides the usual contempt grifters accorded squares, a certain longing for their innocence. It would have been nice to just like clothes.

From Ala Moana she called Cherie, her hairdresser, and wangled an emergency appointment, and also arranged for a facial, manicure, and pedicure at the spa where Cherie worked, at the Halekulane Hotel. The notion of pampering (irritating word!) had never appealed to Marvel; she did not like being touched by strangers in exchange for money, but observing the matrons being pampered around her in spa and salon she found herself slipping, comfortable and chameleon-like, into the guise of a pamperee, and heard herself chatting gaily with Cherie.

This chat directed away from anything personal and toward the hairdresser herself: men, their defects; kids, their achievements and vices; the broken car, washing machine, hopes. This was the world of scuffling, marginal single women that Marvel had lately occupied and never would again, thanks to crime. It was depressing, yet strangely invigorating, the emotional equivalent of the apricot scrub she later endured.

Also, a great haircut; the woman was a genius with Marvel's long, fine hair, producing a layered sort of Italian boy do that would, it was promised, stay in place and look good, even when wet and salted.

"We should highlight it, you think?" said Cherie.

Marvel responded with the Steven Wright line, "Yes, but only the most important hairs," which got a laugh, and when the tinting was done, she hugged Cherie, tipped her a fifty, and went happily off for her facial.

Some hours later, Marvel returned to the Data and ran into Esme and Tanaka in the entry hall. Esme looked wiped out, her hair kinked as if she'd slept in a tight hat, her tan skin frayed, dark smudges under her eyes. They stared at her as abyssal creatures might at a fish from the sunlit reefs.

"You got a haircut," said Esme. "Wow, you look terrific."

"Terrific, yes," said Tanaka, averting his gaze. To Esme he added, "If you should find anything, call me instantly, please." With a tiny bow to Marvel, he disappeared into the garden.

"What was that all about?" Marvel asked.

"Nothing. Just some shit Overby wants." Esme eyed the Nieman bags. "You went shopping?"

Marvel caught the evasion and felt sadness at the friendship leaking away.

"Yeah, Ala Moana, for the party. Want to see?"

"Uh huh. You're *dressing*?"

"Of course. I want to give Sami something to remember while he's hustling bar girls in Hong Kong. Aren't you?"

"I have shit to wear, girlfriend, as you know. Let's see the loot. I got like five minutes."

"You're still working on the legend for the Chinese op?"

"Uh huh, yeah, that," said Esme. Another lie. Marvel suppressed a sigh and led Esme into her room.

Who expelled a small gasp when she saw the Paco Rabanne dress, then cooed about the shoes and looked despondently down at her own feet, dressed in the State Shoe of Hawaii, and declared that she could never get into those, and then they traipsed into Esme's rat's nest of a bedroom and rummaged through her closet, searching for a suitable garment. Marvel cranked up her Girl thing, and in a short while the two were giggling and Esme had stopped looking like the living dead. The best they could come up with was a baby blue ball gown that Esme had last worn to a Filipino social club dance.

"Try it on," said Marvel. She did. They both looked at the reflection in the full-length mirror on the closet door. After a moment, Esme sputtered out a guffaw and Marvel joined her. In an instant they were both hilarious, crying, doubled over.

"I could wear it," said Esme between laughs, "but then no one would look at you. Oh, God, my side hurts." She collapsed on the bed. The hem of the gown stuck almost straight up.

"You could go to the mall and get something nice," said Marvel. "I'd come with you."

Esme stopped laughing and, sliding out of the flounces, said, "No, I haven't got time. The bolohead wants this finished before they leave."

"What is it? Maybe I could help."

Another strange look passed over Esme's face, which she covered clumsily with a fake smile and said, "Nah, nah, it's too complicated. It would take longer to explain than it'll take to finish. And I think I'll just wear one of my Savers shirts and white jeans. You can be the gorgeous superstar just this once."

Marvel went back to her room and set up her virginal Mac as if it belonged to the fictive Alison, tapping in all the details of birth and job and associations she had already devised. She did not turn on the wifi. She set up Alison's email account, and brought up the program, intending to send a message using her new iPhone as a hot spot. It struck her then that she had no one to send a message to, no friends, no relatives. The people she was closest to, if that was still the operative word, would soon be enemies; the whole idea of getting a fresh computer was to conceal her new identity from them. Now a blank moment in which she experienced a loneliness sharper and more insistent than a toothache, and when it passed, and she looked down at the screen, she saw that somehow her fingers had, unbidden, typed Bernard Goodrich's address in the box.

Horrified, she deleted it, and then for a span of time she was not in her room but in a car driven by the deleted addressee, on a country road at night. The car was some kind of large European sedan, warm, comfortable, but she could see snow in the trees and bushes outside. A white road sign peppered with bullet holes appeared, and the car slowed. She heard a question: which way do we go? And she heard her own voice say, "North."

She came back to herself with a start, sweat on her scalp and flanks, hair on end on her arms. With horror she recalled the scene at the beach, the haole couple that had become herself and another man. Now she knew who the other man was. Nausea rose from her belly and burned foul in her mouth, and she dropped her head between her knees until the feeling passed. Although she tried now, the old mode of forgetting what she had always called to herself "weird shit" no longer functioned. This one was too vivid, too detailed, the car, the man, the road seemed as real as the walls of this room and its view of the beach and sea.

She'd read somewhere about the kind of disease that, once you got it, instead of immunity you became even more sensitive to subsequent infections and this was the same. Her head swarmed with upwellings of memories she had thought long buried: her grandmother walking through her bedroom two years after her death. Going into a bar at fourteen with fake ID, seeing a couple at a table who looked familiar, who nodded and smiled at her as she passed. They were her dead parents, she realized a moment later, but when she turned, they were two different people. A conversation with a woman on a bus she was taking to a Van Halen concert in Portland, aged sixteen; she'd gone to the toilet, and when she returned the woman's seat was empty. The bus hadn't stopped.

That one she'd attributed to dreaming—she had dozed off. One of her typical explanations, a waking dream. Another explanation: stress. Oh yes, plenty of that now and there was no one on earth she could talk to about it except *him*. Of course, she could instantly remove all stress . . . but that was something she did not care to think about, and here she found her ability to ditch unpleasant thoughts remained intact.

On the other hand, she could actually be losing it, a rare disease, a little tumor in the wrong part of the brain—it happened. That would be something to check out at her next residence, find a doc, get some pictures . . . scary, yes, but not nearly as scary as the possibility that there was no material cause at all.

Marvel rolled a fat joint and sat out on the little deck that faced the sea and smoked it all. Things slowed down in her head and she discovered a keen interest in the details of the scene before her. The sun had sunk behind the mountains, but the sky was bright faded blue, high clouds above; on the horizon they clumped low and heavy in squadrons--a storm passing to the northwest. It would blow through late tonight or tomorrow morning, and afterwards there would be a couple of days of good breaks and prime kiteboarding.

She sucked the joint down to a spark the size of a Xanax, discarded it on the beach, and then ate a Xanax. Then she went back to her room, lay on the day bed, and let the drugs spackle over her terror until sleep was able to make its welcome entrance.

When she awakened, the window was full of evening blue and her mouth felt like it was stuffed with a very old kitchen sponge. She smelled hot charcoal and roasting pork, heard music coming from the main house, guitar riffs, drums and cymbals, a phrase on a bass. The band had arrived, and the party was gearing up.

She applied makeup, brushed her hairdo back in place, and donned her new outfit. Searching her image in the mirror, she found an unfamiliar difficulty in selecting the proper face from her extensive catalog. Who was she really? Not a question that had ever engaged her for long, but which now seemed important.

But she was a pro; she looked again and the Good-Time

Girl smiled back from the mirror. She strode out on her new stilettos to join the fun.

The 'ohana always threw a big party to launch an operation, and these had become a tradition both among the grifters of the island and the extensive real 'ohanas of Jumbo and the Cars. The caterer (a Honda in-law) had set up long tables on the terrace and the crew, young men and women wearing aloha shirts, heads wrapped in black bandanas, were bringing out plates from the kitchen, all lined with banana leaves and laden with the Hawaiian hors d'oeuvres called pupus, plus salvers of barbecued shrimp and chicken, rice, poi, lau lau, and various kinds of marinated raw fish--poke. A bar had been set up in front of the big traveler's palm and a bartender, Ray Honda's cousin, Donny, was dispensing his famous deadman's punch, and machine-rolled pakalolo ciggies to those who wanted that instead or in addition.

She spotted Ray himself toting a washtub full of ice and beer, gave him a wave and a howzit, brah. He returned a grin, and, resting the washtub on his hip if as if it had been a beach ball, he scooped her off her feet and gave her a wet kiss on the cheek. He smelled of marijuana and beer, which is how he smelled nearly all the time. Ray had never felt the need for a party to party.

"Looks like it's happening, Ray. It'll be a good send-off."

"Hey, yeah, and you lookin 'ono, teeta. Wahfor you all dress up da kine oshare?"

"Oh, you know—make sure Sami dem don't forget me."

"So, aftahs, you gon stick aroun?"

"No, I'm a take me a break. I'm a go to Italy fo two tree weeks."

"Italy. Get some pizza, eh?"

"Probably. You seen Jumbo tonight?"

"Buggah's around. Eh, I got to drop this tub ovah deah. Laydahs, eh, Marvel."

"Laydahs," Marvel replied, and went over to the bar, where Donny supplied her with a joint and a drink of cold mango juice. She stood leaning there, sipping and smoking, feeling over-dressed, but not caring. It was good dope, and soon she had the nice dreamy feeling that could turn to paranoia if she let it, and her face had gone numb. She saw Esme and waved. Esme seemed to see her and then pretended she didn't, and turned away to talk to a couple of locals.

Marvel spotted Jumbo Wedge walking toward the buffet, accompanied by a girl in tiny white shorts and an aloha shirt three sizes too large. Jumbo saw her coming, but, remarkably, pretended he hadn't and began to fill his plate. She picked up a plate and joined the chow line, insinuating herself next to him on the side not occupied by the girl, who looked no more than seventeen, pretty and dim, Jumbo's usual pick.

"Jumbo?" Marvel said. "What's happening?"

He gestured to the spread. "Nice grind, eh?"

"Yeah, nice. What's going on, Jumbo? I just waved at Esme and she looked at me like I was pig shit."

Jumbo glanced meaningfully at the girl, who was loading up on shrimp as if she thought they were an endangered species. He said, low, "Half an hour, in the back, under the tree." He turned his back on her and advised the girl to leave room for the pork.

There was a stone bench under the mango tree, and Marvel sat on it and waited, drinking chilled mango juice and dragging on a joint. She had not, in fact, prevented the paranoia, and she sucked in more dope to let it roam free. Paranoia seemed appropriate at the moment.

"There you are," said Jumbo, almost in her ear.

"Whoa!" she cried, jumping and slopping her drink. The ground was littered with crunchy mango leaves, yet she had not heard him approach.

"How the fuck do you do that? And I wish you wouldn't. It creeps me out."

"My ninja skills. Meanwhile, what the hell did you do to piss off Overby?"

"I didn't know he was pissed. Why doesn't he just come over and talk to me?"

"Yo, do I look like his daddy? All I know, he's been up in Sami's office with Tanaka and Esme since he got here. I heard there was yelling involved."

"Overby doesn't yell."

"Well, then he just started. Then he lets Esme go and calls me in, and tells me I'm supposed to watch you like a hawk until he gets back from Hong Kong, and make sure you stay in the house and don't communicate. No laptop, no cell, and stay out of Data."

"What the fuck. I'm supposed to fly to Italy tomorrow. He *told* me to take a break. I have reservations."

"Yeah, well, too bad. No Italy. No Honolulu, for that matter. You got to stay put. It's a shame—sounds like a nice trip."

Marvel started to cry. She could cry on demand, like any good actor, but this one bordered on the real.

"Why?" she wailed. "What did I do? Could someone please tell me what I did wrong?"

"Something about a cell phone?"

"Oh, for God's sake. Is *that* what this is about? All right, I fucked up. I should have junked the cell I used in the last op, I should have trashed it at the airport, but I forgot. All right? That was it, and when I found it, I got rid of it. It's landfill now, nobody's going to find it."

That was one of Overby's dicta. When caught, offer a small truth to protect a larger lie. She tried to watch Jumbo's face, but it was in deep shadow, lit only by fairy lights and the flickering tiki torches.

"Well, you can explain all that when he gets back. I'm sorry, teetah, I got my orders, eh?" He paused and added, "But it's more than the cell phone."

"What do you mean?"

"You used it. And not just once. You know what a Stingray is? No? It's one electronic spy t'ing Esme has on the property. It picks up dakine electronic transmission, like wifi or a cell call. Esme went over her logs today, and found some email you sent on it."

"Oh God. That was just some dude I was playing, a haole tourist. I even told Esme about it."

Jumbo shrugged. "Hey, I'm just saying what they told me. But I saw Overby, and he wasn't worried about any haole tourist. He was talking about you reaching out to your last mark. Where is he, by the way?"

"How the fuck should I know? This is crazy, Jumbo. Why the hell should I get with a mark? He's a fucking *mark*. Esme must've screwed up, or . . . I don't know, maybe she has it in for me, she's trying to get me in hot water with Overby."

"Why would she do that? I thought you two were best buddies."

"We had a fight. Also, look at her. You notice a little difference in appeal? She's always been pissed I was the star of the show, and now that Overby's dumped me for this Chinese thing, she saw her chance to fuck me up."

That was weak, and she was pretty sure Jumbo hadn't bought it. Should she make a play for him? He'd always had a thing for her. But no, she was an expert judge of the vulnerability of men, and while she might have rolled him if she'd had the time, she didn't *have* time, that was the problem, and Jumbo prided himself on his discipline. Nor did he rise to the bait now.

"Well, teetah, you'll have to take all that up with the man when he gets back from China. And in case you're thinking of an end run, he said he didn't want to see you at all until then. Meanwhile, I better get back to the party before that kid comes looking for me. But also, I meant it about sticking to the house. I don't want to have to, you know, get rough with you."

"I get it, Jumbo. Tanks, eh."

"Minors, teetah. Laydahs."   He disappeared into the dark in his usual disconcertingly noiseless way.

For what seemed like a long time, Marvel sat under the mango tree, listening to the ocean and the burble and thump of the party, recognizing that she was now at the lowest point of her life. She had assumed until this wretched evening that, quite aside from the criminal enterprise there were bonds of affection tying her to these people: a friend in Esme, a brother in Jumbo, a mentor in Overby, and a lover in Sami. What more did a girl need?

Now, in an instant, it had all turned to ash. Unless Sami could save her again. That could work. It had worked once, in Macau; maybe she could make it work again. She went back into the house, using the rear entrance and went to the upstairs bathroom, where she fixed the wreckage of her face and primped her hair.

Back on the terrace, dancing was now general, the band was covering Bruddah Walter's *Sweet Lady of Waiahole*, and the place was scented by the kerosene of the torches and the herbal fug of prime weed. She searched the crowd for Sami, but he was not at the round glass table where he usually held

213

court during parties. Esme was dancing with Pinkie Honda, and judging by the slack look on her face she was some distance down the road to oblivion. Overby was standing nearby, talking to some Asians she didn't recognize.

Marvel reversed direction to avoid his glance and spotted Haulani Ford towering over the normal people, swaying with his eyes closed, a spliff the size of a corona stuck in the corner of his mouth. She went to him and nudged his massive flank. His eyes opened sleepily and he offered a toothy smile.

"Eh, teetah, howzit?"

"I'm good, Ford. Phat party, eh?"

"Da max. You like dance?"

Ford was six foot five and something north of three hundred twenty pounds, but he was surprisingly light on his feet. He grasped Marvel's hand in one the size a fielder's glove and led her onto the floor. Others made a lot of room. Ford was as friendly as ever, which meant he had not been informed of her new poisoned status, that, or he was too stoned to care. They danced to the end of the song and then Marvel asked, "Have you seen Sami recently?"

"Ah, I no wen see him fo maybe an hour. He was wit dat chica from Freddy Azikawa's crew, you know? One pake tita, name I tink Angie Lee? She wen do put-ups fo dakine condo grift. You know dat grift?"

She did. Freddy Azikawa ran a lightweight version of what Overby was planning to run on the Chinese satrap. The pretty girl meets the tourist in the Waikiki bar. They become pals. She invites him to visit her in her time-share condo, which is not her condo at all, and after a certain amount of snuggling, she confesses she can't make her payment this month, and wouldn't it be a good idea for him to ditch his little room at the Hilton and move in her with her for the remainder of his stay? It's cheaper than the hotel, but the owner needs a direct bank transfer. The mark gives up his bank account and routing number, they do the deal, and he goes back the Hilton to get his stuff. When he gets back to the condo, the girl is gone, and so is all the money in his account.

Marvel had a bad feeling about this Angie, so she made an excuse to Ford and went back upstairs to the bedroom she shared with Sami. The door was closed, locked in fact, and from behind it came the sounds--bed creaks and enthusiastic cries--of a girl interviewing for a job. It wasn't the sex part she minded—it was that Angie was a put-up player. They were clearly looking for to replace Marvel, which rendered it unlikely that any move of hers on Sami would be successful. And Angie wouldn't have to take Chinese lessons either.

Now, rather to her surprise, she felt not despair, but rage, not against the gang, but toward the man who'd ruined her life. She ran down the back stairs and out through the garden to Data. In her room, she grabbed her laptop and the freezer bag in which she'd stashed the money and the Alison Hill ID. What else? A pair of good jeans and a cotton sweater, a pair of sneakers. As she passed the door to Esme's office, she stopped, looked around, and slipped in.

She knew where Esme kept her red notebook. She spread it flat, found the written passwords and used them to open the files that delineated the shell corporations and offshore accounts through which the gang laundered its loot. She copied these files onto a thumb drive, returned the notebook to its drawer and, feeling like a thief (a familiar feeling), she headed for the beach. Just let the bastard be there, she thought as she set up her hot spot, switched on Skype, and tapped in his number.

He answered on the third warble. He was dressed for the outdoors, his face reddened with cold. He was out of breath, but smiling.

"There you are again," he said. "That was a short forever."

"Oh, fuck you, and damn you to hell. You ruined my life."

"I'm happy to hear it," Bernard replied, still smiling.

"You're *happy*? What the fuck does that *mean*?" The house was twenty yards away, but Marvel thought that the wind and surf would cover her screamed reply.

In the same maddeningly calm voice, he said, "It means I believe life inside a criminal conspiracy is a miserable life, despite its obvious attractions."

"Oh, now you're my *daddy*? Who asked you to fuck up my existence? Who the hell do you think you are?"

"Who asked me? Well, *you* did. Nobody forced you to return my texts. Nobody forced you to start Skyping me. But if you sincerely desire to return to a comfortable life with a gang of thieves and murderers, there's nothing to stop you from going back."

"What're you talking about. They know about us. They can't read my emails, but they know I sent them."

"Not to mention the Skypes."

"No, they go out from my hot spot, she won't have those. God, I'm not that dumb. But they have the texts and the emails. Meanwhile, I can't leave the island. I can't even leave the house. When Overby gets back I'll be fish food."

"Not so. You could say you realized that when I texted you, it showed that I was still on the hook, and that you could tap me again. They must know that the easiest mark is one who's already been hit. So contacting me was maybe just a venial sin, easily forgiven. And, of course, you could close the deal by telling them where I am. Even if they don't go for stripping me further, they'll need that information to find me and arrange an accidental death. You could even offer to lead them to me, to winkle me out of a place where I'm fairly safe into a place where I'm not. It'd work, I'm sure of it."

"What is this, some kind of half-assed con?"

"No. You're the conman, not me. I'm being perfectly clear, honest, and transparent. And the central fact here, which you keep ignoring, is that you returned my touch. Which means that you understood there was something rotten in your life. You're a thief, but there was a line you wouldn't cross, there was some inherent decency in you. You may have kidded yourself that you were happy in your gang of criminals, but by now you must realize that was all an illusion. There was no real trust, no real intimacy, no food for your soul. You have an opportunity to return to that life, as I've explained, only now you know just how heartless and vicious they are, and, make no mistake, you would have to become just as bad. You have to make an unambiguous moral choice here. And I've just offered to risk my life for you, to keep you safe, so you have to throw *that* into the mix too."

Marvel stared at the face on the screen, keeping silent while her mind raced to figure the angle. It had to be an angle. He was setting her up, setting the gang up for a date with the police. That had to be it, because there was no one who was like he was pretending to be. This was what the marks feel when the put-up is running, she thought, the growing confidence, the sense that this stranger is the One, the rescuer who will fix their broken lives and make their dreams come true. At the same time she was trying to relegate to her amnesia closet the startling fact that he seemed to know how she felt, that he understood what had happened to her. But that had to be bullshit. Had to be.

Her finger tapped the track pad. The red disconnect button appeared. She was moving the cursor to touch it, when he started talking again.

"And here's another thing to think about," he said. "I spent a big chunk of my life in a wonderful, vital relationship, which I imagine is something you've never had. Louise had many virtues, but I didn't know about them until later.

"Strange to say, the love came first. I was in a class with her in college, that's how we met. I couldn't take my eyes off her--the way she moved, how she dressed, those little motions that identify an individual. Her hair. When we started dating, of course, I discovered all these terrific qualities, but that wasn't the *thing*. The thing was *prior* to all that.

"And it allowed me to look inside her, to see the stuff that wasn't so terrific, and could feel this aching sympathy for all her shit, her vices, all the stuff she was ashamed of. I wanted her to feel better, and the same went from her to me, although in honesty, I was carrying a hell of a lot more garbage than she was. What you need to know, Marvel, is that I felt the same *thing* when you came up to me in that bookshop and afterward, when we had that conversation about my star signs and that conversation about your face.

"You felt it too, never mind that you thought you were just there to cheat me. You're a splendid actress, but you're not *that* good. In fact, I was so stunned with love you barely needed to run the con. I would have gone for a perpetual motion machine or the Spanish Prisoner. You thought you were in control, a grifter doing her job, but our meeting had cosmic elements, which is why you couldn't forget me either."

She felt the pulse pounding in her temples and she discovered she was holding her breath. Her finger sagged away from the bye-bye button.

He said, "That's the truth, and the truth is what you're starving for, dying for, and you will die in your spirit if you decide to go back to that life. So, what'll it be, Marvel Gafney? Door number one or door number two?"

"It's too late," she wailed. "I wanted to run, I made plans, but I'm trapped!"

He laughed. "No, you're free," he said.

As soon as he said that, it popped into her head.

"I have to go now," she said, and now she really did break the connection. She tapped keys, bringing up the tide table for Lanikai, for the Kawii Channel and for the western end of Molokai Island. She read good news: with this bright moon and the tide being right, it could work. She hadn't realized until this minute that she had unconsciously provided herself with the canonical second route of escape.

Thirteen

Bernard stared at the blank Skype screen for some moments. He didn't try to re-establish a connection. Instead, he put on his Barbour jacket, called the dog and went out. It had snowed all night on St. Roch and the fresh snow squeaked merrily under his shoes as he trudged up the hill to the gatehouse, bearing Brother Dominic's dinner. The ice cream bar sat in a plastic sack, there being no need now for an insulated bag or any miracles. It was snowing again, or maybe this was sleet, tiny ice spherules that stung his face.

He had been taking the treat to the anchorite monk for nearly a week and had made a habit of staying a while to talk with the old man. Sometimes he would find a pick-up truck or a worn sedan in the driveway, which meant that one of the locals was consulting the sage. On those occasions, Bernard would amuse the dog with a ball until the seeker emerged and drove off, sometimes with a shy nod, never a word.

Then he would go in, present his offering, and watch the monk eat his meal. Dominic attacked his ice cream bar with the concentration and pleasure of a toddler. He had other child-like qualities: the guileless stare, the absence of inhibition, the simplicity of expression. As a writer of fiction, Bernard was ever on guard against the cliché, and here was one, the Holy Fool. This did not, however, prevent him from falling a little under the man's spell.

Brother Dominic had been a monk at St. Roch for almost sixty years, having flunked out of a minor seminary in his home town of Elmira, owing to an inability to absorb Latin grammar, or, it appeared, much of anything else. He had arrived at St. Roch one frigid autumn day, aged eighteen, and asked to join the brotherhood. They duly enrolled him as a lay brother and worked him at a variety of manual tasks until he grew too feeble to do anything but sit and watch the gate. So far as was known, he had never seen a movie, or watched television, or owned anything, or handled money since his arrival.

Today the drive was empty, so Bernard knocked and walked in. The monk was sitting in his rocking chair in front of an old cast-iron wood stove. Besides these, the room contained only a plain pine table covered with worn checkered oilcloth, a straight chair, and a steel trunk. A shelf held a pair of mugs, some plates, a kettle, a Bible, and a breviary. Pinned to the wall were a colored print of the Virgin Mary with Child and one of the Sacred Heart (both in the sentimental style popular before 1960), and a framed black-and-white photograph of a family: father in suit and hat, mother in a dark shapeless dress, and nine children, dressed for church, in size order. One boy, aged around seven and barely discernible as the current occupant, was dressed in a white first communion rig. One end of the room was separated by a green cloth curtain, perhaps once a bedspread, through the gap in which could be seen a neatly made-up iron cot.

The monk had been sitting still as a gravestone and staring out the window, but he turned to Bernard with a smile. Cosmo, the monk's decrepit Dobe, raised his gray muzzle from his mat before the stove and uttered a mild growl.

When the ice cream bar was finished and its stick was clean, the monk tossed it into the blazing stove and said, "You seem lighter in spirit today. Did you get your miracle?"

Bernard had to think about this for a moment. Of course, Brother Dominic knew the whole sad story. It had come pouring out during the course of the first visit. Dominic had asked him how he did and Bernard had found himself gushing in a manner he normally despised, including the tears he had not shed at Louise's funeral. Marvel had been introduced and her adventures recounted during subsequent feeding runs. When the monk mentioned miracle, Bernard recalled their recent Skyped conversation.

"It's strange how the worst sinners sometimes retain scruples," said the monk.

"Yes, it doesn't sound like much, that she's a thief, but not a murderer . . ."

"Oh no, that's not the point, you know. Of course God forgives our petty sins, but that's not what the religion is for. Our Lord spent his time on earth among very bad people indeed. I don't think Christ died on the cross because Brother Lawrence took an extra piece of corn bread. The worse the sin, the more the need, the greater the outpouring of grace. I've listened to people sit in that chair and tell me the most dreadful things. Murder, theft, rape, incest, atrocities done to children. You mustn't think simple country people are immune to vice. The opposite, in my experience. But you say she plans to turn away from that life. That must make you very happy."

"It would, if she could get away. That's currently doubtful. She lives in the midst of some desperate and dangerous men. And then there's no guarantee that she's going to come to me. Even if she does, what would we do then? These people are not about to let either of us go. We know too much."

Bernard laughed and added, "Perhaps we do need some kind of miracle."

"Do you believe in miracles?" Dominic asked. Bernard had slipped the question and answered, "Karl Rahner said, 'I don't believe in miracles, but they sustain me.'"

"Is that a friend of yours?"

Bernard explained that Karl Rahner was one of the great Catholic theologians of the twentieth century. Dominic shrugged and said, "I don't understand theology. It all seems so simple to me."

"You must think I'm stupid or crazy, involving myself with a woman who cheated me and whom I barely know."

"I never knew any women that way--but I don't imagine this is all about lust."

"No. And I don't really know what it *is* about. Or whether it's a good thing or not. And I keep thinking, why *me*? I had a perfectly ordinary, successful life--a home and a wife I loved, work I was good at, that was rewarded. I was rich, in fact. And suddenly, for no apparent reason, not only did I lose most of that, but I find myself desperately wanting to be with a woman with whom I have nothing in common, a genuinely bad person who utterly betrayed me. I realize it's stupid to ask why, but *why*?"

"Yes, that's what everyone wants to know, but it *is* stupid to ask, as you say, and the question has no answer. There was a woman who lived a long time ago, in England, I think, and the people were suffering from a great plague and a war, and everything was ruined. She lived like me, an anchoress, except they walled her up in a little cell and people came and asked her why, why these horrible times had come to them and she said, 'Wouldst thou witten what thy Lord means by these things? Wit thou well: love is His meaning.'"

"Yes, Julian of Norwich," said Bernard. "Fourteenth century. It was the Black Death."

"Oh, you heard that before? I learned it from a sampler my mother had on the wall. When I was a kiddie I thought she'd made it up. So that's one answer. God's love is beyond human understanding and sometimes it causes great pain. And the other answer is that the Holy Spirit has a sense of humor. There's a saying, if you want to make God laugh, tell him your plans, but of course, God knows our plans and everything else.

And He must be laughing all the time at us creatures, scurrying around, chasing the things of this world like squirrels after nuts, fearing death, pretending we're not holy beings tied to Him by unbreakable shining cords."

"I'm not sure I believe all that."

To Bernard's surprise, the monk laughed and slapped his thigh, like a guy in a bar at a dirty joke. "Oh, you don't? Well, neither do I, from time to time. What, you don't think religious have doubts? Oh, we do, we do. We're not like Cosmo and Murtagh, are we? They have no doubts about their masters, but we do about ours. It's part of original sin, I believe, but don't ask me to explain that. I just know it's so, and looking at the world as it is—why, you'd have to be a fool *not* to doubt the goodness of God." He paused, his mouth opened as if for the next word, then snapped shut and he seemed to be listening to nothing, or to the wind or the tick of sleet on the window. Then he said, "She'll come to you."

"You think?"

"Yes, as I say, God does like His joke. She'll come, and then your troubles will really begin." He laughed, and after a stunned moment, Bernard did too.

"What did you think of that, Murtagh?" Bernard asked as they walked back to the monastery.

<That dog is very old. He hardly has any real smell left, just old smell.>

"I meant the man."

<The same. Also, he has no fear at all.>

***

Marvel was in the water-fun equipment shed, working by the light of a mini-flashlight gripped in her teeth. She heaved the stuff-bag of a ten-meter sail from the shelf to the ground, then the tackle bag and the twin-tip board. She slipped from her beautiful dress into an old Speedo, donned a wet-jacket. She corseted herself in her harness, strapped on an inflatable life vest, and attached Jumbo's Garmin GPS to her left wrist.

She found Jumbo's waterproof backpack and stuffed the beautiful dress and the other clothes into it, then a freezer bag with her money and fake ID. The terrific shoes? So hard to abandon these, but you couldn't wear stilettos on a kite board, so off with them, and add to the backpack a pair of rubber slippers from a box of odds and ends. Arms into the backpack—no, first attach the camel water bag to the backpack with its straps, then put on the pack, then pick up the board, sail bag, and harness bag and stagger out to the beach. The moon was up, near the full, and bright. She'd forgotten the pump and had to run back and grab it.

Unpack the kite, spread it, colorless in the moonlight, kick sand over the windward edge, trail out the lines downwind, straighten the tangles. Connect the pump. It started its low-pressure whir and the ribs began to plump up. Time pressed, she could hear the sound of music from the party, in a few minutes or so someone might miss her, but she made herself be careful, each lark's-head knot just so.

She checked her watch: twelve-thirty a.m. Not that great. She figured three hours for the journey, and by then it would be high-water slack tide at her destination. Sunrise was at six-thirty, which meant that although she would not be able to see her landing, the barrier reefs guarding the target beach would be under water. She'd once seen a kiteboarder dump on an exposed reef and lose all the skin from the back of his head to his heels. It was far better to land by moonlight than take a chance of getting hurt on a reef.

The wind, a steady northeast trade, was feeling the distant storm, and veering south. It was considered imprudent to launch with the wind off the beach, but not this time, because she was not coming back to this beach tonight. Or ever.

She placed the board on the wet sand and switched on the Garmin. The thing reached up into outer space and made friends with the geostationary satellites. Numbers showing her location appeared. Pressing a button brought up the map page and a tiny arrow that showed where she was on the beach at Lanikai. She expanded the map to show the windward coast of Oahu and the blankness of sea between it and the western tip of Molokai Island, then zoomed in on Papohaku Beach, where she marked a waypoint.

That was her destination. If everything worked, the Garmin would show the little arrow moving at an azimuth of about 120 degrees, and all she had to do was keep it on its path by riding the wind across thirty miles of open ocean.

Marvel had never been beyond sight of land on a kiteboard, but she knew that people did it all the time. A kiteboarder had recently sailed from Lisbon to Madeira, a distance of 472 nautical miles, so this was really a piece of cake, except it was night and she was doing it without a support team, and she was scared shitless.

She adjusted her harness, hooked on the chicken loop that attached it to the control bar and the kite lines, snapped on the safety strap. The pump noise changed to the grinding roar that signaled its high-pressure mode. Soon the ribs were hard as a car tire. As she knelt to unscrew the valve, she heard the crunch of steps on sand.

""'Ey, Marvel, what you doin?"

Haulani Ford was standing twenty feet away, clutching a bottle in one hand, swaying like a palm in a stiff breeze.

"What's it look like, brah?" she replied, making an effort to keep her voice light. "I gon kiteboard."

"Fo real? Inna nighttime? You all buss o' what?"

"Nah, Ima gon tak one little ride roun dat Flat Island, come right back, eh?"

"I tink you one lolo teeta, you. You wanna hep wit launch da kite?"

"No, tanks, brah, I wan go practice dakine solo beach launch. Latahs, eh."

With that, Marvel pulled the bar, the lines tightened, the kite threw off its burden of sand and shot up into the starry sky. Marvel shifted the kite into the static zone, where the pull was minimal, walked down to the water and waited for a wave. Lanikai usually had no surf to speak of but the distant storm had kicked it up.

She waited for the moment when the last wave had gone slack and the next one was just showing a white crest. Then she kicked her board into the shallow water, stepped on with her right foot, and gave the kite some power. A little tricky here, but she stayed vertical, wobbled once, and then got both feet aboard and safely in their straps. Once stable, she steered a course for Flat Island, a rectangular acre or so of sand and dry scrub a few hundred yards offshore. As she came around the seaward side of the island, she moved the kite into its power window and headed out to sea.

At the surf-line she edged hard, tensed up her lines, released her heel edge, rose on her toes and flew into the air, rising up above the breakers' foam. Judging distances, she now found, was harder at night, and she landed badly, but then she almost always flopped her butt in the water after getting any serious air, and was at least experienced at recovery. When she was stable, she consulted the Garmin and steered until the tiny arrow sat neatly on the course she'd laid, across the Kaiwii Channel to Molokai.

The tension that had been roiling her gut for the past week faded. She didn't think about Overby, or Sami or Jumbo, she didn't even think about Bernard Goodrich, or what the fuck she was doing in heading in his general direction. This was why she rode kiteboards, to become entirely a physical being, consumed by the natural, the only realities wind, the tension of the bar, the angle of the kite, the angle of the board. Only bird-thoughts occupied her mind.

On the beach, Haulani Ford watched Marvel disappear behind Flat Island. For a few minutes he could see her kite flying above the loom of the island, but soon lost it against the surrounding darkness. He sighed and sat heavily in the sand, and sucked coconut rum from his bottle. He lit a fat spliff and smoked it to a spark. Then he waited for Marvel to reappear around the island. He waited a long time. He had the thought that he should get up, find Jumbo and tell him about Marvel going kiteboarding at night, but there didn't seem to be any big rush about it and besides, the stars were whirling around and it seemed a good idea to take a little rest. Ford leaned back on the sand and quickly passed into snoring sleep.

The seas in the Channel were running around three feet, with a making tide and the usual cross-currents, so Marvel had to constantly adjust her speed and course. The wind had freshened and backed, so that it blew almost directly away from her destination, and the tide and currents pushed her to the southeast. She had to jibe twice, which was terrifying in these seas, in the dark, the precise maneuvering of a kite she could barely see, keeping the correct angle on the madly pitching board.

After two hours of this battling, her legs were dead and shaking and she was nauseated from the constant heaving. The Garmin also had bad news: her leeway and the current had driven her too far to the southeast, which meant she would miss her target, a narrow beach in the middle of the western edge of Molokai, and be swept around La'au Point to the reef-encrusted and inaccessible south shore.

There came a time when she no longer had the strength to fight the situation. She put the kite into its static zone and sat down in the water. It was strangely comfortable. The board was just buoyant enough to keep her feet floating and the wet-jacket and the buoyancy vest and the mild tug of the kite kept her upper body from sinking. She knew she was in trouble, but was not particularly frightened. Just now she was as safe as a message in a bottle, bobbing in the swells. She would miss her tide, yes, but on the other hand it would be light in a few hours and then she would crank up the kite and sail on. In the meantime, there would be floating, moonlight, the elements and solitude. Her life was like that in a way, always alone, self-dependent, mastering the forces.

And this condition had another, weirder effect: it seemed to release once more the springs of her memory. Marvel's memories were largely unpleasant ones, and if asked about her life, she dodged the question, or lied outright, but alone on a board, the memories flooded in. Stuff popped into her head that she'd thought buried—it was like watching a movie, and now, alone on the frothy, star-dappled sea, they came, stronger than ever before.

Marvel leaves her watery couch, and rises. She sees herself floating on the sea, sees her resting kite, bobbing with the swells. She rises higher through the clouds, toward the moon. She's having one of her visions, but she's not disturbed or frightened. The moon is oddly yellow, not moon-yellow, but toy-yellow.

It becomes a nightlight in the shape of a yellow duck, plugged into a baseboard by her bed in her grandmother's house. Her grandmother is seated on the edge of the bed, talking. Something bad has happened that day in school, a bullying jibe about the criminal parents. Marvel had gone after the biggest bully with fists and nails and there had been blood shed. Gran had been called away from work and when she learned what had happened, she gave the teacher and the principal a piece of her mind. Now all is calm, tears dried, a dinner of mac and cheese consumed, TV watched past her usual bedtime, a treat.

Her gran is telling Marvel she's a good girl, that she has nothing to do with what her parents did. Marvel knows she is not a good girl, that she is bad to the bone, as the mean girls in school had chanted. Her gran is saying when people are mean and spiteful to you, when they hurt you, when you think you're helpless, you're really not. There's a magic circle inside you, where the real you lives, and that magic circle is full of love. I'm there and so is your momma. Your momma loved you, although you can't remember her. She made a lot of mistakes, she took up with a man I would not have picked for her, and she had a life that ended badly. But that has nothing to do with you.

Gran says that God's love was in the magic circle and that it would protect her, even if terrible things were being done to her body and mind. Marvel didn't like hearing about God, because if God loved her, why did He make her bad? Now Marvel sees a vision within the vision, she sees what she was thinking when Gran said that about the magic circle. She was four, playing with Gertie, a little mutt dog they had then, black and sharp-nosed, with a whippy tail and a white blaze on its chest. It was a naughty dog, who would jump up on the counter and grab food.

She's playing with Gertie but consumed with desire for the chocolate chocolate-chip cookies Gran has just made and stored on the little shelf above the counter in the jar that came from when Gran and Grandpa who was dead went to Seattle for the World's Fair. It was a glass jar and you could see the cookies and she wanted them so badly (more than one!) and what she did was take a chair and climb up and being really careful slid the cookie jar off the shelf, while Gertie jumped and whined, and just when she had it almost safe on the kitchen table the jar slipped from her hands and shattered on the floor.

Marvel tried to make the broken pieces go together and cut her hands on the glass. She ate a cookie and bled on the other cookies and on Gertie, who was snapping them up as fast as she could, and then Marvel had a thought of a kind she had never had before, which showed how really bad she was. First she moved the chair back under the kitchen table. Then she ate another cookie and wiped her face with a dishtowel very carefully so that there'd be no chocolate marks and wrapped her hand in the towel.

She ran out into the back yard, where Gran was pruning the apple trees, and she told Gran that Gertie had gone up on the counter and pushed the jar down. Her cut hand hurt a little but not bad enough to make her cry. She made herself cry. It was her first con. When they got back to the kitchen, Gertie had eaten all the cookies and Gran burst into tears and took off after Gertie with a flyswatter. Later, Gertie didn't come when called and they found her under the house, stiff and dead. Gran told her chocolate was poison to dogs. Marvel absorbed this remarkable fact, then asked when they could get another dog.

Were there other dogs? If so, she could not bring them to memory. Her grandmother was sick, although she didn't learn about that until later. On the night of the magic circle, she recalled now the intensity of her gaze, and the color of her face in the duck-light. Mind what I'm saying, honey. I will not always be here to protect you, but *that* will protect you. Tell me you understand. She said yes, Gran, but she really didn't.

A thin cloud passed before the moon; Marvel was back on the waves, but only lightly attached to the present. She bobbed on the seas, the kite-lines tugged gently, carrying her somewhere. The GPS was no help, for the little arrow sat on a blank screen, no destination or waypoints showing. She wondered vaguely why she was not more upset. Hypothermia? No, the sea was warm and she had a wet-jacket on, but on the other hand, neither was she exactly *there*. Nor was she exactly alone.

They weren't voices, like crazy people had, more like presences, mighty and benign, connected in some way with thoughts appearing in her mind and with these memories, or visions. They or It was what had made her not throw the Miranda cell phone away, and here was that presence again. This was why she wasn't scared out of her gourd by her situation, it was like heroin in a way, which she had sampled a couple of times, or no, more like opium, which she had come to sort of enjoy in Macau, dreamy and comfortable, like sitting in a cozy chair, mildly stoned, watching a movie on TV.

The moon emerged again, looking pale and lopsided, with smudged eyes, and now it was her Uncle Claude's face, pressing too close to hers. There *had* been another dog, she recalled it now, how could she have forgotten Duffy, a brindled shepherd mix, who was taken away when her grandmother died and she had to go live with Aunt Ethel.

That face, gross and panting, foul breath, hands under the bedclothes, her nightgown. This is the night she takes the steak knife from under her pillow.

Aunt Ethel beating at her with a coat hanger, but she has the knife.

Aunt Ethel taking the bloody bedclothes from her bed and making up Claude's bed with them, while waiting for the ambulance and the police. Then she tells the cops that Marvel attacked her son in his room for no reason, except she has the Devil in her. Marvel stays mum, silent to the cops, to the social worker, to her public defender. There is nothing to say: she is bad, this is what bad girls get. They send her to Oak Creek, to be with the other bad girls.

The moon became the moon again, but paler, because the sky had lightened. Marvel came back to her body with a start. The rocking had eased, the stormy chop now a gentle swell. She checked the Garmin, which told her that it was past six a.m. and that she was just off the southern coast of Molokai. She used the fifth line to re-launch her kite. It shot up into the mild breeze and pulled her up on her board. She saw the white finger of La'au lighthouse just emerging from the gloom, and steered wide of the point, heading northwest on a broad reach.

The wind freshened as she came around the lee of the island but she kept the power on the kite and bowled along, kicking up a little rooster tail, letting the kite pull her from crest to crest of the chop. She felt fine, curiously rested despite the strange night. As the sun rose over the low mountains of Molokai, the world turned pink and she found herself opposite Papohaku and its three miles of white beach.

There was a break in the offshore reef at the center of this beach at high tide, and she had planned to cross it then, but after the hours she had spent drifting in that uncanny dreamlike whatever-it-was, the tide had ebbed and she could see white spume flying above the exposed red-brown lava rock. She cruised back and forth a thousand yards off the beach like a chicken looking for a gap in a fence, but could find no clear path through the breakers.

Or no clear path on the surface. There was plenty of air, however. Marvel realized that she was going to have to fly over fifty or so feet of reef covered with spikes and razors. Unlike most kiteboarders, Marvel didn't much care for flying. She could do chop hops, leaving the water for short distances, jumping off the face of a wave, but she did not like crashing, and kiteboarders who flew a lot crashed a lot too.

The distance she had to carry, moreover, was such that she was going to have to loop the kite, something she had done only once, under Jumbo's tutelage, and it had not gone well. She had slammed into the water from thirty feet up, landing on her back, generating a headache that lasted days.

But there did not seem to be an alternative. She couldn't afford to wait for the turn of the tide. Back at Lanikai, the house would be late to rise after the party, but Jumbo, who seemed impervious to intoxicants of all types, would be up by eight or nine, and he would want to make sure that she was where she should be, and sooner or later he would learn from Ford about her nocturnal excursion. He would guess she had gone to Molokai, the nearest island to Oahu, and with some phone calls he could have men waiting at every airport. So she steeled herself.

To loop a kite, the rider yanks hard on the back end of the control bar, sending the kite into a 360 degree loop that generates tremendous power, lifting the rider high into the air. Every normal instinct tells the rider to ease up on the bar, to bring the kite back to equilibrium, but this is just what the loop rider must not do. Once committed to the air you have to keep pulling. Marvel had no problem doing this in regular life, but this seemed to be different. She kept imagining the result of a crash—a cracked bone, a flayed back, either of which would mean being trapped and ending up in a windowless room with Overby.

She hesitated, therefore, riding up the back of wave after wave, declining to make her move, growing increasingly nervous.

Now. Go now.

It was not her voice that said it, but she obeyed. She edged her board harder and yanked the bar back. The kite dove toward the sea and began its loop. She released her edge, stood up on her toes, and took off.

Lean forward.

Her body screamed at her to lean back, but she obeyed the whatever, stuck her head and upper body out and bent her legs. Looking down she saw that she was forty feet high, traveling across the boiling reef. Slowly, she brought the kite back under control and kept it ahead of her in the direction she wanted to go. Keep the board pointed toward the kite and downwind, Jumbo's words, what she hadn't done when she crashed, but now she did as she dumped power from the kite and started to descend. She landed on three feet of smooth water as gently as an airliner, aching in every limb, weeping.

A short time later, having deflated and rolled up the kite and donned a tee-shirt, shorts, and rubber slippers, she walked through the forest of kiawe thorn trees that rimmed Papohaku Beach, and soon reached the road. She stood there in the sunshine, still trembling a little, smiling with her thumb out. After less than half an hour a car with two Australian boys in it stopped all grins.

This part was much, much easier than sailing from Oah'u to Molokai on a plank the size of a bath towel. Pretty girl Alison Hill charmed them out of their board shorts and they were only too glad to help her bring her kite and gear back to the road, and even more delighted when she offered to trade them a thousand dollars' worth of kiting equipment for a ride to Ho'olehua Airport. She just made the 7:30 to Maui. By noon, she was sipping first-class champagne six miles above the Pacific, heading toward Los Angeles. It took several glasses before she felt herself relax.

Fourteen

Just after one a.m., with the party still going strong, it struck Jumbo Wedge that he had not seen Marvel in a while. He checked the property and questioned the extra men he'd hired to secure it. They all knew Marvel, and knew also that she was not allowed to leave. None of them had seen her recently, and all were sure no car had taken her away. Her Porsche was in the garage, stuck behind the Bentley, so that was all right. He threaded through the revelers and up to the bedroom that Marvel shared with Sami Choi.

The door was thick teak, but through it he heard Sami laughing and a woman's laugh in response and drew the natural conclusion that the couple was grabbing a quickie. Such an excursion was not unknown at the parties here, and at the same moment he heard harsh, combative sounds coming from the patio. He judged that a beef was brewing among some of the rougher brahs, so he hurried down to restore order. After that, he thought no more about Marvel. Sami would keep her under his eye until Jumbo called for him in the morning.

When the party wound up, around three a.m., Jumbo paid off the band, generously tipped the catering staff, checked the property for strays and crashers, called cabs for those too impaired to drive, and supervised Sabine and Dado in cleaning up. He was a neat, orderly man and was scrupulous in this, although it did not come under his mandate as head of security. He had been a Marine non-commissioned officer too long to be comfortable with disorder, and he hated waking up to a filthy house. Overby had left around one, and Jumbo's chief responsibility was insuring that Sami made his flight the next morning. Overby had chartered a private jet, so the schedule was somewhat loose, but he had made clear that he wanted to be in the air by ten at the latest.

After a last look around, Jumbo dismissed his security guards, locked up the house, and went to bed with a seventeen-year-old girl from Pearl City who had compelling identification attesting to an age of twenty-two. Jumbo had wide experience with phony ID, but he let this slide. The girl was hot and he was off duty.

Jumbo awakened quickly, in his characteristic way, one moment blacked out, the next with his feet on the floor, ready for action. Immediately, he felt that something was not right. He checked his phone—7:10. He pulled on shorts and the shirt from last night, slapped the girl on the rump and told her to get up, slid into rubber slippers, and left the room. Entering the big house, he heard male voices in argument and followed the sound onto the patio, where he discovered Haulani Ford sitting at one of the umbrella tables with a can of beer and Ray Honda standing over him, looking pissed-off.

"Whassup, brahs?" said Jumbo.

"Oh, dis moke heah no guru fo nuttin," said Honda. "Lolo buggah. Go head, tell'im what you wen do las night!"

"I wen do nuttin," said Ford, as he rubbed the cold can over his face. "Fuckin teetah wen do. I tot it wen be cool. Da fuck I know she wen go an don come back?"

"What teetah?" asked Jumbo, as dread gathered in his gut.

"Marvel," said Ford, and told the story of her kiteboarding expedition in the small hours.

Jumbo uttered a curse and headed for the stairs at a run. He pounded on the locked door of Sami and Marvel's bedroom until it was opened by a sheet-wrapped Asian woman, grumpy and bed-headed.

"Why don't you just break the door down?" asked Angie Lee.

"Is Marvel in there?"

"Not my style, brah," raising an eyebrow.

"Fuck. Where's Sami?"

"In the shower. Hey, you can't . . ."

Jumbo had already pushed past her and into the steamy bathroom. Over the noise of the shower, he cried out, "Sami, get out of there. Marvel's gone."

The shower did not immediately cease.

"Sami, you hear me? Marvel's missing."

Now the shower stopped. A hand reached out, grabbed a white bath sheet off the rack, and Sami Choi emerged from behind the curtain, carefully wrapped. He walked past Jumbo, said a few words to Angie, who glared at both men and walked into the bathroom herself, slamming the door behind her.

Sami sat on the edge of the bed and lit a cigarette.

"You were supposed to watch her," he said in a calm, dangerous tone.

"I thought she was in here with you. I checked. I guess I should've busted the door down to see who you were fucking."

Sami gave him a look, but remained cool. "How did she get away?"

"She took a kiteboard, according to Ford. He didn't stop her either."

"Okay, she's in the wind," said Sami after a considerate couple of puffs, "so to speak. Where do you figure she went?"

"I was her, I would've stashed one car, some beach parking lot, clothes and shit in the trunk, fake ID. Head for the airport."

"We have people at the airport. They were alerted about Marvel, yes?"

"Yeah, and nobody called in."

"Means nothing," said Sami. "Marvel can look like anybody. But figure she knows the airport is watched and doesn't want to take a chance. Could she have made it to another island?"

"Last night?" Jumbo rocked his hand. "It was blowing pretty good in the channel. She's not that good of a kiter. She'd need a lot of luck, a night like last night."

"If Marvel wasn't really lucky, she'd be dead ten times," said Sami, and added musingly, "Or she could have drowned. That would make things easy."

"Yeah, but let's say she did get to Molokai. Then she would've had to get to the airport and fly out to Maui or HIA . . ."

"No, she wouldn't've come back here. If she made it across, she would've flown to Maui and then the mainland." Sami silently, slowly, finished his cigarette and stubbed it out in the careful manner of a man who has had to scrounge butts in his life.

He said, "Let's assume she got out of the islands. Can Esme get the manifests and gate camera feeds for all the flights that left early this morning?"

"Esme can get anything," Jumbo replied. "But what good would that do if she went through in disguise? And she sure as shit wouldn't use her real ID."

"No. But we can find out what name she's traveling under, if we find the guy who sold her the fake ID."

"You mean a local guy? But she could've bought it anywhere on the mainland."

"No. The only times she's been mainland since she started working with us she's been on operations, and she's watched almost all the time. Everyone she talks to is either a square or working for us. How's she going to find a high-class fake ID guy on the mainland? It's not like you can order on the computer. No, if she had fake paper, she bought it here and there aren't too many guys in that biz on the islands. So. You know what to do--go do it!"

"K, but are you gonna tell Overby?"

"Not unless I have to. Let him stay focused on this new operation. Plus I got a replacement for Marvel anyway." He glanced at the bathroom door. "Speaks Mandarin and Cantonese."

"Well, good," said Jumbo. He experienced an unfamiliar feeling of loss. He liked Marvel. He liked being with her and showing her the water, liked how she treated him, like he was a serious person, a player like Overby, not just muscle. He recalled how happy she was to be part of the 'ohana, which it now turned out was as much a family as a job at McDonald's.

Well, she had fucked up, and everyone understood the rules, and that the whole thing rested on everyone following them. They would find her, he was sure; they could find anyone, and he would see her again. And the mark. He thought he would arrange an accident where they couldn't tell that the mark had been torn up in painful ways before he died. Jumbo was not a cruel man, but he did look forward to the time when he had Marvel and she would think that by putting out he would let her go. That would be one good thing to come out of this fucking situation.

***

Alison Hill, innocent and free as only the dead can be, arrived by cab at her West Hollywood condo. It had the closed, musty scent of a place where someone has died, so she opened the windows, letting in warm, mildly toxic air and the traffic sounds from nearby Santa Monica Boulevard. It was a ground-floor apartment, two bedrooms, with a rear exit giving on to a small patio with pool. She'd paid a local decorator to furnish it, and he had done a quick efficient job, although he'd been a little hurt when she sent a check without actually inspecting his work.

On her instructions, he'd filled the shelves with books and bibelots, the walls with art, colorful prints and paintings in a popular ironic abstractish style and had included, at her request, family photos gleaned from junk shops. There were linens supplied, and simple toiletries, and the bed was made. The closets and bureaus held clothes in her size, supplied by a firm that shopped for people too busy or important to do it themselves. It looked like a real person lived there. Marvel had no immediate plans beyond simple survival. Meanwhile, the condo was a place where she could rest, which she now did, stripping naked, climbing into a terrycloth robe, and flopping on the bed. She slept for fourteen hours.

During these same hours, in her darkened room in Data, Esmeralda worked unsleeping; Jumbo supplied pills to keep her so. She worked not only because it was her job, but because she felt betrayed by her best friend. Marvel had told her some bullshit story about a new boyfriend to cover up she had something going on with a mark, and Esme had nearly spilled the one thing that Marvel was not supposed to know about, the stuff Jumbo and the Cars did so that the marks wouldn't make trouble and the gang could collect insurance.

Esme didn't like to think about that, so she didn't. She had developed the art of memory suppression to a high degree when she was a street kid in Olangapo when nasty things had been done to her and she had done nasty things to others, before she discovered the clean and dependable world of the machines. She often wished she *were* a machine, and now thought that it a good thing that she had lost her only friend; it had been an error to open up, to have feelings about Marvel and Ray Honda and the others. One day soon, she would return to the P.I. and buy a big house and have everything she wanted and take revenge on all the people who had treated like dirt the sad little girl she had been.

She was running facial recognition software on the gate camera dump from Honolulu International. The program supposedly ran by itself, but, unlike the programs in movies, it didn't take three seconds to pick a face out of thousands. Instead, it threw up dozens of false positives, each of which had to be checked out.

The software was ridiculously easy to spoof, and really only worked right on a full-face shot. Anything over twenty degrees off that angle yielded garbage. And Marvel, of course, knew this, the two women had even discussed ways of foiling airport FR controls. Cover the ears, wear sunglasses and a hat. In fact, Marvel had always pretended fascination with everything Esme did, and Esme had revealed all the secrets except one, which was that she monitored the electronic comm around the house with Stingray.

Had this interest, had the friendship itself been a con?

Esme found it hard to believe, although what did she know? It didn't matter now. Marvel the superstar was now a target, and whatever Esme's defects as a grifter, as a hunter she was a superstar herself. Wired like her own machines, she worked on through the hours.

Jumbo knew little about computers—he considered himself more of a people person——and while he knew Esme was good, he also thought that Marvel was too smart to be captured by software of any kind. Therefore, after dropping Sami and Overby at the general aviation terminal for their private flight to Hong Kong, he headed for a particular saloon in Kaka'ako. The district was not as rough as it had been when the fleet and the army were bigger and there were more geese to pluck, but, despite the pace of gentrification, it was still a good place to go when you wanted something illegal. When tourists got ripped off, as they occasionally do in Hawaii, the valuables, cards and papers so lifted often ended up in Kaka'ako, more specifically at a small saloon located between a body shop and a warehouse off Auahi Street.

The saloon was called the Scuttlebutt, or Tiger Jim's, depending on who you asked. Its front overhead, where a name would have been expected, was blank and covered with faded blue paint. It was open to the street under a wide awning, and dark within, the only artificial light emitted by beer signs: Longboard, Primo, Bud, Coors. The bartender was a wide-bodied local named Vernon Pukui, who was called Tiger Jim by nearly everyone.

"Howzit, Vernon?" said Jumbo, taking a barstool.

"Staying alive," said the bartender. "Coasting, you know? Long time, Jumbo."

"Yeah, I'm too good for this place now." He took a twenty from the roll in his pocket, set it on the bar, and ordered a Coke.

The bartender passed over a sweaty bottle and a glass of ice. "What, they no get Coke in Kailua?"

"Yeah, I like one Mexican Coke like this mo bettah, but." He drank his drink, they chatted amiably about mutual acquaintances and the prospects for the team at Kahuku High. Then Jumbo said, "Eh, one noddah ting—you wen spahk dat buggah Blue Hat?"

"Blue Hat, eh? What, you wan score da kine bad paper?"

"Could be," said Jumbo. "Where he stay now?" As he said this he glanced significantly at the twenty on the bar.

"Ah, he go stay inna parking lot mos nights, roun ten. Or later. Byemby the buggah gon be deah, but. Dass one office fo em."

After a few more minutes of chat, Jumbo thanked the bartender and walked out, leaving the twenty on the bar. Driving back over the Pali, he considered his next move. Why Blue Hat? Because while Jumbo had handled a good deal of fake ID in his time, he had never actually bought any.

That was Tanaka's job, and while no one knew that end of the Honolulu underworld better than Tanaka, Jumbo was not anxious to lay the Marvel problem out to the man, because Tanaka would immediately contact Overby directly and tell him what had happened, whereas Jumbo wanted the whole thing cleared up and packaged so that Jumbo would not look like an asshole when Overby inevitably learned of the escape. Also, Tanaka gave him the creeps, something few other people were able to do. Jumbo knew Blue Hat from the kiteboarding and surfing scene. He'd heard rumors that Blue Hat handled phony ID, mainly for kids wanting to get into bars and rent stuff, and he was happy to hear it confirmed by Vernon Pukui.

Blue Hat (so-called because he had never been ob-

served not wearing a faded blue fishing cap with a long, transparent plastic blue brim) was just the kind of guy Marvel
would approach for fake ID. Tanaka would never have dealt
with a character so low on the food chain, and Jumbo himself
never would have thought of him, had he not once seen Marvel
on the beach deep in conversation with the guy, and filed the
observation away. Jumbo's brain was filled with such apparently meaningless connections, which was why he was a very
good security man. He had made a major error in Marvel's case
by underestimating her, something he would not do again.

Jumbo was not exactly afraid of Overby, but the job he
now held was by a long way the best he had ever had or hoped
for, and his fear was that Overby would get rid of him if he did
not repair his error. And he could. He would find Blue Hat; he
would find Blue Hat's supplier (because it was nuts to think
that a surf bum actually produced the kind of high-quality fake
ID that Marvel would use) and he would make the supplier
give up the name of the fake person who was now Marvel. And
he did not think it would be hard to find Blue Hat.

"We wen grab 'em," said Ray Honda's voice on Jumbo's phone.

"Any trouble?"

"Nah, minors. He stay inna trunk. Where you want
'em?"

"Take 'em over the Waimanolo house. I gon be there
byembye."

"K. Ah, laydahs, brah."

When he received this call, Jumbo was doing something he should have done immediately upon learning that
Marvel had escaped, which was examining everything she'd
left behind. He continued, sorting the dump from her closets

and dressers, her desk and cupboards, into neat piles. For a very rich woman, Marvel didn't have a lot of clothes or shoes. Her social life was carried out largely in shorts and t-shirts and all the clothes she wore to work ended up in the trash at the end of each job.

Jumbo examined every pocket, every seam, tapped the shoes to reveal hidden pockets (none found) paged through all the books seeking same (ditto), pulled out drawers and lifted carpets, finding nothing odd or suspicious in any of the places he searched. Clearly, it would be great if they could read the later emails to Goodrich that Esme had detected with her Stingray, but they were encrypted. He knew Esme felt bad about that, just as he felt bad about teaching Marvel to kite board, but who knew? That was why Esme was working so hard and why he was inspecting every waistband. After some hours, having found nothing, he gave it up and left for his interview with Blue Hat.

The house in Waimanolo was a squat concrete box painted faded red, located far up one of the narrow roads that straggled from the little village through thickly forested slopes toward Koolau Ridge. It had plywood nailed over the windows, but sported a white satellite disk affixed to its rusted tin roof. The house belonged to Ray Honda's literal 'ohana, but had been disused for many years following a murder there (an uncle had killed an aunt). Sami Choi slipped Ray the money to pay for taxes and utilities, and it had become a well-known venue for cockfights, a spectacle Sami enjoyed, or at least he enjoyed gambling on the matches. It was also isolated enough to serve as a place for the sort of interviews Jumbo and the Cars occasionally conducted with people who fell afoul of the Lanikai establishment, as now.

When Jumbo walked in, he found Honda and Ford seated on a large mustard-colored velvet sofa watching a satellite feed of an Australian surfing contest on a fifty-inch television. Between them, like a slice of ham in a hoagie, sat a wiry, deeply-tanned haole youth in a sleeveless sweatshirt, board shorts and a blue-visored fishing hat. Jumbo pulled out one of the several dozen folded chairs stacked against the wall, took a beer from a cold case sitting on the floor and sat down.

He watched the surfers for a while, engaging the others in conversation about waves and the styles of the contestants. Blue Hat seemed to have little to contribute. When the show broke for a commercial, Jumbo grabbed the remote from the arm of the sofa and muted the sound. He shifted his chair to face Blue Hat and said, "Howzit, Blue Hat?"

"K," said Blue Hat. "Um, what's this about, brah? I didn't do nothin to you, How come you grab me up off the street, and . . ."

Jumbo made eye contact with Honda and moved his chin a significant inch. Honda slapped Blue Hat on the side of the head, sending the blue hat flying across the room.

"You don't get to ask questions, brah. We not here to talk story. Just answer, eh?"

Blue Hat swallowed hard and nodded.

"Kay den. So—you need to tell us about dakine fake ID you sold to one teetah name Marvel."

"Who?"

Slap.

"Marvel. You wen talk wit her wen you surfin Waimae, back six seven months. Pretty kine haole wahine—I know you memba dat."

"Brah, I sell all kine fake ID, how'm I spose to memba one girl?"

Jumbo said, "Break his arm."

Honda grabbed the surfer's arm, yanked him upright,

twisted the limb and snapped it like a breadstick. Blue Hat screamed and fell to the floor, writhing and weeping.

"You remember now?" asked Jumbo.

"One driver license," said Blue Hat through heavy sobs, "One fuckin license, two hundred dollar, I swear to God, dat all I sold her."

"You know if she wen bought one ID from somebody else?"

"Fuck no, brah. I wen see her one time is all."

Jumbo was a fine judge of when people in this sort of interview had arrived at the truth and he judged that this stupid kid had got there. Unfortunately, it was a dead end. One stolen driver's license was not what Marvel needed to start a new life. She'd have to get a spotless birth certificate on which she could construct a new identity, and this mope was not at that level of the trade. He told the Cars to dump Blue Hat at an emergency room and drove back to Lanikai a worried man. He had no other workable leads on the ID end, and nothing had turned up in what Marvel had left behind, which meant Esme had to come through with something or they were fucked to the max.

But when he dropped by the Data that afternoon, Esme had nothing to show him but a trio of screen shots from the Molokai Airport cameras, three young haole women, approximately Marvel-shaped and the right age, but all wearing hats that concealed or shaded their faces.

"Number two," said Jumbo after a good deal of staring.

"Why her?" Esme asked.

"That's an airport hat, and she bought that straw bag at the airport, too. She took my backpack and she must figure we can get these camera feeds. She knows I'd recognize it."

"I don't know. Tourists buy airport shit all the time."

"What flight is that?"

"The seven-thirty out of Ho'olehua for Maui."

"Can you match that picture to shots from passengers flying off Maui from nine a.m. on?"

"Not a problem. Are you sure it's her?"

"No, but she's the only one coming out of Molokai at the right time who isn't dragging a bag. Let's just see where she goes."

Esme ran a program that matched photographs, and they got a dozen or so matches to female passengers boarding outbound flights from Maui's Kahului Airport. None was wearing a straw hat or carrying a straw bag or wearing the t-shirt and board shorts worn by the woman Jumbo had spotted at Molokai.

"She bought new stuff in the airport and changed," said Jumbo. "Can you make that one bigger? Let me see her head."

Esme caused the image of the woman's head to fill the screen. She was wearing a pale blue Maui ball cap, pulled low, with her hair jammed under it, but a strand had escaped and was clear against her neck. Jumbo thought it might be Marvel's dark brown.

"Where is she going?" Jumbo asked.

"That's the 1:25 to LAX."

"L.A. is a good place to go. You can get lost pretty good in L.A. I could stand out on Hollywood and Vine and hope she walks by, but I think we got a dead end here. Any luck tracing the mark, what's-his-name?"

"Goodrich. No, not yet. His cell is off and I can't get into his computer. He must've had it scrubbed, which is bad news right there, brah. It means he found out about my trojan. I'm monitoring, but unless he uses a credit card or sends a self-ie to Instagram, we're out of luck. I still can't believe we're doing this. What the fuck is wrong with her?"

Jumbo shrugged. "Love is strange."

"You think? You think that's it, she fell for a mark?"

"Or she was trying a private con, which is as bad or worse. Or she found out about our insurance program with the marks and she panicked. By the way, you didn't happen . . ."

"Hell, no. I never said a word to her. But, shit, Jumbo, how come she was the only one of us who couldn't know?"

He shrugged again and said, "Overby thought it would mess her up, working with the marks, if she knew they were the walking dead. It looks like he was right, if that was what it was. Well, hele on, teetah. One of them's got to surface sooner or later. Sooner would be mo' bettah. Before Overby finds out."

Jumbo sat on the bench under the mango where he had last seen Marvel and thought through his problem. Where did Marvel get first-class fake ID? Not Blue Hat, obviously, and not on the mainland. Therefore, someone on the Islands, but who? Tanaka might know, but he couldn't go to Tanaka because Tanaka would tell Overby, so if he did go to Tanaka, he had to have something to hold over Tanaka's head, some edge. And as he thought this a possible answer occurred to him and he laughed. Tanaka's vice was well-known; would he have risked his life to indulge it? Of course he would. He'd endured ruin and exile and life was but a small step further. Marvel knew it too, the sneaky little bitch!

He went to the tool shed, emerged with a wrecking bar and went to Marvel's room in Data, where he proceeded with great energy to rip out the paneling and tear up the floor. He quickly found that one of the particleboard sheets that comprised the floor had not been nailed down, or someone had carefully removed the nails. In the void beneath this he found a gym bag containing a plain Japanese schoolgirl's uniform, a black wig with pigtails, Mary-Janes with appropriate lace-top socks and half a dozen pairs of plain white cotton panties.

Jumbo uttered a curse, then laughed at the insanity of obsession. He packed the things back in the gym bag and drove to Tanaka's house in Kailua. He found the man in his garden trimming a hibiscus hedge. When Jumbo showed him the contents of the gym bag, Tanaka made no attempt to deny the evidence that, in return for her participation in his peculiar fetish, he had provided Marvel with a complete set of first-class fake identification.

"What happens now?" asked the Japanese.

"To you? Nothing, unless I find out you did it again. But I need the name you gave her."

"Of course," said Tanaka, after which they went into the house and Tanaka, consulting his careful records, delivered all the information he had on Alison Hill. The conversation after this was brief, with Jumbo impressing on the other the various bad things that Jumbo would do to him if word of this transaction ever got back to Overby or Sami Choi.

As he drove home, he called Esme. With the name, it was no task at all to find out where Marvel had gone, and since credit card records were an open book to Esme, she even found the address where Alison Hill had gone to ground.

Marvel rose from her long sleep, bathed, gelled her hair into a style appropriate for a hip young person in the movie industry, dressed in a concordant outfit from Alison's ample wardrobe, called a car, and went shopping for an automobile. She bought two, one a silver TT convertible, the sort of car Alison Hill would drive, and the other a late-model used Subaru Outback. The TT she parked in the garage of her building, and she stashed the Subaru in a pay lot a block away.

Back in the condo, she turned on the television, made herself a tequila and soda and thought about the rest of her life. The Alison Hill identity would probably hold up for a while,

251

because Tanaka had a stake in keeping it quiet almost as great as her own. Still, she knew that all hands at Lanikai would be sparing no effort to find out who she was now, and someone might figure out that it was Tanaka who had supplied her new ID. In that case, Tanaka would give her up in a flash, so she badly needed to get a different one.

That was item number one on her to-do list. It would take some time to generate the contacts required to obtain good quality fake paper, but she thought that wouldn't be a problem. Money: she had plenty, but it would be some labor to convert it into an income.

Second item: find a slightly bent broker, someone skilled at laundering funny money into a portfolio of tax-free muni bonds. What else? What *was* there besides safety and money? It had not occurred to Marvel that she was a skilled professional, working closely with other professionals who gave her support and praise, but now it did, and she felt for the first time since her escape a heavy sense of loss. She had no one in her life and nothing to do. She had little taste for being a rich playgirl. The experience she'd had with people whose lives were just that did not incline her to spend a lot of time in their company.

She could run cons, of course, create a gang like Overby had, but after some thought she found she didn't want to. Having seen how a long con operation worked, she understood she did not have the required skill set. She was a put-up girl, not a criminal mastermind. If she tried to run cons by herself, she'd end up in prison, and hooking up with some other, lesser Overby did not appeal either.

During these ruinations, she avoided as much as she could thinking about the purple elephant she had resolved not to think about, with the usual results. But no. Bernard Goodrich was by far the nicest man she had ever met, and he was clearly in love with her, and she thought that ditching him was her life's one good deed. This thought naturally led to an ecstasy of self-pity, and another drink, a stronger one. She turned up the volume on the TV, binge-watched *Breaking Bad,* and drank tequila until she passed out.

The next morning, she awakened too early and too queasy for anything but coffee and toast. At home (her lost life!) she would have walked down to the beach and let the sea wind and the surf blow the fumes away, and while she knew there were beaches in the area, she wasn't sure which ones were any good, and besides, she didn't have equipment. But she brought out the laptop and studied the surfing and kite scene in southern California, making notes on places to explore.

Maybe that could be a life, she could get really good at kiteboarding and surfing, maybe open a shop, plunge into the timelessness of that existence, traveling the world looking for wind and waves. People did it, she knew: Australia, New Zealand, the coasts of Europe. Meanwhile, she could take advantage of the early hour by swimming laps in the condo's little pool while it was likely to be deserted.

She donned bikini and rubber slippers, took her phone, laptop, wallet, and keys, and went down. She swam, but the pool was too short and shallow for good lap swimming, so after a couple of dozen she got out and lay on a lounger reading *The Power and the Glory* on the laptop. Crazily, she found herself feeling sad that she would never get to discuss it with Overby. She'd have to join a book club and see what the suburban matrons had to say about world lit, ha ha.

Marvel heard a car pull into the parking lot that lay on the other side of a ficus hedge standing thick and tall on the edge of the pool deck. A car door slammed, then another, then another. One car, three people, at six-thirty a.m.? Marvel sat up and looked at the hedge. It was thinner at its base, and it was possible to peer through it and make out the general shapes of cars and people.

She saw moving colors, an aloha shirt, but a shirt far larger than any shirt had a right to be, a shirt that could have dressed a cotton bale. Yellow figures on a blue ground. Then another shirt, red on black, almost the same size, then a black t-shirt and the golden-brown skin of huge arms.

Marvel put her slippers on, snatched up her things, and walked out of the pool enclosure. She followed a circuitous path, around the side of the building, down a breezeway, and out onto the street. A few blocks of unhurried walking to the pay lot and her Subaru, and she drove off.

It was a bad situation. She had no clothes except a bikini. She had only the hundred-odd dollars in her wallet; the identification she carried--for Alison Hill and Marvel Gafney--were both compromised. She couldn't go back to the condo. But she had been in bad situations before and now she surprised herself by how coolly she coped with this disaster. From somewhere a message appeared in her mind, with force, so that her small hairs stood briefly on end: the name of the one person in Los Angeles who might help her.

Fifteen

By the third week in November, Bernard was running five kilometers in just under twenty minutes, which he thought was pretty good for an old fart, and he was flinging fifty-pound stones around like throw cushions. His dog had finally learned to release an agitator who struck him, and afterward mastered the other aspects of the protection phase of the trial, so Bernard had decided to put it in for the higher rating at a Schutzhund Association meet at Plattsburgh, two days off. It was something of a long-shot, as most dogs didn't earn on their first try, but Bernard thought pushing the training might distract him from worrying about Marvel, who had gone silent for the past forty-eight hours.

It did not; the worry instead distracted him from the extreme concentration required in dog training at this celestial level. Twice he gave a double command on the down and recall, an exercise that Murtagh could do sleeping, and once he used the dog's name instead of the simple command. The dog picked it up and complained.

<What's wrong with you *now*?>

"I'm sorry—my bad. I keep thinking about Marvel."

<I don't understand. Is she here? Is she in heat? Can you smell it? I can't, and I believe I can smell better than you.>

"No, she's not here, and I can't smell her at all, but she's still on my mind. It's hard to explain."

<A Man thing.>

"Probably, but I don't think I've had it recently. Maybe I'm becoming more human."

<It would be better if you became more like me. That's

the bell ringing.>

"Yes, vespers. Let's knock off and go to choir and get something to eat."

And check phone messages, although Bernard didn't mention that. The monks did not have cell phones; the place was therefore free of the tinkle and burble of those instruments, and there was no air-talking except to God, so that Bernard felt constrained to leave the cell in his cell when he went about the business of the day. He repeated this sorry pun to himself from time to time and shared it with the dog, who was not amused.

When he picked the thing up it told him that someone had called him and left a voicemail. An unfamiliar number; his heart lifted, then fell when he found it was only Jack Bill the bookseller, with a puzzling message telling him to call right away, that it was urgent.

He called, and when Jack Bill answered, Bernard said, "I never got an urgent call from a bookstore before. What happened—you ran out of my novels?"

"No, man, I got your girlfriend here in my apartment. She says she's being chased by killers. It's like the telegram Benchley sent to Ross from Venice—streets full of water, please advise. So, please advise."

"Girlfriend? You mean *Marvel*?"

"Her. She walked into the bookstore first thing this morning wearing a bikini and flip-flops and asked me to help her. This happens all the time in the bookstore biz, as you know . . ."

"Is she there? Let me talk to her."

"Are you sure you don't want me to call the cops? This is the girl with the gang who ripped you off, right? How do you know it's not another scam? You fly to her arms and her pals grab you up?"

"It's not like that, she's running from them."

"So she says. She says she got off Oahu on a kiteboard and somehow the gang traced her to L.A. It's quite a tale. Even to a connoisseur of thriller fiction such as myself it was pretty rich."

"Put her on, Jack Bill!"

"Okay, bub, it's your funeral, but in general, when citizens hear that a criminal is being pursued by other criminals with murderous intent, the smart move is nine one one."

"Please, Jack Bill, put her on and don't call anyone!"

Bernard heard the man sigh dramatically, a clunk as the phone hit a hard surface, and then, after some interminable seconds, he heard her voice.

"I escaped," she said.

"So it seems. You need to get on a plane and come here. Plattsburgh, New York is the nearest airport. Do you have a working credit card?"

"Wait, why should I come to you?"

"I explained this already. We're better off together. Also, it's fate."

There followed a long pause. Bernard imagined she was contemplating fate.

"Okay, say I want to come to wherever—I can't use the credit card I flew here with. That's blown. They'll know practically as soon as I make the reservation."

"Jack Bill can buy you a ticket on his card. Travel as Marvel."

"What? That's crazy, unless you want to tell them exactly where I'm going."

"It's not crazy. They'll be looking for the fake. It won't occur to them that you'd be stupid enough to travel under your own name, and by the time they get wise, we'll have left the airport."

"And then what? What do we do, live in hiding forever?"

"Not at all. If they come after us, we'll defeat them."

"Defeat them? Are you crazy? Do you know who these guys are?"

"Yes, they're a gang of con artists who knock off the old guys they cheat so the victims won't make trouble, and it works because the victims don't know they're coming. But we know they're coming. And we're not victims."

"So what? Do you really think you can beat professional killers?"

"Of course. I have a gun and a trained guard dog, which their other victims didn't have, besides which there's *my* profession."

"You're a writer."

"A *thriller* writer, and you're a woman running from killers. If I've read one plot like that, I've read a thousand, and I've written half a dozen myself. Do you have any idea how much research I've done on this shit? I know all the schemes, dodges and deceptions. I can pick locks; I can make bombs from common materials. . ."

"Excuse me, that's fiction? And we're in real life."

"Fiction *is* real life. Where do you think real life comes from? Where do you think criminals learn how to be criminals? They watch TV and movies. Did you ever watch *The Sopranos*? They spend half their time watching *Godfather* movies so they'll know how to behave. Look, you're coming here. It's the obvious next chapter in this farce. Do you need anything? Clothes, money . . . ?"

"We stole your money."

"Oh, don't be dense. Of course I have money. You didn't get the trust funds at all, and I have a three-million-dollar apartment and a substantial revenue stream from my books. I am far from starving, no thanks to you."

"If you feel that way," she shouted, "why the hell are you trying to help me?"

"That's an interesting question, and we can discuss it at great length when you get here. We can also discuss why a hardened criminal reached out to one of her victims and didn't rat him out to her mob when she had a chance to save herself. It's cosmic, dear girl. You're the famous psychic, you should know."

"That's a scam," she said after a pause, her voice sounding exhausted now.

"Yeah, but this isn't. You're coming."

Another, longer, pause. "Sure, whatever."

"Good. Put Jack Bill back on."

Marvel sat scrunched up in an armchair in Jack Bill's apartment off Santa Monica, ignoring the conversation her host was conducting with Bernard, even though she knew it was about her. She was wearing an old UCLA hoodie Jack Bill had lent. I came down to mid-thigh and she had it pulled down over her knees because she felt cold. Her mind was cranking away, figuring the angles, looking for ways of escape (how much of her mental effort had been so expended over the years!) yet this cranking seemed to be taking place in a distant zone, like the jabber and flicker of a TV show she wasn't really into.

A certain shock still lingered. She had counted on the Amelia Hill identity holding up longer. Obviously, they had gotten to Tanaka, but why had he admitted it? Didn't he realize it was the end for him too, when Overby found out? But maybe Jumbo was keeping it from Overby. That made sense. Tanaka would be Jumbo's guy from here forward with that hanging over his head, until Overby figured it out, which would take ten minutes. Which meant Jumbo was counting on a quick resolution, which meant . . .

259

She didn't know what it meant. She found it hard to care. This was like being on the board in the open sea, that same detachment, the sense of being subject to powerful forces outside anyone's control. Overby was a great proponent of watchful waiting. The instinct is fight or flight, he used to say, but sometimes it's smart to do neither and watch for opportunities.

Goodrich had called her "dear girl;" nobody called her that except Overby. So she was moving into the orbit of another man, under extreme duress, as she had with Overby when he had slipped her away from Reggie Fong. How had he done that? Reggie was a triad guy and no one got away from the triads. He must've made some kind of deal with the big horse of the Lo Chueh, he must owe them, or maybe Overby was a triad guy himself. Probably was, which meant they were doomed. On the other hand, Goodrich was not an ordinary mark. Maybe he wasn't entirely nuts. And he seemed to care about the real her. That would be a change. Unique, actually, in her stupid life.

Jack Bill was off the phone now. He went into another room and came out carrying a short stack of folded clothes.

"I think there must be a fit in there. My daughter's about your size. Put something on and we'll go shopping. The Beverly Center—you can go crazy at Armani. The boyfriend is paying."

"He's not my boyfriend."

"Coulda fooled me. After that, I'll take you out to LAX. There's a 9:15 red-eye via Dulles and Boston that gets you to Plattsburgh tomorrow night. I should call the cops on you, but I'm a sentimental old fool and I like Bernard. I can't say I'm happy he seems to be under your spell, but he's a big boy and I like his books."

"So do I," she said. He snorted and made a what-the-hell gesture, but he was grinning. She said, "Let me use your computer. I need to lay a false trail."

Jumbo hung around Alison Hill's apartment for a day, until it became obvious that Marvel was not about to return. The Cars had been posted in the front and rear of the sprawling condo, Honda in a rented car and Ford on foot, but the hours went by, night came, and the next day dawned with no sign of the fugitive.

She had clearly been here until quite recently. They found the airport outfit she'd worn; the bed was still unmade and the bathroom had been messed in the way that Marvel messed a bathroom. One reason he stayed was because he believed that she'd be back for the cash. Jumbo was well-paid, but he was not a shareholder in the rackets and somewhat more than fifty large in cash was an amount he would himself have been reluctant to abandon.

He split the cash with his brahs, because he was that kind of guy, and they agreed, laughing, that whether or not they found their quarry, the trip hadn't been a total loss. Waiting was a bit of a pain, because they had to keep quiet in the condo in case she came back, or sent someone, so they couldn't party or even watch TV. After twenty-four hours of this, they felt they'd earned the cash.

Late in the morning of the second day, Jumbo got a call from Esme.

"She's moving. Flight from L.A. to Vegas, then to Cozumel via Miami. Also she sent her laptop to Miami. It's live and still pinging."

"I thought we got people at LAX."

"She flew out of Pasadena."

"Smart girl. So what you think? Go to Miami?"

Esme's voice was hesitant. "I don't know, brah. We

running out of time here. Overby dem gonna call sometime and what I can tell 'em, eh? Marvel wen escape and we got no idea where she at? They gon fire all our asses. Or worse, you know?"

"Yeah. So maybe I'll go myself, leave the Cars here in case she double back."

"That's a plan, brah," said Esme.

"No, on second thought I'm taking them with me. She's in the wind, she's not gonna come back to a place she knows we know about. I'll need some help in Miami, assuming we're right. Tell Tanaka to set it up."

"You tell him. He won't listen to me. He might not even listen to you."

"He'll listen to me," said Jumbo with confidence. Then he went down to the street and told the Cars to get ready for a trip.

Marvel went to the Beverly Center Mall with Jack Bill and bought (on Jack Bill's card) a selection of the kind of clothes rich people wear when they leave urban zones, made largely of flannel, wool, ripstop nylon, oiled cotton and Gore-Tex. She took Jack Bill's advice about the kind of temperatures she might encounter in the northeast in November. She bought a pair of boots. When was the last time she had worn boots? A long time, not since she had run off to Portland and met Duane Tillman, who had spirited her off to climes where boots were a barely a rumor. She thought them a symbol, that the life she had known for decades was truly finished. The tears did not begin until the jet she boarded had reached its cruising altitude, and they continued for some time afterward.

It was an uncomfortable flight from Los Angeles to Miami, but then every flight was uncomfortable for men sized like

the Cars, even in first. They were therefore cranky after landing, and Jumbo was cranky with them, but not because of anything physical. When he turned his cell phone on after landing
at Miami International, he found a message from Esme (CALL
ME NOW!!!) which had been posted twenty minutes after the
plane cleared the runway at LAX.

When he got Esme on the line, she told him that the
name M. Gafney had appeared on a manifest of a flight from
Pasadena to Dulles.

"She flew under her real name? Why didn't you spot it
before I got on a goddam Miami flight?"

Esme explained how she hacked into the manifest systems of airlines and how each search of each flight was a one-
off—it wasn't like searching for names on Google—and that
she was focused on the Alison Hill alias exclusively until, finding no hits there, it had occurred to her that Marvel might pull a
sneaky trick like that.

"Is she going to come to Miami from Dulles?"

"No. I got her on a flight to Boston, but she's checked
through to Plattsburgh, New York."

"And what then? She flying around the country to fuck
with us?"

"As far as I can see she terminates in Plattsburgh. But I
think I know where she's going after that."

"Where?"

"I decrypted her emails. I gave her an encryption program, but I kept the private key to it. I just been so busy with
the airline and credit card stuff that I din't have time to run the
decrypts until now. She has to be going to Goodrich."

"I thought you said he went dark after the breakdown.
What makes you think she's going to him?"

"Trust me, brah, that's where she's going. This whole
shit-pile is about him. You should meet the people Tanaka hired

and get them up there."

"Do you know where he's at in this Plattsburgh?"

"No idea, but it's a small place. I'm sending you a map. You gonna need some warm clothes though."

El Salvador is a land rich in gangsters. Oddly, some of these are Chinese in origin, and Mr. Tanaka had made his selection from this peculiar minority. A small brown man was waiting in the baggage claim area when the Hawaiians came through. There was little possibility of confusing this group of three men with any other, so he made a direct approach, smiling, showing glinting gold, hand out, and introduced himself as Chuco Hong. Jumbo looked him over. He wore tan slacks, woven loafers and a black shirt buttoned to the top, and he had the look of a waiter on his day off, which Jumbo thought might be an advantage over the Cars, were stealth ever needed.

"How many boys you got?" Jumbo asked.

"Three, but I can get more. Your man said there were two clients, a guy and a girl, no security."

"That's right."

Chuco looked at his huge new colleagues and said, "Then we should be good. Where are they?"

"Far away. Can you travel?"

"If you're paying, we can go to fucking Siberia," replied the killer with a friendly smile.

When traveling by air, Marvel adopted one of two modes: forgettable or unforgettable. Many people who have been beaten or abused as children have the unconscious ability to disappear by drawing their being into their skins. The eye does not light on them, and if it happens to, the features do not leave even a faint mark on memory. Marvel's forgettableness was to this as a hum is to an aria, for she had cultivated it assiduously for years, and had besides been trained by a man who was one of the great personal camofleurs of his generation.

On this flight, however, Marvel had opted for unforgettable. In addition to the Eddie Bauerei, she had purchased a couple of nice outfits, because why not? As she moved down the aisle, every eye in first class was on her because she was floridly made up and wearing a tight Ferragamo number, in multicolored white, red, black and brown horizontal stripes, and over this an embroidered sweater coat by Rocha. She had Prada boots on her feet, and upon her wrists, two fingers and her neck glittered fake diamonds from Zara. She carried a yellow calfskin Coach tote and wafted gusts of Coco by Chanel. Her dark hair had received a three-hundred dollar cut, and she resembled extremely the Sean Young of *Bladerunner*, except far more charming, not so much the android.

"I love Alaska, she said to the flight attendant as she swooped into the window seat. "Just love it. You know when I first heard the name of the airline, I thought you only flew to Alaska, silly me. But Chuck and I went up there a couple of years back, he hired a helicopter and we flew around Mt. Denali, and oh, I was so happy when I heard they changed its name to the real name, not Mt. whomever, McKinley, yes. And that's when I found out you flew other places. And could you tell me something? Who is the dude in the fur thingee on the tail section? Oh, yes, darling, bring me Champagne. And don't stop until I say so."

And more in this line, plus compliments on hair and makeup for the flight attendants, ("I don't see how you can do it, flying all the time and putting up with all kinds of people, my Lord, my hat is off to you all. I couldn't begin to do that kind of work") and lighting up her seatmate. No dour businessman, no withered lawyer, no wonder woman executive was immune. She drew them out, she showed concern, and on many occasions, she handed out fake business cards to these people in exchange for their real ones, some of which might prove useful in later contingencies. And she told her own story. This was her favorite part, creating the legend, lying ad lib and convincingly, with a smile and, when appropriate, a twinkle and a musky veil of sex.

On this particular transcontinental, Ms. Gafney was a make-up artist for the studios, had been nominated for Academy Awards for her work on several films, knew all the stars, Kate won't go out of the *house* unless Marvel races over and does her, and so on and on. Marvel had an encyclopedic knowledge of celebrity, was an avid reader of *Us,* of *People,* of *Entertainment Weekly,* of *Rolling Stone.* She could talk sports too, and root on demand (Oh my God. You're a Huskies fan too? I just love them. Name-of-quarterback—my man!).

She carried this persona off the plane at Dulles and on to the flight to Boston, and then on the puddle-jumper turbo-prop to Plattsburgh. At either stop she could have spent a brief time in a restroom stall and emerged a forgettable white trash woman, ten pounds heavier and three inches shorter than the stunning creature who had entered. That was the point of unforgettable mode. Not one of the crew or passengers who had lately been charmed would have recognized her. But on this occasion, she kept it going, off the plane and down to baggage claim, where, rather to Bernard's surprise she ran toward, him embraced him in a serious hug, cried, "Oh, darling, how good to see you again!" and kissed him solidly on the mouth.

The dog too received much attention, Marvel dropping to a knee and cooing. Murtagh had not had much cooing recently, and little fondling at any time and he behaved like a pet. Bernard regarded this display with a fixed smile on his face, amazed at the act both creatures were putting on. Marvel, he noted, was not looking at the dog at all but was scanning the surround, making quick rotations of her field of view as she spun around the absurdly fawning animal.

"I think that's enough," he said at last. "You're going to spoil him."

"Oh, please. The poor creature is starved for affection."

"Aren't we all," said Bernard. "What exactly are you doing, Marvel?"

"I'm scanning the crowd," replied Marvel, "for people unusually interested in us."

"*Everyone* is unusually interested in us. They're delighted. It's not often that you see a dog who looks like Murtagh behaving like a Yorkie, and you're quite a spectacle all on your own."

"Yes, keep smiling and check for people who aren't delighted. Where's the car?"

"In the lot?"

"You should've left it on the ramp. Tell me it's not in a garage!"

"No, an outside lot. And it's a ticket if you leave it on the ramp."

"Goodrich, here's a tip: in our present situation, we stop worrying about parking tickets. Okay, let's go."

They went out to the lot. Marvel made a face when she saw the Mercedes.

"A cream antique Benz. Good choice, brah. Not too obvious or fucking practically unique or anything."

"Says the woman who was channeling Gypsy Rose Lee all through a small airport. Okay, we're staying at the La Quinta just outside of town. It's dog friendly. I intend to go there, register, leave you with the keys, drive around for ten minutes and then park outside the delivery entrance in the back."

"That's pretty good, brah," she said. "You must've been on the lam."

"Of course not," he said as he drove off. "I've just written stuff like this for years. I've imagined being on the lam a dozen times."

"How does it stack up to real life?"

"In real life it doesn't stop when you shut down your computer," he said, and she laughed.

Marvel stared out the back window as they drove through the dark streets and onto a four-lane state highway to the motel. Once there, she made herself glow again, filling the small lobby with bright chatter, complimenting the desk clerk on her hair-do, praising the flowers on display, telling the desk clerk she *always* stayed at La Quinta, because they took dogs, and always had such *fabulous* service. Bernard registered as ordered, gave Marvel both key cards, and went back to his car. A short time later he was idling among the dumpsters, when there came a scratching on the window. Murtagh alerted and growled. A person stood there dressed in boots, jeans, a down vest, and a plaid wool cap with earflaps, shouldering a black plastic trash bag. Another tap on the glass. Bernard rolled the window down and was reaching for his wallet to offer a buck, when he realized it was Marvel.

"What was that all about?" Bernard asked as he pulled the car back onto the street.

"You should know. You're supposed to be the big expert on tricky escape plots."

"Yeah, right, you make a big show so people will remember that persona and then you go invisible like you are now—I get that. What I don't get is the next part of your plan. Where do you intend to spend the night?"

"In this car. We want to get as far away as possible from the last place they can trace us to, which would be your dog-friendly motel in Plattsburgh. You want a medium-sized city where we can change cars. Then we hit the bars on the rough side of town. We buy some dope . . ."

"Wait a minute--why do we buy dope?"

"It's the bottom rung of the criminal ladder. A couple of steps up is a guy who can manufacture papers for the new identities that I'll buy off the dark web. Using those, we go to a big city, where I make some money transfers, and then we decide where we want to live and buy property there and hire security and have some breathing space to find out if we can stand each other in real life."

"Bad plan."

"Why?"

"A couple of reasons. The first is that I don't feel like hiding indefinitely. I've explained this to you already, but you don't listen. I'm an author, a public figure, but I am easily distinguishable from Thomas Pynchon or J. D. Salinger. For better or worse, it's simply the case nowadays that publishing the kind of books I write requires public contact. Also, unlike you, I have a family, which makes me vulnerable. If my children were threatened, I would have to come out of hiding. So why start hiding? The second reason is I have to be in Plattsburgh for the next few days."

"Are you serious? Why in hell do you have to be in Plattsburgh?"

"Because they're holding the Schutzhund trials there tomorrow, Friday. Murtagh has been training for weeks for his Schutzhund II ranking and we have to be there."

"You're fucking out of your mind, Goodrich. Let me try to get this into your so-called brain. They know where we are. They are monitoring your card usage as we speak. They will know that you checked into that motel. They will come there, and when they don't find us, they will start looking, and in a place as small as Plattsburgh they will find us and kill us. Then you won't have to worry about meeting your public or any fucking dog shows."

Bernard pulled the car to the side of the road and turned to face her.

"Marvel, you need to calm down. No one is going to kill us in Plattsburgh."

"No? How're you going to stop them?"

"You're not thinking about this in the right way. They can't kill us openly. The whole point of their operation is to keep the secret, to suppress any serious investigation, which means we're not going down in a hail of lead from a drive-by. They'll have to snatch us in secret and take us to a secure place where they can find out if we've told anyone what we know, and then they'll have to get rid of us in a way that won't raise any further questions. That's not impossible, but it won't be easy. It won't be anything like as easy as faking the natural death of a man in a high-risk demographic. It'll take time, and planning, and meanwhile, we'll be planning, too. We'll be planning our attack."

"What attack?"

"I don't know yet. But they're vulnerable. They're criminals and they have to be running scared. Something will present itself, I'm sure, and then we'll make our move."

Marvel was silent after this, for so long that Bernard was moved to touch her shoulder, in case she had fallen asleep or dropped into some kind of coma. She didn't move. He switched on the overhead light and saw that her face was dripping tears.

He handed her a handkerchief and put his arm around her. She felt loose, boneless. He said, "It'll be okay, Marvel. You'll see. We're in a much better position than you think."

She said, "Whatever, Goodrich. You say *think*? I can't think any more. I've been traveling for sixteen hours. I need a bed and a toilet. Could that be part of your plan?"

Bernard started the car and drove back to town, then turned north. It had become colder. Lights from streets and buildings caught low, nasty-looking clouds that seemed to bulge down from the sky. Beside him, the woman had sunk into deep sleep, her temple against the window. He caught glimpses of her face in the lights thrown out by approaching cars, and the sight made him happier than he'd felt in a long time. In the back seat, the dog stirred, mumbled, and placed his muzzle on Bernard's shoulder

"What do *you* think, Murtagh?" he said.

<She's in the pack now. Will you mount her?>

"Not just now. When she's ready."

<You're right. She doesn't have the smell.>

Bernard laughed and drove on, arriving at the monastery just after nine, in a veil of light snow. The gatekeeper was up and appeared to be waiting for them.

Sixteen

Marvel woke to the cessation of motion and the grind of wheels on gravel.

"Where are we?" she asked.

"At St. Roch. I need to find a safe place for you to stay while we're in the area."

"I'm going to stay at a monastery? I thought it was . . . you know, no girls allowed."

"It is," said Bernard. "But there's someone here who knows everyone in the area and might have a suggestion." He pointed to the porch of the gatehouse, where a robed and hooded figure stood, back-lit by the light from within.

They left the car, and Bernard said to the monk, "I'm sorry to be so late, but it's something of an emergency. A refuge situation."

Brother Dominic's eyes fell on Marvel and stayed there for an uncomfortable length of time, until Marvel popped one of her halogen smiles and extended her hand.

"Hi, I'm Marvel Gafney. And you are . . . ?"

"Dominic," he said, and, after the tiniest hesitation, grasped the offered flesh. "I presume you are the one requiring refuge."

"Yes. I'm a criminal and I don't want to be one anymore and my former gang wants to kill me. And Bernard, too."

"Yes, Bernard has told me the story. So, you are the, what should I say? The seductress? We don't use words like that anymore, do we? I'm afraid we can't offer you hospitality here. Bernard can tell you we often bend the rules, but *that* rule doesn't bend. There's a Carmelite establishment in Delmar, but I'm not sure you'd be comfortable there. They're all quite old. Unlike me." He smiled, then seemed to notice that he was still holding her hand and let it go.

"I suppose you could stay with Mrs. Klotz," he added after a moment's thought.

"Who's she?" asked Bernard.

"A friend. She seems to think I've helped her in the past. A good woman--she ran the dairy from which we used to get our milk. Wonderful butter. She has two of our dogs, our failures, I should say. I suppose she would take in another stray. But, oh dear. I'd have to call her and I'm not sure I could make it to the telephone in the prior's office. But I would be happy to try, if I could lean a little on you, Bernard."

"We have cellphones," said Bernard. He took out his burner phone, but it was out of juice. Marvel gave him the Alison Hill iPhone, earning a surprised look from Bernard, to which Marvel replied a shrug.

"Oh!" said Dominic, slapping his head dramatically. "Yes, I always forget about them. Wait, I'll find her number."

The monk rustled through the books on his single shelf, mumbling to himself. Bernard said, "You think when it lights up, they'll be able to trace it, and you don't care."

"Right. I drank your Kool-Aid, brah. You're right, running sucks. Let them find us, and we'll see if you've got the stuff."

After some minutes, Dominic returned with a smile on his face, and a piece of paper flapping in his hand.

"I knew I had put it in Butler, but I couldn't recall where until I remembered St. Bridget was the patron of dairy workers. Could you dial it for me?"

Bernard did so and handed the ringing device to Dominic.

"Oh, Martha? Hello, this is Brother Dominic. Sorry to disturb you so late. Oh, that's good then. How are the dogs? Um-hm. Yes. Mm. I always use cod liver oil. Yes. Oh, that's wonderful--the rash is all cleared up? Wonderful. Well, yes, I have been praying, but I would hesitate to call it a miracle in the strict sense. No, not at all, but thank you. Ah, well, the reason I called, I wonder could you do me a favor? Oh, thank you. I have, or we have, a guest here, Bernard, a charming man, very devout, and he has a friend, a young woman, who seems to be in something of a fix, and I wonder if you would be so kind as to put her up for a day or so.

"Oh, no, nothing like that. She seems to be on the run from some very bad people. No, actually, as I understand it, they're a gang of murderous villains. I take it she used to be a villainess herself, but now wants to turn her life around and devote herself to charity. Yes, it *is* just like a movie. Um-hm. Yes, you have the dogs. Well, no, I don't think it will come to shooting. Yes, well, that's splendid, Martha, a very Christian act. Thank you so much. I'll send them right over."

Dominic handed the phone back. "It's all arranged. It's a large house and all her kids have gone off, and her Eric died some years back. An excellent woman. Here, I'll write down the address. It's in East Mooers. She said she'll leave the yellow porch light on for you."

"Let me understand this," said Marvel in the car. "I travel six thousand miles to hook up with you and you're leaving me in the middle of nowhere with an old lady, because you have to put your dog in a show?"

"That's an accurate description, if unkind. Mrs. Klotz is an excellent woman. Wonderful butter. She might be able to help you turn your life around and devote yourself to charity."

"Fuck you, Goodrich," she said, but without heat.

They drove through a scrim of hard granular snow that made it possible to see road signs, but Bernard had entered the address into Marvel's iPhone and confidently followed the directions of the robot lady, until it said, "You have arrived at your destination. Your destination is on the right."

They looked out the car windows. Nothing. The headlights made tubes of glowing snow through utter blackness and lit up a yellow road sign with black arrows pointing right and left.

"Betrayed by Apple yet again," said Bernard. "No, unfair— must have entered it wrong. Well, what now?"

"Oh, my God!" cried Marvel.

"What?"

"I've been here before," she said in a breathless voice. "You and me in this car in the dark. I said, 'Go north.' But . . . no, this is too crazy."

"You've been *here* before?"

"No, it was in Hawaii. I had like a . . . a vision. I was thinking about you and suddenly I wasn't in my room, I was here, and I had a feeling we were lost and I said 'north.'"

"Interesting. Well, let's try it."

"Seriously?"

"Yes. It's no crazier than our present lives." Bernard brought up the compass on the iPhone. North was to the right. He turned the car and drove for what seemed like a very long time, but was only fifteen minutes by his watch. A sign loomed: East Mooers, Pop. 102."

"A dairy-oriented place, apparently," said Bernard with a laugh. "Now let's see if we can find a yellow light."

East Mooers consisted of a gas station and general store, a feed and agricultural gear emporium, and a score of houses. One of them had a bright yellow porch light shining, and as they pulled up the drive, they heard big dogs barking.

The front door opened, and out stepped a large woman wearing a canvas barn coat over a chenille bathrobe. Her thick gray hair stuck out from a center parting like a pair of Brillos, beneath which sat a rough-featured but kindly face bearing thick, clear-framed glasses.

Bernard said to the dog, "I think you'd better stay in the car, guy. We don't want to upset this lady's dogs."

<They fear me, as they should. If you're too long, I'll bark.>

Martha Klotz ushered them into her kitchen. She fussed over the terrible weather, said it was too late for coffee, offered to make cocoa, asked if they'd care for a drop in the cocoa, not you, Mister, because you're driving, showed her arms where until lately she had suffered a horrible itching rash that Brother Dominic had put to flight, a holy man, a saint, everyone in the neighborhood knew it, all the way to Vermont; after which a catalog of known cures, man and beast, and they all agreed that Brother Dominic was a gem. The cocoa was excellent, although Bernard regretted his absent drop, which was Jameson's. The dogs, Magnus and Bluto, fawned, sniffed, begged cookies (denied!) and settled, entwined, on their bed of feed sacks in the corner.

Bernard and Mrs. K chatted about dogs, a safe topic, considering, and Bernard put in that he was taking his dog to the trials the next day. Mrs. Klotz said she'd been to one a while back, and wasn't it amazing what they got those dogs to do, her own were dumb as posts, although lovable, which you had to admit was the main thing with dogs. Marvel was largely silent during the conversation.

"I should get back," said Bernard presently. "They start pretty early."

"I'll go get your room ready," said Mrs. Klotz to Marvel, rising. "You'll want a hot water bottle. Those sheets will be like ice."

When she had gone, Bernard grasped Marvel's hand, which he found icy as well.

"I'm sorry about this," he said, "but it was your idea to leave the hotel. Are you angry?"

"I'm terrified," she said, proving it with the look on her face. "See that stove? My grandmother had a stove exactly like that, and that cat clock with the swinging tail—she had one like that too, and this enamel kitchen table and the fucking linoleum . . . or maybe I'm just imagining it and I'm already around the bend. Plus, that thing with the car, the vision or whatever the fuck it was. I don't want this. I want my life back, but without the killing."

"Tough luck, kid. That's gone. You'll have another kind of life."

"What, with you? Christ, Goodrich, you have no fucking idea what I'm like. I'm a grifter. I lie, cheat and steal. By now it's an instinct, and I don't know if I can change. And I think I'm going nuts."

"Because you're having visions."

"Yeah, visions. AKA, schizophrenia, psychosis, whatever. A ticket to the locked ward."

"You know, you have enough real troubles without inventing fictitious ones. You're not crazy. Stressed? Yes. Confused, disoriented? Yes, again. Basically, you're experiencing a form of intense déjà vu, stress-related. You're seizing on coincidence and attributing causality. It's a common mistake. I'm sure you've taken advantage of it many times as a grifter. Don't fall for it yourself."

"You sound just like Overby. Everything is under control; the world makes perfect sense. Do you even really believe that? I thought you were a Catholic, speaking about believing weird shit."

"I'm more of a Catholic *fan*, although the belief seems to cause good behavior at least, as witness Brother Dominic and your hostess."

"Yeah, her. Are you really going to leave me alone with her in this creepy house? Christ, it even *smells* like Gran's."

"Evidence only of the international confraternity of old ladies. It seems comfortable enough to me, but the main thing is it's safe."

"Actually, Esme probably has my iPhone located as we speak."

"Yes, but it's extremely unlike that the bad guys will capture us and torture the truth out of us before tomorrow morning. Look, the snow might get serious and I don't want to get stranded if it does. You'll be fine here."

"Damn it, Goodrich. I thought the whole point of this was we couldn't live without each other. You could stay."

Here she gave him a Look and tossed out the sexual net, more out of curiosity than any felt desire. To her surprise, he laughed.

"Yes, that," he said. "But now is not the time. As you know. Nor would Mrs. Klotz approve."

"I'm amazed that you care. We're consenting adults."

"True. But your screams of delight would disturb her honest slumbers. Not to mention the dogs."

"Screams of delight, eh? A proud boast, Goodrich, especially from a man who won't put out."

"Good night, Marvel," he said. "I think I'll retain your iPhone."

"Why?"

"Because if they get a location off it, I want it to be me, not you they find."

"That's . . . what, you're like risking your life for me?" Her eyes widened in disbelief. He brought her close in a brief hug and kissed her cheek.

"Yes," he said, "and you're just going to have to get used to it. I'll come by after the trials. It'll probably be past five."

She shied away from the import of this last and said, lightly, "Okay, take your time. I'm sure there's loads of stuff to do in East Mooers. I might even get into Mooers itself, see a show, check out the Neiman-Marcus . . ."

Mrs. Klotz returned, waving a red rubber hot water bottle like a landed bass, and attesting to the chill in Casey's bedroom, but it won't be too bad, she added, and they predict warmer tomorrow, the snow won't stick this time. Under cover of this blanket of chatter and good cheer, Bernard made his escape.

Ordinarily, when Jumbo went on an operation, he would arrive at a venue that had already been scouted by a local team. The client would have been located, and in some cases a scam to draw him to a particular spot would already be underway. Jumbo would arrive with his guys, go to the spot, and do the guy in a fashion that Overby and Tanaka had already worked out. He felt himself a cog in a smoothly functioning machine, and liked it. He went in, made his contribution, followed the protocol to the letter, and got out. It was like the Marines, except not as much chickenshit and a vastly larger paycheck.

On this particular clusterfuck, however, he was not a cog, because there was no machine. He was coming into a strange city with no idea where the clients were located, or if they were still in Plattsburgh at all, nor was there a team in place providing valuable local intel. Tanaka would help on demand, of course, but without enthusiasm, and of course he was a cog, too, just as dependent as Jumbo on direction from Overby. Ironically, the only member of the Lanikai outfit who was expected to improvise regularly was Marvel, who (ha-ha!) would be no help on this one.

The Cars were uneasy, too. On the flight to Boston from Miami they drank more than they normally did when working, quite a bit more, until Jumbo felt it necessary to cut them off. They were even more cog-like than Jumbo, had been hired specifically because they knew how to follow orders, in normal rather than Hawaiian time, and they understood by now that the present operation was making it up on the fly. He knew they were bothered that it was Marvel, and he thought that would make them unreliable when it got to the wet phase. He thought he himself was reliable enough, but he was glad he had the Hongs along for that.

The Hong group was another unknown. He presumed they would follow orders, if he could think up the right ones. Unless Tanaka had hired them to kill *him*, a possibility he could not dismiss; so that was one more thing to watch. Beyond this, the whole group should not have been traveling together on the same plane, three Hawaiians, two of them immense, plus four Spanish-speaking Chinese, an assortment bound to stick firmly in the minds of the flight attendants and other passengers in first.

In real operations, the participants filtered into the locale over many days, always traveling alone. But there had been no time for that, and to make things worse, the stolen credit card he had tried to buy the fares with had been called in by its owner and when it bounced he'd had to use a different card, one that could be traced back to a business connected with the Lanikai outfit. It was a bad violation of protocol, but what else could he do? Roller skate to fucking Plattsburgh?

Esme was the only one he could rely on completely, because she was even more avid to nail Marvel than he was. This had surprised him—the best pal, after all—but that datum could be stuck in the can labeled Women and ignored. Jumbo didn't like depending on Esme, and tried not to bug her when she was slow getting him the intel he required, but he understood that she too was working under unfamiliar constraints.

The outfit had a network of bribed or extorted telecom employees who could provide Esme with CDRs, pen registers, and tower dumps, and there were similar useful subbornees in the credit card companies, but absent the normal operational planning, Esme had been obliged to set up a complex tracking op on the fly and this was creaky, uncertain, and slow.

He was relieved therefore when, upon landing at Logan and turning on his phone, he saw that she had left him a text:

BG Visa lit up: La Quinta on Rte 3 res 2 nites. Nailed both cells. Call.

Jumbo read this with relief and immediately got Esme on the line. There followed a complex and barely comprehensible description of how she had obtained access to the burner phone Goodrich was using and the iPhone Marvel had bought as Alison Hill. She could now track the location of both phones, and so it seemed the advantage had shifted to the pursuers. Maybe they were finally catching a break.

Or so he thought until the gate person for the puddle-jumper to Plattsburgh informed him that he and the Cars could not all go on the same flight because the plane could not fly that much weight. Jumbo surprised himself by remaining calm. He smiled, he pressed the urgency of the flight—a crucial business issue—and the agent managed to get all of them on a regional jet leaving for Burlington, Vermont, that evening. That meant they would miss Goodrich at the hotel, but Jumbo thought that with Esme's new tracking ability, it would not be that difficult to run them down. It was a small place and he had seven guys. He would have to look for vehicles and a place to do the interrogation and disposal, but that was no big problem. Assuming no

further glitches, he thought it shouldn't take more than a couple of days.

Marvel awoke to the sound of her grandmother's voice: "Marvel? Marvel?" with that characteristic interrogative at the end. She swung her feet out from under the quilt and was feeling around on the chilly floorboards for her pink kitten-faced slippers when she discovered she occupied a woman's body, rather than that of a girl of nine.

It was the smell, she told herself after the shock had subsided. Camphor, old paint, the smoke of ancient fires pickling every object, all under the more immediate scent of bacon and coffee. It took her a moment to distinguish memory from the reality in which she found herself, the room bearing the melancholy look of abandoned childhood—faded wallpaper with a sporting theme; hung upon it a framed photograph of a high school football team, who displayed a banner naming them regional champs, 1970; a maroon mortarboard with tassel pinned to the opposite wall, a line of trophies standing at attention on the bureau and a foot-long crucifix on the wall above the head of the bed. An embroidered sampler on the other wall prayed, "May His wisdom guide you, His strength uphold you, His care protect you and His love enfold you."

Marvel experienced her usual repugnance at such displays and went to the window, which showed a dead garden white with frost and across the rimed fields a line of oaks bearing yellow leaves going brown. Her breath frosted the windowpane. With a finger she wrote "HELP" and then rubbed it off.

In the hall she found a bathroom. She wanted a shower, but the claw-foot tub was not so equipped, and the thought of waiting for a tub to fill did not attract. She did a quick whore's bath, brushed her teeth and her hair and then

dressed in one of her new rustic outfits—jeans, wool socks, jersey, down vest, and those boots.

She went downstairs and found Mrs. Klotz in her kitchen, preparing a breakfast scaled for a husband and three growing sons. Marvel had spent a lot of time in rural kitchens and recalled well the script for morning conversation in such places. How good it smelled. How much food. Your own eggs? Yes, far better than store-bought. She once baked every day, but did not do so any more, except for bake sales and such. Terrific bacon. A friend still kept hogs. The weather: it won't snow, but it'll get colder. The roads will ice. Anecdotes about how miserable the winters are. Eric Junior, we call him Buzz, our oldest son--in Houston, free of snow, very successful, wife and three, darling, sees them in the summers, he wants me to go live but she can't, she'll die right here and be buried next to Eric.

Does she want to see pictures? Off course. There's all four of her men at the cabin: Buzz, he's holding the bass he caught, and then her husband Eric, she lost him six years ago, cancer, still misses him every day, then Buell the middle kid, with the bandage on his ear, a fishing lure snagged, and that's Casey, the baby, he lives down the road in Champlain, our wild one, had all kinds of troubles with drugs, but now he's settled down, thank the Lord.

Hard on Eric because he worked for the prison system his whole life, never could figure it, we treated all of them the same. Buell was in the Marines, came back from Afghanistan, never the same boy after, lives in the woods now, somewhere down in the Park, in a place she's never seen, calls himself a survivalist, thinks everything's going to come crashing down, collects canned food and guns, always such a sweet child, couldn't stand to see an animal hurt, wouldn't hunt hardly, and now this, all twisted from the war.

Here was a picture of an all-American kid in dress blues, the kind the services provide for the home folks, with the flag in the background, and on the face a look of pathetic formality. Sorry we killed your kid, the picture says, but here's something to remember him by. Mrs. Klotz attests that if it weren't for Brother Dominic and the Church, she would've gone crazy long ago, like these women you read about, hoarders and a hundred cats.

The breakfast was wonderfully good. Marvel hadn't eaten a breakfast like this for a long time, and she ate like a fullback in training, strips of thick hot greasy bacon, fried eggs over easy, just the way she liked them, fresh, airy biscuits, with homemade strawberry jam and creamy butter, and between bites she said the encouraging and sympathetic words that were required to keep up the old woman's flow. The persona she occupied was entirely content to sit in this warm kitchen, rich with remembered odors, and let the actual Marvel spin around in a cage like a trapped rodent, a distant well-padded cage from which the screams of terror barely escaped. The rodent screamed get out get out run hide they're coming they're driving here they're at the door door door…

"You seem to be in a lot of trouble, young lady," said Mrs. Klotz, a remark that came out of nowhere, and a phrase she had heard more than once in her life. It shook Marvel right out of her cozy performance.

"I'm all right," she said. "These biscuits—how do you

make them so fluffy?"

"Lard," said Mrs. Klotz. "Like I said, my husband was with the prisons for a long time and he helped me get a job in the parole office after Casey left home. I seen a lot of girls in trouble. And you have the look. Brother Dominic said something about a gang of murderers? How did you ever get yourself mixed up with something like that?"

A story immediately appeared in Marvel's mind, together with the expressions and emotional effusions that would turn her hostess into an ally. She knew she could do it, it would be trivial to roll this nice old lady, but oddly, disturbingly, the words froze in her mouth and she felt herself blush.

Which told her something was seriously amiss. Marvel never blushed without device. She had mastered the blush. She could blush on demand, a most effective ploy. The marks thought it a seal of authenticity. She felt disarmed.

She choked out the words: "I can't . . . I'm sorry, I don't want to talk about it."

"Well, I'm not your parole officer, dear," Mrs. Klotz said. "You needn't talk to me at all. But one thing I've found— you can't keep things tied up in you. They tend to curdle. I know. When Casey was having all his trouble and Eric had the cancer so bad, I just got so I didn't want to talk to anyone, and I was all alone with it.

"Then Buzz, God bless him, he came all the way from Texas and arranged for respite care and I could get out again, and the first place I went was to Brother Dominic, and it all poured out, you know? Why was God punishing me so, and why was he torturing a decent man to death, and all the things you say when you're so down.

"I can't even remember what he said to me then, but it was like a cloud lifted. I knew my honey was going to die, and I knew I was going to die, and that Casey was in God's hands

285

and either he would come out of his affliction or die of it and somehow I was all right with that, too. It sounds funny to say it just like that, but it was so. I was a different person after. You do yourself a favor and sit down with that man; that's my advice. In fact, I could run you over there today."

"That's a real good idea," said Marvel, miming an expression of gratitude and allowing her eyes to dampen. "But I was in an airplane all day yesterday and I'm really too tired to sit down with anyone. And I'm all crampy, you know? I think the best thing would be for me to take a long walk and then spend a quiet day inside."

Mrs. Klotz gave her a long, un-hickish, penetrating look and said, "Well, suit yourself, dear. You need anything, give me a holler."

Marvel offered to help with the dishes, was refused, insisted and then helped, clumsily, until she felt it was decent to leave. Mrs. Klotz said it was chilly out and did she have a warm coat? She did, a pink quilted parka with a hood, and she threw it on and went out. She had forgotten to buy gloves and a warm hat, but she pulled the hood up over her ball cap, thrust her hands into the down pockets, and set off down the street.

Walking, she considered her entrapment. She didn't own a car, had no access to her money; her credit cards were blown, and she had no way of obtaining new ones; she was completely dependent on a man she had cheated and despoiled. She examined the place where she had now cast up. A certain irony here: she had fled small-town Oregon for the high life, and here she was stuck in a place that made Dogpatch look like Hong Kong. As in Dogpatch, people here were clearly scrabbling. The houses seemed well-built, substantial, yet most of them needed painting. The cars in the driveways were old and worn and seasonally filthy.

Some people had hung hopeful signs in their front windows. Alterations. Firewood $50/cord. Psychic Readings, Horoscopes. Massage and Waxing. Doreen's Hair Styling. She should patronize each with her last hundred as an act of charity. Goodrich would like that.

She wondered how long it would take them to get here. Had they brought Overby into the hunt yet? She suspected not, and this was an important advantage. No one knew what contacts Overby had, no one really knew where his loyalties lay, if the term could even be used for someone like him. They would want to clear up the Marvel problem without involving him, which meant Marvel and Goodrich were up against a team without a coach. Of course, it was still the Mooers High School Raccoons (withered Go Raccoons. signs showed on several of the lawns) against, let's say, the *Patriots*, playing without Belichick. That didn't generate much confidence.

But here she was at the town's center of commerce, the Chevron station-cum-general store. She went in, and yes, it smelled the same as the ones in little Oregon towns, possibly a central office shipped in the air in special vessels, a mix of gasoline, cheese, warm wood, and old coffee. Marvel had done of lot of shoplifting from such places and felt right at home.

At the back, they carried a small selection of dry goods, where she selected a pair of yellow leather work gloves lined in flannel and a large one-hander clasp knife, and bought them for cash from the stern old woman behind the counter. Warm hands, big knife: it was something. The woman stared at her so intently that Marvel worried that the word was already out to look for someone like her, but then decided it was a combination of stranger in town, the shiny new clothes and some residual shoplifter aura that clung to her from her youth.

She walked to the end of town—no great trek—then back along the other side of the street. She didn't need a massage, Doreen would never touch her hair, and her clothes fit fine, but the Psychic sign, in pink neon script, drew her. She was bored in the way she'd been bored as a teen, a boredom familiar to those confined to tiny towns where they don't fit in, a boredom aggressive and suffocating. She'd escaped for a while and now here it was again, yawning wide, showing fangs.

Psychic Readings. She felt a visceral repugnance at the whole classless, clueless hick effrontery of the cheap local "psychic," and was about to walk by, when she found her fingers reaching, almost without volition, to the doorbell. It was a lite version of what had happened when she tried to dump the Miranda iPhone in Kailua, and a chill went up her spine.

The bell sounded distantly in the house and, as if she had been expected, the door opened at once, revealing a blocky, middle-aged woman with the heavily incised face of a chain smoker. The woman wore (of course!) a turban in multicolored silk, a floor-length front-zipper house-coat, and harlequin glasses freckled with rhinestones. Around her neck, on a tarnished metal chain, hung (yes!) a faceted crystal the size of an egg.

This woman looked Marvel up and down and, still unsmiling, gestured her into the hallway. She clearly expected Marvel to follow her and she did, taking in the furnishings as she went. The décor was Early Rural Tacky: kitschy wallpaper featuring classical figures and cancerous blossoms, much faded; a mismatched set of living room furniture, heavy, graceless pieces upholstered in colors that, had they ever appeared in a decorator's catalog, might have been named Mold, Humus, and Snot; a kitchen none too tidy, with ancient sink and appliances, the kind made with white enamel that chips black with age, standing on cracked linoleum in that acidy green shade that announces low-rent and absence of taste.

A smell of cigarette smoke and ancient cooking hung in the air. Marvel thought that the psychic business in East Mooers did not bring in much folding money. Maybe the woman worked for eggs? Maybe she should offer some tips from a higher-level grifter. Like, lose the turban and those glasses!

The woman conducted her to a room in the back of the house that might have once been a bedroom. The single window was covered with an old chenille bedspread and the walls had been painted dark maroon. In the center of the room was a faded Oriental rug, upon which sat a chrome and Formica kitchen table flanked by two chrome and plastic-covered chairs from the same set. A low pine bookcase held a few books and a box of tissues. No crystal ball. Lighting came from an overhead fixture equipped with one of those parchment-paper shades that rotated when warmed and projected little dots of colored light across the walls and ceiling. Dust hung in these beams and produced a confetti-like effect, but without cheer.

Marvel recalled her own days as a low-end grifter and thought that even at her lowest she had never been quite this pathetic.

"Sit," said the psychic, indicating one of the chairs. When they were both settled the woman said, "I am Eya. What should I call you?"

"Alison," said Marvel.

The other looked at her for what seemed like a long time. Marvel returned her gaze and took the interval to study her face. Squarish, heavy browed, with a lumpy jaw and a small hooked nose like a parakeet's beak, a tired forgettable face, like the invisible women who check out groceries or bring you coffee in cheap diners. The eyes, however, hardly went with this anonymous face, for they were memorable: large, smoky, deep-set, luminous, and amused. This was what startled Marvel, that amused look, unique in her experience of marginal fortunetellers, who invariably tried for a haughty, intense digni-ty. Eya looked like she was about to crack a coarse joke.

"Alison, huh? Okay, whatever. So, you have a question for Eya?" Her voice was deep, cigarette-warped and marked by the accents of New York City's outer boroughs.

Marvel made her voice light and innocent. "There's a man I'm involved with. I don't know if he's good or bad for me."

"Oh, really?" said Eya. "No, the question is which of the men you're involved with will get you. You're in great danger, but you already know that. One man wants to kill you, one man doesn't, but will try anyway, one man wants to save you, but you might reject him. Why is this? Because you're damaged, dear. You were damaged at one, and damaged again at ten, and damaged again at twenty, and now you're thirty something and here is the final crisis. Your real question should be, do I heal the damage and become the person I was meant to be? What blocks you from this? I'll tell you. It's not the dam-ages. It's that you think you're smarter than everyone else, you think that you control the game. What's your day and month of birth?"

"March first," lied Marvel. Eya sniffed, and Marvel stared at her, at those eyes, which had somehow become larger than eyes were supposed to be. The little moving dots of light seemed to distort her face, smoothing away the marks, making her younger, vital with energy. There was a new smell in the room, flowery and medicinal, like geraniums.

"See, you can't stop trying to outsmart," said Eya. "You give me a phony name, a phony birthdate—fuh!" The woman flapped her hand as if dispelling a stench. "Listen to me, dar-ling, you're not so smart. You're not nearly as smart as you think you are. What you are, is you're a really, really powerful psychic."

"Oh, please. That's bullshit!" cried Marvel.

"You think?" said Eya and laughed. "Then how about *this*?" She smiled, showing gold. Her face seemed to grow larger, then impossibly larger.

Everything dissolved.

Seventeen

Marvel couldn't stop crying. It was the kind of infant howl that most people leave behind at age four, but here it was again, hopeless sobbing, tearing her throat raw, spurting liquid from eyes and nose, shaking her whole frame like dengue, and in a corner of her mind she wondered if this were a Thing, that some people really couldn't stop crying and had to be put away in a quiet, drug-rich environment. Something had happened, this woman Eya had caused something to happen, but exactly what this comprised seemed unavailable to whatever in Marvel remained rational.

Yes, magic casements opening on faery seas forlorn, all that acidy stuff, but that wasn't the important part. It was that everything she thought she knew about the nature of the universe and her place in it had been overturned. What she had considered aberrations—her visions, her voices, her uncanny ability to understand and manipulate marks—were now revealed as the very center of her being. There was in actuality an unseen world as real as this table, this chair, this awful woman sitting across from her. Worse, there were entities in this world who *knew* her, who wanted to guide her, and she realized that she had worked her whole life to shut them out. But shutting out was clearly no longer an option. It was all blooming, buzzing confusion now: that's why she was crying like a baby.

Eya was smoking, sending thick plumes of gray vapor into the color-spangled air. Marvel howled and put her hands over her eyes. There were faces in the smoke. There were faces everywhere; everything writhed with uncanny life.

"What did you do to me?" Marvel wailed.

"I didn't do anything," said Eya. "I just opened the door. This has been going on your whole life, except you stifled it as much as you could, except where you used it to screw people over."

"You know about that?"

"Yeah. My line is Madame Eya knows all, sees all, but we're way past that. It should be obvious that you were guided here. I mean, for crying out loud, this place is not exactly Grand Central, is it? They wanted you to wake up and now you're awake. The rest is training. Have a Kleenex."

Eya reached behind her and handed Marvel the box of tissues. She grabbed a wad and honked and wiped up most of the fluids.

"Who *are* they?"

"Don't ask me, darling. Spirits? God? It's like your higher power in A.A. I once knew a drunk who said his higher power was his pick-up truck. It doesn't matter—they're just there. Or Him."

Marvel worked to fight the panic in her mind. Yeah, They were there. She had just been someplace where their presence was very strong. She'd felt them as paradoxically incorporeal *and* massive, on the scale of the Graf Zeppelin or a 747, an immense presence, more real than matter—a source of pants-pissing terror. She really, really wanted to get on their good side. Also, she was drowning in remorse, the bottomless sadness of experiencing for the first time the evil she'd done.

"About this training," she said between sobs.

"Uh-huh. Stop crying."

"What?"

"I'm training you. Stop crying. You're a control-master, you haven't lost any of your talents or abilities--get control of yourself!"

Marvel responded with rage.

"Oh, fuck you! I didn't ask for any of this shit, I don't like this shit, I am scared shitless by this shit. And take off that stupid turban!"

Eya laughed, a smoker's baritone croak. "Very good. Anger usually restores the ego. You're back among the living?"

Marvel felt the oppression lift, but she also had the clear sense that the misery was just taking a breather and would be back for many more rounds.

Eya said, "Okay, you're going to be like that for a couple, three weeks, crying, going to pieces. It's just part of the deal, and it passes. Part of being open to our thing is being open to ourselves. All the horrible shit you've done, that you denied and rationalized and packed away so you could feel good about yourself, now you have to live with it. It's hard and some people don't make it. It's a gift and any gift can be rejected."

"What happens then?"

"The gift fades and disappears. But you're not going to do that, are you?"

Here a penetrating look, and Marvel shook her head.

"So, back to training. The most important thing to understand is that all this is not for you. It's for them, or it, or Him, and whatever people they want to help, for whatever reason. You can use it to do evil, and you have, but then you end up in the kind of pickle you're in now. What else? Oh, yeah—learn how to breathe. The contact comes easier if your mind is empty, and the traditional way to start that is conscious, controlled breathing. There's a place you go in your head when you're scared shitless, right?"

"The magic circle," said Marvel in wonder.

"That's one name for it. So, you already know. Okay, you're trained."

"Seriously?"

"It's not like learning the violin," said Eya after a thoughtful pause. "It's more like learning to talk. It's wired in, but you can influence how it grows. You talk to a kid a lot, and listen to her, she'll learn to talk a lot faster and better than some kid who's stuck in front of a TV all day and no one ever talks to her. Or like sex, without the grief and the fluids. The more you do it the better it gets.

"In line with that, you need to get yourself a spiritual practice. The default in our culture is to block psychic information with monkey chatter, you know? The mind talking to itself, regretting the past, worrying about the future, and so on. You can learn to stop that. It isn't that hard. God, the library is full of books on how to do it, the wisdom of the East, and all that blah-blah. It doesn't have to be organized, although obviously there are psychics who work through religions. Just find something and stick with it. It's not optional, by the way. As far as how you're going to use your gift, don't worry about that. You'll be informed."

"So, basically don't do evil, pray, and wait for orders?"

A phlegmy chuckle. "Right. Just like the Girl Scouts. What's your day and month of birth? For real, now."

"August 29th."

"So, a Virgo, like I thought." Eya faced away to the right, shut her eyes, and slowly rubbed her left temple. After half a minute, she popped her eyes open, straightened in her chair, and said, "I don't often guess people's signs, but sometimes it comes to me, and when that happens, I'm always right. But it's interesting that when you lied, you picked Pisces. Your moon might be in Pisces. You have a powerful emotional self, very unconventional. Now it's expanding. What was selfishness crosses over and becomes love and generosity?"

Marvel started crying again. "I can't believe this. I'm sorry, not fucking astrology."

"Oh? What do you have against astrology?"

"I have against it that it's total bullshit. There's no such thing as a Pisces or a Virgo. They've done studies—you assign phony birthdates to a thousand people and you get astrologers to do their charts and everyone says, oh, how wonderful, that's just like me."

"You're right. Ninety percent of it *is* bullshit. But so what? Ninety percent of art is bullshit. But Monet isn't. Mozart isn't. It's like looking at a bunch of patzers, clothesline artists, and from that you conclude there's no such thing as great art. The point is to get where you're *in* the ten percent that *isn't* bullshit. Which exists.

"Look, you have to forget the normal laws of causality. We're way beyond that. Astrology, cartomancy, oneiromancy, they're all just tools. They're ways of focusing the uncanny information we get from whomever so that it's not a confusing mess, and over the centuries people who can receive that information have found it useful to handle it through the so-called occult practices. I ask a client what their month and day of birth is and somehow, I reach out to the whatever, the cosmic file drawer with that date on it, and information flows into me. Or doesn't, like when you give me a phony date. You don't like it, don't use it. Use a crystal ball."

Another heavy chuckle. "Meanwhile, I tell you things about yourself that are true, that you know to be true, and so what if I arrange them using astrological terms? I could use Jungian terms, or Vedanta terms, and they'd be no less true. For example, I say you have a typical Virgo personality. On the down side, you're contemptuous of people you think aren't as smart as you, and you thought you were entitled to cheat them for that reason. You're hypercritical and picky and hard to please. On the other hand, you're vastly intuitive and you have untapped reserves of compassion. That's what's making you cry now, not astrology. You see the pain of the world and all the pain you've personally caused and it's unbearable. Oh, yeah, I almost forgot. You have to fix that. What I said about not doing evil with the gift, that's a retroactive thing. You have to apologize and make restitution for your crimes."

Marvel's weeping increased. Yes, it was true, in the depths of her misery, a little self-satisfied voice had been whispering, yes, what a wretch you are. But you still have *all that money*. Outraged by Eya's latest demand, it started another line: really, you don't need this crap, you're a grifter, you don't have to listen to this crazy bitch, you only have to look out for yourself, you can fake psychic better than she can, you can split now, you don't have to think about all that depressing shit . . .

If you lie for a living you don't have a real life. Do you want to end up like Overby?

Did she think this thought, or did it appear in her mind from outside? In any case, it shut down the nasty little con-girl trying to take control, leaving the real Marvel exhausted and resigned. There was no escape from this. She recalled vividly the real Overby, who had burst hideously from the avuncular mentor in that Kailua Starbucks, and whom she had spent a lot of emotional energy trying to ignore. And, no, thank you—she didn't want that at all—but how could she construct a new person from what she now saw as a sludge of lies, evasions, and self-deception?

This is the bottom, she thought, I have nothing left, I should kill myself or call Jumbo and tell him to get me, I'm ready for the concrete shoes. But then, almost like the reflex in which we shoot our arms out when we feel ourselves falling, she closed her eyes tight and reached out to it, or them, or Him, in helpless, wordless supplication.

Immediately, it was as if she was back in the happiest day of her life, maybe a sunny summer's day, looking forward to her sixth birthday, a party and presents, and playing with her little dog and everything just perfect, perfect contentment and bliss. She basked in this incredible joy for several minutes, until the world and its infinite agonies returned to her consciousness. But the world did not affect her as it had; it was no longer a hostile fortress to be conquered, but a poor invalid needing care. And that was now her job, to make things right, to make the horrible old planet a little better, even if only temporarily. The image of the globe as a cantankerous, dirty old man lying on a disgusting bed appeared in her mind and she barked out a laugh.

"Feeling better, are we?" said Eya through her smoke.

"I don't know," Marvel said, unable to keep a smile from her face or a giggle from her voice. "I never . . . I mean, what the fuck?"

"They zapped you. Nice, but it doesn't last. And never think you can *make* it happen. Everybody in the world would be a saint if they got one of those every time they made a decision to do good instead of evil. They could close the damn jails. But no, they keep those in a little jar, and it's probably a cosmic pain in the ass to toss them, who the hell knows? I mean, there's a real contentment with doing good readings and healings and so on, whatever you're given to do, but not *that*."

"Have you . . .?"

"Yeah, a time or two, and I've been doing this shit for thirty-eight years. Stingy bastards!"

Marvel had a thousand questions, but sensed that Eya was not going to answer them. Already the woman seemed distant, fidgety. Marvel asked one anyway.

"So, okay, restitution. After that, what? I get a pink neon sign and start doing 'you will meet a dark stranger'?"

Eya rolled her eyes and sighed. "You still don't get it. You're not in control anymore. You'll be informed about what they want you to do. You'll get guidance. That thing you did, before the bliss bomb, that reaching out? That's what you'll do when you do your practice. You'll seek guidance and sometimes you'll get it, although it's not exactly e-mail. Sometimes it'll be gnomic, or Delphic. How about, 'left leads to right after right was left'? I got that for a client once."

"What did it mean?"

"Oh, the usual. The client was a lonely middle-aged woman who was going around with a rat bastard, and all the time there was a really nice guy who admired her in an apartment three doors down from hers. To the left. He'd just gotten through a horrible divorce after his wife left him. His name was Wright, needless to say. It took us months to figure that out. Most times, though, I forget what I receive. I mean I have no idea. The client has to remind me. I should have said that the stuff you get for clients is confidential, but it's kind of moot, since it gets erased, just like dreams. I wish I could say you're in good hands and everything will be all right, but I can't. They may tell you to spend your time in a crummy hole like this one, who knows?"

"If you don't like it, why do you stay?"

"Who says I don't like it? It's my fate. Thirty-eight years ago, I was a psychiatric social worker. Then a voice told me to go to an ashram in India. Everyone thought I was crazy. Maybe I was. After that I was in Germany for twelve years, and in Buenos Aires for five. Then I came here. It tends to be an adventurous life. I'm still hoping I'll be directed to start up again in a nice beach resort, someplace warm."

Eya breathed out two dragonish plumes of smoke from her nostrils and stubbed out her cigarette. "Well, I think we're done here, don't you?" she said.

"I have to leave? Wah!"

"Uh-huh. This guy you're with can do you a lot of good while you put your life back together, but it's not going to be easy. What's his day and month of birth?"

"October 15."

"Oh, brother. It's going to be a slugfest, all right. And there's something about a dead woman. And a dog."

"Yes, I know. Is there anything else I should watch out for?"

"You'll see dead people. That can be disturbing. This house, for example, it's real old, 1887. Lots of people have lived and died in it and some of them may still be here. Can't you feel them?"

Marvel felt a chill and the hairs on her arms and on the back of her neck stood up. Chicken skin, as they say in Hawaii. "Yes, yeah, that's right. I can feel them."

Eya said, "That's funny. I can't. This house has never been haunted." She broke into her gurgling laugh, and after she stopped coughing, she said, "God, are you gullible! And now you need to pay me fifty dollars and scram out of here. I got another client going to call me in an hour and I have to prep."

Out in the chilly street, feeling like a baby abandoned on a church doorstep, Marvel reached into her bag for her cellphone. She wanted to talk to Bernard, she wanted to talk to a sensible decent man and he was the only one she knew. How sad was that? But Bernard had her phone. She started crying again as she trudged back to Martha Klotz's house.

***

On deplaning at Plattsburgh, Jumbo found that his optimism had been a transient thing, and so he was anxious to talk to the only person who could sympathize. As soon as his phone connected to the local network he called Esme.

"What've you got?"

"The Alison cellphone is live—it's at a high school field less than five miles from the airport."

"A high school field? What, she gon play soccer? Are you sure?"

"That's what the technology says, brah. And it's not moving. Suggests she's on foot."

"K. We're going now."

Now proved to be over half an hour, as they had to wait in line at the rental counter, where they found that they could only get one SUV, a Toyota 4 Runner, and had to settle for a Hyundai Santa Fe as their other car. Yet another example of how fucked this operation was. All that shit was supposed to be handled by Tanaka's on-site crew, which in this case they had not got.

The Hawaiians took the Toyota and gave the Hyundai to the others, and drove off in a depressed and anxious mood. Another thing: Jumbo never arrived at a venue without previously scouting routes, nor was there an escape plan in place. Overby always insisted on an escape plan—a safe house, a depot with extra money, weapons, and ID—but now they were flying naked, and if something went wrong they'd be trapped in this crummy burg, and Jumbo had no illusions about the ease of concealing his current posse in this corner of white-bread America. Best case—they'd find her, lift her with no problems, get out into the country, find a crappy motel somewhere, make her tell them where Goodrich was, and get him to come to them. He had no doubt that Marvel could convince a man to meet her anywhere given the proper encouragement.

Worst case? He decided not to think about that, although this in itself was a violation of protocol. No plan survives contact with the enemy, Overby said often, and in normal ops there was always an exfiltration procedure available. Of course, they didn't actually *have* a plan, so that was cool. Also, speaking of cool, they were still dressed for the tropics and the temperature was in the forties outside. Thinking thus, Jumbo started to laugh.

"What's funny, brah?" asked Honda from behind the wheel.

"This clown show," said Jumbo. "Stay left. There should be a bridge ahead."

Bernard and his dog's dog day dawned brisk but clear, patchy clouds, weak sunlight in short breaks that made the people on the field sigh and lift their shut-eyed faces to the sky. It was a small trial, the last of the year, only a few dozen dogs (four Dobes, the rest German shepherds or Malinois) outnumbered by their handlers and the volunteers who judged or who pretended villainy, and by the spectators assembled on the edges of the trial grounds. These comprised the high-school playing field, now marked as a football gridiron, and a larger empty field to the east of it. The former acted as the venue for the obedience phase and the latter had been set up for the tracking and protection phases. Hides had been set up on this area, little red teepees arranged in two precisely separated, evenly spaced lines, as if the field were an encampment of miniature Germanic Sioux.

The morning had gone splendidly. Murtagh had aced the obedience trial, heeling, sitting, staying, and retrieving in the prescribed manner, and without staring up at Bernard's face while moving, which some of the other dogs seemed to think was darling. Murtagh dropped and came and walked as if on rails, flew up the A-frame barrier like an angel, brought the wooden barbell without chewing it, all as if he had thought up the difficult routine as a personal amusement. He scored ninety-seven points out of a hundred: *Vorzüglich,* as they say in Schutzhund circles.

"You're officially an excellent dog," said Bernard, scratching his dog behind the ears. "How about that?"

<You must have known it already.>

"True, but confirmation is always nice."

<For you, maybe. I go with my instincts. That dog is losing it entirely.>

Bernard looked out at the tracking field, where they were awaiting their turn. A German shepherd had completely dropped the scent and trotted back to its handler as if it had completed the course and wanted a pat.

Bernard watched the debacle and cast his eye further, to the small crowd beyond, looking for forms and faces that did not fit. Everything seemed normal.

The judge blew his whistle to signal disqualification and gestured to Bernard to move his dog into position behind a screen. Schutzhund II requires stranger tracking, which meant that a volunteer would stamp her feet to lay a concentrated scent in a two-foot square of the field's brown grass and then walk off on the course, dropping an object like a scarf or sock imbued with her scent in two different places as indicated by the judge.

The handler of the errant shepherd, a red-faced, middle-aged man in a windbreaker and corduroys, picked up his line and led the bad dog away with just that air of nonchalance that Bernard had observed in the city amongst dog walkers retreating from a shit-pile their sweetie has just deposited on a sidewalk in front of a doorman.

"Number six," said the judge, looking up from his clipboard and acknowledging Bernard and dog with a formal nod. "You're working free?" he asked. Almost all Schutzhund tracking trials are run with the dog harnessed to a long line, but Bernard thought it impugned the genius of his dog to do it and so Murtagh had been trained to track free. The judge looked past the screen, directed the volunteer on the drops, and gave Bernard the signal to start.

Murtagh took off, nose to ground, picked up the track, made the long turn perfectly, and dropped on the object, a pair of rolled socks. Bernard retrieved this, told the dog he was brilliant, and sent him off. As the dog approached the far turn of the tracking rectangle, moving closer to the spectators, Bernard happened to glance past the dog. There is a paranoia common to people who actually have deadly enemies that heightens the ability to detect excursions from the ordinarily benign, and that brief glance told him he was in trouble.

The dog, sensing the loss of focus, took a break of his own, casting for the scent and then, having found it, took a leak on the field. Ten points off. Bernard refocused, brought the dog back to his duty with a sharp word, and the rest of the trial went off without a problem.

"Honestly, Murtagh, you slut, how could you pee during a trial?" Bernard said this as they walked to the protection trial area.

<Another dog did.>

"Really? If another dog attacked a little girl, would you join in?"

<What little girl?>

"There's no little girl. That was just an example of a bad thing to do."

<What does biting little girls have to do with peeing? I don't understand.>

"Forget it, Murtagh. We've got to move to the protection trial now. If you would just remember to let go when I tell you, we should do fine."

<I always let go when you say.>

"Good dog," said Bernard and turned his attention to the crowd. There were three of them, he thought, two Asians and a huge tan guy who was probably Hawaiian. They all wore black hoodies without coats, which did not suit the current weather, and the big guy's hoody was about two sizes too small. When Bernard stared at them, they all pretended interest in something else, but when he observed them from the corner of his eye, their attention was fixed only on him.

He was prepared for something like this—the Escape from a Gang in a Crowd, having dealt with it a number of times in his fiction. He judged that they would not try to snatch him in front of hundreds of witnesses, nor simply shoot and run. Their play was to grab him on the road somewhere and extract from him the location of Marvel, who must be their primary target. His was to escape observation, reach Marvel and move out of Mrs. Klotz's. Aside from everything else, he didn't like the idea of these people getting close to that nice old lady.

While they waited for their turn at the protection trials, Bernard used Marvel's phone to do a little research. The geography looked right, as did the weather and the phase of the moon. A certain electricity ran through him as he contemplated testing his writer's imagination against grim reality. He called both of his children, to tell them . . . what? That he was about to risk his life? Fortunately, neither of them was picking up, so he left a message telling each that he loved them and that he was fine.

The judge called their number and, in a moment, they were off, Murtagh coursing on a zigzag run around the six red teepees, Bernard hustling in his wake, glad he had taken up running again, not sweating much, breathing easily. The dog found the concealed helper and barked. Bernard moved forward, heeled the dog, ordered the man to come out and raise his hands. He patted the man down, told Murtagh to guard and went into the hide to "search" it.

The helper bolted. Murtagh caught him in two great strides, grabbed the man's canvas sleeve and dragged him off balance.

"Out!" Bernard ordered, and, God bless him, the dog dropped the sleeve. He even dropped it after the man whaled away at him with a stick he'd pulled from his jacket. The rest of the trial went the same way. The helper attacked Bernard with his stick, and Murtagh defended him without actually drawing blood. After the helper had been subdued, Bernard and the dog conducted the mock malefactor to the judge on a winding path, Murtagh snarling and showing teeth all the way. Bernard presented the stick to the judge, said his name and the dog's and stated that he had just completed the protection routine for Schutzhund II.

"Ninety-eight," said the judge. "*Vorzüglich.* Congratulations. We're having a little celebration after the trials, a private home, dogs invited."

"Thanks," said Bernard, "but we have a prior engagement."

He returned to his car, ignoring the two Asian hoodies following at a discrete distance. In the car, he brought up a map on the iPhone, made a phone call and drove north a few miles to the Champlain Mall. The place was jammed with Saturday shoppers and decked out for the holidays. He parked illegally just outside the south entrance, ran in with Murtagh at his heels and trotted through the main corridor; people showed varying degrees of alarm, but all moved smartly out of their way. Out the north door—this was the diciest part of the plan, depending as it did on the efficiency of a stranger, but . . . there he was, a cab idling just where he had directed. He opened its door, the dog jumped in, he followed.

The driver, a small sand-colored man, said, "I don't know about the dog. Does he bite?"

"Yes, but not you," said Bernard, dangling a stiff hundred-dollar bill over the man's shoulder. "I need to go the Chase Bank at Consumer Square and then to Assurance Motors, on Route Three."

An hour later, Bernard was behind the wheel of a three-year-old Jeep Grand Cherokee, the yield of perhaps the fastest sale the young man who sold it to him had ever made, although somewhat disappointing in that no financing would be required. The Chase man had been all smiles when Bernard showed him the special matte black card his bank had given him, and he'd walked out of there with twenty grand in hundreds and fifties.

After getting his car, Bernard drove a circuitous route, making sharp, fast turns, pulling into suburban drives to wait and watch. There seemed to be no pursuit. On the way to Mrs. Klotz's, the mirrors showed only the sparse, normal traffic behind him.

"I think we did it, Murtagh. I wrote a little non-fiction just now. And by the way, I have to tell you how proud I am of you. Schutzhund deuce. You're an almost perfect dog."

The dog stuck his head through the space between the seats for a pat.

<And you too are almost perfect, my beloved.>

"You should have three cars for a thing like this," observed Chuco Hong.

They were sitting in their cars the parking lot of the Champlain Center, the cars pointing in opposite directions so they could talk through the windows.

"Yeah," said Jumbo irritably, "I know that, but we're playing by ear here. The guy made us and he split. It happens. Meanwhile we know where he's going because my associate is tracking the cell he's carrying."

"He'll dump it, if he's smart."

"He hasn't so far. Maybe he doesn't know we're on to that phone."

"So we're going to go wherever he's headed?"

"In a while," said Jumbo. "But first we need some warm fucking clothes. And this is a mall."

"And guns," said Chuco. "Unless we want to slap them to death."

"What's wrong?" said Bernard, when Mrs. Klotz opened the door and he saw her face.

"Something happened to Marvel," Mrs. Klotz replied as she let him in, casting a nervous look over his shoulder into the empty street. "She went out for a walk and came in a couple of hours later, crying like her heart was broke, and she won't say what it is. Do you think it was that gang?"

"I doubt that," said Bernard. "Where is she?"

"Up in Casey's old room. I asked her and asked her what was wrong, but she wouldn't answer. I asked her if . . . "

But Bernard failed to learn of these further futile queries, for he had raced up the stairs to the little bedroom. He knocked, said his name, asked for entry. Interpreting the groan he heard as permission, he went in.

Marvel was on the narrow bed, lying atop the quilt, which she had dragged over her body. This was crunched into a fetal position, and she had stuck her head partly under one of the pillows. From beneath, sobs issued.

Bernard put his hand on the back of her neck, a hot and sweaty span of flesh, and said, "Whatever it is, you're not alone. I'm with you here, until the last act."

The sobs, if anything, increased.

"Come on, Marvel. Roll over and tell me about it. What's wrong? What happened?"

A groaning mumble that he interpreted as, "Everything."

He plucked away the pillow and gently tugged her supine. Her face was unattractively blotched and swollen.

"Okay, let's have it," and in fits and starts, with many a tearful interval, he coaxed it out of her.

"Have you considered the possibility this Eya character worked a con on you?" he asked. "Maybe drugs, hypnosis . . ."

"No, Goodrich, this was real, as real as this bed, or you. I *was* someplace else. I *was* communicating with . . . *things*, that are not like us. As far as drugs, Jesus, that bliss bomb I got . . . if they had a drug that did that, no one would give crack a second look. The only possibilities are one, that the universe is not what I thought it was, or two, that I'm crazy. But I don't *feel* crazy. I feel okay. Better than okay—I feel real, solid for the first time."

"Then why do you appear to be weeping uncontrollably?"

"Oh, that's for the past. They're tears of remorse. I thought that was made up, in novels, tears of remorse, but here they are. She says it'll go on for a while."

"Your psychic, this is."

"Yeah, her. Look, brah, I detect by your artificial calm and your careful tone that you're humoring me. I don't blame you. I'd do the same in your place. But that shit all went down just like I said, and now I'm a believer. If that freaks you out, do what you have to do. Take off if you want. I'll be all right."

"Don't be stupid. It would take a lot more than a cosmic transformation to run me off. But, look, we can figure out the ontological stuff later. We have a more immediate problem: your ex-friends are in town. They'll probably show up here soon, so we have to leave."

"I guess. Any ideas?"

"Well, my instinct is to head for the hills, find a place we can defend and let them come."

"That's your plan? Me and you against . . . how many do they have?"

"I spotted three. I expect there could be more. Come on, get your stuff together. We need to talk to Mrs. K."

"This is insane," said Marvel, nevertheless rising from the bed.

"Yes, but I have a good feeling about it. This is the way the thriller ends, a confrontation in a deserted cabin or an abandoned factory. You've seen it a thousand times in the movies. The good guys win."

"Goodrich, do you hear yourself? This isn't some plot you concocted. It's real life. Real blood will squirt out of us and no one will yell 'cut!' after we're dead."

"For someone who's just conversed with the airy powers, you seem to have a inordinate hankering after mundane reality. That's a second big advantage we have. You're a psychic. You know what's going to happen."

"You believe all that?"

"Don't you? Go ahead—peer into the mystic realms and tell me we're headed for disaster."

Marvel opened her mouth to object, then let out a sigh. It was all too much. The sense of moving in a cosmic game she did not understand returned, as it had in Eya's room, and, with it, resignation. In fact, she was no longer afflicted with dread. The world had been revealed as something vaster than Overby's realm of greed and murder. She had a deep confidence that there was a future before her such as she had not imagined, and that it did not include death by violence in an isolated cabin.

She smiled at Bernard and said, "Okay, brah. The cosmic forces are go."

Then they were on the bed, where, despite Marvel's assurances, they kissed like the doomed, tearing at clothing, fingers digging for warm flesh.

Downstairs, a car door slammed. Murtagh barked; Magnus and Bluto took up the cry.

Bernard leapt away from the bed, tugging his clothes into approximate order, and grabbing his pistol from his jacket. He snapped a round into the chamber and advanced slowly and silently down the stairs. The barking stopped. That was odd. He took the last three stairs at a leap and swung into the living room, where he found he was aiming at Mrs. Klotz, who stood on her hooked rug with a cardboard package in her hands.

He made the pistol vanish into the waistband in the small of his back.

"I'm sorry, I heard the dogs and I thought . . . "

"It was the UPS man with my seeds," said Mrs. Klotz.

"Right, sorry. Look, these people who're after us? I saw them in Plattsburgh, and we have to leave. Is there any place you can go? I don't think it's safe for you here."

Mrs. Klotz's soft mom face turned steely. "Young man, I've lived in this house for almost fifty years. No bunch of thugs are going to run me out of it. I've got a shotgun and I know how to use it."

"Really, ma'am, it's not a good idea."

"Sonny, it's not worth arguing about. If it comes to it, I am seventy-eight years of age, and getting shot on my doorstep is as good a way to go as any. I seen a lot worse. And they may not bother with me at all. But what will you do?"

"I thought we'd head into the park, find a cabin and hole up."

"I guess you can use our place on Bailey Pond. It's the one in those pictures."

"Oh, no, we've imposed on . . ."

"Don't be silly. I'll get the keys and make you a map. You need to zip your fly."

Ten minutes later, Bernard, Marvel, and the dog had left East Mooers behind, heading south into the vastness of Adirondack State Park.

"Nice car," said Marvel. "I had one like it for about forty minutes back in L.A. Where are we going? Not that it matters."

"Mrs. K.'s fishing shack. We turn left at Ellensburg onto Bailey Pond Road. She drew me a map. She said the propane tank is full, there's wood cut and there's food in the pantry."

"Sounds cozy. Do you think there'll be a chance to whip off a quickie before the murderers arrive?"

"Perhaps we'd better stay alert until they're dispatched."

"Well, I admire your self-control, if not your sense. How are you going to dispatch them? With that little pistol?"

"I'm a much better shot than any of them, for one thing, and for another, I have a dog. And you, of course. Mrs. K. says there are weapons in the cabin, a shotgun and a rifle. I assume you can use a shotgun."

"Oh, yeah. I'm a country girl. How do you know you're a better shot? One of the men following us was a recon Marine."

"No, I mean I'm a *really* good shot. There aren't many people on the planet better than me with a small caliber pistol at ten meters, and none of them is a thug, as far as I know. The moon is full. I'll set up outside and pick them off as they approach."

"Did you ever shoot a man before?"

"No."

"Apparently, it's different, at least according to at least one of your opponents. He's done it a lot."

"Maybe, but he doesn't have a second-degree Schutzhund. What do you say, Murtagh? Are you ready for the real thing? Ripping throats? Crunching bones?"

<I have always been ready.>

Eighteen

The killers found a gun show in a strip mall parking lot off 22 just outside Beekmantown, where Jumbo bought half a dozen semi-automatic pistols and a couple of knock-off AR-15s that the seller assured him had been modified to fire full-auto. He bought a bunch of magazines and enough ammunition to assault a pillbox. He also bought a chrome whistle and a K-bar knife. Jumbo considered himself fortunate to dwell in a nation where a gang of criminals could arm themselves with automatic weapons, no questions asked.

Goodrich had abandoned his Mercedes at the mall, which meant he had obtained another car. He must know they'd be able to trace his credit cards, so he probably hadn't gone to Hertz, and he did not seem like the type to steal one. Fortunately, the motor vehicle bureaus of the nation were as an open book to Esme, so it was not hard for her to pick up Goodrich's new registration. They were looking for a dark green Jeep Grand Cherokee.

Esme had also kept him informed about the movements of Marvel's iPhone and given him the GPS coordinates of its current location. He'd looked it up on his tablet—a log cabin in the middle of nowhere, lake on one side, road and wide field of grass on the other. There was a garden adjoining the house to the south, and a small yard and outbuilding on the other side. Beyond this clearing, on either side between the road and the lake, a wide belt of woods stretched in both directions.

It was a simple tactical problem. Night. One car above, one below the cabin, personnel to slip through the woods on both sides, hold at the woodline and behind the outbuilding. On a signal, both groups will rush forward, kick in both doors, fire off some rounds into the ceiling, and that would be it. The lake, Bailey Pond, sat nearby, convenient for disposal of remains. So it *would* all work out; with a little luck he could be back on the beach in Oahu by the day after tomorrow.

The cabin was indeed cozy, and pretty, too. It had been built from a kit, clearly the work of a man who loved to use tools and his hands—polished logs, red shingled roof, the walls inside all paneled, the floors hardwood. Bernard felt uneasy at the thought that anything bad might happen to it.

He looked through the big picture window at Bailey Pond, actually a substantial lake, its riffles now reddened by the setting sun. He thought about the family that had once en-joyed this view and the grimness of its fate, and about fate in general, and the particular fate that had brought him to this spot. It felt right: insane, perhaps, but where he was supposed to be.

Meanwhile, Marvel strode around the main room of the cabin, looking in cabinets, then checked out the rest of the house: master bedroom and kids' room (bunk beds, birds nest collection, stacks of board games), and the small, tin-showered bathroom. The dog did the same.

"This is quite a love nest, Goodrich," she said when she had completed this inspection. "Or death nest, possibly. I haven't seen a phone like that in a while—with the dial? Do you think it works?" She lifted it. "Dial tone. We could call out for sushi."

"I'm still thinking about love nest."

"Yes. I see there's a gun case. Did she give you the key?"

She had. Inside the glass-fronted cabinet stood a Win-chester Model 70 and a Mossberg twelve-gauge, together with boxes of the appropriate ammunition. Bernard handed her the Mossberg and a box of number three shells.

"Load this," he said. "I'm going outside to take a look around."

The telephone rang, the old sound that almost no one heard anymore, strange and nearly shocking. After five rings, Bernard said, "I'll bet that's Mrs. K checking to see we got here okay," picked up the receiver and said, "Hello?"

"Dad?" said the voice.

"Lawrence? How did you get this . . ."?

"Dad, just listen. You're in serious danger. You need to get out of there ASAP and come here. Leave now, and bring that woman."

"Come where?"

"To Boston. We can protect you."

"You can *what*?"

Bernard heard his son take a deep breath. "Look, Dad, I'm not kidding. There's . . . well, there's a contract out on you and this woman, Marion Gafney. I can't talk about it on an insecure line . . . "

"Just cut the bullshit, Lawrence. What do you know and how did you find out about it?"

"Okay, your whatever she is, Gafney, is not some average grifter. She's connected indirectly to the worst people in the world. People who deal in drugs and human trafficking and terror. They move the money around that makes all that possible."

"That's nonsense. What's your source?"

"I'm supposed to say, 'national technical means.' Um, you know who I work for, right? The NSA? Do you know who they are?"

"They eavesdrop on everybody."

"Right. And my part of it is finding ways to penetrate the dark web. That's why it was weird when you asked me to look into it after you got ripped off. So I looked. I found the con jobs and the murders of the old guys. Then I followed the money. This kind of long con requires moving a very large amount of money untraceably, to the gang to pay them off and afterward to secure the loot. I had to tell my management what I was doing."

"Why? I thought you were doing me a favor."

"Dad. For crying out loud, these are federal crimes, wire fraud and money laundering, for starters. Concealing knowledge of federal crimes is a felony, quite aside from my professional obligations. Let's say my management was interested. When I traced the money transfers back to a certain source, they got *really* interested and they kicked it up to Ft. Meade and the NSA got the FBI and the counter-terrorism people involved. It's a big deal now. That's why you have to come in."

"Sorry, kid, this doesn't make any sense. How do you even know I'm here?"

"We're tracking her cellphone. The one you used to call me? And, believe me, the bad guys are tracking it too. You should disable it immediately and leave."

"Not a good plan. There's one route out of this place, and if you're right, I expect they're already on it. I would not want to meet them on a deserted road. I think we'll be all right here."

"Are you insane? You're in a cabin with a known criminal, killers are coming at you and you think you're all right? Do you want to make us orphans?"

"Marvel is a grifter. She's not involved with anything like what you're describing. In fact, she ditched the gang at great personal risk when she found out about the killings."

"Really? Ask her if she knows who Hamid Liu is."

"I will. Thank you for calling, Lawrence. I appreciate the heads up. Goodbye for now."

Bernard put the receiver back in its cradle.

"That was your kid?" Marvel asked.

"Yes. He says there's a contract out on us."

"Not a big surprise. Wait, how does he know? I thought he was a computer geek."

"He is, but he has national security connections. Apparently, you're connected to the worst people in the world."

She shrugged. "Was connected. Although considering the shit that goes down in the world, fleecing rich guys doesn't seem the absolute pit of humanity. *Killing* them, that I'll give you is fairly bad."

"No, he wasn't talking about that. Do you know someone named Hamid Liu?"

"Sure. He's the money guy. He moves funds during operations and arranges our pay-outs. He's the one that set up my BVI account. Why?"

"Because the feds are after him big time. Not a sweetheart is Hamid; he's got his finger in a lot of really dirty pies, according to Lawrence. Lawrence wants us to come in out of the cold and be protected."

"No, thanks."

"I thought you'd say that."

"What do *you* say?" He saw her stiffen; the animal in the headlights look came back into her eyes.

"I told you. The only side I'm on is yours."

"Why?"

"I have no idea. I used to plan my life carefully. Now, not so much. Your swami told you the same thing, essentially. I'm living a different kind of life now, the kind of life I used to imagine as fiction. And it's fucking crack cocaine. I love it. I was half dead—now I'm super alive, and if it ends soonish, then so what? It's the only sure cure for Alzheimer's. Meanwhile, I'm starving. We should get some food in us before the show starts. How are you in the kitchen?"

"I burn everything."

"Not a good recommendation. Fortunately, not to toot my own horn, but I can cook pretty well. Let's see what's in the house."

What was in the house, besides a lot of beans, dried soup, dog food, and canned fruit, was a pack of spaghetti, a tiny bottle of olive oil, an onion past its prime, a withered hunk of what is known in those parts as store cheese, a jar of home-canned tomatoes, and a frozen pound of hamburger, from which Bernard assembled an edible shadow of a pasta Bolognese.

"This is terrific," said Marvel, "it's like restaurant food."

"I'm glad you like it. Maybe we should open a restaurant. You could work the front and I could cook."

"Could I steal credit card numbers? It's been a long time since I worked square."

"Of course," said Bernard, "but only from people who ask for ketchup."

They ate like lumberjacks. There was plenty of Bud Lite in the refrigerator to go with the pound of pasta they consumed.

"So continue the story," said Bernard, cracking his second beer. "You stabbed your wicked uncle and your aunt had you thrown in the clink. What happened then?"

"I did eighteen months. It wasn't bad, kind of like kid's camp, in a way. Dope was pretty easy to get and the hacks didn't give us a hard time. There was a program, a lady came and gave classes, and I finished high school inside.

"And I made a friend inside, a kid from a nice family, dad was a lawyer, mom was some kind of professor. She was in for boosting. She'd been arrested dozens of times and given every kind of break, but she couldn't stop. I mean she could've had a life, but no, she had a taste for it, you know, crime and living on the edge. Anyway, she taught me about stealing stuff, what to take, how to fake out the store bulls. It was all about how to look. We were white, which was the main thing, but there was a way of carrying yourself, a way to dress and make up your face that made you invisible in Nordstrom's. That was the first time I became someone else. It hit me like smack."

"A place to hide. Me too."

"What?"

"What do you think writing fiction is? It's hiding behind characters, essentially a cowardly act. At least you did it in real life, at the risk of your body. Go on—what happened next?"

"She got out a week or so before I did and found a squat in Portland, and I met up with her there. She went out and stole some classy outfits for me. I got a job in a restaurant, bussing tables, and after work we hit the stores. I did mostly fancy leather and perfumes, designer stuff, anything we could fence, and also things we could wear. It was actually a shitty life when I think about it now, living with druggies and street kids, everything dirty, fights all the time, and always being a little scared. I mean, *she* was scared. I was just wired. I got into downers, not like a junkie, but enough to take the edge off so I wouldn't look nervous when I boosted. But I must've been, because I got caught. That's how I met Duane."

"In jail?"

"No, I didn't go to jail. Duane was a store dick. He grabbed me when I was booking out of a store in downtown Portland with a couple of Prada bags inside a Nordstrom's shopping bag. He took me to his office and locked the door and I figured, okay, a blow-job or a quickie bent over the desk, no big deal, but that's not what he wanted."

She paused and shuddered.

He said, "What did he want, then?"

"Me. Duane Tillman was a grifter. He got the job on a false ID, and he was there to rip off the store a lot worse than *fifty* little girls with shopping bags ever could. He thought they were on to him, and he was making plans to split town, but he wanted to set up his next grift and he needed a pretty young girl. I didn't find out what he was until later."

"What was he like?"

"A snake. He had slicked back brown hair and a rough kind of skin, you know, thick and pocked? And these white eyes, almost no color at all. He went to tanning salons, always had a tan, so the eyes really stood out when he stared at you. And fascinating, in a sick way. After his shift was over, he took me back to his place. He had an apartment in the Pearl, the whole place full of stuff he'd ripped off. I'd never been with a man before, just boys who didn't know much more than I did, so it was sort of a revelation. Orgasms, you know? He knew how to push buttons. I thought I was in love. I'm sweating talking about it. Do I have to go on?"

"I don't need the moist details. What did you do next?"

"We moved to Seattle. We ran the badger game on guys around the convention center, dudes from out of town, married, looking for action."

"That still goes on?"

"Eternally. I'd check into a hotel, the Hyatt maybe, or the Sheraton, on a stolen credit card and hang around the bar being friendly until I got picked up. We go up to his room. I strip down, I undress him, we go at it hot and heavy and then the breakdown: Duane comes in on a pass key, he's mad, he's got a gun. He starts screaming he's gonna kill both of us. My part was to sell the con."

"How did you do that?"

"I had to act like I was scared to death, you know, so the mark doesn't have a chance to think."

"How did you do that? Show me."

"Really? Okay, but it works better if I'm naked."

Marvel screamed, a sound as high and disturbing as subway wheels, and flung herself off her chair to the ground. The tears came, her face became red, her nose dripped, she scuttled on her side into a corner of the room, pleading, sobbing, holding her hands up in defense, exactly as if being stalked by an armed man."

"God, that's enough!" cried Bernard.

Marvel emerged from the fictive terror in an instant, went to the sink, washed her face, dried it with a dish towel, and resumed her seat.

"I used to piss myself--it was a terrific closer. Anyway, Duane would tell me to get dressed, and then he'd tie up the guy. We'd take his cards and hit the ATMs and buy expensive and fenceable shit, and then go back to the motel in Tukwila and fuck our brains out. I thought it was a great life, but Duane thought it was chump change. He was just using the grift to sock away money for his big score. You want to hear about this?"

"Very much. You know, I made up people like you, but I never thought I'd actually meet one. You're like Pirate Jenny. Do you know who . . ."

Marvel sung, in a convincing imitation of Lotte Lenya: "'*And a ship, a black freighter, with a skull on its masthead, comes into the bay.'* It was a great favorite of Overby's for obvious reasons. He thought Mack the Knife was a role model, I guess."

"I guess. What was this big score?"

"Duane had a pal in Macao who said he could get him a job as a pit boss at the Golden Pheasant Casino there. He had it all worked out. I'd work as a dealer. They were always looking for cute white girls to deal for the big players. I'd skim high denomination chips and he'd cover it up."

"That sounds a little dicey. So to speak."

"It was crazy. Like they didn't have people watching the people watching the dealers? It lasted maybe ten days and then one night after work Sami Choi showed up at our room instead of Duane. He was a shift boss with casino security, and he told me that his guys had picked Duane up and that they were coming for me. When I say casino security, I don't mean square-badge guys, I mean people who were into a knife across the neck and a dump in the harbor. It was a triad place, the Pheasant. You know what a triad is, don't you?"

"I do. So how come this Choi was willing to help you?"

"My winning personality? What can I say? We needed more scratch when we got to Macao, because of course, Duane needed to be a player, and a chunk of his stake went to betting long odds at craps. Not to beat around the bush, he pimped me out, very high-tone, escort services, and Sami was one of my regulars. That's how he knew me.

"Anyway, Sami was sort of a made guy in the triads and I guess he cleared it with the White Paper Fan of the Lo Chueh. Also he wanted to keep on fucking me and he couldn't do that if I was dead. The triads are pretty flexible in that regard. It's all about favors and face and *guanxi*. Anyway, I had to turn over Duane's cash and stuff, so Sami could save face, and I got out of there with the clothes I was standing in. He brought me to Overby's place by the Kun Lam Temple. Don't you think this is weird, by the way?"

"What do you mean?"

"Oh, just yakking about my hard life while a gang of killers is driving toward us. Why aren't we shaking and moaning?"

"Do you feel like shaking and moaning?"

"No. I feel calm and totally alive. I'm thinking, this is the last plate of spaghetti I will ever eat, the last beer, and it doesn't bother me. I mean, what the fuck, right?"

"We've become warriors, I think. We're on the other side of terror. Our pal, Jack Bill, ran a rifle platoon in Vietnam, and he talks about the same thing. After a while, you can't be scared anymore and you get into the zone of *what it is*. You exist in the moment, like Murtagh, or the sages, and you stop worrying about anything, even imminent death."

"I guess. Well, to resume. I remember being impressed by Overby's place. I'd never been in a private residence that looked like a hotel lobby, big white rooms with ceiling fans and thick Chinese carpets and celadon urns. We had an interview. He asked me if I was scared and I said no, I wasn't. I didn't get scared, I said. I said, I figured I would always find some way of getting out of the shit. He asked me about my life and I told him my sad story, making it kind of funny, because I thought that would make me attractive. I was picking up what he was like and changing myself to be someone that kind of person would want to have around.

"He asked me what I wanted to do with myself, if I wanted to keep dealing, and I said, 'probably not at the Golden Pheasant,' and we had a laugh, and I said, 'Really, what I liked to do was flim-flam, being someone else, but for real, not just in front of a camera.' And he gets this big grin and he goes, 'My dear, I can't express how delighted I am to make your acquaintance.' It turned out he was looking for an intelligent, pretty white girl he could train as a grifter, but at a much higher level than what poor old Duane had in mind. Basically, the two of them bought me from the triad. Basically, they saved my life."

"And you didn't grieve at all for poor old Duane?"

"Not much. To tell the truth the bloom was off the rose by then with Duane. And his scheme was dumb, even *I* could tell that. Anyway, I owe both of them, big time."

"But not enough to condone murders," he said.

"So it would seem." Marvel rose abruptly and started to clear the table. Confession time was apparently over for now. She said, "You know, there's someone living here. The bathroom has been used recently. And there's a pair of boots in the bunkroom with fairly fresh mud on them."

"Well, Mrs. Klotz probably . . . "

"No, it's a guy."

"How do you know?"

"I'm a psychic. Also, the toilet seat was up and there were piss spatters on the rim of the bowl."

"A squatter, maybe," said Bernard, looking out the window at the twilight gathering above the lake. "I should go out now. Remember to load the Mossberg."

"Where are you going?"

"Into the woods on the north side of the property."

"Why there?"

"Because the line of sight from here on that side is blocked by the shed. But anyone coming from the south has to cross the garden and pass across a clear field of fire. You can shoot them from that window."

They stood at that window and embraced for what seemed a long time.

"We're not going to die here," she said, pushing away, looking at him straight on.

"I'm happy to hear it, because I would really, really like to jump on your bones at least once before that happens. Turn off the lights when I go."

Bernard kissed her then, nothing heavy, just a so-long kiss, like the one he'd given Louise the morning she'd been murdered, a thought that briefly crossed his mind and was instantly snuffed. He whistled up the dog, took his pistol and a couple of extra magazines, put on his coat, a knitted cap and a scarf, grabbed the small flashlight he spotted lying on the counter by the stove, and walked out of the cabin.

"Dog, this is serious now," he said as he walked across the yard and into the trees. "These people we meet are real bad guys, not fake ones. When I tell you to go, you really need to tear them up."

<I understand.>

"Do you? I wish I knew if this was a hallucination. Not that the rest of my life isn't one. I've become more fierce, it seems. Now I wish I had taught you how to kill."

<I know how. You always make me stop.>

"Point taken," said Bernard. He walked carefully through the young maples, birch and beech between the road and the lake as the light faded. He was looking for the easiest way through the close-set trees and the viney undergrowth. He found a likely path and a couple of places where he could shoot from cover at anyone who walked along it, and where he was not too far from the road, in the event that the visitors chose to walk that way.

He settled Murtagh in a hollow at the base of a large tree and then circled around it, clearing the area of fallen branches and dead vines, picking away anything that could constrain his movement in the dark or make a noise, then returned to where the dog waited. His back was to the lake, but by turning he could just see the slate-blue expanse of the water.

It was cold, but he was out of the wind, and dressed for the weather. Night fell. The moon rose, shrunk now from the full, but still bright enough to see a path or shoot a man.

He heard the sound of cars passing on the road and saw their headlights and at each car he felt the tension grow and then fade as its sound diminished. Then he heard car sounds that did not pass, but slowed, and then the gravel crunching sound of a car pulling onto the shoulder fifty yards up the road. Its headlights went off. He heard four doors slam. A moment later he heard a car park further south, and more slammed doors. So, a probable four bad guys up close to him and another group to the south. They were going to rush the cabin from both sides, a good plan, probably devised by the ex-Marine that Marvel had mentioned.

The dog alerted, whining softly and sniffing, and then came an unexpected and unmistakable noise from the lake, the clang of a paddle on an aluminum canoe. Bernard felt an instant of fear, then dismissed it. There was no reason for the enemy to go for an amphibious assault—it was just some poor schmuck out for a cruise in the moonlight. The dog made another, deeper growl, and in a moment even Bernard's inferior ears could hear the sound of crunching footsteps on the path. There were four of them, walking two abreast, chatting quietly in Spanish. One of the first pair was carrying a long gun.

Bernard was trembling, but not as much as he had after winning a fencing match, swimming two hundred meters, riding a strange horse over a dozen jumps, and running a kilometer, something he'd done routinely in pentathlon. He used the familiar mental discipline to freeze his nerves, to move into that exalted space that only top athletes know, the zone of absolute focus. For reasons obscurely connected to his athletic career, he consulted the luminous dial of his watch: 2:52.

He waited until the last two men were a dozen feet past his tree, then stepped out onto the patch of ground he had carefully cleared, and fired twice, striking both men in the back of the head. Bernard stepped back behind his tree as the two men fell crashing into the undergrowth.

Bernard crouched and observed through a gap in the foliage. One of the two men shouted out in Spanish. He ran back to the two fallen men, cried, "*Chingada!*", turned to the other man and yelled something, of which Bernard only caught, "*muerte.*" The other man ran up, unlimbering his piece, an assault rifle. They spoke, and then the man with the rifle backed into the shadows, while the other man vanished into the woods on Bernard's side of the trail. Bernard stepped back to get a different angle of view, and brought his boot down on a dried branch that snapped like a shot.

The man with the AR immediately began to fire long automatic bursts at the sound. Bernard made himself small and hugged the ground. He heard slugs striking his tree and cleaving the air about his head. Bits of snapped-off twigs showered him. He heard crunching movement through the woods in the near distance. The other man was clearly aiming to circle around behind Bernard while he was pinned down by the fire from the AR. A good move, which might have worked were it not for the Secret Weapon.

The second man was clearly not Deerslayer. He was making a good deal of noise as he bushwhacked. Bernard said, "Get 'em, Murtagh!" The dog darted like a snake through the undergrowth and in ten seconds there came a woodsy crashing from some yards away, a shrill scream, the snarling of a big dog and the repeated cry, "*¡Ayuda!*"

The man with the AR stepped out of cover, perhaps to go to his comrade's aid, perhaps because he was not a trained infantryman used to night operations, but in any case, Bernard was able to put four quiet shots into the center of mass. The man staggered, let off what remained in his magazine in the direction of some upper branches, and collapsed.

Bernard walked forward cautiously and inspected the casualty. He was curled up on his side, groaning softly. Your . 22 long rifle is not a man-stopper, Bernard thought, but four hollow-points through the breadbasket will slow most down a good deal. He retrieved the AR from the ground, a 30-round magazine from the man's pocket, and a 9-mm pistol stuck in the man's waistband. He flung the pistol away, loaded the AR and walked off, tracking the sounds of canine mayhem.

"Out, Murtagh. Heel," he said, and Murtagh did. The foliage was thicker here and the man on the ground was just dark lump. Bernard knelt by him and switched on his flashlight. One of the Asians, it seemed. His face was knotted in agony for good reason: the dog's teeth had torn up his forearm. Bright bone showed through a mangle of flesh. Murtagh's muzzle was dark with blood and he kept licking it with disturbing enthusiasm.

Bernard gestured with the AR. "Stand up," he ordered and the man did.

"What's your name?"

"Tipazo."

"Okay, Tipazo. We're going to walk over to your pal now. If he's still alive, you're going to use your good arm to drag him back to your car, and then I would advise you to travel to the hospital in Plattsburgh. Or drive into the lake, I don't care, but if I see you around here again, you will end up like your other two pals. Do you understand?"

The man indicated that he did and they all walked back to where Bernard had shot the other man, with Murtagh guarding and snarling and otherwise having a great time. The other guy was coughing now and spitting blood, but Bernard did not waste time worrying about him, because just after they got to the path, he heard the blast of a shotgun from the direction of the cabin. Bernard took off at a run down the path, with the AR at high port.

When Marvel heard the chatter of automatic fire, she picked up the shotgun and stood by the wall next to the window that faced the garden. She was excited, but not nearly as much as she had been in the past, during an operation. She had a calm assurance that this sequence of events would not end in her death, one of the advantages, she supposed, of her new status, if indeed that was real. Still she did feel a thrill of fear when she saw a red spark blossom on the far side of the garden, and the window dissolved into flying shards; followed an instant afterward by the percussive banging of an automatic rifle. Peeking out around the riddled window frame, she saw two figures running hunched over about ten yards apart, heading toward her. She fired her Mossberg at the one on the right, aiming low, and was rewarded with a cry: "Ow. Shit. Fuck. I'm shot!" Ray Honda's voice.

Another burst of fire came through the window, peppering the wall behind her and shattering Mrs. Klotz's collection of souvenir plates. The shooter (Haulani Ford, from his bulk) expended the magazine and paused to put in a fresh one. Marvel aimed her shotgun at him, but before she could squeeze the trigger, she felt the weapon gripped from behind, and a powerful arm lifted her off her feet. A point stabbed into the soft flesh at the base of her throat and Jumbo Wedge's voice said into her ear, "Come on, teetah, you don't wan shoot nobody. Let me have the gun."

Marvel released the shotgun. Jumbo let it slide to the floor. He yelled out the shattered window, "Yo, Ford—go round the back, see what Chuco dem are up to."

Marvel found herself remarkably free of fear. Instead, she feared for Jumbo and the Cars, for whom she retained tender feelings, despite her current status as their intended prey.

"Jumbo," she said, "you should get out of here while you have the chance. Ray's wounded. You should get him some help."

"Oh, fuck you, Marvel!" said Jumbo. "You shot him and now you're all worried about him?"

"I'm worried about all of you," said Marvel.

"Yeah, right. We'll see how you feel in a little while." He grabbed her arm and pulled her through the front door of the cabin.

"Let her go!"

Jumbo whirled, bringing Marvel with him as he did, pressing the blade deeper into her throat. It broke the skin and she felt a warm trickle run down her neck.

"Drop the knife," said Bernard, taking an aiming stance with his pistol.

"Drop the gun!" shouted Jumbo.

For a few seconds the two men stared at one another.

Then Haulani Ford stepped from the shadows of a fir tree, pointing his AR at Bernard.

"No, you drop it, motherfucker," said Ford, and Jumbo laughed.

Bernard let the pistol fall to the ground.

Jumbo said, "Find some rope in that shed or tape and tie this bastard up. Then help Ray get back to the car. Where the hell are Chuco dem?"

"I shot two of them and the others split," said Bernard.

Jumbo said, "Bullshit!" and began to drag Marvel off across the garden in the direction of his own car.

Marvel said, "Jumbo, please, this is not going to end well for you."

331

"Shut the fuck up," said Jumbo. From behind them came the crack of a rifle.

"There goes your boyfriend," said Jumbo.

"Not really," said Bernard from behind them.

He was standing twenty feet away, aiming his pistol in the approved Olympic stance. Ford was a dark mass on the ground. Marvel had an intense feeling of déjà vu, as if this scene exactly were already in her memory, the three figures arranged as if on a stage set, with the pale theatrical moonlight pouring down, bright enough to cast shadows. Jumbo yanked Marvel close again with the blade at her throat. Bernard could see his eyes glinting as he searched for his companion.

Jumbo yelled, "Drop it or I'll slice her, I swear I will!"

"That only works in movies," observed Bernard quietly, and fired.

The bullet struck the middle knuckle of Jumbo's knife hand, exploding it into fragments; a microsecond thereafter, expanded to almost the diameter of a dime, it penetrated his hand, struck the wooden handle of the K-bar, levering the blade away from Marvel's throat, and, ricocheting off the wood, tunneled up Jumbo's wrist for several inches. The knife fell noiselessly to earth.

Jumbo had always considered himself something of a stoic, but the pain he now felt as his ulnar nerve shredded was far worse than anything in his experience. A howl he barely recognized as his own voice erupted from his mouth, and he found himself down on his knees clutching his gushing arm.

After a moment of shocked paralysis, Marvel ran to where Haulani Ford had fallen. She saw the moonlight reflecting in his open, frozen eyes and felt a sob rise in her throat. She closed the eyes with her finger and walked over to Ray Honda.

"Howzit, Ray?"

"My leg's fucked. Was that you with the shotgun?"

"Yeah. I aimed low. I'm sorry."

"How's Ford?"

"He's gone."

"What you mean, *gone*?"

"I mean dead. *Maké* dead forever. I'm sorry."

Honda's face twisted up like a baby's and he expelled several organ-like groans. "*Maké* dead? *Maké d*ead fo'ever? How am I gonna tell his mom? What the fuck, Marvel. I thought you were 'ohana. Why you do like this, running away and ratting us out?"

"I never ratted you out and I never will. I ran because of the murders."

"You wasn't supposed to know about dem."

"Yeah, but I did," she said, at which point both of them became aware of the sound of a helicopter, getting louder.

"That's probably trouble. You need to *hele* on out of here, Ray. Wait one . . ."

Marvel rose and went to where long, stout wooden poles had been arranged in tripods to support beans, took one, brushed off the dried vines and brought it to Honda. Using it as a crutch, he struggled to his feet.

She said, "Go back to your car, Ray." The man hobbled away, groaning. Jumbo was already walking slowly across the furrowed garden, bent over his wounded hand, like someone carrying an awkward, dense weight. The hand was wrapped in a scarf, she saw, which shone black in the moonlight, as if it had been soaked in tar rather than blood.

As he passed her, Jumbo said, "Overby's gonna do something real bad to you, teetah, and I hope I'm there to watch."

"He'll have to catch me first," she said. "Aloha anyway, Jumbo."

The two men trudged slowly across the rutted earth like the wounded of an antique war until they vanished into the shadows on the far side of the garden. The helicopter was now directly overhead, its racket maddening. Marvel looked back to where she had left Bernard and saw him kneeling on the hard furrows with his hands in the air. In front of him, a bearded man, an older and more battered version of the one in the framed photograph Mrs. Klotz had shown her, was pointing a deer rifle. The man was dressed in camo and boots and had a soft Ranger hat on his head. His eyes were pale and crazy. When she approached, he pointed the rifle at her.

He shouted for her to put her hands up and get on her knees, but instead she said, "Hello, Buell. Put the gun down and we'll figure out how to help you."

Nineteen

Buell's mouth moved, but they couldn't hear him above the racket of the helicopter, which passed directly over them at less than a hundred feet and started to settle in its own tornado of dust onto the field on the other side of the road. Marvel was surprised she wasn't more frightened, because Buell Klotz was screaming at her, bright dots of spittle flying from his mouth, obscenities and orders to get down, get down, and she imagined he'd done this a good deal in Afghanistan and thought that maybe an important part of him had never come back from that sad nation. He was psyching himself up to do something dire, and her gentling words seemed to be having no effect, so she reached out to the Thing in her head or maybe in an alternate universe and asked for advice, and got back a "don't worry everything is fine" sort of message. She looked over at Bernard and was surprised to see his face was wet with tears. Buell had his rifle four inches from her forehead. He was yelling that he was going to shoot and she believed him.

In the shadows beneath the hydrangea bush where Bernard had stayed him, Murtagh's doggy brain struggled with a problem in moral philosophy. Bernard had given him a down stay, and such a command meant that he must not move for any reason until released. In the City he had held stay for hours while Bernard had vanished inside buildings, as calm and immobile as Anubis on a frieze. On the other hand, he was supposed to protect Bernard, and the man with the rifle was certainly attacking, shouting and pointing a stick at him and exuding a sharp odor of menace. And he couldn't hear anything except a horrific racket from above. So he waited, patience having been trained into him, and whined softly, and set his eyes on the source of all order and rightness.

The sound from the sky diminished and he could hear again, he could hear the slight wind in the foliage and the scuttling of small animals and the shouting of the not-right person and the soft voice of the woman talking and then the sound he had been waiting for without knowing it, a finger snap from Bernard's upraised hand and the welcome release from the stay.

He's going to shoot me *now*, Marvel thought, as if she was somehow plugged into the damaged psyche of Buell Klotz. It was the helicopter, he's terrified of a conspiracy in his head and choppers in the night are part of it, and at the same time she knew (without knowing quite how) that the decent kid that Buell Klotz had once been was still in there and that, given time, she could reach in and get him back in control of this particular body. That was peculiar enough, but just as strange was the drawing out of time; it seemed that she'd been standing there talking softly to the man who'd just killed Haulani Ford for a good half-hour when she knew that it had been mere seconds. She'd seen the scene so many times in movies, and that was something movies did, too, drawing out the scenes of violence so the viewers could get their adrenaline circulating, and she thought that her last thought would be regret that she and Bernard would never share the next chapter.

The rifle fired and Marvel felt a blow on her face. She had shut her eyes when she realized she was going to be killed and after the shot she didn't feel any different and wondered whether this was what death was like, you just feel the same and sort of stroll away from your body to whatever the next thing is, and then she heard the sounds, growls and cries of pain and opened her eyes to find Murtagh savaging Buell on the ground. The dog had come out of the darkness like a toothy missile, ninety-five pounds of bone and muscle traveling at over twenty miles an hour, and, grabbing an elbow in mid-flight, had knocked the man flat.

The rifle went flying. Bernard picked it up, ejected the remaining rounds in its magazine and tossed it aside. He looked at his watch: 3:02. The whole thing. from the first ambush until now, had gone down in an absurdly tiny interval. He had heard about the illusion of time compression during violent action, had even written it into his books, and now he had experienced it. His entire being was lit up, as if he had lived a whole lifetime in those few minutes. Yes, a cliché, but also the ultimate drug, the great addiction, why men did war and sports, too, and he recalled that at the height of athletic exertion there was this same feeling of unearthly calm, but still a mere shadow of what he now felt, because even in the Olympics they didn't actually kill you when you lost.

Bernard gave Murtagh the out, and the dog dropped the shredded, bloody sleeve and went to heel, still snarling. He saw Marvel kneel by the head of the downed man and talk to him; her face close to his. Bernard couldn't hear what she was saying and didn't really care to know what it was. He watched the helicopter disgorge a number of men in helmets and black jumpsuits, observing them as he might have rubbernecked a wreck on the highway, a portentous event that did not really concern him.

Now came the shakes and the sweats and the nausea, knees like jelly. He knelt and embraced his dog, leaning on the animal's dense bulk. He had cried; he resumed crying. He had

337

enough of the writer's distance left to reflect that they never told you about this part in the thrillers.

Marvel was also having a new experience. Although she had never met Buell Klotz before and had heard only a scrap of his life story, she found that she knew the man. This knowledge had appeared in her mind as soon as she looked into his eyes, and it was odd in that it lacked the coherence of narrative. It was more like she had dreamed the truth about him, a life spooling out of a set of disconnected but vivid images.

The middle brother, fighting for a sense of who he was, not the baby, not the leader, finding that sense in sports, in being the best fisherman; in the Marines, the peculiar joy of submission to the group; pride in the Marines; his comrades, the unspeakable closeness of men under fire; the terror of driving the roads, of fearing the next moment, the bombs exploding, his mangled friends; the villages, the terrified brown people, what they did to them, what *he* had done, how he had *felt* doing it; and afterward; the homecoming, all those nice people who didn't understand, the departure of the comrades who did understand, the toxic loneliness, the sense of being used up, doomed; the drinking to oblivion, the nightmares within that state, the paranoid fantasies, the suicidal ideas. All this and more had come to dwell in Marvel's mind and she detected in the inexplicable confidence of that knowledge a ghost of what she'd felt when working a mark, that instantaneous understanding of precisely what combination of looks and words would roll him.

Now she did the same to Buell, and as she did, she understood that in helping someone the gift was different, was more powerful then when on the swindle. She told him things that no one knew but him and two guys who were dead. Even in the moonlight she could see his eyes pop. That established, she told him he was a hero, he had just saved their lives, the two of them were friends of his mother's. The helicopters had nothing to do with him. She wanted him to take his rifle and get into his canoe and go away and drop the rifle in the lake, and then seek out his mother. His mother needed him, that was the part she stressed, that he had a family who loved him, who didn't care what he'd done in Helmand province, he was a hero, he was one of the good guys, there was a place for him with his family, his family needed him.

And on and on, in a tone she'd perfected as a grifter telling lies, and again she found that it was even more effective when the content was true. It was not exactly hypnotism, but neither was it a nice chat. She stood and so did he. Without a word or a backward glance, Buell Klotz picked up his impotent rifle and walked off down the graveled path leading to the lakeshore. Marvel watched him go and only then noticed the lugubrious noises coming from either Bernard or his dog, she couldn't tell which.

Coming closer, she saw it was the man, sobbing.

"What's wrong, Goodrich?" This was disturbing. Prior to this evening, Marvel had only seen men cry in movies and news shows, and now both Ray and Goodrich had broken down. "Come on, man," she said, "the evil ones are dispersed and we're still alive. Get a grip!"

"I killed two people," said Bernard. "I ended two human lives. I just did it, without hesitation, pop pop, just like in the fucking movies. But this isn't like the movies. I want it to be like the movies. I want to make a cute wisecrack and kiss the girl."

"You could still kiss the girl."

Bernard moaned and said, "How do you do it? How do you not regret? Here's a plan—why don't *you* train *me* to live in the animal now, without remorse?"

"I don't know how to do that," said Marvel.

"I wasn't talking to you," said Bernard and clutched his dog like a kid with a teddy bear.

<If I could, you wouldn't be a man, only a very incompetent dog. It would be like teaching me not to have a keen sense of smell. You're squeezing me too hard.>

Bernard released the dog and grabbed Marvel. "Maybe I will kiss the girl after all."

They were still kissing when four armed men in black jumpsuits arrived and made them stop.

The men were remarkably polite. They did not shout or order them about. They allowed the couple to retrieve their bags from the house and did not comment on the corpse in the garden. A fifth man, who wore a suit, introduced himself as Warren Cole, and said he was from the FBI's anti-terrorism organization, and that the men in the jumpsuits were an FBI hostage rescue team. His mission was to remove both of them from the danger that they were in and bring them to Boston, where some people wished to question them about money laundering.

They wanted to put Murtagh in a crate, but Bernard said the dog was entirely under control, despite the blood on his muzzle, and displayed his Schutzhund II certificate to prove it. There followed a brief helicopter ride to the military area of Plattsburgh Airport, where they boarded a comfortable Gulfstream jet. Its eight seats—vast armchairs--were arranged in two rows. Marvel took the seat across the aisle from Bernard and the dog plopped down on the ample, carpeted space in front of his feet.

The plane seemed to have an almighty priority, for as soon as the doors were shut and they were buckled in, it rolled to a runway and shot into the air like a rocket. A steward circulated and took drink and snack orders. Except for having their cellphones confiscated, it might almost have been a vacation.

Marvel was certainly acting as if it were a fun excursion, rather than a gentle version of arrest. This Marvel was all chat, and flirting with the agents, and asking the flight steward for little favors, and squealing with pleasure when these were received. She was delighted with the experience of flying in a private jet, just like Beyoncé.

For a good half-hour she engaged the steward in a lively discussion of the various contestants on *The Bachelorette*, then pled total exhaustion and asked for blankets. The steward supplied several. She curled up in her giant seat, cocooned herself in them, and became a pale blue mound. This was vexing—Bernard had imagined more whispered confidences during the flight. Perhaps the Marvel he thought he knew was as fictional as this bimbo, another player in a reality show?

In a few minutes the blue mound that was Marvel began to rise and fall in the even rhythms of sleep. Bernard looked out the window and watched the sun turn the sky to rose. The dog picked up on his irritation and raised its head to rest on the man's knee.

<What's wrong now?>

"She's ignoring me. Why? Maybe because I cried, she thinks I'm a wimp. She could probably blow away a battalion dry-eyed."

<No, she wants you to mount her, but she has to check your running and scenting abilities to see if you're fit to breed her puppies.>

"I doubt that."

<You wouldn't, if you'd pushed your nose up against her vagina like I told you to.>

"Also, I haven't written anything in over a week. But you don't care about that, do you?"

341

<No.>

"Thus speaks man's best friend. Get off my knee, dog!"

Murtagh produced a heartbreaking look of rejection and slid down to the floor. Bernard stepped into the aisle and retrieved his laptop from the overhead. He looked over at the FBI people. Several had laptops out too, and some were dozing. Apparently, he was just one of the gang now.

When he switched the box on, he found, somewhat to his surprise, an open and unlocked wifi server, to which he connected. He brought up the draft of *Sleeping Dogs Lie*, read over the chapter he had written and tried to slide into the zone. After staring at the words on the screen for a good long while, he wrote a couple of sentences: *Noreen and Bingo walked through the door of the fraternity house and into a large, high-ceilinged room. The walls had been painted brick-red, which might have appeared fetching by candlelight, but now, with the clear sunshine of an autumn afternoon streaming through grimy windows, the room looked unpleasantly anatomical, reminiscent of what a minnow might see as it slid down a heron's gullet.*

Vintage Goodrich, but oddly unsatisfying. He recalled what he'd said to Marvel about the difference between writing thrillers and living in one. The difference between phone sex and sex, it now seemed. The preposterousness of the plot struck him anew, the preposterousness of all thrillers, but wasn't this life just as preposterous? Maybe he should switch to nonfiction. A sour laugh appeared in his throat, and then he noticed the little icon that told him he had a message from kitegurl21:

You in?

Seconds passed, and Marvel felt a pang of irritation. The guy had to know what she was doing, and why, and be willing to back her play. Would he? She could not help wondering as time slipped by and there was no reply. Obviously she could not explain the thing to him, because text was forever and they were in the clutches of the Feds, who could find out anything.

That was the problem with Bernard, or at least she feared it was a problem: that he was essentially a mark and not a grifter. His virtues were mark virtues—decency, honesty, grit, the whole list—but maybe that meant he would be useless in getting out of the current jam, which meant that regardless of how it felt to be with him, she would have to dump the jerk. There was also the irritation that, after having been smart enough to swipe one of his burner phones and secrete it in her underpants, she was not actually going to be able to nail down . . .

Yes. Hey, pretty neat plane. Maybe they'll put us up in a hotel. I could sure use a shower.

Well, that was a relief, and the trivial comment was a nice touch, confirming that he knew what she was doing, that he would back her play and that their communication was probably being monitored. She typed in some random crap in character about her hair and nails being a total disaster and how she couldn't wait to get to a salon, and added she was going to take a nap. Then she really did.

Bernard was six hundred words closer to completing his book by the time they touched down at Boston's Logan Airport; Marvel slept the whole time, unless she was secretly texting someone else under those blankets. He found that in order to write he had to put himself into a kind of trance, in which he could pretend that what had happened to him recently was also fiction. It sort of worked.

Marvel emerged from her blankets, went to what she fetchingly called the little girls' room and returned with her makeup amped high, a wiggle in her walk and a giggle in her talk. They all left the plane and found a SUV waiting on the tarmac. It was early morning, chill and overcast, execution weather.

The Federal heavies departed here, presumably for somewhere requiring more violence, leaving Bernard and Marvel in the keeping of Agent Cole and a tall, copper-haired woman with the big hands and broad shoulders of a competitive swimmer, whom Cole introduced as Agent Delamare. The two agents held a brief private conversation with the SUV's driver, and Bernard took this opportunity to approach Marvel and have one of his own.

"It's hard to talk to you with that goony expression on your face," he said.

"I can do goonier. Watch."

She did one that made Goldie Hawn look like John Maynard Keynes.

"Or I could go with stupid and sexy. Like this."

It was not merely the change of expression or the tone of voice or make-up or the way she moved, Bernard thought as he watched this display. It was not even acting. While a great actor can make you believe he's a character other than himself, you still know that the autistic genius on the screen is *really* Dustin Hoffman. But there was no *really* with Marvel. She had disappeared entirely behind the persona. He thought, that's why she couldn't be a theatrical performer. No one wanted to see that. It had a freaky quality, located somewhere in what the CGI guys call the uncanny valley, where an image meant to look human instead makes you uneasy, even slightly nauseated.

"Knock that off, Marvel!" he said, whispering what he wanted to shout. "You're freaking me out. And you're disturbing Murtagh."

She bent her knees and caressed the dog's black velvet ear. "Are you disturbed, Murtagh?" she cooed, "A big strong dog like you?"

<Yes. You but not you. It does disturb me.>

"I get that, but you'll just have to bear it for a while. Think of it as having to wear a choke chain. Can you do that?"

<If he says.>

She rose and looked him with her weird bicolored stare. "Well?"

"I guess this is it," he said, "where I decide if I've gone crazy or if the world is genuinely not as I'd imagined. You can really hear him?"

"Of course. I've always heard animal stuff in my head. I thought everyone could, and when I found out they couldn't and were going to treat me like a freak if I said I could, I clammed up on the subject. It's not really words. We put it into words, because that's how *we* think, but they think in a different way. So, as to the dog . . ."

"The man says to do what she wants," said Bernard. "Did you get that, Murtagh?"

<Yes. Go with the smell.>

Bernard said, "Well, sweetheart, what's your plan?"

"What makes you think I have a plan?"

"Dames like you always have a plan, and we poor jokers spend our lives trying to figure it out. You're the brains of this outfit, sweetheart, and I guess that makes me the muscle. I'll back you all the way, but remember this—I won't be your sap. Get one inch out of line and I'll send you over so fast you'll come right out of those fancy shoes."

"Damn, Goodrich, that was a credible Bogart. You never cease to amaze me. Well, the plan . . . the plan is you stay put like a good citizen and I book. I'll contact you when I can."

"Veto that."

"Oh, don't be an idiot. All you have to do is tell them the truth. You haven't done anything wrong, and your kid has an in with national security. But my dumb cunt act won't stand up to serious interrogation, and if they're going after Hamid Liu, there will be *extremely* serious interrogation, and I'm not going to let that happen."

"You could give them Overby. Then they wouldn't need you."

"I'm not going to let that happen either . . . you know I would personally kill for your hair. And I *love* your styling-- butch, but hot at the same time!"

Agent Delamare had approached from behind Bernard and was stopped short as with a blow by Marvel's cheerful rays. By the time they were all in the vehicle, Marvel was going on about hairdressers and Agent Delamare's answers were becoming shorter.

Marvel was pouty and more subdued during the ride into Boston, contenting herself with singing Gnash's *I hate u I love u* under her breath and tapping out the time on the armrest with her fingernails. Everyone stayed silent during the ride and no one told her to shut the fuck up, although Bernard was tempted.

They drove into the garage of an anonymous office building in Kenmore Square and arrived at an office equally anonymous, its name mere letters on the door. Agent Delamare took Marvel off with her and Bernard found himself deposited with his bag and his dog in what appeared to be a windowless conference room, containing a polished table, a whiteboard and six chairs.

Agent Cole asked him if he wanted anything and Bernard asked for and received food and water—a packaged turkey sandwich, a bag of corn chips, a chilled plastic bottle, and a plastic bowl. He gave the dog water and half the sandwich, then, after tasting it, surrendered the rest. He didn't share the chips.

"How's that, Murtagh? Pretty good?"

<Terrific. I prefer your food, but it's not very filling. This place is wrong.>

"Yeah, but I don't think we'll be here too long. Right now I need you to stay and be quiet, whatever happens."

<Yes. Quiet, but ready to tear your enemies.>

They waited. Bernard had heard and written fictionally that the guilty often fell asleep in rooms like this and wondered whether he should risk it. He felt like he had just completed a pentathlon and wanted to sleep for a day. As he mused about this, the door swung open admitting Cole and a stout man with the costume, face, and bearing of a senior bureaucrat. Cole introduced him as Stan Baker, from Washington.

"What agency?" asked Bernard.

"I'm with Justice just now, but I tend to float," he said, chuckling. "How're you doing, Bernard? Nice dog."

"Thanks, but please don't pet him," said Bernard quickly, as Baker extended a hand toward Murtagh's head.

"Why? Will he bite?"

"Not unless I tell him to, but he doesn't like touching from strangers," said Bernard. "As to how I'm doing, I'm a little confused. My friend and I were attacked by a gang of criminals and we were able to fight them off, with no help from the authorities, I hasten to add, and after that we were—I won't use the word 'abducted'—but let's say 'compelled' to come to this place, which is clearly not an agency of government, against our will, and held incommunicado, with no explanation. So, in answer to your question—I am not doing well at all, sir."

Baker kept nodding his head during this, a smile on his face, as if he sympathized with Bernard's complaint. He said, "Well, I'm sorry to hear that, Mr. Goodrich. I believe you were caught up in a national security operation that has nothing to do with you personally, and we hope we can have you answer a few questions that may help us, let's say, untangle you from this mess, and send you on your way. With your dog."

"I don't like the idea of answering questions without my lawyer present."

Baker said, "Bernard, this is a national security matter, and you are in no way a suspect. I don't think there's any need to bring another party into the conversation. Unless . . ." Here a smile and an ameliorative wave of his hand.

"Unless what?"

"Well, your son, Lawrence. He's already familiar with the situation and he has the necessary clearances. Perhaps you'd be more comfortable if he participated in this discussion."

"Lawrence's here? Sure, bring him in."

Baker said, "Walter, if you would?"

Cole got up and left, returning in a few minutes with Lawrence Goodrich, who looked wan and nervous.

Bernard rose and laid a typically awkward hug on his son. He had not seen the young man since Louise's death, and while he had anticipated a reunion at some future time, he had not made any move to schedule one, nor had he expected that when it came it would be as a participant in what looked like a federal interrogation. An uncomfortable silence when they were all seated again--clearly there was not going to be any family small talk. Bernard said to his son, "Okay, L., what's going on here? I take it that all this activity, and the recent derring-do with the helicopters and the strike team has to do with your interest in some Arab money guy. What I don't get is how I'm involved, or Ms. Gafney."

Lawrence looked at Baker, who answered, "Indonesian, not Arab. His name is Hamid Liu. As far as we can determine, he hailed originally from Surabaya and his family were small-time bankers there. Of Chinese extraction, as his name suggests. During the anti-Chinese massacres of 1965 and later, the family fled and settled in Macau, where there was a place for their expertise in discrete transfers of funds. Liu was just a child during this exodus, but he grew up in the business. They sent him to Princeton and the Wharton School, and he graduated with honors. He spent some years at HSBC in London and then returned to Macao, where he entered the family business, Liu Brothers International, Ltd.

"Around the turn of the century, he dropped out of sight. No one has seen him since then. We don't know if he's still in Macao, and obviously our abilities to operate in Macao are quite limited. The PRC government is distinctly uncooperative with respect to Mr. Liu. Meanwhile, over the last ten years, his name has turned up in various investigations of terrorism, drug trafficking, and human smuggling. He seems to be connected with the Lo Chueh Triad. I don't want to sound overly dramatic, but we have reason to believe he is one of the world's premier financiers of evil. Obviously, we would very much like to get our hands on him. I take it you'd never heard his name before your son mentioned it last week?"

Bernard shot a glance across the table at Lawrence, who averted his eyes. Bernard had the impression that Lawrence had not been authorized to talk freely on this matter, had stuck his neck out to help, and felt a surge of love and gratitude.

"No. I bank with Citi," said Bernard.

Cole rolled his eyes, and in a more aggressive tone asked, "But your girlfriend knew who he was, didn't she?"

"Yes, as a matter of fact, she did, although she's not my girlfriend."

"Oh, really?" said Cole. "Then how would you describe your relationship?"

"Ms. Gafney was until quite recently a member of a confidence gang operating out of, I believe, Honolulu. I was a victim of that gang earlier this year. I'd rather not go into the details here. I don't believe it's germane to your interest in Hamid Liu, nor for that matter is my relationship with Ms. Gafney. The long and the short of it is Ms. Gafney contacted me something like a week ago to warn me that my life was in danger. She had just discovered that her gang was in the habit of doing away with its victims. As I was the only surviving victim, as far as she knew, she wanted to save me.

"At the same time, she asked for my help in escaping the clutches of this gang. Unfortunately, they discovered our communication and were planning to eliminate her as well. Fortunately, she did manage to escape at great personal risk to herself and came to join me where I was staying, in upstate New York. Unfortunately, this gang discovered our hiding place and sent a group of killers after us. Fortunately, we were able to dispatch three of them, and the others fled. That's really all I can tell you. Ms. Gafney, as I think Mr. Cole here can attest, is the furthest thing from an international conspirator. Hamid Liu is just a name to her, and I doubt very much if she has any substantive knowledge of his doings. My impression is that's she's some sort of actress, whose main roll is softening up the gang's victims."

Cole and Baker exchanged a look, and Cole said, "Yes, and you were one of them. It makes me wonder why you seem to be palling around with her. Especially since you say it's not

350

a hookup. So what is it? Intellectual? You sit around and drink coffee and discuss Proust until the hit team arrives?"

"Again, I'm not sure how the details of my relationship with Ms. Gafney relate to national security, or your interest in Hamid Liu."

Baker said, "It speaks to your veracity. You'll admit it's an unlikely connection. I mean, the person who ripped you off approaches you and you don't call the police? Maybe there's something else involved, maybe you've been promised your money back if you, let's say, help further some greater criminal scheme?"

Bernard said, "You know, Mr. Baker, I believe I've been entirely forthcoming on a matter that causes me a great deal of pain, and I can't help it if you prefer to concoct some outlandish explanation for what I regard as a simple act of Christian charity. This young woman decided to turn her life around, she asked me for help, and I gave it. End of story. And if you're suggesting in an official capacity that I'm involved in some criminal conspiracy, then I decline to talk any further without advice of counsel."

Cole said, "There's also the matter of the three bodies you and your girlfriend left up at that lake. The state police would like to talk to you about those. The initial report used the words 'execution style' for the two found in the woods. Both shot in the back of the head at close range with a small caliber round. That doesn't sound like you were defending yourself, does it?"

"I was opposing six armed men," said Bernard. "I set an ambush. And I would be happy to speak with the state police about those events. But I don't care to speak with you anymore. I've told you what I know."

Bernard stood up. "So . . . unless you're prepared to ship me to Guantanamo or to some torture cell in Bulgaria, I intend to walk out of here right now. Lawrence, nice to see you again. I'll call you later."

Baker shrugged and held out his hands, palms up. "Suit yourself, Bernard. But if we check and we find you've withheld anything substantial to this investigation, then we're going to come after you, and then you really *will* need a lawyer. And don't expect that Gafney will be going with you."

"I assure you; she knows little more than I do about money laundering."

"I doubt that very much," said Cole. "We unlocked the cell phone she registered under a false name. There are some files on it that are protected by pretty fancy crypto, something we don't expect to see on a bimbo's cell phone. We're just waiting for a warrant that will compel her to open those files, and then we'll see how innocent Marvel Gafney really is. Or you are."

Bernard did not respond to this. He called his dog, opened the door--and was almost knocked down by the inrushing Agent Delamare. She looked wildly around the room.

"She's not here?" she cried.

Cole shot to his feet. "Of course she's not here. You were supposed to lock her in a room."

"I did," said Delamare, who looked close to tears. "The room's still locked, but she's gone."

Twenty

The problem with confining a person in the offices of a high-tech security firm, Marvel thought, when the door shut behind her and she had a chance to take stock of her surroundings, was that such firms tended not to think seriously about low-tech security. The lock on the door was a joke. She reached into her big Prada bag and took out a thin steel shim. Thirty seconds, a few practiced motions, and the lock yielded. This impotent device was supposed to secure a room containing the paper files required by even the most paperless of enterprises, racked in cabinets that lined the walls; these in turn were secured by cabinet locks just as feeble.

Marvel picked one of them easily, pulled out a three-foot high stack of files and with these teetering in her arms, her bag slung behind her, and her aura dialed to zero, stepped out into the corridor, kicked the door closed, and strode off. She passed several people, but no one stopped or questioned her. Gaining the reception area, she placed the files on a coffee table and walked out.

On leaving the building, Marvel found an enclosed mall with a subway entrance in it. She took the T to Copley Place, where she checked into the Marriot, went to her room, swallowed both of the bottles of tequila supplied by the mini-bar, ordered and ate a meal from room service, and went to sleep. Rising just after nine, she had a room service breakfast and hit the Copley Place mall.

She used Alison Hill's credit card to buy a clutch of warm outfits, a quilted parka and a rolling suitcase. With her purchases packed into the suitcase, she next visited the Apple store on Boylston Street, where she bought yet another Mac Air, iPhone, and laptop case.

Back in her hotel room, she set up the laptop with her Hawaii email account and downloaded a program called TaskMan Pro that Esme had told her about, and worked with it for a couple of hours. She did some research on her computer, made several significant phone calls and received satisfactory responses. After that she futzed around for an hour or so, trying on the clothes she'd bought, making faces in the mirror, being other people to herself. She made and drank a Bloody Mary with two of the mini bottles from the mini bar, then dialed a number known to fewer than half a dozen people in the world.

"Who is this?" said a familiar voice.

"It's Marvel, Overby."

"Well, how nice to hear from you at last," said Overby in a cheerful tone. "What a lot of trouble you've caused!"

"All I did was leave. You were the one who sent the killers."

"Not so. I didn't know a thing about it until recently. And they're retrievers, dear heart, not killers. You know the rules. We don't have a retirement plan. Why did you, by the way? Leave, I mean."

"I found out you were killing the marks."

"Really? Elderly gentlemen passing away from natural causes hardly seems . . ."

"Oh, cut it out, Overby! You *killed* them."

"Supposing we did. What does it matter if a few old men died who would've died soon anyway? I mean, there are so many people."

"It turned out that it mattered to me."

"You mean one particular man mattered."

"So what? It's my life."

"You *owe* me your life, Marvel. You seem to have forgotten that."

"No, I haven't. That's why I called you. Two things: one is I just walked away from a couple of FBI agents. They were asking questions about Hamid Liu. They were coming in their pants at the prospect of interrogating me on the subject."

"That's distressing. How did the FBI get involved?"

"I don't know, but they're also on to the long cons with those widowers. It's not just a lone PI anymore. I'm giving you a heads up, Overby, and I'm suggesting it might be time for you to get small. God knows you have enough money to buy a new identity and disappear."

"Thank you for that, dear. I see you retain some loyalty to a beat-up old man. What was the other thing?"

Marvel hesitated, took a long breath and released it. "You need to leave us alone. Just forget about us."

Overby laughed, as if she had just made a joke. "I'm sorry, dear. As much as I might like to give you a pass, I'm as bound by the protocol as anyone else. There are others involved, as you know, and they have a particular, we might even say *Oriental*, distaste for betrayal. If they found out one of my people had skipped and I did nothing about it, they would come after *me*. You know how the yakuza boys chop off their fingers to pay for some mistake? It would be like that, but they wouldn't stop with the fingers. I can't tell you how sorry I am about this, but . . . "

"I'm sorry too, Overby. Remember when you found me with my laptop in the Starbucks in Kailua and you accused me of writing my memoirs?"

"Yes. I expect you were communicating with your pet mark."

"I was. But I just got finished *actually* writing my memoirs, the chapter about you and about the long cons we pulled--names, dates, details. I also dipped into Esme's computer before I sailed away. I have all the corporate details, your account, passwords, everything a federal agent would need to build a case against you and Liu and your associates. How do you like that?"

She heard a long sigh over the line. "That was a serious mistake, Marvel. A genuine treason."

"Call it what you like, Overby. I call it insurance, and it's all up in the cloud now, in a program that's designed to send a message unless I tell it not to on a regular basis, using a password. I guess you can figure out where the message goes, should anything happen to me. Or Goodrich."

"A good plan, although I'm surprised you don't detect the flaw."

"You mean if you did happen to grab me, you could make me give you the password and you could go in there and erase the whole thing. But TaskManPro lets you set up multiple task managers with different passwords, and you can set up shortcut keys that send your messages immediately. If I knew I was going to be killed anyway, I would give you the shortcut sequence as a password and let you cut your own throat."

Another laugh. "Hoist by my own petard. Or by my own pupil, I should say. But here's the real flaw in your plan, darling. You forgot the first principle of this kind of work, which is not to give a shit about anyone, and especially not to be sentimental about particular human beings. Everything is easier when perfect selfishness rules. I've just sent you an email with an attachment. When you've had a chance to consider the offer made in it, call me and we'll make arrangements. As always, a pleasure."

Marvel heard the line go blank. She tossed the phone on the bed and dashed to her laptop. There was one message in her mailbox. Its subject was URGENT and its message was a video link. She opened it.

A slim woman of around twenty sat on a chair. She had Eurasian features and would have been lovely had her face not been gripped by terror. She first held up a copy of that morning's *New York Times*, as proof of life, and then read from a sheet of paper:

"If you want to see me alive again, I can be traded for Marvel Gafney. Wait for a call for further directions. Any attempt to engage the authorities will result in my death."

The words came choked; slow tears dribbled from her eyes. A man's chest, clad in a brown leather jacket, appeared in the frame. A hissing sound, like a thousand snakes. A gloved hand reached out and grabbed a hank of her hair. Another gloved hand appeared clutching a lit blowtorch. The woman writhed in the man's grip. She raised a hand to guard her face. The terrible blue flame drew closer to her face. She screamed. The video ended.

Marvel watched the foul thing again, stopping it at intervals to study the woman and her immediate surround. The woman was clearly Goodrich's daughter, Leslie. The chair was just an ordinary wooden folding chair. Dark wooden paneling showed behind Leslie's head, and the light was wan and ghastly, shining from some overhead fixture, probably fluorescent. Marvel felt her own eyes tearing, but suppressed the impulse to cry or surrender to the grief and guilt and self-pity she felt boiling up in her.

Instead, she thought of Eya and breathing and being scared shitless and the magic circle. So she sat cross-legged on the hotel bed and breathed in and out in careful rhythm, until she relaxed and then entered a place beyond relaxation. Nothing dramatic altered her appearance except a movement of her eyes to the upper left: an observer would have thought she was deep in thought, or bored.

Thoughts floated through the blackness like floats in a parade, some hideous, some luxuriously seductive. They tugged at her; she wanted to trip along the street following them, but she pulled herself back, allowing them to glide by. Gradually her consciousness traveled to another place, above the clawing thoughts. Of course she knew the kid's birthdate, as she knew everything about Goodrich, and she did what Eya had told her to do, a version of what she'd done spontaneously with crazy Buell Klotz; she reached and she found.

It was like rummaging through an enormous clothes closet, except the garments were psychic phenomena—thoughts, desires, emotions, memories, fears—vivid but inchoate, flapping in her notional face then falling away. There was dark stuff there too, because it turned out that even nice, well-brought-up young women who went to Bennington had the Shadow, but Marvel ignored this. She was searching for the source of this psychic reality in real space, something she had done many times without thinking much about it. Around her grandmother's place, it had been a thing: if you wanted to locate something lost, Marvel was your girl.

Then she was flying over terrain, as in a video game, a green carpet splashed with the autumnal colors of oak, birch and maple, threaded by dark roads. A kaleidoscopic dissolve, and there appeared what seemed to be a loaf of bread, brown and rectangular, sitting on a roughly woven patterned cloth. After a timeless interval, she understood that she had mistaken the scale. It was not a loaf but a building, a double-wide brown mobile home sitting in a clearing in the midst of a wooded plot. She could see the details as if she was really a sparrow flying above it, the white frames of the windows and the brass handle of the door.

Yeah, but where is it? She sent the question out and the Thing answered unhelpfully: *You will find it.* At that, the real world, if *real* meant anything anymore, reassembled itself. Marvel found herself sitting cross-legged on the hotel bed. She immediately picked up her phone and called Bernard.

On the announcement of Marvel's escape, Bernard found himself left alone in the room with his son, who apparently felt no need to join in any pursuit. After a brief, uncomfortable silence, Bernard said, "I hope this isn't going to get you in trouble with your firm."

"No, chasing fugitives isn't my department. And to the contrary, I'm something of a hero. Our basic task is to figure out the structure of the dark web. The goal is to penetrate the system of cut-outs and proxies that conceal the identities of the bad guys, and we also do some cryptographic analysis. When you asked me to look into the trail of the people who ripped you off, a track to this Hamid Liu showed up. Plus evidence of an actual series of crimes linked to his operation.

"I didn't even know the name before, but when I brought your stuff to my boss, her eyes got real big and she yanked the emergency cord. Apparently Liu handles money for the people who ripped you off. We've never gotten a clear lead from a live meat person to him before, so it was a major thing. All this is way over my pay grade."

"I don't see why they didn't just take us to FBI headquarters. If Marvel is so important, you'd think they'd want to take her to a place where there's a real jail."

Lawrence actually looked around the room, the instinctive motion of one who is about to reveal something confidential. "I really can't talk about this stuff in detail, but basically they think there's Chinese government complicity in Liu's operation, and they're not entirely sure the FBI computers are secure from Chinese hackers. Any workable lead on Hamid Liu has to be kept really close until they can see if it plays out. So using a NSA contractor as a front makes sense. But now that your girlfriend is in the wind, that may change."

"What do you mean?" Bernard asked. "And she's not my girlfriend."

"Then why are you . . ."

"Lawrence, I explained all that to the agents. You were here. I don't feel like going through it again."

"Fine, Dad," said Lawrence, his face closing down in the familiar way. "I guess this clambake is over until they find your . . . until they can locate the Gafney woman. So, well, I need to do some things at my desk."

"You mean I can go?"

"Not my call. But if you turn left out this door, there are fire stairs."

They stood and shook hands, and Bernard picked up his bag. Neither of them was a big hugger, or at least not of each other, but Bernard felt the urge to embrace his son now. In the moment, however, he settled on an awkward pat on the shoulder. Lawrence patted Murtagh rather more enthusiastically and both men made their separate escapes.

Out on the chill streets, Bernard made himself stop thinking about why his son didn't like him and considered his next move. Marvel was going to contact him and she was still in Boston. Therefore, he should stay in Boston. Therefore, he needed a hotel that liked dogs. And a place to collect himself. He found a coffee shop, settled Murtagh under a table, ordered an Americano and a scone for himself and a scrambled egg sandwich for the dog. He unlimbered his laptop, found a hotel, and made a reservation, imagining Lawrence and his fellows watching every keystroke, but what could he do? They were going to track him, obviously, in hopes that he would lead them to her, and he was going to have to rely on her to thwart their efforts.

He needed a spare identity but, even though he had imagined obtaining false ID any number of times, he had no idea how to proceed in real life. It was one thing to write about contacting Fast Eddie down at the Blarney Stone--the thing itself was in a different universe. But Marvel would know.

"How do you feel about staying in a hotel named for another breed of dog? The Doberman Arms was full up, so we're staying at the Boxer."

<I hate hotels. The smells are confusing.>

"You'll have to put up with it. We have to stay here until we find Marvel."

<Give me something of hers to sniff.>

"There's only my heart," said Bernard, to which the dog had no comment.

They took the T to Bowdoin and walked to the hotel. In their room, Bernard filled Murtagh's collapsible canvas bowl with water, sat on the bed and wondered how long it would be before Marvel called him. It turned out to be about thirty seconds.

"Can you talk?"

"Yes, I'm in a hotel room," he said, as blessed relief washed through his veins.

"Check your email and call me back," she said, "and don't worry. This will all turn out okay."

"What will turn out okay?" he asked, but she had already closed the connection.

Bernard turned on his laptop and watched the video attachment the monster had sent. For the second time in his recent life (the first being Louise's murder) he experienced an emotional typhoon unmediated by the writerly persona. He didn't think, how interesting—this must be what it feels like to have your child threatened with death by torture, he felt it without that comfortable padding and it made him howl. He howled until the dog stopped him with its whines and growls and sympathetic agitation. He found it helped to tell the dog what had happened.

<I could find her. Give me the scent.>

"She's too far away for that," he said, "but I do have something of hers to sniff."

Bernard went to his suitcase, brought out Otto, the blue dinosaur, and they both sniffed it. Then Bernard called Marvel.

"You must be going crazy," she said. "I'm sorry."

"Numb, mostly. It's not your fault."

"Yes, it is, ultimately. I colluded in the chain of events. That I'm different now doesn't let me off the hook. I have to make this right."

"How will you?"

"I have a plan." He listened while she told him what it was, after which he said, "That's crazy. You can't do that."

"It's the only way to protect Leslie."

"They'll kill you."

"They won't. I keep telling you that I know what's going to happen and it's not me dying."

"That psychic . . . stuff."

"Yeah, that psychic *shit*, as you were about say. I know you don't understand, and I can't really explain it, but I just know things and this is one of them. Have I been wrong since this business started? Did we not escape from the cabin of death? Am I not at liberty? Just relax and trust me, Goodrich."

"I don't seem to have much choice. I guess I could throw myself on the mercy of the FBI."

"They would kill her for sure then. They'll keep her alive as long as there's a chance of trading her for me. Once they have me, she's of no use to them and they'll let her go."

"Why won't they kill both of you?"

"Because it's Overby's operation. He had a principle— minimize illegal acts. They don't need the heat that would come down on them if they murdered a kid just because they could. No, they'll play it straight. They're crooks, not sadists. Well, Overby is a sadist, but not that way. So, are you in?"

"I guess. Where is this gadget you want me to pick up?"

It was not Fast Eddie at the Blarney Stone, but it was clearly quasi-legal. Bernard rented a car and drove out of the city to a bar off 128 near Hanscom Air Force Base, where, in exchange for two thousand cash, he received from a furtive youth a tapered spindle in white plastic about the size of a Bic lighter.

"Do you know how to use it?" asked the youth.

"I don't even know what it is."

Eye-rolling here. "It's a GPS tracker that links to an iPhone app. Let me see your smartphone."

Bernard handed him the new iPhone he had bought ear- lier on Marvel's instructions. The youth took it, thumbs flew, beeps sounded. He handed the iPhone back to Bernard. It showed a large-scale map of the local neighborhood.

"Turn on the tracker," said the youth. "No, the other end. It's recessed. Now, see the button that says 'track' on the app? Press that."

Bernard did and a flashing red light appeared on the map. The youth snatched the iPhone back and moved his fingers on the glass and now Bernard could see the building they were in, with the red light blinking in it.

"You can set it to continual send, but that just wears out the battery. The case is a solar recharger, so if you just use the track function it should last essentially forever, or at least until the collapse of industrial civ."

"Is that coming soon?"

"Soon enough. Although the Singularity could come first. In a couple of years this thing will be small enough to implant and run on bio-energy. Cyborgs are merely a transitional phase. After that, hyper intelligent machines take over and upload the human race. Then it's game over."

Bernard thought about the game being over as he drove the rental car back to Boston. Eschatology, a constant interest of mankind; of Bernard's, not so much. He'd always considered the present world and its fictional shadow sufficient to occupy a reasonable man; thinking about what comes next seemed otiose and even disrespectful, a view shared by St. Paul. The ghosts of childhood religion plucked at him as he drove: heaven, the communion of saints, choirs of angels, the throne of God, no dogs. You couldn't believe all of that, but neither could you believe that kid's world—technology as ruin or salvation—which might have been more convincing had the kid not been wearing smeary fourteenth-century tech in front of his eyes.

Bernard felt a shift in his consciousness, as if one door had opened and another shut. The dun, car-tormented landscape beyond the windshield seemed to stutter and then resolve. What was this, a mini-conversion? Not really.

Having spent much time recently with people whose faith enlivened every cell of their bodies, he knew he was not of that fortunate, unfortunate species. He believed in his daughter, and believed that she was going to die unless he believed in Marvel, and so he came to believe in her out of pure necessity, as the church fathers had believed in the God that supported all of being. He believed in her voices and in whatever produced them, he believed in a universe not entirely composed of forces and particles, a universe penetrated at every level by uncanny beings and subtle influence. Crazy, but there it was. She could talk to his dog.

"Do you think it's strange that Marvel can talk to you?" he asked Murtagh.

<Anyone can talk to me. Listening to what I say seems to be more of a problem. She knows how to listen with different ears.>

Marvel was waiting in his hotel room when he entered it, although he had not given her a key. He decided not to ask, but greeted her with an embrace and handed over the gadget.

She hefted it in her hand and asked, "Do you know how it works?"

"You don't know?"

"Of course I know. I want to find out if you do."

He told her what the kid had told him, demonstrated on the iPhone, and added, "It has solar recharging built in."

"That's nice, but I intend to put it where the sun don't shine."

"Won't they check that?"

She shrugged. "If they do, I'll just have to be resourceful. Besides, Overby's an analog guy and he's winging it now, because he can't let on that this is happening. Beside Esme, he has no tech support and . . . "

"Excuse me, why doesn't he have . . ."

"Because if the people he works with, including Hamid Liu, knew that someone on the inside—me—had gone rogue, they'd snuff him out. If Sami found out, for example, he'd rat out Overby in a heartbeat to stay cool with the triads. That's what he's thinking about, not a vaginal beacon."

"How come you knew who to go to for this?"

"We did an operation in Boston and that kid supplied some of the tech. Tanaka has technical people on retainer all over. They think it's a Chinese piracy thing."

"Wait, I thought he was Overby's guy."

"He is, but I have him on a line."

"Like you have me."

She looked surprised and barked out a laugh. "You? You're something completely different, my boy. I don't know what *you* are at all, but I'm sure not pulling your strings. Probably the opposite, if you want to know. We're involved, we're entangled, we're compelled."

"Yeah, right, it's bigger than both of us, as they used to say. But do you *like* me?"

"Oh, Bernard, don't be stupid. You know I love you. I'm literally crazy about you, as my recent actions have amply demonstrated. No, get your hands off me, we don't have time. . . okay, maybe a little bit, but no wet stuff. No, really, Goodrich!"

After an interval, she sat up on the bed and adjusted her clothing. "None of that until this thing resolves and we're free."

"Who says?"

"They do. My Guys. I'm supposed to abstain from drugs, booze, and sex until this passage is complete. After that, I intend to rip your clothes off with my teeth. They'll have to pry me off you with an impact wrench."

"Unless she dies. Or you do."

Marvel said, "Neither of us is going to die. Nobody is, this time around."

They drove north on 91 toward Vermont, through the ancient heart of the nation, past yellowish landscapes rimmed by gun-like black trees, under oatmeal skies that occasionally spit a sparse, granular snow. Beneath the stupor of freeway driving, Bernard slid again into doubt. He worked hard at trying to believe Marvel and came very close, especially when she began including Murtagh in her conversation. To distract himself from the crazy ontology and the worse pain of imagining what was happening to Leslie, he focused his attention on the plan.

"Tell me about the actual exchange again," he said.

"I went over this already. There's nothing complicated."

"I want to hear it again."

She sighed. "Fine. I will be in my car, which I will have rented at the Keene airport. I drive west on Route 9 until I hit the junction with Route 8 at Searsburg, where there's a gas station. At one o'clock I pull into the gas station and wait. If and when they're convinced I'm not being followed, a car will pick me up and drive me to the location where they have Leslie. If not, I'll get a message to drive to a different location. If they're satisfied and they bring me to Leslie, she'll get in the car and they'll drive us to a remote location in the Green Mountain National Forest, where they'll release her. At that time you'll get a text with her location. You'll enter it in your GPS and pick her up."

"And meanwhile, what's happening to you?"

"I'm explaining to Overby how the both of us can get out of the fix we're in."

"How're you going to do that? The guy is a demon, by your own report. That area is full of lakes and caves and

367

ravines. Why wouldn't he just kill the both of you and take off?"

"He won't."

"How do you know?"

"I just do."

"Oh, bullshit, Marvel. It's my *daughter*."

The car had swerved on the road during this exchange and Marvel put her hand on Bernard's shoulder, saying, "I know it's your kid and I'm sorry as hell that she got sucked into this, but you have to stay calm, and for God's sake resist the impulse to do anything but what you're supposed to do. Are you going to calm down now?"

Her hand moved warmly on his shoulder and on the back of his neck. To Bernard's surprise it seemed to be charged with Xanax; he felt the churning in his belly and the suffocating tightness in his throat start to fade.

"Okay, I'm calm. Could you please tell me why you think this bad guy is going to be such a sweetheart? That's the part I don't get."

"Because you don't understand me and Overby. He may use me, he may abuse me, but he won't kill me. I'm his finest creation and the closest thing he has to a child. He's enraged that I left him for something as petty in his eyes as an objection to mass murder. He wants me back, not dead, but he thinks he has to kill me to get him square with the people he answers to, the triad bosses, and I'm going to show him he's wrong, that there's a way out for both of us. He'll go for it. In a strange way, we love each other."

"You're saying you're lovers?"

"No. But, yeah."

"What the hell does that mean?"

"We did do it once. It was just after we moved to Hawaii, about a month after he rescued me. He was working me hard, all day, from dawn practically, way into the night. How to walk, how to talk, memorizing faces, memorizing sequences, all his trade-craft, picking pockets, picking locks, spoofing alarm systems—everything a girl had to know to put up a long con, plus unarmed combat in case things went sour.

"And I had to read books and talk about them, because he needed a cultured woman, not a half-educated hick, and he was not a gentle teacher. It was incredibly hard, and one time, I broke down, total hysterics, told him he could kill me or send me back to the triad, I said I'd rather whore on the street than do another torture session."

"What made you break down?"

"Oh, nothing really—an observation exercise. Walk through a hotel lobby and describe everybody in it. Do you know there's a car following us?"

Bernard checked his mirrors. "Yeah, I do. A black Suburban. It's been on our tail for the past hour. Gangsters?"

"Probably. It makes sense. There are going to be other cars strung out behind us, looking for tails. Anyway, I couldn't do it. I always left someone out or made someone up. It's a lot harder than it sounds. And for once he didn't mock me for a dumb yokel or yell at me. He hugged me and stroked my hair and told me I was wonderful, his best student ever, and he'd taught for years at the Agency's spy school in Virginia. Okay, he was manipulating, but it was such a relief that I melted and I started to kiss him, and the rest followed. He knew what he was doing, too, speaking of manipulation.

"After that, lying in bed, he talked to me in a tone he'd never used before, like he was showing me an inner person, a kind of exhausted candor, if that makes sense. He said that pleasure was all well and good, but power was more important than pleasure. With power you could have any pleasure you fancied, including some not available to the weak. He said this thing we did we won't do again, but when a man and a woman work together long enough a sexual tension builds up and we just discharged it and so now we can proceed without all that smeary haze getting in the way. Then he told me to get dressed, because we were going back to work."

"Sounds like a real prince."

"Yeah, but he was the closest thing to a prince I'd ever found. I worshipped the man."

"Then you found he had feet of clay."

"No, I knew what he was from the get-go. Overby doesn't care for romantic illusions and he didn't put any on me. I would still be on the team, with him, if . . . "

"If not for the murders."

"Yeah, I tell myself that, but If I hadn't met you, he might have convinced me that it was all still cool. It was you, Goodrich, not mere moral qualms. I'm not sure I *had* moral qualms about the other marks, if I'm honest with myself, but I wasn't going to let them kill *you*. Basically, I'm a follower. I used to like being told what to do by Overby, and now, after the thing with Eya, I seem to be working for cosmic forces, who also tell me what to do. At the end of the day, I'm a pull-toy on a string. Are you hungry? I'm starving. I can't remember my last sit-down meal."

"We have to get off the freeway at Brattleboro," said Bernard. "We can eat there."

The exit appeared. Bernard rolled off it and headed east on Route 9. In a short distance, roadside restaurants appeared.

"What kind of food do you like?" he asked.

"I eat anything."

"That looks like a Thai restaurant on the right. It must be a federal law. Every community above twelve hundred people will have daily access to *pad thai*."

"Not Thai, not any Asian. I lived there for years and I never got to like it. I mean, really, you have no idea what you're eating in that brown goop. Plus it all tastes sort of the same."

"I like Asian food."

"Oh, right, your late wife. Am I a bad person for not liking Asian food?"

"No, you're a bad person because you're a career criminal ruining the lives of innocent people."

"That was mean."

"Yes," he said. "I'm a little testy."

"Why are you testy? You don't believe me when I say I've changed, that I'm a different person now? When I say everything will be okay?"

"Of course I *believe* you. I wouldn't be here if I didn't believe you. But the belief offers me no comfort, do you see? It's not like believing in God, where you can say to yourself, okay, the world is a horror show, but underneath there's a moral order, and all will come right in the next world. This is, like, the opposite. I feel like I've been sucked into a world I don't understand, a moral order turned on its head. I'm thinking maybe I'm part of a con so long it approaches the infinite, and now it's come to this cockamamie scheme of yours. And I'm helpless. That's why I'm testy."

"Look, there's a diner," said Marvel. "Pull in!"

Bernard whipped the car over somewhat more forcefully than the traffic situation demanded.

"I bet they make a good burger and milkshake," said Marvel. "In my opinion, the fabled East has nothing that compares to the American burger. I would bet Murtagh agrees with me. What about it, Murtagh? Burgers are your fave, right?"

<I like road kill best. Old dead things. Men never let their food get old enough.>

371

"You never ate road kill in your life, you phony," said Bernard.

<Yes, I did, a groundhog with maggots in it. It was the best thing I ever ate.>

They left the dog in the car with the driver's window open and went in. The diner was a diner—stainless and red leatherette, patched in places with peeling tape, the air warm, smelling of toast, coffee, and bacon, that ineffable diner pong, and boasting the two canonical diner waitresses, the pretty sullen teen and the over-friendly gray-permed matron, of which they got the latter.

When she had taken their order and had her ears filled with lies in response to her cheerful interrogation, Bernard said, "Did that really happen? Out in the car, the burger discussion . . ."

"No, it didn't *really* happen. It was a mutual fantasy, characteristic of the *folie à deux* in which we find ourselves. That, or your dog talks. Either one is inexplicable, so we choose to believe the latter. It's nicer for the dog. Meanwhile, get a grip, Goodrich!"

"So I take it you weren't impressed by my *cri de coeur* out there on the road."

"It's neurotic bullshit," she said. "Look, you're either in or you're not. I asked you on the plane and you said you were in and that was it as far as I was concerned. When you're *in*, it means you stop thinking about all the shit that led up to the con and all the shit that could go wrong. You clear your mind and solve the problems that come up. Just *hele* on. That's how it is in my world.

"You know, whether you believe it or not, I've changed since I met you. I've become more like you. I grew a con-science or got one blown into my head by forces from beyond, you pick. What you don't get yet is you have to become more like *me*. And it's there. I see it in you. So stop being such a mark. Drop the fucking *waha* and let's just run our con."

"But we're not running a con."

"You don't think so? In a few hours I'm going to try to roll the smartest man I ever met, a totally ruthless world-class manipulator, and the stakes are my life and the life of your girl. If I thought about it for one second, I'd be curled up fetal position in a pool of vomit. So I fucking don't."

"Plus, your voices say you'll crown the Dauphin at Rheims, and so you will."

"You got that right, brah. Oh, good, here's our food!"

Marvel had the burger special with a chocolate milk-shake. They ordered take-out for the dog, double cheeseburger hold the pickle, lettuce, and tomato. Bernard went with the homemade beef barley soup, because he wasn't hungry, in fact was faintly nauseated by the nice smells in the diner and the sight of people unconnected to murderous violence digging into their chow.

But with the first spoonful, animal spirits flowed back into him, and he found himself ravenous. It was wonderful soup, fantastic. He finished it all and the bread that came with it and poached Marvel's fries. As he did, he realized that the advice Marvel had just given him was the same as what he'd received from both Brother Dominic and the dog, stupidly simple and banal. Be faithful to those you love, run your racket and don't worry.

Marvel looked up at him and gave him a major smile, a Miranda smile, except real.

"Finally got it, eh?" she said.

"You read my mind."

"Uh huh. You and Murtagh are as an open book to the Marvel. But did he really eat a road kill?"

"Yes, how could I forget? It was up at our country place before he started serious training, and technically it wasn't road kill. Someone had shot a groundhog and it had crawled into its hole and died. Murtagh dug it up, rolled in it and consumed most of it. He bought the rest home and laid it on my bed.

"Well, the stink was life-changing. We threw him in the bath and washed him down and the stench would not leave. We tried dog shampoo, human shampoo, my sister-in-law's really expensive shampoo made with virgin's tears and ambergris— nothing worked. Finally, my brother came in and said that the only thing to use was tomato juice. So—and you can imagine the arguments—we bought a case of tomato juice and filled the bath with it, and we're talking about an extremely amusing experience here as you may imagine, the dog drinking the juice and getting sick off it—well, anyway, it worked, to an extent, in that Murtagh afterwards smelled of tomato juice rather than old groundhog corpse. I believe most people would prefer it. On wet days he still has that Bloody Mary waft."

"I was wondering what that was," she said. He thought her honest laughter was the best thing he'd heard in a while.

She said, "So we're good now."

"Yeah, we're good."

"Let's go, then," she said. "Don't forget Murtagh's burger."

Twenty-one

In the Hertz at Keene International Airport, they did not make much of their parting. Marvel rented a white Chevy Cruz, they embraced hard and too briefly in the parking, lot and she was off, but not before she extracted from him a promise to stick with the plan, to keep at least twenty miles away, and to put completely out of his mind any thought of personal heroics.

As he waited in the lot, he realized he had no intention of keeping this promise in full. He understood that every plan failed at some point, so that heroism was *required* to save the mission. It was a common trope in thrillers; now he saw for the first time that it also governed real life. That's what heroes *were*: people who risked their bodies to save the wreck of a collapsing plan. Like most people, Bernard recoiled at thinking himself heroic, although he thought that when the need inevitably came, he would not disgrace himself. But he would give the plan a chance.

He was supposed to wait for half an hour in the parking lot, to let her put some miles between their two cars. At that time, he was directed to ping her vagina (her phrase) and follow discreetly the moving red dot. He had time to think and what he thought was that this thing was strangely reminiscent of athletic training. One of the things that separates great athletes from regular people is their ability to literally embody some abstract ideal of perfection. It exists in the mind first—the perfect leap, the perfect backhand, the perfect pitch—and then, with enough talent and effort, it becomes real in the world of sweating flesh.

In the same way, he felt that years of imagining thrillers had prepared him for a life of risk and danger. Stories teach us how to live, as Anatole France once remarked, and our lives proceed according to plots invented by people working alone in quiet rooms. So in this one he was the Sap, torn from normal life by the Plot, and on the lam with the Bad Girl. They were heading for a confrontation with the Villain in an isolated region. So far, so conventional. The only remaining question was would it be a feel-good potboiler or an arty, dark piece, Raymond Chandler or Patricia Highsmith.

Because the villains, too, were caught in the same tyranny of art. Unconsciously, they were hoping for arty, noir, a *Chinatown* ending, where the bad guys got away with it. Bernard didn't think they were in arty just now. He thought that actual bad guys were oppressed by having watched the fate of innumerable bad guys in films and TV shows, and that this must give them pause during their malefactions and weaken their resolve. Or he hoped so. He thought about what his life would be like were both Marvel and Leslie to die. He thought he would either retire to the monastery or become one of those pulp thriller avengers, shooting down the bad guys until they were all gone or he himself was dead; he hadn't yet decided which.

The alarm he'd set on the iPhone went off, startling him out of his doze. He pinged and observed that the red dot that was Marvel was moving toward the rendezvous point. He put the car in gear and followed, keeping the distance she had prescribed.

Marvel reached the referenced gas station before time, and, as directed, pulled into an alley, where she parked on a scruffy patch of asphalt amid Dumpsters. It was ten minutes to one. She wished for drugs, but the Guys had made it clear that she was to stay clean until further notice. She did the thing where she opened herself to the Whatever, but they were apparently busy serving another customer. Nor did they play classical favorites while she waited. It occurred to her that the assurance she'd received of a good outcome depended on what "good" meant to beings beyond her comprehension. If there were such beings. If she were not mad.

I've become a sucker in my old age, she reflected, I'm basing my entire life and the lives of others on something that happened in a tacky room presided over by a sloppy old lady in harlequin glasses. How dumb was that? She actually laughed at herself and recalled what she'd told Goodrich: when you're in, you're *in*. She felt a certain energetic vibration in her body, not unpleasant, and discovered she was not at all afraid.

At a few minutes past one, a car pulled into the lot, a huge black Yukon SUV. Jumbo Wedge and an Asian man she'd never seen before got out. Jumbo had a cast around his hand and his arm in a sling. He opened her door and told her to get out.

She said, "Hello, Jumbo. How's your hand?"

"Fuck you, Marvel," he said. "Turn around and put your hands behind your back!"

"Is this really necessary?" she said but complied. The Asian man efficiently bound her hands with cable ties.

"Who's your friend?" she asked.

"Not your friend anyway," replied Jumbo. "Your new pal iced two of his cousins. Now shut up and get in the car!"

They made her crouch in the foot well of the SUV. The Asian guy threw a blanket over her head. The two men got into the front seats, the Asian man driving. As they drove off, Marvel did what Overby had recommended long ago during one of those interminable tradecraft sessions. If you're ever snatched and can't see, you should sing *Row, Row, Row Your Boat* to yourself. Eight recitals equal approximately a minute. If you know how long the trip took, and you keep track of the turns, and when they occurred, you have some idea of the radius within which the location you are taken to must lie, assuming normal driving speed, and assuming you manage to escape or are able to convey this data to friends. Besides, doing so tends to keep fear at bay and occupies the mind.

Marvel reached three hundred and thirty-six repeats of the ditty before the car came to a stop, thus forty-two minutes, at which point it had become reasonable that life *was* but a dream. There had been only two turns during the ride, which meant they hadn't bothered trying to confuse her. She'd felt some rise in elevation during the ride and when they popped the doors, she felt a deeper chill in the pine-spiced air, and she supposed, therefore, that they were somewhere in the Green Mountains National Forest.

They kept the blanket draped over her head as they led her from the car. She stumbled up two shallow steps, a door shut behind her, the blanket was yanked away. She was in the mobile home where the video had been shot, that she had seen in her vision; and there was Overby.

"Sit down, Marvel," he said, indicating the folding chair.

"Can I have my hands back?"

"Not just yet."

"Where's the girl?"

Overby laughed. "My line is, 'I'll ask the questions,' isn't it?"

"That would be banal. Really, where's Leslie?"

"How did we come to this, dear girl? We're supposed to be on the same side."

"I had a change of heart. It happens. You know, all deals are off if you hurt the girl."

"Deals? How can you not understand your situation? Didn't we have a lecture on betrayal? All networks are subject to subversion and betrayal, and what follows?"

"There must be a sleeper network in place, completely separate from the original, and a different system of codes and contacts arrangements must exist, ready to be mobilized at need."

"Very good. Very close to the book answer. And don't you think I had such an arrangement in place? And don't you think that as soon as learned about your moonlight cruise I mobilized my backup network? All that information you stole is useless, all the shell companies and accounts are dissolved and their traces erased."

Marvel shrugged and said, "Well, Overby, I guess you outsmarted me. You're still the king of the con men." She looked him in the eye, and smiled and saw a small flash of dismay appear on his face, quickly suppressed.

"You think you've got something else, don't you?"

"Not at all," she said. "I had one pathetic ploy, organized on the spur of the moment, and you've neutralized it. Partly. The feds will know that a person named Freeman W. Overby is not a retired government official with investments, but a criminal mastermind. That'll get out, and it's not going to help your project with Zhou Feng-yi."

"Perhaps, but in any case, you won't be sending anything out while we have the girl, will you? And of course, you'll give me the passwords that disable your scheme, because you know what will happen to our little miss if you don't. Again, this is the problem with caring about individuals, do you see? It's like running a race with a concrete block chained to your leg. There's no way you can win."

Marvel laughed. "Hey, don't rub it in. I'm totally beat, except there might be a fat envelope sitting in some mail center, and I might have given the clerk a couple of grand to ship it to the FBI unless I come there in person to pick it up. Or there might be five envelopes. It's something to think about."

"That's a bluff."

"Maybe. But all it takes is a phone call to Mr. Zhou, and you're sunk. In fact, if I were you, I wouldn't go back to China at all. In fact, now would be a good time for you to retire. As I keep reminding you, you have enough money. Buy an island. Build a house. Get a yacht."

"You're thinking Goodrich is going to save you."

"Not really. It's just that your chart is full of trouble. Mars is in transit square your natal Pluto in the Eighth House. It says danger and violence. Why don't you just tell me where the girl is and take off?"

Overby laughed and said, "That's pathetic. You're talking like a suck. . ."

The sound came from a distance but it was still loud enough to startle: a shotgun. It echoed off the hills. Overby had excellent control of his face, but Marvel was very good at reading faces and observed a twitch of dismay. She thought it was probably because none of his people had a shotgun.

Bernard spotted the black Jeep a little east of Wilmington on Route Nine. He sped up, the black Jeep kept pace. He slowed down and pulled into the parking lot in front of a general store. The black Jeep sped by. Bernard didn't think it was a false alarm, because he had recognized the license plate. Since the Jeep had passed him, it meant they had another car in play. He thought about going into the general store and buying a gun. It was hunting season and they probably stocked shotguns and ammunition.

Then he recalled what it had felt like to shoot the two Asian men and decided he didn't want to go into whatever he was going into packing heat. He went in and bought a coffee and a packaged cake instead. He sipped the thin brew, ate a bite of cake and gave the rest to Murtagh.

Then he waited, trying not to let his eyes rest on the frozen dashboard clock. The numbers changed: one o'clock. She would be meeting the car now. One thirty. She was moving. He traced the red dot on the map, south on Route Eight and then into an area that seemed to have no roads, a red beacon in the middle of a green field, like a jelly apple dropped on a lawn. There it stayed as the minutes rolled by. Two-ten. He found he was grinding his teeth from the tension.

"What do you think, Murtagh? Should we break the stay?"

<There must be a finger snap.>

"Yes, I know, but I'm going to be a bad dog and snap my own fingers. I can't bear this not knowing."

He followed the road the red dot had traveled until he came to what looked like an old logging road and took that east. When he came within what the map said was a quarter mile from the marker, he found a wide spot on the road and nosed the car into the brush.

"You have to stay, Murtagh. But I'm going to leave the window open and I have the dog whistle."

<Whine.>

"No, really. There's going to be people with guns and I don't want you hurt."

<I'm not afraid of guns.>

"I know, but stay anyway. Stay!"

Bernard took his down parka and a wool hat from his suitcase. It was past three now and the bright spot in the overcast had sunk to a hand-span above the line of the western mountains. It was chilly and about to get colder. In the pocket of his parka he found Leslie's little blue dinosaur, and decided to treat that as a good omen.

He walked along the dirt road, occasionally checking the iPhone app, whose little dot hadn't moved. Less than a hundred yards from his car, he found fresh tracks veering off into the woods. Pushing past a springy stand of young sassafras, he found the black Jeep, empty but for a locked aluminum suitcase and a nylon bag containing a satellite phone. He walked on until a violent noise froze him: the blast of a shotgun, close, twenty yards or so, he estimated, coming from the woods on his right. He waited, unsure of what to do, until a voice just behind him said, "Put your hands on your head, and turn around slowly!"

Bernard obeyed and found Jumbo Wedge with his right hand in a sling and the other pointing a nine-millimeter pistol at him.

"You fucker!" Jumbo snarled. "How about you stick out your right hand and I'll show you what it feels like."

Bernard slowly extended his hand and looked into the other man's eyes. They seemed unfocused, and his face was slack. Doped to the gills.

A voice shouted, "Drop that gun. Do it now!"

They both looked up the road. A black man in a camo coverall and yellow sunglasses was standing at the edge of the woods twenty yards away, pointing a shotgun at Jumbo.

Who whipped his pistol around and got off a shot. The man with the shotgun cried out and fell back onto the road. He had not lost his shotgun and was starting to climb to his feet. Jumbo extended his arm, and prepared to kill the man.

Without consciously willing the act, Bernard found himself leaping and wrapping his arms around Jumbo's extended gun arm, his hands clenched as hard as he could on the man's massive wrist. Bernard flexed his knees and threw his weight backward and Jumbo, unable to use his other arm for balance, fell heavily onto his back.

It was a case of fighting a man who could beat you with one hand tied, who actually had one hand tied. Bernard was on his back gripping Jumbo's arm across his chest. It was like holding an anaconda. Jumbo sat up, got his feet under him, and stood slowly, bringing Bernard along with him as if he were a haversack full of marshmallows. Then he began to rotate his arm and wrist, to bring the muzzle of his pistol to bear on Bernard's head.

The man was immensely strong. Resisting his movement was like resisting a backhoe. Bernard sank his teeth into Jumbo's wrist and felt the man tense his arm muscles. In another second he would think of smashing Bernard against a tree and that would be it.

A voice cried out, "Goodrich. Get away from him!"

Bernard saw the camo man pointing his shotgun from a sitting position. He let go of the arm, which flew up into the air as Bernard fell back on his butt. Then came the vast noise. The shotgun charge took Jumbo in the chest, neck and face. He collapsed on the road, expelled a few bloody bubbles and died.

Bernard didn't look at Jumbo or pick up the pistol. Instead, he walked toward the man who had saved his life, now lying on his side. His tan face had become a mealy gray.

"Mr. Ewell," Bernard said when he got close enough. "This is a fortunate meeting. How did you know to find me here?"

"The girl called me. Listen, I'm shot. My car's in the woods about a hun . . ."

"I know where it is. And you'll want your sat phone."

"Yeah, cellphones don't work too good here in the boonies."

Bernard took off at a run, retrieved the nylon bag with Ewell's sat phone, and ran back. he was glad to see he was barely winded. He couldn't fight a gorilla but he could still turn in a respectable two hundred meters.

"Are you bleeding badly?" Bernard asked, as he set up the phone's antenna under Ewell's direction.

"Not so much. He got me in the hip. But it hurts like hell."

"You said she called you?"

"Yeah. Told me the whole story, said she was going to pay back my client. She gave me the name of this tracer app and the codes to connect it." He pulled a smartphone out of the breast pocket of his jacket and showed Bernard the familiar map and the blinking dot. "I got here and parked and started walking. I ran into a, some kind of Asian guy with a pistol and took him out and then I walked through the woods and I spotted you and the big guy. I'm assuming they were the people who took your daughter."

"Right. Then you know you have to give me a few minutes before you call. If the cops and all show up on this road, these bastards might, you know . . . "

"Shit. Well, take your time, man. Take a gun, too."

Bernard walked back to the corpse and reluctantly picked up the pistol.

In the mobile home Overby and Marvel heard the sound of a pistol shot, followed a few minutes later by another shotgun blast.

Marvel said, "It sounds like you've got a small war going on out there."

"I'd say it's my people taking care of your boyfriend."

"He's not my boyfriend," said Marvel, "but he's certainly not dead. His chart shows a Jupiter transit of the sixth house, which suggests a fortunate turn in his life, expansion and beneficence."

"Oh, don't be stupid!"

"The stars never lie, Overby. I bet your Mr. Zhou is studying your chart right now and not liking what he sees. I expect the cops will be arriving soon. Your best move now is to cut your losses and leave. It was you who taught me to always have a clear plan of escape. You probably have a chopper stashed somewhere nearby. Where's Leslie?"

Overby said, "Honestly, Marvel, maybe you should have gone for a brain scan. You seem to making extremely poor decisions lately and . . . "

He stopped because heavy running steps were sounding outside and Overby was just reaching under his jacket, Marvel could see his Walther coming out of the holster, when the door flew open and Bernard appeared, his face in a snarl and his pistol pointing at Overby's face.

"Put the gun on the floor!" he ordered, and after a long moment Overby complied.

"Where's my daughter?"

"I have no idea," said Overby. "My men hid her somewhere. Not close. You could ask them."

"They're dead," said Bernard. Marvel let out a shriek of anguish.

"You're not going to kill me," said Overby with confidence.

"I suppose not. Unlike you, I find it stressful to end a human life, even yours, and even after what you've put my daughter through. Fortunately, I have this."

Bernard reached into his shirt and withdrew a thin, chromed whistle on a chain. He held it to his lips and blew. It made no audible noise except a hiss of air.

"Did you kill Jumbo?" Marvel asked.

"No, although he tried pretty hard to kill me. It was Ewell who shot him. He got the other one, too."

Tears ran silently down Marvel's cheeks. She said, "Get me loose, Goodrich. There's a knife in my pocket."

Bernard found it, snapped it open one-handed, knelt and slit through the cable ties. While Marvel was rubbing circulation back into her wrists, Murtagh leaped through the open door and came panting into the room.

"Murtagh and I are going to find Leslie," said Bernard. "Pick up that pistol and watch him." He went out with the dog.

When he was gone and the sounds of man and dog had diminished, Overby said, "You're not going to shoot me either."

"Not unless you try anything fancy. You deserve to be shot for getting Jumbo and Ford killed, but I'm not the one to do it."

"They knew what they were getting into."

"That's your excuse? That they were trained mercenaries who knew the risks? In your sick fantasies, maybe, you and your fucking protocol. Ford was a Waimanolo stoner who had no business playing with guns, and Jumbo was that plus a short career in the Corps. You're a grifter, Overby, a simple thief. You're not a secret agent anymore, you can't just terminate with extreme prejudice anymore. There was absolutely no need to murder those old men, and no need to come after me."

"The protocol I devised kept all of us safe for many years," said Overby, "and your friends would be alive now if you hadn't betrayed us."

"But I *didn't* betray you. I resigned. Or you could say you fired me. I never ratted you out. I escaped from the FBI so I wouldn't *have* to rat you out. And I will never rat you out as long as you stay out of my life from now on."

"How do I know I can trust you? And there are people, as you know, who would frown on letting you run free."

"You never *know* if you can trust someone. You just have to believe, you have to take that leap. Otherwise your life will remain a pile of gilded shit. I learned how to do it, and maybe that's one lesson the teacher can take from the student. As far as the triads go, you can buy them off. You can say that you stake your life on me not talking. It might even do you some good. Now get the fuck out of here before Goodrich comes back, because if you've harmed that girl, he *will* shoot you like a rat."

"You're letting me go?"

"Yes, go now. Get in that car and drive away!"

"What's your angle?"

"Jesus. There *is* no angle, you horrible old man. I love you. Did you think I worked like an animal for you all those years because I wanted money, because it was my girlhood dream to be the world's greatest put-up artist? You're the only father I ever had. I get that you don't understand that, but it doesn't matter. For better or worse, you made me and I owe you. But I can't be with you anymore."

After a period of tense silence, Overby walked to the door.

"You should really shoot me," he said. "I don't forgive. I'm sorry, but that's just how I'm made."

"And you have no idea what a sad and pathetic thing that is to say at the end of a long life. Goodbye, Overby. Thanks for my brain."

"You know, it's not going to work, whatever idyllic future you're planning with this meathead. You'll be bored out of your skull in six months and you'll betray him. You'll never be a taxpayer, you silly bitch. You're a grifter to the bone and you always will be."

She let him have this last word, and sat there until she heard him get into the SUV and drive off.

"This is Leslie. You know Leslie, don't you, guy? Take a good sniff."

Bernard was holding Otto the stuffed dinosaur for Murtagh to smell, and after he was sure the dog had it, he gave the command to seek and off they went, out of the clearing where the mobile home sat, down to the road. They

heard the sound of a car departing, going away from them, north into the national forest. They ignored it. The dog began to sniff the earth.

The dog knows very well who Leslie is and has picked up the scent in an instant, but with the patience of love allows the man to wave the toy under his nose. The dog moves through a dense smell-scape and struggles to orient himself in this new and fraught environment. The most important smell is that the Man is frightened, which is distressing, and this is connected to the man he just passed on the road, who was once an enemy and here he is again, smelling of blood, down, therefore safe, not worth a sniff, then another enemy, dead, safe, but another smell on him, detectable even under the death stink, a familiar person; then the house, stink of formaldehyde, gas, under that of the woman, Marvel, and also the smell of sexual desire when the Man comes in, also the smell of a strange man, not safe, fear, hatred and enmity against the Man, and the dog's lips begin to curl before he stifles it, having received no order to guard, and that familiar personal smell, Leslie, she's been in the enclosed space and all around the door, and fear is there, and a paper towel with her vomit on it underneath the house, and the track is faint, too faint to follow, he has to cast shamefully in all directions. The ground is damp and cold and the wafts of scent are sluggish.

The dog runs back and forth on the road's edge, nose properly down in the dirt, ignoring everything it brings him, pine rubber oil squirrel deer droppings dead things, except the thin traces of the girl. Something is wrong here, the dog knows what a walking scent is like, he is trained to follow one, and this is not a walking scent, she is here but not here, but the scent of the dead man, the enemy, is cloaking her scent, they are not the same scent but they have the same track.

The Man is agitated and is talking, encouraging, but the dog does not want to talk and now the woman has come and talks to the man, which distracts him and so the dog can concentrate on this hard problem. It is much harder than the problem in the field trials when the distance changed: two trails, together but not the same person and Leslie's scent is so faint —how could this be?

"He's confused," said Bernard. "Why is he confused? He picked up the scent back at the trailer but he keeps losing it."

"Maybe they took her somewhere by car," said Marvel.

"No, because he keeps finding her trail along the road. Come on, Murtagh, for God's sake, *seek*!

The dog is surprised because the Man never doubles commands, it is almost the first thing they learned in training. Of course he is seeking, he is seeking Leslie but this other powerful scent is so mixed in . . .

Murtagh stops and has a memory. He recalls running by the dead man and smelling Leslie on him and now he performs the dog equivalent of solving Fermat's Last Theorem and puts it together. He plants his nose to the ground and dives into the bushes following a fat nose-glow of a track. He seeks, he finds. He spins in circles barking: the heroic dog!

"He could have carried her," said Marvel. "Look, the dog's onto something!"

Bernard and Marvel crashed through the whippy tangle of maple saplings, honeysuckle, bearberry, pursuing the dog. The tangle thinned and they realized they were on an abandoned road, blocked by deadfall, pierced by young jack pines. They could see the dog's black shape leaping through the thicket of a downed ash.

The ground dipped and fell to a rocky stream bed. The former road crossed over a galvanized culvert lacy with rust; part of the road had fallen onto the rocks. The dog was dancing and whining in front of the culvert's open end.

Jammed inside the culvert was a 55-gallon oil drum. Bernard grabbed at the cover, tearing his fingers on the rough steel. He pressed his ear to the icy steel. Nothing, a void. His heart hammered. He picked up a smooth stone from the stream bed and pounded on the rim of the oil drum until the top clattered down.

Inside was his daughter, bound like a mummy in gaffer's tape, freezing, battered, but alive. The two of them dragged her out and cut the tape from her. She was barefoot and bare-headed, still wearing the sweatpants and t-shirt she'd been wearing when captured. Her skin was waxy and bluish.

Bernard carried her to a patch of dry ground and laid her on their coats and they lay down on either side of her, warming her with their bodies until she started to shiver and cry. There they stayed until the sirens came, and all the helping strangers. Bernard surrendered autonomy, except that he would not release his daughter's hand, not in the ambulance, or beside the gurney, until she was whisked away to an examination room at Southwestern Vermont Medical Center in Bennington.

Marvel stayed with the dog. She called Bernard several times over the next twenty-four hours while he sat next to Leslie's bed. They were like phone calls from a dream, not a bad dream, but not real life either. He asked her about what was going on between her and the authorities. Her answers were vague. Many interviews with officials, and with people not so official. He gathered that she was constructing a new life, and trading on the intel she had stolen from the Lanikai computers. Despite Overby's recent actions, there was still a trove of information there about the elusive Mr. Liu, and the feds were delighted.

But most of their conversation was her cheering him up, her voice like a lifeline to a strange future that he was apparently destined to share with this odd but singularly compelling woman. She tried to get the dog to talk to him over the phone, but that seemed to be outside even Murtagh's repertoire.

"Was that her?" Leslie asked after he had completed the last of these calls. With the resilience of youth, she was up and about and anxious to get back to her theater program. She had refused trauma counseling and further medical attention. She had been a victim, she said, but she was not a victim any longer and refused to be so treated. Bernard thought she was splendid. He had imagined that she would take a break and live at the House for a while, but she shot that down. She had a play in rehearsal and the idea of submitting to Aunt Mary's ministrations did not appeal.

When he said that it had been Marvel on the phone, the girl issued a classic teen sniff of deprecation.

"You don't approve?"

"It's your life, Daddy. But L. says she's a dangerous international criminal."

"She was. Now, apparently, not so much."

"Are you in love with her?"

"I wouldn't crank it up that far. We've barely spent any time together, I mean, besides when she was stealing my money. But there seems to be a connection there. We're in each other's hearts. She risked her life to be with me. She offered her life to rescue you. That must count for something."

"I wouldn't have *needed* saving if she wasn't in the picture."

"That's true, and I'm deeply sorry for it. As I know she is. All I can say is that people change. I know I have. Do I seem different to you?"

She favored him with the clear-eyed and merciless appraisal of the young.

"I don't know—you look tighter, and, I don't know, more dangerous. Not as baggy and Dad-ish. It's a little scary, if you want to know. Are you going to, like, live with her?"

"We haven't exactly made plans," he replied, "but it looks that way. We'll probably have a different kind of life than the one I had with your mom in the city."

"Oh, Mom!," the girl cried. "I miss her like crazy, but she's fading. I have to look at pictures to remember her face. After she died, I used to call her, just to hear her voicemail message, but now I get the telecom 'no longer in service' thing. A black hole. Do you think it ever gets filled?"

"No. But on the other hand, life goes on. You think you'll never laugh again, but then you do. You think you'll never love anyone again, but then you do. Or so it seems."

"So you *do* love her."

"She's an unusual woman. There are some difficulties. I agreed with your mother on just about everything, but Marvel is always pulling stuff that astounds and disturbs me."

"Is that her real name—*Marvel?*

"Reality is not one of her main things, I'm afraid. But that's what you call her."

Leslie was quiet for a minute and then said, "I want to meet her. I mean I met her already when . . . when I was rescued, but I should talk to her."

"I could have her come by. We could have dinner when . . ."

"No, just send me her contacts," Leslie said. "I'll arrange it."

Later that afternoon, Bernard was dispatched to Leslie's dorm to bring back a package of clothes prepared by her roommate. When he came back to the hospital room, he heard laughter spilling out the door and found Marvel sitting there regaling his kid with some tale, certainly embroidered, that had lit up the dear face as he had not seen it lit for some time. Leslie stifled it somewhat when she saw Bernard, under the principle that the young cannot admit that their elders have anything on the ball.

While Leslie dressed, Bernard got Marvel alone in the hallway and said, "What was that all about? You have a new best friend?"

"I was just being charming. She's a neat kid."

"You just being charming is like LeBron dropping in on a half-court game down by the playground. You conned her out of her socks."

"Con implies some nefarious purpose," Marvel said, "And I don't have one. I wanted her to like me, you wanted her to like me, now she likes me. It's a talent I have. Implying I shouldn't use it to smooth my path is like implying you should stop writing because too many people like your books."

"Completely specious logic, but let that pass." He had another thought, suppressed it, but she said, "What's wrong?"

"Nothing."

"Something. There was a shadow on your face when I said that about your writing."

"You're reading my mind now?"

"Uh-huh. What was it?"

"I can't do it anymore. I mean, write Noreen and Bingo books. I'll limp through *Sleeping Dogs Lie*, but that's it. No more."

"While millions wail. Why are you quitting?"

"All of this, what happened over the last few months. Being inside a thriller seems to disable one's ability to make one up. Or it does with me. Also, the damn things were getting too cozy and flaccid. Twenty-four novels about the same person, who never changes and whose dog never gets old and dies, well, it's not enough anymore."

"Mm, yeah, and my former profession has lost its appeal as well." She smiled brightly and said, "We'll just have to think up something different to do."

After Leslie was settled back in her dorm room, Bernard and Marvel walked through the elegant campus, kicking up leaves. "This is sweet," Marvel remarked, "Look at all the fresh faces! It's a far cry from the School of Hard Knocks, my own alma mater."

"Yeah, but it has a better football team than Bennington. So, what's the plan, Marvel? I ask because I haven't got an idea in my head about what to do next. Maybe we should find a place and sit down and have a drink or three and a meal. My stomach is growling. I can't remember my last real dinner. And we could discuss."

"We could do that," said Marvel, "but I would prefer to stroll over to my hotel room and fuck our brains out."

"Actually, come to think of it," he said, "I'm not really all that hungry."

"That was worth waiting for," said Bernard, as he attempted to scoop up his brains, which were scattered across the room, along with the clothes that they had ripped off like teenagers, or like people in a movie.

"Are you fishing for a rating?" she asked.

"Are you inclined to issue one?"

"Yes. I have had a lot of sex, but nothing in the same class as this."

"No? I guess you were dazzled by my mastery of exotic Eastern techniques. Also, I was happy to note that you were able to extract that thing from your vagina."

"Only one object at a time in my vagina has always been my rule," she said, "but let me add that I have had more experience than most with exotic Eastern techniques. I spit on exotic Eastern techniques. Sometimes a girl does not wish to be played like a flugelhorn. Sometimes she just wishes to be seen."

"And yet your whole life has been about disguise."

"Just my point. Basically, that's what started this whole caper. I was conning you; I was being someone else, and yet you *saw* me. You saw what I didn't even see myself. And this, what we just did, was an extension of that. It was connected to what happened to me at Eya's, stripping away of all the accumulated bullshit until only the glowing center remains." She

395

gave an uncomfortable laugh. "It's hard to explain, but I never want to be without it, ever."

"That can probably be arranged," he said, squeezing her and kissing her until she gasped. "But beyond that, what are we going to do now?"

"You mean long range or short range?"

"Start with the former."

"Okay. I've been thinking and talking to people. It occurred to me that I'm a grifter, and you're a pro at making shit up, devising stories. You just told me you're burnt out on thrillers, yes? Well, we seem to have a basis for an enterprise."

"Really."

"You're so cute when you get that doubtful frown on your kisser. But listen: the world is full of people ripe for the plucking, people who have stolen for years, people the law can't reach. Kleptocrats. Cartel guys. Cheating corporate scumbags. What about taking those guys off?"

"An unbelievably stupid and dangerous idea, even for you. It sounds like a good way to get killed."

"No, really--we would have the tacit and entirely unofficial support of the Feds. Recall we have a friend at the NSA. A relative, in fact. And we could give the money back—that's the beauty part. As well as taking evil assholes off the court, unofficially. Besides, my guys want me to do it."

"Your guys. Will you still love me if I have problems with all this psychic business? The astrology? I mean, I can't quite get my head around it."

"That's a problem with your head, not the mystic realms. Murtagh has no problem with it. Do you, Murtagh?"

The dog, who had been dozing in a corner despite the recent excitement and strange noises, lifted his head at the sound of his name.

<No. No problem at all.>

"See?" she crowed. "You're outvoted. So, are you in?"

He looked at her, and she supplied one of her crazy-wonderful smiles.

"Yes, yes, God help me, I'm in."

"And while I'm doing that, you'll . . ."

"Be the muscle. Also, I just this minute thought of what I'm going to write next."

"What?"

"This, what just happened to me, us, these past months. Fictionalized, obviously."

"Writing n muscle n sex. It's a trifecta. Good. Now, as to short-range plans . . ."

"Something to eat? We could call room service."

"We could," she said, and slid a warm thigh across his groin. "Or. . ."

"You read my mind," said Bernard.

Made in United States
North Haven, CT
19 February 2023

32869810R00222